MW00364758

GHOST WAVES

Also by James McManus

Antonio Salazar Is Dead
Curtains
Out of the Blue
Chin Music

GHOST WAVES

James McManus

Grove Press
New York

Copyright © 1988 by James McManus

All rights reserved.
No part of this book may be reproduced, stored in a retrieval system, or transmitted in any form, by any means, including mechanical, electronic, photocopying, recording or otherwise, without prior written permission of the publisher.

The name Grove Press and the colophon printed on the title page and jacket of this book are trademarks registered in the U.S. Patent and Trademark Office and in other countries.

Published by Grove Press
a division of Wheatland Corporation
841 Broadway
New York, N.Y. 10003

Portions of this novel previously appeared in *The Review of Contemporary Fiction*, *Formations*, and *New American Writing*.

The author wishes to thank the NEA, Wang, SAIC, the Illinois Arts Council, and the Shifting Foundation (twice) for support while this work was in progress. Thanks also to Barney and Lisa Rosset, Textor and Pepe, W, S, and db.

Library of Congress Cataloging-in-Publication Data

McManus, James.
Ghost waves/James McManus.—1st ed.
p. cm.
ISBN 0-8021-1029-0
I. Title
PS3563.C386G45 1988
813′.54—dc19 88–14766
CIP

Designed by Paul Chevannes

Manufactured in the United States of America

First Edition 1988

10 9 8 7 6 5 4 3 2 1

GHOST WAVES

1

A DETECTIVE was following Linda. She was watching him watch her in the smudged oval mirror of her compact while pretending to powder her forehead. Her Bentley was waiting at Jackson and Wacker. It was the fifth red light in the last seven blocks that had caught her. She still had another twelve blocks to make it to The School of the Art Institute, where for reasons known only to them the photographers wanted to shoot her. She was doing her best to stay calm by reminding herself she was home. Didn't work. She wasn't sure where home was anymore. She wasn't sure anything would.

She had just crossed the river. She seemed to recall being told it flowed backward. No, she had read that somewhere: in an *Artforum* piece about three Chicago painters whose names she no longer remembered. The notion had sort of tied in with a thing about rivers—canals, actually—in one of the songs she was writing. Her reaction right now was: so what.

If she craned her neck and looked out the tinted side window, she'd be able to see the lowermost quarter or third of Sears Tower. She didn't. She turned around and looked out the back. The detective was two cars behind her in a robin's egg blue Saab convertible. With his mouth shut and sunglasses on, he did not look unlike Shane MacGowan. He'd been there when she got off the plane at O'Hare Wednesday morning, and maybe since long before that.

"And you're sure you don't want me to lose him." This was Chas, her chauffeur, on the intercom. He had permits for both of the handguns he carried, but he still made her nervous. He often made pseudo-discreet reference to persons his "mates" had "had whacked." Was one to infer hardass Chas might have whacked them? His hair was moussed back on his block of mick skull, then curled up in moist little rings at his collar. There were not many stunts she'd put past him. She couldn't help picturing herself participating involuntarily in a demented chase scene through the Loop: running lights, scattering schoolchildren, fishtailing through U-turns, Chas playing chicken with oncoming traffic, her recently customized Bentley whanging off cars both parked and still moving, forcing other cars up onto sidewalks, sheared-off hydrants geysering potently as they tore along under the el, winging steel girders at sixty, metal on metal on metal, the blinding glare through the tracks overhead strobing it all into black-and-white slow-motion rushes scored by Bernard Herrmann with CSO brass patched with blared GM horns and bursts from M-10s, the whole issue finally settled with totaled police cars, maimed passersby, the low boom and roar of a twelve-gauge.

"That's okay, Chas," she whispered. Weren't aspirin supposed to reduce inflammation? She'd just taken six, but her vocal cords still were on fire.

"Just so's you're sure, Ms. Krajacik."

Samuels, her manager, who was sitting beside her, told Chas not to make her repeat things. "Just drive," he said, brusquely.

In spite of the fact that they were fellow South Siders, Linda could tell that her Bridgeport chauffeur did not take real kindly to reprimands from her U of C MBA manager. But now that the words had escaped Samuels's lips and pricked Chas's sensitive ears, she didn't see how she could do much about it. Saying something unfriendly to Samuels, or friendly to Chas, or vice versa, would only make things about seven or eight times as complicated. So she sat on her hands and shut up.

She had three shows to do in Chicago that weekend. The one Saturday night was a benefit for homeless South African black kids and would wind up her twelve-city seven-week tour. None too soon, either. She'd been hoarse since the three-hour show in Toronto last Monday. She just hoped her voice would hold up. Declan was flying in Saturday and would join her onstage for the encores. They planned to do "No Man's Land" on acoustic guitars—maybe the last verse or two a cappella if she had any voice left at all—then bring back her band and turn up the Fenders for "West" and "Pursued by the Ghost."

She and Declan had been more or less living together since April, when his Asian tour ended, though since her tour began they had seen one another three times a month at the most. Photos of them—at the Hans Haake opening in Cologne, on the set of her movie *Crillon,* playing miniature golf in Kyoto—were starting to appear in the *Post, Match, La Stampa,* the *Mirror.* Even both *Times*es were apparently no longer above printing unfocused, badly lit "candid" shots whose subjects could only be identified by reading the captions. And that was the good news. Half the articles had her as pregnant, which made Linda laugh. If only they realized how far off the money they were, though she knew this was hardly the issue. The one thing they always got right was that Declan was legally married and would be till after the trial, which was why this detective was tailing her. Wasn't it? According to her security people, he'd been hired by Declan's wife's lawyer.

The sunlight was blocked by a cloud or a building as Chas nosed the Bentley through the T-shaped intersection at LaSalle Street and Jackson. The Saab was still two cars behind them. Motherfuck lawyers, she thought, though she knew that vice versa was likelier. The sidewalks around her were teeming with lawyers, in fact, plus bankers and traders and brokers: gray pinstriped suits, aluminum attaché cases, gumball blue and chartreuse traders' jackets. As the crowd filtered past, she could see the stretch Bentley's reflection in the Bank of Bahrain's polished window. She could even make out, when she squinted, an identical crowd scene reflected back into the bulletproof pane she was looking through.

They'd be running the sound check in less than an hour —the guys in her band were already at the Horizon—but she still had the one final interview and "photo opportunity," both of which, according to Samuels at least, were crucial to Sunday night's show. Seats in the first fifteen rows would cost five hundred dollars; the cheap seats were one twenty-five. (The scalpers, she knew, would get at least twice that.) But she couldn't help making a last-ditch appeal: that her voice and the traffic and shortness of time were sufficient excuse to cancel the shoot and the interview. "Plus I couldn't be less in the mood," she told Samuels.

He sighed and restated what he'd told her all week. "You want to get that much per ticket, raise those kinds of dollars, you've got to show face with these people."

"So then how come Keith tells me we sold out last Wednesday?"

"We did."

"So—"

"So who do you think has been forking over that kind of yen for those tickets? Your 'fans'?"

Linda groaned.

Samuels cursed, shook his head. "You've got quite an imagination, you know that?"

"Yeah yeah," she said. They'd been through all this countless times. Why did she even give him the satisfaction of arguing? She mentally punched herself, hard. Samuels had too many figures and facts, all of which tended to demonstrate . . . whatever he wanted them to, in this case that something like 92.29 percent of all tickets for big-money benefit concerts were purchased as writeoffs by political action committees, multinational agribusiness cartels, and big local radio stations—plus scalpers, kabuya, and dinks. Yeah yeah, she thought. But who gives. The strongest comeback she was able to muster was, "So what else is new?"

Samuels ignored her rhetorical question: he *loved* to make this kind of point. "People who read the *New York Times,* girl. People who read the *Wall Street Journal,* who insist—"

"In other words, assholes like you," Linda said. She'd almost said "plasma-sucking sphincters," but in the nick of time had concluded this was slightly too vicious for the sort of debate they were having. Besides. She didn't mind Samuels all *that* much.

"Assholes like me." Samuels nodded. "You got it."

Minutely, perceptibly, Chas nodded too.

"Because," Samuels said, "if the rock-and-roll business has taught us anything, girl, it's that—"

"What?" Linda said. "That you can kill anyone?"

Chas nodded harder.

"It has taught us," Samuels said coolly, "that assholeric

behavior is clearly acceptable, even highly desirable and profitable, so long as the behavior in question is *spectacularly* assholeric."

Yeah yeah yeah yeah. She'd heard all this too. Samuels's maxims.

"In other words, to continue my point, it's assholes who like to pick up their morning paper and read about what a bodacious idea it was for them to have donated all of their hard-earned dinero, so that *next* time, next *cause,* they'll be likely to see their way clear—"

"Oh," Linda said. "So it's 'for a good cause' that you're letting this worthless cheeseball harass me."

Samuels sighed. "Remember the last time you stiffed him?"

She nodded and winced. She wanted a cigarette desperately but knew it would not help her voice. Then she lit one up anyway. Screw it.

"Remember?"

She did. She remembered. She said so.

"Good," Samuels said. "I refrain, by the way, from ironical dig on the cigarette."

"Good."

"Indeed, I take this not unanticipated opportunity to indulge my own fearsome craving and light one myself."

And he did.

Long moments passed as they sat in the traffic. Her old school was still about ten blocks away. Were students she'd had classes with, hung around with in dorm rooms and nightclubs, still there? She'd only been gone nineteen months, after all. In any event, she would try not to be condescending.

The sun came back out. Samuels coughed. "Ten, fifteen minutes, kid. Tops." He covered his mouth with his dinky white fist and coughed harder.

She sipped some Bombay from the platinum flask that

Declan had sent her from London. *Buzz, buzz,* it said. The one she'd sent him said, *You say so.* Neither inscription used names because even initials might be brought up against him in court.

"You promise?" she said. Exactly what she hoped to accomplish by appeasing her manager was not all that clear. Apparently, though, she had done it.

"Promise," said Samuels, crossing his blue-blazered heart.

"We promise," said Chas.

Samuels and Chas exchanged glares in the mirror. It was just what she needed: guys in her entourage, inside her *car,* trading bomb threats.

She took two more sips, then a drag, then sat back and tried to relax. She had gotten up less than three hours ago but was already wired and thirsty. She knew she was drinking too much, but she hadn't slept well the whole tour. And she *hated* Manhattan reporters.

Samuels cuffed her left shoulder, then squeezed it reassuringly with his miniature fingers. "Don't *worry,*" he told her. "He'll dress up and lick you all over."

She blew a tight smoke ring into the conditioned air of the Bentley. It spun back around on itself as it rose and expanded, then wavered, slowed down, and got crooked. Clips from the bloodbath that had ended the car chase kept flashing back to her—gore leaking onto the asphalt from seams in a rocker panel, eyeballs bugged out in a death stare, a balding head unneatly severed—as she watched what was left of the smoke ring disintegrate against the crushed gray velour of the ceiling.

"That's what I'm afraid of," she said.

Absence makes the heart grow fonder. Familiarity breeds contempt. And all that. It is strange.

RICHARD BAUM traded futures. He was good at his job and he knew it, but his ears were now ringing and he'd started to sweat second thoughts from his crotch to the back of his scalp. It was time. He was standing on tiptoe on the second octagonal tier of the pulsed seething Board of Trade wheat pit with both palms thrust outward, offering 300 Dec at eleven. The tendons and veins in his neck were erect as electric guitar strings. The 1:14 bell had just rung, which meant he'd been at it for four hours straight, slamming the wheat the whole time, but with only this one long last minute in which to consolidate his new short position: 2.86 million bushels. His forehead and temples were throbbing. No sweat, Richard told himself. None. He glanced for the briefest of seconds toward the spot three tiers back where Honora, his runner, was supposed to be standing (but wasn't), then focused into the din and the chaos before him, using precision RBaum avionics to phase out the shouting and shoving and waving white palms of the sellers and zero in hard on the backs of the hands of the suckers. You bet. He was pumped, just ecstatic, and desperate, which averaged out inside his balls and his brain as a fierce deadly calm. Now's the time. He clenched both his hands and bellowed "*Three hundred at ten!*" at the top of his lungs, meaning three hundred thousand more bushels, while jabbing his fists past the ears of the local below him to show the whole world just how anxious he was to be going a full fucking cent even lower. When you had to you had to, he figured, which helped him keep punching and waving and hoping. Somebody elbowed him, hard, and he elbowed them back even harder without really looking and keeping both fists up and thinking *you sleaze piece of shit you* and growling (but hoping it wasn't Glenn Beckert he'd elbowed) and yelling "*At ten!*" even louder. And then, just like that, from directly across the mad pit and just as the pulpit bell sounded, he spotted Jack Carter, the hedger for General Mills (and Mr. ex-President, Jr.), getting ready to hit on his offer. Richard made positive eye contact, waited a fifth of a second, then fired. You got it, their eyes said, together. Carter then closed out the deal by scooping a hand toward his body while touching the top of his head, then rechecked the size of the order by extending the last three fingers on his right hand and crossing his raised cocked left forearm. Done, Richard thought, nodding back, and about fucking time, as he whipped out his cards and his pencil and wrote up the order. Done done and done, you lame cracker. He smiled. You want it you got it, you poor dumb sad lame motherfucker.

From the observation deck a floor and a half above the huge grain room, Maggie Krajacik could see into all seven pits but had lost sight of Richard in wheat. They were going to be married that Saturday evening, but this was the first time she'd seen him in action at work. And what action! It was frantic enough to begin with, at least since she'd got there at noon, but since the 1:14 bell had gone off it had seemed to get way out of hand. It sort of made her wonder how any business at all could get done—or, if it did, how a person could ever keep track of it. Because into this one single pit designed to hold seventy, maybe eighty-five people, about two hundred gonzo berserkos had been jammed to transact their strange business. They all were decked out in preposterously boisterous jackets (hot pink, sunkissed orange, magenta, chartreuse), and nine out of ten were maniacally waving their hands and their elbows and shrieking in each other's faces. People were being literally thrown into and out of the sides of the pit, and what looked like a six-on-one fistfight had erupted across from where Richard had been. To Maggie it looked like a brawl in a gumball machine, just one manic orgy of moxie. If you multiplied the whole thing by seven . . . although even *that* wouldn't tell the whole story. Because in the crosshatch of aisles between wheat and the other six pits and the phonebanks there also were hundreds of runners, a lot of them good-looking girls or young women, all of them wearing the same awful jackets, all dashing madly in seven directions at once. In all her born days she had never seen anything like it. The way these people were swarming all over each other reminded her of the time she had pried up a flagstone in her grandfather's patio and surprised both herself and a whole little city of translucent maggots. The only real difference was that the crew now below her was louder, much much more colorful, and not really quite as disgusting.

She at last spotted Richard again. He was outside the wheat pit discussing some point face to face with a pretty young redhead who was wearing a chartreuse jacket like his. Richard looked angry, downright ferocious in fact, and the redhead looked scared.

Then they both burst out laughing and hugged.

> I ain't superstitious but a black cat just crossed my trail. No I ain't superstitious but a black cat just crossed my trail.

GIN-GLAZED and trembly, Linda leaned back in her chair. Another degree she'd tip over. She was conjuring up her reflection in a green plastic folder, the kind you put term papers in. It was also the color of Tanqueray bottles, she'd noticed; it was also about as translucent. When she made it concave her face would appear right side up, upside down when she made it convex. What she wanted to do was to get it faced both ways at once. She thought she could do this by controlling the curve of the plastic with delicate, untrembly twists. Didn't work. She figured the trick was to catch it between merging curves, but the best she had managed so far was diagonal pairs of her faces that warped back and forth between quadrants: upper right/face upside down, lower left/face right side up, then vice versa, vice versa, vice versa.

She sipped more Bombay: no tonic, no lime, just some ice. She was sweating. For some goddamn reason her suite in the Whitehall was like deep fucking jungle. She had called the desk twice. Both times she'd gotten obsequious apologies and absolute promises to deal with the problem immediately. The last call was forty-five minutes ago.

She got up and went to the phone, lit a Merit. Should a girl in the state she was in be calling, at this hour, Hank Rendeck? The guy who was probably Declan's best friend in the States? The blind, brilliant poet who'd helped discover her? Plus who also was happily married?

She felt calmly frantic. Why not.

So she dialed.

Two rings. No answer. She smoked and sipped gin with one hand while she listened. He'd certainly seemed interested that night in Sag Harbor, although how could you tell with a blind guy, especially when he was your legally married lover's happily married best friend, plus (sort of) your own friend as well?

Well?

No answer.

Though if Hank *had* been interested, wouldn't she still have been able to tell, blind or not, during that very strange week on Long Island? He had, after all, been twirling the ends of her bangs while Jill, Mrs. Rendeck, was sitting right—

Then, out of nowhere, detonating into her reverie, came the click of a message machine, followed by three or four seconds of tape hiss, followed by Rendeck's deep voice, sounding tired: "This here is Hank. Please leave a message." Then six or eight seconds of tape hiss. Then *beep.*

Her nerves turned to grease as her options flashed past her. She held the Bombay in her shaking right hand, the Merit and phone in her left, cursing herself for not having planned a routine. She tried to say "This here is Linda," but only "This here" would come out, followed by diphthongal groaning.

Good going, she said, to herself, hanging up.

Real good going.

Dirt plus sweat equals mud. Which is exactly what the inside of her right calf and ankle were smeared with. Some mud.

How did it get there, she wanted to know. Posing for stills in that dumb "installation"? She realized that not to remember was bad.

She sipped more Bombay. It was good. She crossed her right leg like a guy would, resting her ankle across her left knee, and, in the light from the end of a steak knife commercial, examined the mud on her calf. It was streaky and gray and it itched her. There also was short light brown stubble poking up through it, like—what? Like a rice paddy. Like some stubble through mud. Like a jungle. Like miniature rice paddy on steep slope of ankle . . .

Yeah, right.

"You's a mess," she concluded out loud to herself as she scratched through the mud with her nails, feeling crazy and lonesome and cruddy, then dug through the mud even harder.

Then, feeling better, she told herself, "Girl, you are *drunk*," and stood up. She tasted the mud on her finger with the tip of her tongue. It was chalky and salty and bitter.

She swallowed more gin and began to get out of her clothes.

"You are wasted."

In the bathroom she yanked back the curtain and checked out the tub for her father before getting totally naked. He had died on this day nineteen years ago. She hadn't even fucking been born yet.

She looked at herself in the mirror. Her breasts, even drunk, looked quite swell. Did they not? Her buttocks in three-quarter profile looked wholly, entirely splendid. Her hair was . . . he in here without being visible? Just the idea of that rocked her. It wasn't that she didn't want to talk to or deal with her father. She did. It was just that—

She pulled her damp underpants and T-shirt back on in a hurry, feeling clammy and scared but also a little bit silly.

And then she could feel him behind her. And froze.

She looked in the mirror.

Behind her.

The intense satisfaction she derived from picking a dry little scab off her forearm was almost all lost when a droplet of blood emerged underneath, surrounded by moist pink new skin. A three-year-old Wimbledon match was on cable: two guys. The tall one, a cute jerky redhead with lips even bigger than Mick's, was "now down a mini-break." The announcer went on to point out that the white lines within which the two guys were playing were actually composed of titanium dust—not chalk, as his partner had called it. The partner said, "I stand corrected, I guess." The announcer responded, "Indeed."

Linda groaned loudly and turned down the sound. She liked what she heard now so much that she turned off the sound altogether. Okay. This was better. She slid on her black-on-black shades. This was def. She was tempted to go get her boom box but realized she was not in the mood for loud music. Besides: she was comfortable just as she was, was she not, here in her luxury suite, overlooking the Magnificent Mile of her Dirty Old Town, with her gin and her ice and her cigarettes, watching two bonny jockstraps play tennis, in silence.

She worked the scab into a loose lumpy ball and rolled it around between her thumb and her index finger, smoothing it, making it harder, then licked the fresh blood from her mini-wound. It tasted like blood, nice and salty, ideal for a chasing by elixir of juniper. So consider it chased then, she thought. And she chased it.

The screen said the tennis was coming to her via satellite cable, but that it was taped and delayed. Just what did that mean? She looked at the clock by the bed: almost two. So that made it what time in London? Were Prince Chas and Di sleeping peacefully or was Chas still out talking to pansies while Di sucked off guardsmen in bear fur? And what about all those underpaid blokes at the Royal Distillery? Huh? Were they already there, hard at work, diligently preparing the next precious batches for export? She hoped so. If not, could some gin waves be shipped via satellite?

She tried to watch tennis. The biggest problem was that it was almost impossible to follow the flight of the little white ball against the glare of the sun off the dead grass and dirt of the court. The high camera angle didn't help things much either. Was it also the Whitehall's, the set's, the delay's, or the satellite's fault? Her shades'? The Bombay's? So then why was she watching, she wondered. Changed channels. CBC documentary: skeletal African children with distended bellies were brushing the flies off their faces —or, worse, not brushing them off. Other stations had news, a gay televangelist, commercials in Spanish, a commercial in English, old movies.

The room buzzed cold blue when she boosted the F on the blinds, then matted pitch black when she killed the TV.

She tried not to think about Declan. She sat and stared out with her chin on her knuckles, not drinking. The Loopline was sporting some Big Fucking Buildings. She knew that without even looking.

Could Rendeck have told she was flirting the time she had asked him for help with that phrase in her IRA song? Hadn't hers, *country matters,* made sense the most interesting ways? (Declan had told her it had.) The other thing was: would Rendeck be able to make out her voice from the two mumbled words she had left on his tape? Would answers become more apparent if she knelt down and masturbated? Much less if she didn't? She was certainly too drunk to fuck. Rendeck had told her to read *Station Island,* and so far she hadn't. She was all mouth and trousers, she was. Plus, wouldn't voices be what he was best at? This was her punishment then: no groupies, no Declan, no Rendeck.

So what. She pictured his hand—his veined hairless wrist, his calloused and extra-long fingers—extended to track the deep groove in the small of her back, be surprised by the smooth of her abdomen, the backs of her knees, and not being able to find them.

She stood up and took off her shades, just to spite him, then stretched. As a matter of fact, she was glad. She opened the little square fridge and took out more ice. The bright shaft of air dense with mist made her squint and chilled the inside of her unslashed left wrist.

It felt good.

She turned on the tennis again, sipped her gin. The best she could do was deduce where the ball was by watching each player run toward it and the way he behaved when he got there. Such fun. No sound and no ball: just the players' response to the speed and the spin and the angle. Then all of a sudden it hit her: Hank had used tennis to try to explain how a particle physicist could describe things like messenger bosons and quarks, which were too small and fast to be visible. If you watched, or as Hank had put it, "observed," tennis players, even if the ball they used were invisible, you could still get a decent idea as to what *kind* of ball they were using—its size, weight, shape, texture, etc. —if you knew what to look for and looked hard enough and were smart. You could tell it wasn't a football or basketball from the size of the racquets they used, but that it wasn't a golf ball or marble since it didn't go through the holes in the net. You could tell it wasn't a shotput. You also could tell, since it didn't always move in straight lines, that it was shaggy and light enough to be moved by the wind and have spin. Things like that.

She started to watch with real interest. The score was love-thirty. The redhead was serving. He tossed the ball up, swiped at it viciously, charged toward the net. The ball stayed invisible. The other guy lunged to his left, half lost his balance, then stood there. An ace.

Linda clapped once. Her reward for this insight was two more wide fingers of gin. She felt pretty proud of herself. She could bring all this up when Declan arrived for the concert.

She finally passed out, didn't dream, then came back to about ten minutes later, when the telephone rang. She jumped. What the . . . tennis was still going on. The ember of one of her Merits glowed in the two-thirds-full ashtray. She sat herself up at the table and winced when the phone rang again. Her tongue felt like smoked cardboard crud.

She stood up and lurched toward the sound. The sixth ring she heard was louder but shorter than rings five and four: whoever had called had hung up. But she answered it anyway, knowing full well that all she would get was a dial tone. The dead certainty of its uninvolved drone at least would confirm what she already knew, she supposed, and would please her.

It did. She listened for eight or ten seconds, then gently hung up. It was time—what she didn't yet know was: for what? She didn't feel dizzy or sick, only chilly and sweaty, exhausted. She did not want a cigarette either.

She got down on her hands and knees and stared at her upside-down thighs. Closed her eyes. She could feel the blood rush to her head, the damp strands of hair that were stuck to her neck and her face. Her teeth chattered hard. She inhaled. She could smell her own breath. Her whole grotty body, in fact. She could see things in back of her eyelids.

She realized her knees hurt and heard herself groan as she rolled on her side. She was smart.

She curled herself up on the cool warped linoleum floor.

Fell asleep.

21

RICHARD'S BIG Wang beeped and whirred day and night, on its own, comparing Brazil's daily rainfall with China's, Australia's with Canada's, analyzing six different ways in which rubles and rupees and yen were continuing to be a factor in revitalizing Argentina's port facilities and general transportational infrastructure, charting the relative strength of the American dollar, the size of the most recent PL480 shipments of wheat to Ethiopia, that morning's gold fix in London, the Nikkei cash options, the subsidized sales of BICEP and EEC wheat to the USSR, algebraically summarizing USDA figures on the rates of disappearance in Iowa silos and desertification in eastern Nebraska and the subsequent widening of cross positions on the Kansas City Board of Trade, encoding succinctly in quantified precis Paul Volcker's most recent pronunciamento, enhancing as well as digesting the implications of EROS's latest remote multispectral satellite photographs of the hard red fall wheat crop in the Azerbaijan Soviet Socialist Republic while tracking the ethnobotanical research results on their A92 strains of sorghum, and other such fresh fundamentals. It printed out ten or twelve inches per day of conclusions and recommendations, folding them page after page into the wire receptacle at the far right-hand edge of the twelve-foot-long walnut table that functioned as Richard's main desk. Centered above this receptacle were two handsome samplers handsewn by two different women. The top one said *When you live among wolves, you must howl like a wolf. —V. I. Lenin.* The one on the bottom said *Wheat fields were rolling like waves in the wind.—V. van Gogh and N. Khrushchev.* Both of these mottoes had been factored into the calculus, along with everything else, by the Wang. Of all the programs that Richard had written, these had been the trickiest to come up with and had taken the longest to expunge all the bugs from, and therefore the pair in which he took the most pride. The entire RBaum master program and all of the incoming data were protected from thieving broker-hackers by a custom GW Peepbuster, the bottom line being that the system could only be interfaced with via ten-character alphanumerical passcode, which was changed every Sunday at midnight.

At 5:56 Friday morning Richard typed FOOTSIE-16, heard the affirmative whir, then took a small sip of his tea while he waited for the index to appear on the screen. He was riding a rampaging wheat bear and loving each plunge and each dip. Yes siree, Bob. He just loved it.

Maggie walked in on him just as the index came up. He drummed four tanned fingers and exhaled.

"So what's on the menu this morning?" said Maggie. She was wearing the powder blue SIOUX FALLS HIGH T-shirt she'd slept in, and she hoped she hadn't disturbed him.

23

"Good morning," said Richard. The light off his face was pale green. Is that how disturbed people look, Maggie wondered. He sniffed.

"Get it?" she said.

He didn't and did. Didn't say.

Maggie stared past him for five or six seconds, watching dawn come up over Wolf Point through his curved picture window. The Marina City towers were both still dark gray, but the light off the buildings downriver was a cool milky pink. She wondered if Richard had noticed.

Richard typed VOLCKER and tried to recapture his lost train of thought: it had something to do with the dollar.

The Wang churned and ticked. It was ready.

Moaning and stretching, torquing herself at the waist, Maggie shivered. Her vagina still ached from their screwing the previous evening. She yawned.

Richard looked up, not at Maggie, at nothing, then back at the brightening screen. He hit SRCH.

"Search for what?" said the Wang, right away.

Richard typed $M1.

The Wang churned and ticked. Maggie came around behind him and started massaging his shoulders. His thin spot was showing. She kneaded his lateral tendons. Churn, tick. Some figures came up on the screen. Richard leaned forward and squinted.

"Come to think of it, honey," she said, "what *is* on the menu this morning? I'm starving."

"Actually," he said, "this is work time."

"Fine, fine," she said, feigning mock insult, jerking her hands from his neck as though scalded. Once they were officially married, she wondered, would mornings be different? What about lunchtimes? Would evenings be better or worse? "I can, I suppose, take a hint."

Richard just stared at the columns of figures displayed in small dots on the screen. His eyes said it all. He just loved it.

My mother is a guppie.

LINDA MOANED, ripped a G chord, paused for three beats with the pick held high in the air, then slashed a quick bar chord while grinding her hip toward the mike stand. Feedback, two rimshots, a bass chord. Then all the stage lights went out: except for one cough and the tiny red exit signs, the Horizon was silent and dark. The next thing you heard were some tasty legatodelic notes being toggled by Linda with wah-wah. Guys whistled. Twin baby spots glinted off the chrome of her upside-down sunburst red Strat as the SRO crowd yeahed and hollered its pleased recognition: she had segued (without any intro and with typical deadpan irony) from "The Wait" to her spooky new cover of "Voodoo Child." Clicking the digital wah-wah with the ball of her foot, she soft-touched the rest of the measure, then signaled her drummer and bass player and hammered home two monster D chords. They loved it. Declan still hadn't arrived, but all that really meant was his charter was late—there was no way he wouldn't make *this* show. She stepped back from the mike as more lights came up, glancing stage left at the bevy of roadies and groupies, and showed the Horizon her profile. No flexes or smiles or bandannas, no makeup or jewelry or shoes. All she had on was a loose but too-short velvet bodice soaked through with ginsweat and Jasper Johns knickers crosshatched by hand by old Jap in the primary colors on white, plus the Strat. The guys in the front rows were creaming. Linda pretended she just didn't notice—or, if she did, could care less. She windmilled a G chord and let it feed back on itself while boosting her treble and aiming her Strat at the Voxes, then jangled her bangs from her eyes and sang: *Well I'm standing next to a mountain . . .*

Her room was a shambles. Torn shade, no curtains, not-quite-plumb walls stripped and peeling. Dusty fragments of cobweb hung from three of five corners. The paint was a yellowish gray interrupted by lighter, rectangular clean spots inside ancient brown tape marks. There were also graffiti, some tackholes, a handprint, dripped gray encaustic, bad drawings: Les Pauls, Giacomettis, Borofskys, self-portraits. The floor was more colorful: magazines, paperbacks, canvases, gessoed cafeteria trays, paper plates spattered with steak sauce and paint, a pillowless sheetless stained mattress. A Coke can. Cassettes and LP sleeves were strewn every which way. And clothes: cyclist shorts, blue and black Levi's, handpainted jackets and dresses, a Fearnley tartan kilt, a skindiver's suit, a red vinyl sheath dress, a blue rubber hiphugger miniskirt quartered by oversized zippers, a hysterical green one so narrow no *way* she could ever get in it—all this plus white Y-front undies, plaid anklets, a couple of frayed lacy camisoles, booties, a big black brassiere, low and high heels and above-the-knee boots and Air Jordans, T-shirts and gym shorts and sweatshirts. A sty.

Higher up, on the bookshelves and dresser and desktop, were seventeen fifths of Bombay, all of them with sunglasses, vertical hair, and great cheekbones drawn in green fine-tipped marker onto the face of the queen on the label, all of them empty but one: the one right beside the cassette deck. And, on the dresser, an in-progress still life of startling verisimilitude: a lime and a quarter, three tiny Taco Bell ashtrays, a Swiss army knife and an ice tray, reflected back into the mirror.

Closer at hand, on top of the speaker behind her, the glass: tall, cool, inviting, and sweating. Like Linda. Who now that her flash power solo was over, reached back and drained what was in it.

Her mother knocked hard on the door.

"Not home," Linda yelled.

Her mother knocked harder.

She put down her glass. "Yeah, come in."

Maggie opened the door and came in. She was wearing her pearly gray trenchcoat; underneath, Linda knew, was the blue shift she'd bought to get married in. She winced at the volume and exhaled, surveying the room with concerned resignation.

"What," Linda said.

"Could you please turn it down for a second?"

Linda moved toward the dresser, then stopped. She and her mother looked hard at each other. Hendrix repeated himself—*Don't be late*—then burned through some proton-fast riffs. Linda blinked twice, but Maggie had looked away first.

Linda hit REWIND.

Big silence.

The tape whirred and clicked in reverse.

"Listen," said Maggie.

"Don't you look nice," Linda said—with just enough English, she hoped, to let Maggie know what she thought.

"Why thank you."

The silence that followed was not quite so large but was denser, more urgent.

And longer.

"So," Maggie said. "We're going now, okay? Gonna do it."

"Okay?"

"You have enough money to last you, you think?"

Linda considered the question. That Maggie was good for a twenty or three was clinched by her just having asked it. If, on the other hand, Maggie assumed she—

"I'm good," Linda said, doing her best to sound tough, self-sufficient, and sober.

"Okay," Maggie said. In a hurry. She moved next to Linda and kissed her damp cheek. The same height exactly, they were also in much the same shape. With heels on, however, dressed up, Maggie looked leaner and taller. "I'll call you."

Exhaling gin and tobacco, inhaling Chanel number something, Linda did not say don't bother. What she did say was something that sounded like "Yeah."

They did not hug each other.

"See you Sunday," said Maggie.

"Okay," Linda said.

"Trades futures with who" had been all Linda wanted to know when His Lowness and Maggie had made their engagement official. It was over some big fancy brunch at the Drake the Friday before this last Easter. She had ordered eggs Benedict, her mother and Dickman the sushi. It could not have been too much more awkward. She had seen this day coming for months, basically since their dates started lasting all weekend, but hearing her mother pronouncing the actual words ("So that what we are planning to do, Lind, so long as you have no objections . . .") had still pissed her off, made her sick, and surprised her. The key word, she realized, was *we,* which helped her decision to leave her objections unstated—plus that way, she knew, they would have much more impact. She politely froze Richard, pointedly left what she'd ordered untouched, and gave Maggie the treatment she knew would combust her the most: "Or maybe I should say, with whom."

Since then she'd had no further comment. She'd made some vague plans to find her own place and move out but was too broke to do much but plan. She read *Hamlet* twice (once for a lit class, the next time to savor the sarcasm), started drinking even *more* like a carp, reread "The Dead" at Hank Rendeck's suggestion, stopped painting and doing her schoolwork, then read parts of *A Portrait* (again, for a lit class) and painted again, mostly self-portraits on trays, worse than ever.

Nothing much happened. She decided she wanted to kill him, but didn't. Elaborate plans—for the wedding, the move from the Northwest Side to Wolf Point, and the honeymoon—got frantically made. She ignored them. She started a journal using splashy black fountain-pen ink on flesh-colored 3 × 5 cards. *Tattoos,* she called it or them. She restricted herself to zero or one card per day, turned them all horizontal, used only the sides without lines, and tried conscientiously not to write any smaller than normal. When she ran out of card she was done. There was still always room for her entries, however, since, one, she had planned it that way, and two, she didn't have that much to say. Silence, daydreams of exile, and sarcasm: the recalcitrant daughter's three watchwords. Pathetic, she knew. Just pathetic.

By refusing to go to the wedding, however, she could tell that she'd got to them good. There was that. Because for the last several days both Maggie and Rick Dick Rich Richard had been going way out of their way, in their own special way, to make nice to recalcitrant daughter. They told her straight out what it was Richard wanted (her mother), let her know where he was coming from (Schaumburg), downplayed his age (twenty-seven, only nine short years younger than mother, almost nine long years older than daughter), revealed that his parents were dead (great, so were hers), displayed—and displayed and displayed—how much money he had (enough to buy dugout-side seats to weekend Cubs road games *and go,* a jet black Mercedes 250, a graphite black Porsche DP-935 cabriolet convertible, a black-hole black Lamborghini Countach that looked like something George Jetson would drive, and apparently five or six buildings, including the airplane hangar of a loft on Wolf Point where he lived, along with a bunch of bad art), and made futile attempts to explain where his money had come from (making killings, it seemed, on E Systems, bullion, and AIDS stocks in order to buy and or sell financial or food futures contracts either over the phone to New York or while standing in person in pits in the Loop, or vice versa). They told her in so many words that Rick Dick Rich Richard was undyingly anxious to be Maggie Krajacik's betrothed, to becoming recalcitrant daughter's unwicked and generous stepfather, and to make them one rich happy family of Baums. Yes indeed. They told daughter everything except what his problem was. Plus whatever they told her was always much more than she wanted to hear, about Richard. Or perhaps it was less than she wanted to hear. Linda could never decide. And so all they had told her, she figured, was more or less what she had wanted to hear.

About Richard.

oooooooh waaaaaaah
oooooooh waaaaaaah
oooooooh waaaaaaah
sing a song
play guitar
make it snappy

THE BRIDE was not pregnant as Maggie and Richard stood before Judge Mel McGuigan. She was wearing a circlet of baby's breath, earrings and necklace of uncultured pearls, a Dodger blue Nam Uong Dong shift hemmed one inch above the tops of the backs of her knees. Her daughter was not in attendance.

The groom's cocoa suit was unpinstriped flannel. His navy silk tie was knotted in a taut four-in-hand: a convex equilateral triangle. He had just had a haircut that made him look less thin and several years younger, and a very close shave with a straight razor.

They had never been buddies, but he and McGuigan had known one another since their days at DePaul. McGuigan had taught at the law school and Richard, a sophomore, had scalped him some student-rate Blue Demons tickets. Richard was now twenty-seven, McGuigan a year short of twice that. Both of their hairlines had started receding. McGuigan had found once that Baum Richard F. deserved supervision instead of conviction for a third violation in twenty-two weeks of the statutes prohibiting speeding five business days after Richie gave Mel one hot wheat tip. Plus their Cubs season tickets were both in Box 117.

Hitchlessly, deadpan, McGuigan recited the ninety-six words of the ceremony. From the windows on the LaSalle Street side of his chambers, twelve floors above Daley Plaza, the Picasso looked less like a hound than a woman. From the window on Washington, the State of Illinois Building did not look like Darth Vader's helmet. Faint strains of salsa rose up from the uncrowded plaza.

Richard sniffed, cleared his throat, then slipped a gold ring onto Maggie. With the medium heels she had on they were much the same height as they looked into each other's eyes. Then she slipped a ring onto him.

Three of their West Bank Club friends, plus Richard's best man and his wife, stood behind them. No one was crying. Both men had noticed that Maggie was not wearing nylons. Two of the women were smiling.

"You may not kiss the bride," said the judge.

Roughly two-thirds of the 397 receptiongoers at the West Bank Club were dancing to "Be My Baby." They had just danced to "Miss You," "(Dawning of A) New Era," "What's Love Got To Do With It?" and "Girls Just Wanna Have Fun." The band, the Tropes, from LA, had a skinny young black guy on vocals who could make himself sound and behave black or white, male or female, cockney or Motown or haircut, ska, house, or chutney and western. He could even do young Ronnie Spector.

Busboys were clearing dessert plates. Most were all business, but two helped themselves to champagne whenever they got half a chance. Another was mopping up vomit. Tuxedoed waiters were making the rounds with champagne, Frango mints, the last of the wedding cake, bottles of Corona and tall cans of Old Style, and coffee. One, a tall blonde with taut facial muscles, was allowing himself to be flirted with by well-to-do businesspeople. Another took time to make eyes at the Tropes' bass guitarist. One of the stockier ones had just helped to break up a fistfight.

Some people ran, one guy while yelling that others should do so, in terror, when a trio of jumpsuited trainers arrived with a bear on the end of three chains. Women screamed. Another stepped forward and ruffled the fur on the bear's huge black head. At the opposite end of the hall, as the Tropes segued into "Respect," nine other trainers were steering a black Andalusian bull down the ramp of a trailer. Its flared chocolate nostrils, the conical tips of its four-foot-wide horns, and the muscular hump on its shoulder made it seem very capable of wreaking real havoc. Most people backed off and gawked. The ponytailed videographer Richard's accountant had hired was taping the bear while her boyfriend, the stills guy, was snapping the bull, which was pissed.

With a mock-caustic glare, between the heads and over the shoulders of seven or eight of their guests, Maggie asked Richard: were large, live, and dangerous beasts really necessary?

Richard shrugged hopelessly: at least these two were.

But still: were they not a bit much?

Richard shrugged helplessly: yes.

A little bit obvious?

Hope so.

Bit hokey?

You bet.

Plus, *plus,* she told him by pinching her nostrils together: they stank.

That they did, he admitted.

They danced. Richard loved her right now, very much, but well understood he should not try to prove it by arhythmic shuffle and mince. The goddamn fast dancing was always his least favorite part of receptions; he liked it even less when how *he* was dancing was the center of half the attention. He kept staunchly at it, however, reminding himself there were much better ways, and ways he was good at, to let women know that a lovemaking session with him would be worth it. Maggie, for her part, seldom looked much more bodacious than when she was dancing, and knew it: simultaneously cool and high-energy, lean and curvaceous, mature but still youthful, streetwise and proper and wicked. She loved it.

A bond options trader cut in. Another pretended to give the chained bruin a Moe-style poke in the eyeballs. The Tropes' backup singers hitchlessly rendered the sock-it-to-me chorus while the lead guy did perfect Aretha. Jerking conservatively, Maggie lipsynced the chorus and worked at ignoring the drunk, frantic bonds guy, who had more or less straddled the bride of his colleague in grains and was twisting. Richard pretended he couldn't care less—to be watching, instead, the flirted-with waiter get coaxed to continue his decent Max Headroom impression. He could not see the waiter real well from where he was standing but could see the people who coaxed him. He could not tell what Maggie was thinking.

Some doctor's beeper went off as the bull, albeit briefly,

got loose. Nyuck nyuck nyuck nyuck. There were screams, savage laughter, and mad frantic dashes for cover.

There was none.

"Vell, Maggie Baum, can I borrow a few hundred grand now?" This was Angie Lovullo, who had processed figures and words next to Maggie at Shearson in the pre-Richard days and had followed her into the john. They had also escorted each other to their daughters' eighth-grade graduations. "I did, after all, know you when."

"Tell me you're happy for me," Maggie said, feeling tipsy. Plus she needed to pee rather soon.

"I'm happy for you," Angie said.

"How happy *are* you, for me?"

"I'm *so* happy for you."

"Yeah, right."

"No really. I am."

And they hugged.

"I know," Maggie said.

They occupied two empty stalls. The chaotic graffiti in Maggie's, among other (much worse) words and pictures, said GROAN, DON'T LOOK DOWN, PANT, YES, ISIAH, DON'T LOOK NOW BUT, DELUBED, IT WOULD COST ME A GROANING TO TAKE OFF HIS EDGE, WOULDN'T COST HIM A FARTHING TO TAKE OFF MY PANTS with the *h*'s crossed out with a different-colored marker, and TUSS. She heard Angie groan and wondered what hers said, then realized—

"Where's Linda?" said Angie. "Or shouldn't I ask."

"Groan," Maggie said.

"Still sulking?"

"She wants us to crash, burn, and die."

"She'll get over it, kid," Angie said after missing a couple of beats. "Don't you worry, okay?"

Maggie nodded.

"Just don't you worry."

"Who, moi?"

"Yeah, vous. Don't you worry."

"I'll try," Maggie said.

They stood at the mirror together. "A girl can get over a few million quid pretty quick," Angie said.

Maggie said nothing. She felt Angie sizing them up, comparing their faces and bodies, deciding which one had deserved to be suddenly rich.

"Let me tell you," said Angie.

Four younger women waltzed in. College kids. They were raucously cursing and singing but cooled out as soon as they saw who was in there. They all said congrats, lucky you, then disappeared into the stalls. Maggie did not know a one.

From inside a stall, one of them *psst* to her friend. "Which one was it?" she whispered.

The friend quickly shushed her.

"Hey," Angie said, loud enough for all concerned women to hear. She caught Maggie's eye in the mirror. "You sure you don't want to adopt me now, kid?"

Maggie just puckered and checked out her lipstick. She pretended that all she could hear were the shushes and whispers and pissing.

A bean oil trader was telling a joke in the men's room. Three guys are arguing about which is the oldest, the premier, profession: surgery, art, or the law. The surgeon says, What about Adam and Eve? When God opened up Adam's chest and pulled out that rib to make Eve, it clearly established surgery as the first, most creative profession. No way, goes the artist. The most powerful act of creation was clearly when God forged everything in the entire physical universe out of chaos. And remember: He did this a few days before putting the knife to old Adam. The surgeon admits this makes sense. The lawyer, however, just snorts, shakes his head. That's all well and good, he allows. But who do you jokers suppose created . . . *the chaos?!*

There were snorts, croaked guffawing, and strenuous nods of approval. Even the lawyers were hooting.

"You see that bull's balls?" someone said. "Or that fucking hump of muscle on its back? Jesus Christ!"

One of the endocrinologists asked, "You guys hear about the Ethiopian woman who *didn't* have AIDS?"

No one had.

But so where did the traders fit in, Richard wondered.

Maggie danced with a Taiwanese banker whose reverse-English name she had caught but forgotten, with a couple of less raunchy bonds guys, then finally danced slowly with Richard. The song was "Chances Are," Johnny Mathis, one of the very few covers the Tropes didn't nail to perfection. Our Song, she figured, pressing against her new husband. She remembered a few of her boyfriends, Janos and Kenny especially—she tried not to think about Michael—about how much or little she'd want them to see her right now. A robin's egg blue XJ6 wrapped with yard-wide white ribbon and tied with a curlicue bow had been parked by their table when she returned from her powder. Its plates said 4MAGGIE. From Richard. She loved him, she told him now, rubbing her cheekbone along his smooth jaw. But t'would cost you a Jaguar to take off my pants, she was thinking. Just kidding. She did. Did she love him as much as she thought she'd loved Michael? Not really. It wasn't the same, though. She was older and much more mature.

Some things meant more to her now. Plus she might want to start a new family. She could see Linda's point about some things with Richard, but all things considered, she thought she was acting real selfish. The biggest thing was that she'd never—

"I love you too," Richard told her, then hugged her and spun her around. The centripetal forces took her off guard and siphoned some blood from her brain. It was strange. When she opened her eyes her vision was fisheyed and hostile: almost half the men at her reception, she noticed, were older by over a decade than the girlfriends or wives they escorted. They also had much larger noses. She couldn't spot one single couple in which the woman was older. A few of them *looked* older, sure, but all that really meant was that this was how things had turned out. She was scared. Most of the women were blondes: waxed, flaxen, plastic. Like her. Or too skinny. She knew who they were, *what* they were, every one: secs, aides, or nurses, students or runners or phone clerks. Either that or the dark, curly, curvy type. Coke sluts with nose jobs was how she was tending to think of them now, just about every last one, as she held tight to Richard and followed his effortous lead, though maybe, she hoped, it was just the champagne or the Style. She did not want to be that way, really.

She was now Mrs. Richard F. Baum.

They left the reception at 10:45 to good-natured boos and applause. No fanfare, no rice, no JUST MARRIED crap on the bumper. They drove Maggie's present the block and a half to Wolf Point.

Richard read *Insight* while Maggie went into the den area and tried to call Linda. They made love on the floor unspectacularly but without too much pressure. She took a fast shower, then tried to call Linda again, this time from right in the bedroom. While she combed her wet hair out, Richard watched Tokyo grain ticks on unscrambled CBT cable. He told her how wicked she'd looked. She told him that he'd been a beast. What? The best. He turned off the lights and TV, and they kissed. She thanked him again for the Jaguar, made a joke about choker chains, curlicue bows, and McGuigan. He winced.

They agreed that the day had been fun.

Married today in some courtroom over bride's daughter's (coolly unstated) objections. Bride's daughter not in attendance. Invited, made nice to, but not in attendance. No way.

THE GHOST of her father was crouched on the edge of the tub, leaning over, moving its hand through the water. Linda had just run a bath for herself then gone down the hall for clean clothes. When she came back in, humming, and saw it, she exhaled, one very hard pant through her teeth. Didn't blink. Then another hard pant. Then she shivered. She had seen it before, several times, but only in daydreams or nightmares. Now it was here, the real thing, a dense shroud of virtual presence before her own eyes. Mike Krajacik. He'd been killed by some new kind of mine near Khesanh. Nineteen years ago. The platoon leader's letter arrived about seven days later. Linda hadn't even been born yet.

He lifted his hand from the bathtub, and clear water trickled back in. It was him. Linda had heard Maggie's stories, read the platoon leader's letter, pored over all the old pictures. A guy with a Brian Jones haircut, by himself or with Maggie, smoking hookahs or Winstons or reefers. A kid on a tricycle, crying. A lean blondish man in jungle boots, camouflage, big baggy pockets on the thighs of his pants, not that much older than she was: nineteen. Same color hair, same nose, eyes, and forehead. Her father. Half of his features were covered with sweat and burnt cork; the other half ran with wet gore. He was handsome. One of his shoulders and both of his arms were just gone, and flies buzzed around the dark wounds. Was he smiling? Focusing on him as hard and as sharp as she could, Linda still couldn't be sure.

What her father was doing, she realized, was trying to talk. Because now there was noise in the room, though it was more of a hoarse moaning sob than a voice, and distorted by echoes and reverb. It was *his* noise, however. His voice. That much she knew. She never had heard it before, but she knew. It was way out of sync with his mouth and was coming from somewhere behind him. She was doing her damnedest to make what it said make some sense, but she couldn't.

And then it got louder: a deep growling yell wrung with terror that punched Linda's breath from her chest, left it caught up in back of her throat. She could not sob it out. She could taste it.

The next thing she knew he was gone. Just like that. Though the voice lingered on for a second or two as ripples spread out in the bathtub, and Linda just watched them get wider.

Date unimportant.
Temperature ditto.
I *saw* him.

2

FRANK BAXTER, Linda's Time Design teacher, was barking in her ear like a crazed, drunken Bear fan. She danced. He was dodging and growling behind her and shouting things at her. "Reaction Formation" by Dick Holiday boomed from the person-sized speakers. He had to.

A film loop of the last ninety seconds of *High Plains Drifter* was projected onto the wall of the basement performance space. The projector was set on the small plywood stage she was dancing on. The stage was designed so that the harder she danced the more the film wavered and shimmered.

She danced. A grid of trapezoids and trapeziums had been masking-taped to the floor of the stage in roughly the shape of two crosses. The task was to keep your feet inside the grid, one shape per step, while you simultaneously watched the movie, listened to "Reaction Formation," and danced. While the *point,* Baxter had instructed the class, was to relate what went on in the film to the words of the song to the grid to yourself to the music—either that or *ignore* the grid's pattern (or the film, or the music) in provocative ways while paying *even better* attention to the four other things. To make things make new kinds of sense.

She could see Baxter clapping but couldn't quite hear him. He was sticking his tongue out at her as she tried to change times with Dick Holiday. Her classmates relaxed on the bare wooden floor. The tips of two cigarettes glowed in the dark. They were watching.

Her dancing, she hoped, was a smart person's version of hopscotch. Sideways, backward, diagonal hopscotch. Hopscotch with verve, edge, and wit. With Clint Eastwood.

Baxter curtsied and minced, mocking the halfassed plié she had foolishly tried to incorporate, though she knew he was merely "inciting" her. He'd been telling the class that he wanted them to use their "muscular" imaginations "with a vengeance." He'd also been playing them videos of Michael Jordan "driving the paint" in slow motion. Now he apparently wanted Linda to explode through the air with *her* tongue out.

She did.

"*That*'s how to move like a sister!" he yelled.

Some of her classmates applauded. Some whistled.

"See how she drops that trick butt?"

She continued to work at it, hard, doing her best to keep toes and heels inside the grid. It hurt but felt good. What she wanted to do was express some cracked but still juicy geometry—to go wild and stay under control. She was pumped.

Baxter yelled "Whoa!" and she paused, out of breath. Her shin splints and lungs were on fire.

"No no—keep *going!*" he yelled. Shook his head.

She sucked in more air and kept going.

Baxter turned back to the class. "I'm like, just, *whoa*—"

as he blew on his sizzling fingertips, shaking and cooling them off. "This little cracker's like, *wha?*"

There was laughter.

"Plus always remember," he shouted. "Irresponsible behavior will be appreciated only so long as it is *terrifically* irresponsible."

What?

"That goes for you too, girl!" yelled Baxter, his index finger extended point-blank in her face. "Pull the trigger!"

She danced irresponsibly. Terrifically, she hoped, irresponsibly. Hard. Like indigenous tribeschick in war party throes had gone nuts. Like she no longer knew from no shit.

Her classmates were whooping and hooting and whistling. Two guys got up and were barking and snarling with Baxter. She was making a spectacle of herself, and they loved it. It was killing her. *Ah.* And damn the trapeziums too! Gay men, Frank Baxter, gay and straight, women and guys were thinking about having sex with her. She suspected her sweat smelled like gin.

For the sixth or eighth time, Clint and his pinto disappeared into the wall. The Holiday's rave-up was just about over. Everyone knew what was coming. Get down.

The vocalist whispered "reaction formation," making her voice sound like Clint's.

Linda listened.

GHOST WAVES

> Once you have given up the ghost, everything follows with dead certainty, even in the midst of chaos. Amen.

HEAVING AND grunting, cursing hard under their breath, two huge young movers had the six-foot-long navy blue crushed velvet couch about a ninth of the way out the front door. It was up on one end, turned sideways and tilted a little, jammed good and tight in the doorframe. The movers, however, seemed like they knew what to do. The guy on the inside was white and the guy on the outside was black. The white guy was fat, and his beltless Levi's had slipped down too low, exposing his raw hairless crack. He was sweating.

Even if Linda had wanted to help, there was simply no way. The movers had taken both doors off their hinges, so there wasn't even something to hold. She stood there and watched. The couch wasn't budging from the angle they had it at now, but she sensed that they wouldn't give up. Not these guys. The couch, after all, must've fit through this fucking door *once* . . .

Maggie came into the hallway. Linda could tell she'd been crying, but she didn't look sad. In fact, she looked strangely euphoric. She was wearing a pleated white tennis dress and holding a pair of brass lamps: their cords had been neatly bound up and taped to their bases—which was Maggie all over, she thought. She also was wearing the ring.

"Would you take these?" said Maggie.

She took them.

Maggie glanced at the men and the couch, then went back down the hall to her bedroom.

Their apartment was just about empty. They'd repainted four rooms (all except Linda's) only eight or nine months ago, and the walls and the ceilings were still crisp flat off-white. Linda remembered that paint job: masking the windowpanes, using the *Reader* to cover the things that were too big to move into her room, how much her wrists and her back and her shoulders had ached after doing her share of the ceilings, not to mention the sick fishy smell of fresh wall paint that hung on for days and days after—even if it *was* the best painting she'd managed to finish since then.

Maggie came back lugging two more big lamps.

"You told me this place had track lighting."

Maggie shrugged. "We'll see what we need when we get ourselves settled. We can always just toss them, I guess."

The blue couch had finally slipped through. The white guy hoisted his end up and was easing his way through the door. His pants had slipped down even lower.

Linda and Maggie waited a moment, not looking, then followed the couch and the men down the steps, first quickly, then slowly, forming a motley four-person procession across uneven patio flagstones, down the short driveway, and up the steel ramp of the van.

They loaded the new XJ6 with things like old china and records, then turned in their keys to Mr. Sadlowski, their landlord, who lived right upstairs. They had lived in the apartment on Eastwood for seventeen years, during which time Mr. Sadlowski had raised their rent twice: they'd started out paying $65 a month and ended up paying $160. Mr. Sadlowski was too sick to come to the door. His great-grandson Paulie accepted the keys and gave them both kisses goodbye.

Maggie had last-minute shopping to do. She was packing, Linda noticed, a shiny new platinum credit card with M. BAUM on the signature line: she wouldn't leave Dick's side without it. What she "needed" this morning was a white Prince ceramic tennis racquet, so she stopped at the West Bank Club pro shop and picked up some ankle-high training shoes, a white Fila warmup, five pairs of socks, and, incidentally, the racquet, which she left in the shop to be strung. She tried to buy Linda some outfits, but Linda refused even sweatsocks. Linda also had noticed—but had so far resisted the temptation to mention—that Maggie now seldom missed chances to stock up on pricey new tsatskes: hammered white gold candelabra, a Russian white lynx calf-length coat, a leather hippopotamus, a Roger Brown multiple, "joke" chandeliers for the parking area. She even had managed to get the recalcitrant daughter herself to the post office to apply for her passport ("never know when you might need it," she'd said), though her actual purpose was so that Richard could take them to Paris. And Linda's tuition, including the $3675 she still owed from last year, was now paid in full. Plus Linda could pick out a car if she wanted.

She didn't. Nor was she going to Paris, at least not with Maggie and Richard. When she did go to Europe she would go there alone or with friends, and to London. Nor was she taking—

"No really," said Maggie. "Why don't you?"

"Why don't I what?"

"Get a car."

"What? So it's part of the deal that he's gotta be buying us *cars* now?"

"We just thought you might like to have one. I mean, talk about looking a gift horse—"

"No chance. Unless I could sell it and use what I got to move out. But I guess that's not part of the deal."

"It isn't," said Maggie.

The deal was real simple: if recalcitrant daughter would be good little girl and move in along with her mother, her material needs would be all taken care of; if she didn't, they wouldn't. A neat little trade, fair and square. Her counter-proposal, that Maggie could lend her a few hundred dollars to help get her started in a place of her own, had been turned down by Maggie as "silly."

"Exactly what's silly about a twenty-year-old college student not dying to live with her mother? At least half of the people my age live in dorms or apartments."

"Nineteen. Besides. Believe it or not, I still love you."

"That's hardly the point and you know it. I mean gimme a break."

"But that's where you're wrong," Maggie said. She had taken the tone Linda hated the most: thoroughly confident in its old-fashioned wisdom—smug, safe, and snug in the driver's seat. "Because if you'd really like to know, that's the *whole* point."

That had been Maggie's big pitch all along: she would

miss her too much if she didn't come with her. She loved her. No one was making a deal, no one was "trading her future," no one was forcing anything on anyone. It might *seem* like they were, but they weren't. And Maggie still needed her daughter around "to provide continuity," just like Linda still needed to be with her mother, "now more than ever, in fact," blah blah blah. She also insisted that Linda was "still just too young" to be off by herself, trying to work to pay rent *and* tuition and still have some time left for schoolwork. Besides: it was "just for a couple more years," till she turned twenty-one, by which point she'd have her degree and would therefore be better prepared to decide what she wanted to do. And besides: sooner or later she'd realize how wrong she had been about Richard. In the meantime, with her own little wing in the back of the loft, she could paint, play her music, have friends over, and come and go pretty much just as she pleased, which was how it had been back on Eastwood. "It'll be just like a dorm," Maggie said. "Only better."

"Yeah, right."

"Just one other question," said Maggie, and Linda could tell what was coming. "Is it too much to ask of—"

"—of one's only daughter?" said Linda. "The one person left in one's life? Just this once, let's skip the close-little-family routine. I mean, you of all people . . ."

"Well is it?" said Maggie.

Well was it? She had to admit, although never to Maggie or Richard, that the plusses were real tough to beat. That school would be paid for would eliminate the number one hassle she'd had—until Richard. She would also get thirty-five dollars a week for her "other expenses"—Maggie had not said "allowance," but that clearly was what it would be. There was also the fact that the loft was so close to the School: the Ravenswood el went right there from the Merchandise Mart; she also could walk it in twenty-five minutes. Plus, since she'd live right downtown, there would also be plenty of places to waitress close by, like Debevic's, Ditka's, or Heyday. She would not have to take the allowance *or* the new car. She would not have to work at Large Bob's anymore, go scrounging for loans and half-scholarships, or take Maggie's last hard-earned dimes for tuition.

The only real minus was Richard: having to live right there with him, beholden for just about everything to the very last person on earth she wanted to breathe the same air as, right upstairs from where he'd be fucking her mother, let alone *owing* him something, the little ass-miserable prick. It was hard to say which would be worse, being there with them or having Maggie there all by herself, when just the idea of him touching her mother turned her nerves to hot grease and shut down her brain altogether.

Her bottom-line assessment of the deal was that if she had any balls she would turn them down flat and move out. Quit school, maybe be poor for a while, find a good roommate or get a small studio, start waiting on tables full time. Just do whatever she had to. And *show* them. The truth was, however, at least the way things stood right now, that she didn't.

Richard's three-story building was set on its very own little peninsula, which jutted into the Chicago River where the three branches merged at Wolf Point. A half-block-square fortress was what it amounted to really, nestled down low among all the new River North buildings—and more going up by the minute.

From across the river, at the corner of Wacker and Wells, it looked like a cross between a slate-and-glass chessboard and the Toyota/Cadillac dealership it had been before Stanley Tigerman got his hands on it. From the West Bank Club sundeck its green-tinted glass both reflected and echoed the warped convex face of Nuveen's William Pedersen building; it also caught part of the river.

Closer up, approaching the building by boat or on foot or by car, you were faced with a sheer twelve-foot wall of putty-colored cement. No doorbell, no mailbox, no windows. Vandalproof cameras (with floodlights at night) were aimed at all three of the walk-, float-, and drive-through steel doors, which, if the person inside so desired, would slide open sideways, admit you, then quickly clang shut. To those who'd approached uninvited, what the building proclaimed loud and clear, Linda thought, was FORGET IT.

Inside was something. Maggie and Richard had been working with a designer named Garth or Greg something to "achieve 12,650 square feet of unified living space that was contemporary, casual, and extravagant, all at the same time," this according to the *Tribune*'s recent "Tempo" feature on Richard.

The main loftrium was two and a half stories high. A twenty-five-foot rhomboid grid of windows looked south toward Nuveen, southeast toward the rest of the Loop, and east down the river—at, Linda noticed, a slightly less floppy, much much less colorful version of the Red Grooms sculpto-pictorama of this part of town, in reverse. It was something.

All the furniture Greg or Garth had selected had names. The H's alone included Stan Houlberg, Steven Holl, Ho S. Kim, Holly Hunt, and Keith Haring. The den space (den area?) had synthetic cheetah-skin carpeting, authentic antelope hides on the wall, and live trout and perch in between.

The master bathroom was more like a spa than a place you would go to floss your teeth, bathe, or relieve yourself. It had two sinks, two showers, a black sunken tub with a whirlpool, a bidet, and two toilets. The fixtures were hammered white gold. There was a fireplace, cacti, his and hers

Nautilus, *Jokes for the John, The New Yorker,* and dozens of large scarlet towels. The floor had an art deco pattern of light amber granite inlaid with dark amber onyx. Two entire walls and half of another were mirrored. Things would recede from you quickly, repeating themselves isometrically, getting smaller and smaller but never—not quite—disappearing. Which basically gave you two choices: keeping your eyes closed or watching yourselves taking shits. Unmirrored square pillars were hung with a series of Hockney lithographs featuring tanned young men with white buttocks cavorting together in sparkling cerulean pools, taking showers alone and together, jackknifing up off warped boards into well-rendered blue-and-glare nothing.

Richard parked his cars in an area just off the living room, if that's what you'd call the center of a vast open space where a TV and sculpture and Italian leather couches and fireplace were, but which was apparently not to be confused with another large area fifteen or so yards beyond it, vaguely demarcated at one end by a freestanding two-sided bookshelf and on the other by a massive aquarium in which more perch and trout (no alewives?) cavorted, and between which were cacti, a wetbar, a fig tree, a beige pre-Columbian globe, a black bearskin rug, a Nakamichi stereo system, a couple of oversized Infinite Slopes, another (identical) fireplace, another TV, and more leather couches, so that when Linda and Maggie's two movers had unceremoniously deposited *her* couch, at Richard's impatient behest, in the middle of an empty and carpetless and more or less undefined space about ten yards beyond these two areas, it looked more than a little ridiculous.

"That'll be fine," said Richard. "For now."

"Can say that again," Linda said, more or less under her breath.

Maggie said, happily, "Huh?" She was pleased that her husband and daughter had finally agreed about something. She wanted to know what it was.

The movers gawked at the loft, saying nothing.

Richard said nothing.

"Nothing," said Linda.

The room designated as Linda's was upstairs and under the roof, in a part of the building that had not been remodeled and where the spaces were much less wide open. The room itself had once been an office in the service department, and apparently not the big boss's: it was L-shaped but not very large. A third of one wall was composed of translucent glass bricks. (What would she look like undressing, she wondered, seen through these bricks late at night from the street, with a light on above or behind her?) There was also a small clear-glass window that looked east past the Merchandise Mart and the el, down the river. The rest of the walls were cinder blocks painted the same glossy gray that the door was. The floor had been covered with industrial wall-to-wall carpet, slate gray, that was several shades darker and cleaner where the cabinets and floor mats had been.

As she stepped farther into the room, gauging wall space for posters and mentally arranging her furniture, Linda suddenly felt something behind her. She turned her head, saw it, and screamed. *Jesus Mary and Joseph!* Because standing there waiting to welcome her, leaned up against the near wall, was a uniformed man with a smile on his face.

Mr. Goodwrench.

She exhaled and calmed herself down. She prided herself on not being chicken or jumpy, and the fact that she'd screamed pissed her off. Although now that the shock had subsided, she had to admit she was pleased. The room's only drawback, in fact, was that it did not have a closet: there was no place to hang things except for some hooks on the walls and the back of the door. After doing a little exploring, however, she came upon what must have been a broom closet a few steps away down the hall. And then just around the corner from the closet she discovered a small *but her very own* bathroom. It was only a toilet, a sink, and a medicine cabinet, with not enough room to change clothes, but she still was ecstatic to have it. It even had its own little north-facing window. She figured she'd put up a curtain and be able to bathe from the sink, European style —or bathe not at all, if she had to. The point was that now she would not have to share one with *them.*

She test-flushed the toilet and grinned—couldn't help it —when it gurgled and whooshed into action, losing herself for a tick in the hard clockwise suck of the water.

It worked.

She hooked up her stereo and put on WSAI while she unpacked her records. Could she live here? She couldn't decide. "Do You Know What I Mean?" by Lee Michaels and Frosty was playing. Okay. The movers had brought up her mattress and dresser and desk, along with the parts of her bed frame. Everything fit, but just barely, and her easel was still in the hallway. Her clothes and the rest of her stuff were piled up in boxes and Jewel bags or spread out on top of the mattress. Oink oink, she thought. Just like home.

As she transferred her T-shirts and sweaters from Jewel bags to drawers, she firmly resolved that, at least as far as the chaos of her room was concerned, there would now be a whole different Linda. And while she was at it she figured she might as well also resolve to start painting again. What the heck. Then she further resolved *with the help of Thy grace* that she'd drink less.

The SAI reception was bad, but it got a lot better when she found, then attached, the antenna. Voilà. She spread out the ends of the T and moved them around, tuning in, then taped them in place to the wall.

"These Things Happen" by Peter Gordon and David Van Tieghem came on, and she turned up the volume and frugged a few steps by herself. Like a ditz, but who gave. She grabbed Mr. Goodwrench, pressed his smooth cardboard cheek against hers, paused for dramatic effect, and then tangoed. The rhythm, of course, wasn't perfect, not quite 4/4 time, but was Goodwrench complaining? No way. He didn't dance bad for a grease monkey, either. A little bit stiff maybe, but since when did a girl let that bother her? And Van Tieghem and Gordon were cooking now, old Mr. Goodwrench was holding her up close and personal, step step step *close,* extra tight, when all of a sudden the music was interrupted by a hodgepodge of distant male voices, all shouting. And then, just as suddenly, the shouting got quantum leaps closer. There was also some maddening static and what sounded like—what? A machine gun? She knew "These Things Happen" by heart —these sounds weren't on it. Her first guess was that it was probably interference from a passing police car. Or maybe she was simply too close to the Merchandise Mart, where the station was broadcasting from. Or maybe—

And then, through the static, one of the shouting male voices became more distinct. Even calm. It said, "Linda?"

She held Mr. Goodwrench. Say what?

And then, again: "Linda."

Her father? She thought so but couldn't be sure.

She waited and listened. Far in the background, in another whole world, she could make out Van Tieghem's tattoos on the high hat and P. Gordon's faint strains of sax. Closer in, on the frequency where all the shouting had been, there was nothing but feedback and droning.

She listened and waited, noting: *I am now sober.*

"These Things Happen" gradually began to get clearer, then louder, but she waited until it was normal.

Okay.

Tensed up, collected, she listened.

> And so all of a sudden we're rich. And it isn't all bad. But Baum (pun intended) is a name I won't go by. No way. I'm still a Krajacik, however M. Baum wants to play it. And at least from now on always will be.

RICHARD WAS trying to concentrate. His Exportkhleb contact was due to be calling from London; he wanted to know how the satellite photos had matched with their actual yields. The Koncertina Kid had moved in and was making more waves with his wife. The subsidized EEC wheat was now seventeen dollars a ton under his, yet Tradex had not made an offer. He had a sore throat and a headache. The dollar had been murdered again in Tokyo, London, and Bonn. He'd also been having these dreams. . . .

He spread his mail out on the desk. *Crain's*, *Futures*, *Grain*,

BOMC News, and the *Journal.* Lynch, his accountant, requested his signature on seven new leases. The Zara Baines Gallery was pleased to announce an opening three Fridays hence for Togrul Farmanovich Narimanbekov, an Azerbaijani painter. Chemlawn was having a sale on crabgrass retardant. Field's, too, was having a sale. Air France had expressed him the honeymoon tickets. Via one real slick flyer, the International Society of Wang Users requested his attendance at their annual Technetronic Conference in Boston: write-offable fees were $640 for non-ISWU members (like him), $590 for members—before April 15; after that they went up to $690/$640. Since the annual membership dues were $85, which included a subscription to . . .

He'd been doing fantastic at work, had finally found and latched onto the woman he thought he wanted to settle down and have kids with. . . . The thing was, he'd badly discounted the Kid factor, underestimating by a couple of orders of magnitude what a contrary and obstinate cunt she would turn out to be. How *could* have RBaum been so wrong? Scoping the likely untoward was his specialty, his main claim to fame, and his failure of perspicuity (and balls) in the case of the Kid was haunting him now day and night. He'd gone out with Maggie three times before she had mentioned her seventeen-and-a-half-year-old daughter. Not that she'd lied to him or anything, or gone out of her way to keep it a secret; the subject just never came up. (They'd met at a Monday Night thing at the Ultimate, and their first couple of dates had been Bear games, some dinner—no sex whatsoever, however, until date number four: about average.) At first he hadn't thought he'd mind being a stepfather, especially since the real dad and husband was so thoroughly out of the picture. Even after five or six months had gone by, and Maggie invited him to Linda's graduation (with the graduate, of course, acting sullen as hell in her mortarboard, pearls, and blue gown—though he'd had to admit she looked "darling"), he still hadn't taken the hint. His only consolation was that he *had* had the good sense to hedge, pretending to Maggie from the very beginning that having her daughter fuck right off out of their life was the *last* thing he wanted to happen. He also thanked Christ that he'd taken this position early enough to be able to sell it to Maggie. Because right off the bat he'd been able to tell she'd insist, so he'd made goddamn sure that Linda moving in with them had been his idea in the first place. The trouble with this position, as well as the beauty of it, was that all he could do now was wait for the Kid to decide on her own to move out. What he couldn't help wondering was whether she'd sensed this somehow and was countering, waiting him out, doing her best to cast *him* in the role of the Homewrecker Asshole Supremo. She was spooky enough, with a big enough chip on her shoulder, that there wasn't too much he'd put past her.

But what the fuck else could he do? He'd gone out of his way from day one to make nice to her and she'd repaid the favor by busting his balls ever since. Even when she blew off the wedding and soured the whole day for Maggie, he'd tactfully defended her behavior as being "perfectly understandable for a young woman in her position" and as something she would "get over." He'd even suggested that *Maggie* had overreacted: chancy at the time, to be sure, but a real savvy play in the long run. The clincher, he'd figured, was suggesting to Maggie that they invite her along on the honeymoon. When Maggie had balked, he'd insisted. After all, he had argued, what a marvelous chance it would be for a student her age, an art student no less, to be able to travel to Paris, see the Louvre, the Rodins, the Pompidou Center, not to mention the opportunity it would provide for the three of them to spend some quality time together on neutral territory and really get to know one another, to make a fresh start as a family. . . . He had to admit that in pitching the plan he had waxed pretty eloquent, but he'd still been a little surprised when Maggie had bought it. He'd been floored when the Kid bought it too. But so now that the tickets were written, the hotel rooms booked, the itinerary worked into his schedule and his dates with Kerenyev confirmed . . . now that Maggie was enthusiastically committed to the idea, wouldn't really be happy, in fact, unless the Kid tagged along . . . now that the whole thing was settled, the Koncertina Kid was making noises to suggest that she just might not deign to accompany them, that she appreciated the offer and all but still might not be able to make it. . . .

The telephone rang, but he sensed it wasn't Kerenyev.

Correct. It was Lynch.

"What," Richard said.

A Polaroid snapshot clipped to a thin stack of grocery receipts fell from the sleeve of her leather as she emptied onto her mattress the black plastic bag that her jackets were packed in. She fingered the twist-tie, testing its sharp wire point, and stared at the upside-down picture. She couldn't help wondering where it had come from but was not all that anxious to see who was in it. She was not in the mood for surprises.

The picture showed her sitting on Maggie's lap in the driver's seat of their old maroon Nova; you could tell they'd just bought it because the sticker was still on the window behind them. The Nova was parked alongside some bushes and Linda was pretending to drive it. Her hair was still long and light blond. She was squinting. Maggie had a modified Rod Stewart haircut and had made herself cross-eyed for the person who was taking the picture. Since Linda was seven or eight, Maggie was at least twenty-five, but she looked like she was still in high school. Linda could vaguely remember seeing this picture before, but she didn't have any idea who had taken it. She also could not figure out what its connection might be with the ten-year-old grocery receipts.

She picked through the rest of her jackets, looking for clues without really thinking that one would turn up, then surprised herself more than a little by finding a lime green school folder from which the picture and receipts must have fallen. Real strange. Inside the folder were four other stacks of receipts (the kind of thing only a person like Maggie would save), an eight-by-ten glossy of her second-grade class, a crisp dollar bill with a dime and three nickels Scotch-taped to it, and an L-shaped sheet from which four of nine wallet-sized prints of her squirrelly, gap-toothed school picture were clipped. There was also a waterstained sheet of typing paper, folded twice like a letter, mimeographed in smeared purple ink.

LINDA K.

I was strong when I was in my mom's stomach. I kicked my mom and she ate pizza and got sick. One night my mom did not feel good. In fact my mom felt awful because she was having me then. She had me. When I was first born the doctor held me upside down and I wasn't breathing. So he was shaking me to get the air out and then he put an oxygen mask on my face and then they cleaned me off. I was my mom's only baby and they said, "Is that all?" and she said, "I think so." My dad Mike was dead. No one saw him get blown up by a mine, but he did. He was dead. Then I came home and stayed in my crib for like three days and my mom just carried me around.

When I was two I never slept. My mom had to pick me up and run around the house and sing me a song while she's running around the house. I was always naked. I laid on my mom's tummy before I went to bed. And I ate everything my mom gave me. I was always snacking. I was at my mom's job in a crib. I went on a roller coaster when I was a baby, but not one that went upside down.

When I was four I just wandered around and I always

went to my best friend Pammy Szabo's and we always bit each other and then we'd make up. I always ate whatever was on my plate except for broccoli and tomatoes. I only liked the good stuff. We lived in an apartment with one bed and I was helpful. I was scared of dogs. When I went to my uncle's I saw his dog Abbie. She got run over by a car.

In kindergarten I met my friends Dana and Lydia. I learned how to play nice and learned not always to bite people. When we were doing a project we always got to paint a picture of it. I liked to paint a lot.

In first grade I hated the spelling tests. I didn't have enough time. Made a lot of friends. That's the year Lydia wasn't in my class and that was the year I was the trouble-maker. But first grade got easier for me. The spelling tests were not that hard. In silent reading I always looked at the pictures. I liked that.

Now I am in second grade. I am seven and a half years old. My favorite color is blue. My favorite animal is a cat. My favorite sport is blamball. My four best friends are Liz, Birgitte, Dana, and Lydia.

She still could remember dictating this to Ms. Guenther, her second-grade teacher at Kizer. She even had heard half the words in her second-grade voice as she read them. My favorite animal is a cat. Always naked. Because she was having me then.

How something as large as this folder had found its way into the bag with her clothes, or inside the sleeve of her leather, she did not have a clue. She had packed by herself, stuffing her clothes into garbage bags the morning they'd moved; all Maggie's clothes had been sealed up in boxes for days.

She went through her jackets again, looking for more stray mementos, then emptied out four other bags and sifted through her clothes. That was it.

She sat on the mattress and stared at the Polaroid. She wanted to see if, by concentrating hard on the upper left corner, a third face might start to develop.

61

If I had any balls I'd move out, but I don't. If I had any balls I'd play a whole lot of things pretty different.

RICHARD WAS pissed that he'd had to put the honeymoon plans back on hold while he waited to see how the Russian wheat harvest developed. Maggie did not seem to mind, though. She said it would give her and Linda some time to get settled. Which figured.

He gazed at the willows outside, sipped his tea. Where *was* his new wife, by the way? Didn't she sense that he wanted her to come to his office now and bug him?

No, he concluded. She shouldn't right now. He was thinking.

The metaphysics of futures, of options on futures, of calls and strike prices, making money when price structures fell *or* got boosted, did, he admitted, intrigue him, but the sex life of wheat was what drove him. The tasselization of polyploids, GB2 strains of sorghum, how mature parts of male seedlings under certain uncertain conditions were bonded together with the complementary parts of the female. It was truly a discipline, the sex life of wheat, although marrying Maggie helped, he decided. The better he got at it, the better his own had become.

And now that he thought about it, he decided he wanted her daughter to sit on his mouth, on his tongue, just to smother him, grind him, and twist without mercy. He wanted to lap her deliciously bitter perineum, to be helplessly at her—

He felt someone watching him. Froze. In the hallway behind him. But who? Maggie was still at her tennis lesson; she wouldn't be home for another ten minutes, he'd thought. He also had asked her—had *told* her—not to sneak up behind him like this, especially when he was working. And he knew it couldn't be Linda. Since the day she'd moved in she had strenuously made a point of avoiding the part of the loft he was in, especially when Maggie was out.

He could still feel the presence, however, and was sure it was female. He was pissed off and turned on and scared in just about equal-sized lots. It was strange.

There was nothing to do now but turn around and look.

There was nothing.

Linda had tried several gins but liked to be loyal to one. Tanqueray packed the wickedest punch, 94.6 export-strength proof, and came in the prettiest bottle. The Beefeater bottle was easy to handle, but its overall vibes were too stodgy: it reminded her of sloshy dink farts with martinis. The cheapo American gins, like Burroughs or Seagram's or Fleischmann's, were fine for the odd gin and tonic, but sipped straight they tasted like something you'd rub on sore backs. Which was how, more or less, she'd got started. It was at a Fourth of July block party the summer between eighth grade and Steinmetz. It was almost a hundred degrees out, and she'd just gotten done playing volleyball. All she had on were some shorts and a tube top. Jimmy Nawrocki's old man had come up behind her and pressed his ice-cold gin-and-tonic glass into the sweaty and sunburned small of her back, and she'd screamed. Then, just to show him, she grabbed it and drank it straight down. It tasted like very cold, very wet Christmas trees and made her feel instantly great. She'd discovered her magic elixir.

What she liked about gin in general was that, except in the summertime, no one else drank it, or hardly. She liked how it looked and smelled clean. It made her feel smart, cosmopolitan: exotic and urban, that is, not meringue-brained and cleaved like the magazine.

Bombay sort of struck her as the most international. To make it they used coriander seeds from Morocco, licorice and angelica root from England, orris flowers from Italy, juniper berries from Germany, lemon peel from Spain, and almonds and cassia bark from Indochina. She was often convinced she could taste each ingredient. They distilled it from a special 1761 recipe in London, the home of most great rock and roll. The red, green, and gold on the label reminded her of Christmas trees, and she liked Queen Victoria's picture: she looked sassy and fat and in charge.

There were also the lines from that Campion poem, "Gin and Tonic," she could never exactly remember. Something like:

I stank, of lime I thought, and chattered from the ice
While craning my neck off the hammock to kiss her bare knees
She tapped my thrilling ganglia with a lemon croquet mallet
And I'd prod her with wickets till her back glowed ultramarine
Until it would cost her a something to . . .

Something. She took a big sip of Bombay and tried not to think about sex. She wondered, instead, about Christmas trees: what they had or did not have to do with St. Joseph. It was too hot to picture him clearly, so she took two more sips. She still couldn't picture him clearly. She could not picture Christmas trees either.

She pictured herself onstage at the Cabaret Metro singing "Pursued by the Ghost," a song from her most recent album and one she had written with two of the Pogues. She had written the lyrics herself, and she, Jem, and Declan had worked out the music. For some bizarre reason Declan had not received credit from ASCAP when the album came out, which had led to their first major fight: it was hard to be lovers when your lawyers were trying to shred one another, and you along with them, and were charging you big for the privilege. She tried not to think about that.

She was still "from Chicago," she guessed, but all the time she'd been spending in London and Dublin and Glasgow of late had added a slight lilting brogue to her voice, which became more pronounced when she sang. The Metro was shoulder-to-shoulder with rowdy young guys; the girls who were there were on dates. Several rows back, by himself, drinking a toast to her voice, was Hank Rendeck. The glare of the stagelights off the polished blond wood of her Martin was reflected into his eyes. He was squinting.

She was wearing the same cornflower blue prairie dress Suzanne Vega had worn on "Saturday Night Live" to do "Luka" and "Marlene on the Wall." Her voice hadn't been very strong for that show; she'd seemed kind of nervous. But she still had looked stunning. Even in close-up, with all the TV lights, her skin looked translucent and flawless, with two little nonacne scars on her cheek. (Which meant all the chanting she'd done for clear skin must have worked.) When she played at the Bismarck she'd worn black, black, and black: shoes, stovepipe trousers, and a loose-fitting open-necked sweater that coyly revealed one red bra strap. From the second row in the balcony, Linda could see she looked good, though from her hips to her knees she hadn't looked overly skinny. She'd also made time to tell jokes: about being a Puerto Rican Avon Lady, who Luka actually was (and was not), New York City, and "dating." Linda remembered how much harder and tighter "Straight Lines" had sounded that night, compared to the studio version.

She took two small sips. That was it. She couldn't think of a single famous woman painter who also was beautiful. As. Someone like Georgia O'Keeffe didn't count: it seemed like she'd always been ancient, more handsome and venerable than big-star-type gorgeous. Barbara Kruger didn't paint, Barbara Bysshe couldn't. Vera Klement? What about Moira Dryer, or someone like Lisa Milroy? Should Jenny Holzer count? Cindy Sherman? Who knew.

She stared at her racks of cassettes, her five plastic milk crates of albums, her neat stacks of canvas board, canvas, and swiped cafeteria trays. Nancy Haynes? Nah. Hollis Sigler?

She wanted to get a CD player but did not want M. Baum to help pay. Everyone had one but her. (Janet Cooling.) Plus you couldn't even *buy* tapes or albums these days . . .

She noticed that the cluster of empty Bombay fifths had uniform layers of dust on their shoulders.

She wanted to be irresistible.

then listen now
to what I say

SHE WAS drinking and snooping, sifting through Rick Dick Rich Richard's desk drawers and file cabinets, rotating his Rolodex, checking out letters he'd opened. She knew if she had any balls she would open some *un*opened ones, but she didn't. She swallowed a belch that did not taste like Christmas trees, swigged more Bombay, unfolded a letter from *Esquire.*

Item thirty on the questionnaire from the editors of their annual Register wanted to know how many people he'd slept with. (1) Fewer than five? (2) Six to fifteen? (3) Sixteen to twenty-five? (4) Twenty-six to thirty-five? (5) Thirty-six to forty-five? (6) More than forty-five? He first had checked (5), then whited it carefully out and checked (2).

Undecided.

Although wasn't that a somewhat unusual way to feel for

a member of a select group of American men and women who were under forty years of age and who had already made significant contributions to their respective fields of endeavor? For a man who was being saluted as part of a generation unmatched in idealism, energy, and accomplishment?

And what about *one*, Linda wondered.

She tossed the sheets back on his desk and stared out his accomplished, select picture window. A plane and two clouds were reflected, upside down it sure looked like, in the concave and shimmering face of Nuveen, the "333 Wacker Building."

Or none.

She lit a cigarette, blew a long plume of smoke toward his Wang, an imperfect ring toward his copier, then flicked the match onto his carpet.

Fuck *him*.

There was something about him she hated. She could not put her finger on it, but it always was there. She could taste it. The browns of his eyes tried to hide it, to maintain his cover—no chance. It reminded her of static electricity, the no-taste of lasers or glass. It also was faintly metallic. Waves of it zapped her whenever she saw him or pictured him down in his pit, or with Maggie. He did not even have to be there.

Other things bothered her, too. His pores, for example. His thin blowdried hair. The way he winked at you to say that the joke was on somebody else—or vice versa. The way he sandwiched both clammy hands around the one he was shaking, or blew ropes of snot from each nostril before he came in from a jog. And what about his shirts with the collars that were not the same color, plus all his red ties and suspenders. Or the way he checked out his nails: instead of making a turned-in half-fist, he extended his fingers and turned out his palm like a girl. The very big deal that he managed to make of not flaunting his credit cards, cars, and six buildings.

The fact he was fucking her mother.

And why would a clueless, latex, hotshit twenty-seven-year-old trader of futures want to marry a thirty-six-year-old data processor in the *first* fucking place? Because she was broke and he wasn't? To be her knight in shining armor? Her omnipotent and beneficent savior? . . .

How *did* men see her mother? Maggie's face wasn't movie-star caliber, but she could probably pass for an anchor. She also had stayed in great shape. Her body, in fact, was probably Mag's prize possession. Ms. Torso. Even naked, in daylight, it still wasn't all that disgusting, though she couldn't pull off going braless. She also had outstanding legs, which were always the last things to go and the first things that guys like the Dick Man would notice. But still. If you wanted to fuck someone gorgeous, why not go hit on some model or starlet? Plus you didn't have to marry them, either.

And what about Maggie? Aside from his dollars, what could she *see* in this guy? He was nothing out of the ordinary lookswise: no bolts through his neck or scars with the stitches still in them, but certainly not the new Bono. He was not, by any stretch of even the most vivid of imaginations, a squeeze; in Linda's very humble opinion, he barely could pass for a handshake. He was an available male heterosexual, but there wasn't much else you could say for him. (Was there something she hadn't picked up on: some huge cock or astonishing sexual technique? She did not even want to consider it.) She had to admit that he wasn't a drunk or a crack fiend. He didn't grab waiters' or waitresses' asses. He tipped well. He wasn't real stupid. Wasn't fat, wasn't skinny, wasn't real wimpy or studly. He probably didn't have AIDS. But if the best you could say for the guy was he wasn't too much of a bozo, what else could it be *besides* money? Because it wasn't just that he had money —everyone had it these days—it was how fucking *much* that he had. Five million? Ten million? Hundreds? She had no way to gauge things like this. But owning six River North buildings, plus the cars and the art, told you *something.*

What confused her was that not being rich never had seemed to bother her mother. It never had seemed that they were poor. The way they had lived, to Linda at least, had always seemed perfectly normal. Plus Maggie had ditched guys with money before. Mick the Greek, for example: all gold chains and Bronx breath and hair spray. And what about Dr. Patel? Though she had to admit that you couldn't seriously see yourself strolling down the aisle (or even a side street, at least no more often than necessary) with monkeys like Dr. Patel, no matter how many orchids he bought you. Now could you. Besides. If you had to go out with a primate, better to swing from the vines with Danny Rayhall, one of the truly great apes of Maggie's (not uneventful, the more Linda thought about it) pre-Richard love life. Danny had certainly qualified as a specimen. He'd also been younger than Maggie, but only by one or two years. Linda had sort of half-cottoned to Danny, though she'd only been twelve at the time. The main thing she remembered was that he let her take sips from his Schlitz cans. When he finally proposed, though, Maggie had several objections. His "ride," as he called it, was a T-top Camaro or Trans Am or something equipped with six bangers, six lifters, six speakers, six cams, and six heads or headers—Danny was godawful proud of it, whatever it was it had six of. He'd also been proud of, and often at pains to expose, the smudgy tattoo of "The Nam" on his biceps. (Had he ever known Michael? Linda remembered that this had been one of the issues. In any event, he had not.) There was also the issue of "prospects." Of the three jobs he held in the ten months he went out with Maggie, the highest position to which he had risen was with the 7-Eleven corporation as associate evening branch manager.

So compared to the grottiest, most loserly dregs of the Greater Chicagoland Area, she supposed she could see how a Richard might come off not looking half bad. But who wouldn't! And did everything have to be relative? Wasn't a guy either appealing or plain flat-out *not?* To Linda it always had seemed like a straight yes-or-no proposition.

Like the fact that he was fucking her mother.

At first she had given Maggie the benefit of the doubt, ignoring his age and his loathsome plasticity, doing her darnedest to see him from her point of view. A rich younger man had proposed to her mother. Was this such a hideous crime? Was it *his* fault he wasn't her father? Besides: she soon learned that pointing out defects only made Maggie more eloquent and emotional praising him. For a while she had tried to ignore the whole business, assuming her mother would soon see the light. After eight months of dating, a six-month engagement, and now with the move and the wedding, it had finally dawned on her that it just wasn't going to happen.

In bed, late at night, she daydreamed of ways of getting him out of the picture. She could threaten to leave, for example. (Granted she just had moved *in,* but so what.) She could wait until Maggie was feeling guilty about something, then just lay it right on her. "Him or me, Mag. Take your pick." She knew it was melodramatic, plus maybe not real fair to Maggie, but if she thought it would work she'd've tried it.

She could introduce Maggie to some other guy: sexually irresistible, a "successful professional," not too unintelligent, and above all available. Like *who* was the question. Mink Toffenetti? Dr. Patel? Doug McKnight? Maggie had already kissed these guys off, Dr. Patel at least twice, and Linda could not really blame her. The fact was that most of the half-decent guys Maggie's age had already long since been taken. But did that mean you settled for zipmonger sleazeballs like Richard?

She could say he had tried to molest her. Or, better yet, pretend she was letting some dark little secret just slip. "Isn't our Richard's . . . oh nothing." Yawn, change the subject, blow a few smoke rings while Maggie demanded to know what she'd meant. "Never mind." Even more deviously, she could mention he'd tried to seduce her and pretend she had found it amusing. "Here I am shaving my pits in the bathtub, Dick Man just barges right in and starts . . ." He'd deny it, of course, but the rat would be planted in Maggie's thick skull. "Just thought you might like to know."

She could fuck him and let Maggie catch them. This would be upping the ante a bit, and it gave her the willies even to briefly imagine it, but she guessed it would sure do the trick.

All of a sudden it hit her. What she really wanted to do to this wally was kill him. Lace his zinc capsules, or his vitamin E, with the same stuff they'd put in the Tylenol. Spike his wetting solution with turpentine. (Would that kill him? How about industrial-strength ammonia?) She could somehow get hold of a gun and just waste him, or hire a hit man to do it. She could run his ass through with a forklift, then dowse him with lead-free and torch him. It thrilled her to realize she meant it. There'd be problems, of course. Reducing her husband to ashes and gas fumes would probably piss M. Baum off, not to mention the crimp it might put on her chances of landing a decent replacement. Plus, wouldn't *she* stand to handsomely profit by her zillionaire stepfather's murder? She would probably end up in prison getting groped by cruel bulldykes with truncheons, forced to perform oral services on orifi crawling with mange and disgusting diseases, gagging and puking, refusing, resisting, knowing they'd kill her if she didn't submit, although not before all seven women had repeatedly violated . . .

Her nerves and her brain were hot grease, popping and sizzling with each new idea, but it still made her shiver a little to understand that *she was serious.* She was going to kill Richard Baum. Whatever the consequences, the important thing was that she would no longer be just pathetically sitting around, acting sulky and tough, doing nothing. From this moment on she'd be *biding her time,* lying in wait till the right opportunity presented itself. Victim gets home from the pits at 2:10, mother's still out at aerobics class, stepdaughter's taking a shower with bathroom door (slightly) ajar—then reverse-*Psycho* time on Wolf Point. *Eeek! Eeek! Eeek!* Did she actually hate him that much? Yes she did. Enough to be able to knife him? You bet. Maybe give herself a few cuts and bruises beforehand, manufacture some tears later on. It would be the first violent act of her life, but so what. She tried to remember a previous instance; aside from a few tiffs with second-grade girlfriends, she couldn't. She'd been brought up by Maggie as a good little seventies hippie, an artsy and sensitive peacenik, and she relished the thought now of changing all that with a vengeance. A spontaneous throat-slashing rage brought on by his efforts to rape her—oh yes! The more wanton and reckless the act was, in fact, the easier it would be for a person like her, with no record, to plead self-defense, PMS, temporary insanity, whatever—to get rid of him *and* get away with it. Kathy Crowell Webb, Hamlet Jr., Lizzie Borden, Anthony Perkins, and her. By the time the detectives arrived, the warm sudsy water plus the heat of the battle would have washed off all traces of semen. All they would find were the body, the Jasper Johns handprints and abstract expressionist drips of fresh gore on the walls, more of it still swirling clockwise down the drain of the shower, the innocent stepdaughter cringing in tears and in shock. She always had wondered how good an actress she was—what tougher screen test than a grilling by homicide detectives?

She would have to be practical. She couldn't leave traces of premeditation: no poisons or failed brakes or hit men, no chainsaws concealed in her pillow. Even stashing a knife in the bathroom, she realized, might end up appearing a bit too convenient. Could she do it just using her hands? He was stronger than she was, more vicious, and probably better at fighting; even if she caught him off-guard, she doubted she'd be able to kill him. There were classes she could take—karate, jujitsu, tai kwan do—but these might be brought up against her in court by the lawyers. In the *kitchen,* however, or anywhere near it, she could always grab one of the steak knives. . . .

She fell asleep slashing him, stabbing him, sickened and weakened by warm salty droplets of gore that sprayed off his hands and his face as he tried to fight back, but somehow she managed, just barely, shrieking and panting, lunging and thrusting with all that was left of her strength, to continue.

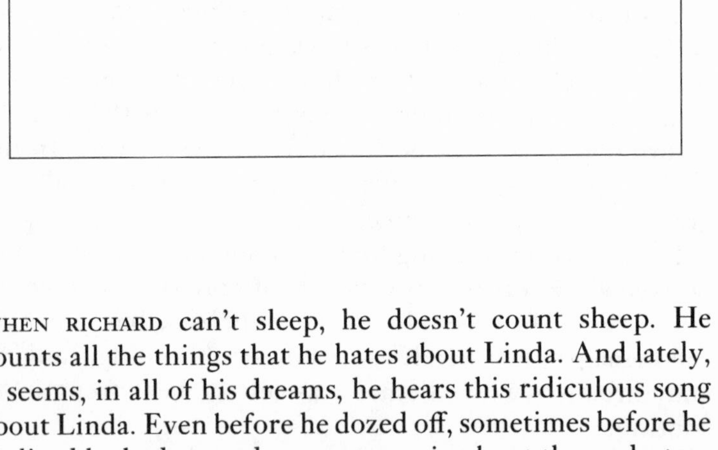

WHEN RICHARD can't sleep, he doesn't count sheep. He counts all the things that he hates about Linda. And lately, it seems, in all of his dreams, he hears this ridiculous song about Linda. Even before he dozed off, sometimes before he realized he had started to worry again about the undertow she was creating in his relationship with Maggie, Jan and Dean's dippy and sickening melody would make its way onto his soundtrack, and he'd think about loving he'd missed. About Linda.

That the song played involuntarily made hearing it twelve times as maddening, but what irked him the most was that he did find—her body at least—quite attractive. Not more than Maggie's, of course, but sometimes the call was too close. To ignore or deny this was futile, he figured. Why try to? He was also convinced that admitting these kinds of things freely, even if only to yourself, kept you more in the black in the long run.

In the meantime, however, dealing on a daily basis with his stepdaughter's provocative physical presence and subversive vibrations was costing him. Even the most basic conversations, like buzzing her in when she'd forgotten her key, not to mention sharing the same refrigerator and doorways and city, was always a face-off with Linda. Then there were the shots that you couldn't help getting when you lived underneath the same roof. It was bad enough seeing her knees through the holes in her blue jeans, but a couple of evenings ago she had come down to Maggie's bathroom to borrow shampoo. She'd been wearing a towel and some raggedy, baggy gray sweatpants. The towel had covered her shoulders and chest well enough but had left the cleft small of her back exposed. And the way the frayed purple shoestring upholding those sweats round her hips, hitched in a crimped little bow at her navel, with no help from any elastic, had almost been . . .

Anyway. Her most unignorable feature, he thought, was the ultrafine grain of her skin. Translucent through two or three layers, then flushed milky pink underneath, it appeared to have no pores at all. And no freckles. Except for some pale flaxy strands on her temples and forearms, it seemed to be perfectly hairless. Or the taut but plush way that it fit her, or the way that in some lights it shone. He'd never seen any skin like it. He could only imagine what it felt like to touch. What it looked like you'd feel was the moist fragile surface of moth wings, something that bruised if you breathed on it hard and registered prints if you touched it. Though apparently it wasn't *too* fragile, since no amount of cigarettes, gin, cheap soap, cheap makeup, no sun, bad air, no exercise, pastry, fajitas, bacon cheeseburgers, tacos, spare ribs, cold cuts and white bread could blemish or thicken or dim it. If there were other good ways to ruin your looks or your health, he was sure she would try them. He also assumed she used drugs.

Another big problem was how old she was. Most guys his age, and ninety percent of the traders he worked with, showed up at parties and bars with nineteen- or twenty-year-old snatch on their arms. And while it certainly didn't embarrass him to have Maggie as a wife—far from it—he realized that if everyone *else* wanted young stuff, people were bound to assume he did too and ipso facto was angling to grapple his recent bride's comely young daughter.

Maggie had not brought it up yet, but Linda sure seemed to assume it. The contemptuous looks that she shot him whenever all three of them were in the same room seemed clearly designed to suggest he'd made offers that *she* was disgustedly nixing. As though he'd be clueless enough to get cute with his wife and her mother right there. All this in spite, or because, of the dozens of ways he'd *already* improved her shit life. Though as soon as he started to mentally list them (great place to live, paid tuition, allowance, rich charming husband for her poor widowed mother, first-class trip to Paris, chance to find out firsthand from a master how wheat markets worked, about art . . .) the Jan and Dean song would rev up again in his brain and he'd have to chill out and refocus. Or try to, at least. Because keeping from dwelling on the grain and plush fit of that skin was sure getting harder and harder.

Am I so complex that I cannot respond to real danger?

3

LINDA HAD made herself smaller than life. She was nervous. She was drawing her face in three-quarter profile, shifting her weight on her workbench, and smoking. She wanted to know what a penis felt like deep inside her, to be clenching it tight with those muscles. She glanced at the mirror, the drawing. She had made her lips fuller than they actually were, but they still looked like hers. She looked like a black girl whose hair had been straightened: Jill Richard, the drummer from Klymaxx, or Tina. She could do that, she knew: she was capable of such an effect and it was also considered permissible, in some cases even desirable. She was trying to make her eyes glint using very dark lines around where the light would come off. It was working. She felt pretty proud of herself. She was also a little bit drunk. Technically this was called chiaroscuro, but Linda preferred to think of the unnervous flicks of her hand that produced these nice glints as a kind of negative capability, hers, a term she had learned just last week in Aesthetics and

Physics. Some poet named Keats (not that other one, Yeats) was the guy who had coined it. He had died very young, she had learned, but not before he'd come up with a bunch of great poems, or great odes, and that term.

Her Life Drawing teacher, Chuck Nash, had a penis. She never had actually seen it, but she always assumed it was there. Chuck Nash was married, or at least wore a ring, but did that make that much of a difference? He was standing right next to her now, helping Sasha. (Rachel and Tommy were watching him too, she could tell.) She could not see the front of his jeans, but she could see the back. There were smears of dried ultramarine on his pockets, the size of large thumbs. The paint was no more than a shade or two darker than the almost new denim, but when light hit it right you could see it.

She stubbed out her cigarette, licked the dull point of her pencil, squinted across at the mirror. Her face looked okay, but the one on the paper looked better.

She blew her bangs up from her eyes and kept working.

Penises were much in the air that semester at SAIC. In her Wednesday 2D class a sleek straight erection had been stylized as a red-white-and-blue MX missile: the Piecekeeper. A graduate student who signed her work simply Ophelia had painted a museum-scale portrait of John Wayne Gacy in his clown suit holding a lariat (or maybe a whip) in his right hand, his little pink dick in his left. One of the commonest lines of the resident graffitists was POWER TO THE PENIS: HARD ON! As if to illustrate this motto, the wall by the Kotex machine in the second-floor john now featured a six-foot-high model inscribed—in various inks, handwritings, and sizes—with dozens of names for that organ, some of the more original of which included Holmes, Daddy, dipstick, private eye, tootsie roll, boinker, trouser trout, porkbelly, Mr. D, Dr. C, Mikey, Tuss, gizzpistol, Johnson, snatchsnatcher, thangwhanger, gashhammer, muffstuffer, Trubba, meat, moonbeam, puppydog's tail, puddingpop, pearlpusher, clitstinger, tuskmusker, and a half-dozen others that Linda could either not decipher because of the handwriting (or spelling) or ever begin to imagine. It was also a list to which she had nothing to add.

Hanging downstairs in the undergrad sculpture gallery was a humorous little contraption entitled *Ronnie and the Purple Penis.* It consisted of two latex figures dangling by strings from opposite ends of a hanger: a miniature Ronald McDonald and a grinning purple penis with a Reagan-style wave on its head. (Did penises really get purple, she wondered.) The artist was the notorious Jiffy Lube Man, who was actually a guy named Hank Rendeck who happened to be in her A & P class; she'd been checking him out since day one.

This Jiffy Lube Hank guy was also one of the founding members of a mini-anti-movement within the School that called itself Vas Deferens. She had just seen a picture of *Ronnie and the Purple Penis* and read about Vas Deferens in that week's issue of *F,* the SAIC student paper.

The headline said VAS DEFERENS: AT WAR WITH ART. "Know your enemy: Art" was their "rallying cry for the coming apocalypse." The article was accompanied by two black-and-white reproductions: *Ronnie and the Purple Penis* and a piece by Chester Treasure called *Jesus On A Tray (Part One of a Series),* which was the crosshatched face of an African-looking Jesus goopily painted onto a cafeteria tray. There was also an interview with Vas Deferens's four founding members: Chester Treasure, Mr. Electricity, Artist With No Name, and the Jiffy Lube Man.

F: "Why is Vas Deferens 'at war with art'?"

Chester Treasure: "Because, okay, the attitudes prevalent in contemporary art are too avaricious and grotty."

Mr. Electricity: "It's our duty to make art so hot that it melts down the wax in folks' ears."

Chester Treasure: "In their rears?"

Jiffy Lube Man: "Don't forget their museums."

Mr. Electricity: "In their galleries . . ."

Artist With No Name: "I mean, the whole art-star system is really pretty lame."

F: "Lame?"

Jiffy Lube Man: "Yeah, lame."

Mr. Electricity: "Well, pretty lame."

Artist With No Name: "Lamer than last year, at least."

F: "Okay . . . What, in your opinion, makes for a successful piece of art?"

Jiffy Lube Man: "A successful piece of art is penetratingly executed, titled, and signed."

F: "Ahem. You are at war with art, yet you make art. Why?"

Jiffy Lube Man: "We're only at war with contemporary art. After all, the Old Masters *are* the Old Masters."

Artist With No Name: "Art today has gone astray. Pun intended. We must forge a new direction for artists."

Jiffy Lube Man: "Pun intended."

F: "Ahem."

Artist With No Name: "As art gets worse it appeals to less people. Prices go up by a factor of ten every year. It will quickly reach a point where no one, not even artists, will like it."

F: "So Vas Deferens is trying to stop that from happening."

Chester Treasure: "No, we're trying to *help* it to happen."

Jiffy Lube Man: "When it does we'll begin to rebuild it using less corporate, i.e. less infantile, principles."

Mr. Electricity: "A little less anal as well. Like no more

of this six-months-per-square-inch Imagist craftsmanship horsebleep."

F: "And what would those principles be?"

Jiffy Lube Man: "Sorry. Can't tell you. You'd immediately start putting up roadblocks."

F: "But—"

Jiffy Lube Man: "End of interview."

Chester Treasure: "Goodbye."

F: "Goodbye."

Jiffy Lube Man: "Pleasure talking."

She crumpled up *F* in disgust; she was sick of their schnabelling attitudes. And apparently it went without saying that everyone knew what Vas Deferens meant. Linda assumed it was German, as in *Vas iss going on arount here?* Plus deferens sounded German as well. Wrong again. Her biggest mistake, however, was to casually ask Sandra, the mulatto hepster she sat next to in Intro to Lit, what it meant.

"How do you mean?" Sandra said.

"You know," Linda said. "Like what's 'vas deferens' German for?"

Sandra winced like she couldn't believe it, then replied much too loud for the supposedly private conversation they were having: "Would you listen to her talking 'bout German! Are you kidding me, girl?"

Unfortunately, she was not.

"The vas deferens's the thing that carries the sperms from guys' balls to their—you know. Mean, girl, where you been?"

Well excuse *me,* Linda thought. She could feel herself blushing. "I guess I've been examining just a few less vas deferenses than *some* folks round here."

"Well I *guess,*" Sandra said.

And they laughed.

"I mean, you know, as in vas-ectomy?" said Sandra, forming scissors with two of her fingers and snipping the blades together.

"Gotcha," said Linda.

"As in Vas-eline?"

"I gotcha," said Linda.

When she got home that night she broke out some gin and looked up vas deferens in the dictionary. Where else, she considered, thumbing back to UV and then carefully turning the pages. She found it. *A spermatic duct especially of a higher vertebrate (see also Wolffian body) forming in man a small thick-walled tube about two feet long greatly convoluted in its proximal portion.* Say what? Greatly convoluted perhaps, but what's this about two feet long?

Her other dictionary had it as *the deferent vessel or duct of the testis that transports the sperm from the epididymis to the penis.* Okay. Getting warmer. Looking up deferent, she found *conveying away; efferent,* while deferential, just below, meant *respectful,* the very illogic of which led her (somehow) to understand that there was indeed a vas deferens between a man and a woman. Ha ha. Boost the guffaws on the laugh track. Ho ho.

Sipping more gin, she looked up epididymis, which turned out to be *the elongated organ on the posterior surface of a testis that constitutes the convoluted beginning of the vas deferens,* which led right back to—what? The issue, or tissue, she thought, was getting more and more convoluted and certainly less and less sexy. It reminded her of the time back in high school when she'd discovered, purely by accident, while paging through some architecture magazine, that the curved edge formed by the intersection of two vaults was called, of all things, a groin: rather useless information perhaps, but something she would remember. The irony was that four or five months after this a problem involving the groin of a vault had actually turned up on the math portion of the SAT test she was taking to get into SAIC. Some facts were funny like that, she supposed.

She lit a cigarette and turned back to vas. In addition to vas deferentia, the plural, there also were vascular bundles, vascular cylinders (in Boston they'd be vascula cylindas), vascular tissues, vasoconstrictors (found deep in the Amazon jungle), vasodilations, Vaseline, and vasectomies. And while she was at it, she figured she might as well look up erection: in the event that she ever happened to come across one in the course of her studies, she wanted to be able to distinguish it from, oh, say, a vascular bundle. What an erection turned out to be was *a: the state marked by a firm turgid form and erect position of a previously flaccid bodily part containing cavernous tissue when that tissue becomes dilated with blood, b: an occurrence of such a state in the penis or clitoris.*

Hmm.

She blew a small smoke ring, watched while it billowed and warped, then tried to blow another one through it. They simply destroyed one another.

Ho-hum.

Definition *a,* she decided, would be her contribution to the list in the second-floor john. Definition *b* she'd reserve for some other, less public, contingency.

She sipped some more gin and anxiously riffled the pages, looking up Wolffian body.

Rick Dick's new nickname for me is the Koncertina Kid. Don't I know it. And of course he still thinks I don't (know it).

THE NEXT time A & P met, on Tuesday, Linda, on purpose, arrived about ten minutes late. That way it would only be natural for her to slip unobtrusively into one of the seats by the door near the back of the room, where the Jiffy Lube Man always sat. And it worked. He was still sitting two seats away, on her right, but nobody else sat between them.

Jonathan Strobe, the professor, had chicken-scratched four barely legible words onto the blackboard

POSSIBLE
PROBABLE
VIRTUAL
ACTUAL

with a short violent arrow slashing down on their left and a shorter, even more violent one, slashing up, on their right. "And so," he was saying, "for one *ve-e-ry* brief instant . . ."

A few of the students, including the Jiffy Lube Man, started laughing. They were supposed to be discussing "In The Mind of Some Eternal Spirit," an essay by some Sir named James Jeans. Linda had skimmed it that morning coming down on the el but had not really gotten too much of it. She pulled out her copy and wrote down the words from the board at the top of the first Xeroxed page, then drew both the arrows. She had taken a right-handed desk chair, so she had to turn sideways, toward Rendeck. Okay. This was the last time the class would be meeting before the field trip to Fermilab. According to Strobe there was some just incredibly juicy analogy between what Sir James Jeans had written and what they would see on this field trip, though she couldn't recall what it was.

Rendeck was not taking notes. She hadn't actually looked at him, of course, but still. She could tell. She figured that to stop taking notes now herself would tip off the fact that she'd noticed.

"Sir Jeans's central proposition, then," Strobe was saying, "is that God is a mathematician." He repeated this, paused for effect, carried on. "That mathematics, in fact, is the poetry of logic. So that whatever pictures or metaphors we may come up with to help us apprehend the way the world works—however insightful, however poetic—that any or all of these nonmathematical pictures will turn out not only *not to be accurate*, but will in fact lead us one step further *away* from the truth, i.e. from an accurate understanding of the way the world really works. . . ."

Linda wrote *G = mathematician* and *math = poetry logic.* She heard Rendeck's lighter click open, then five seconds later smelled smoke. She wrote *pictures or poems never work.*

Strobe had gone on in his usual ebullient, jittery, fast-talking manner: ". . . just as in Plato, where we sit imprisoned in the cave of our senses with our backs to the light, so that all we can see are what amounts to reality shadows —as Sir Jeans now points out, a position which Plato developed in response to his own age's tendency to interpret physical reality, or nature, in purely anthropomorphic terms, gigantic gods and goddesses hurling thunderbolts about at each other . . ."

She was dying for a cigarette now. She had her own pack in her purse, but what she (sort of) wanted to do was get one off Hank. The best way, she figured, would be to coolly and subtly get his attention (whisper his name? just say "yo"? clear her throat? wait till he happened to look at her?), then nod toward his cigarette while holding her two cigaretteless fingers up to her lips and say with her eyes what she wanted. But of course she did not. What she did was write *Plato,* then *thunderbolts (anthropomorphic).*

". . . until a thousand years later or so, after Descartes had taught us to mistrust the evidence presented to us by our senses, Bishop Berkeley hypothesized that . . ."

Hank cleared his throat rather loudly. Linda was writing *Descartes,* but she stopped and looked over his way. He was staring at Strobe with his right hand half raised, not really making all that much of an effort to get the hand noticed, and was exhaling thin plumes of smoke. It was the first time she'd seen him, really looked at his profile, up close.

By now Strobe had glanced at Hank's hand more than once, but he had not acknowledged it yet. Linda looked back and forth between her notes and the board and the two of them as Strobe kept on talking.

And talking.

Her original impression of Hank was that he looked like James Dean, only harder and smarter and darker: less pretty. Same wicked eyebrows, however, same swept-back hair, pretty much the same blasé attitude. Up close he looked a bit older (twenty-six, twenty-seven) than he had when she'd watched him from farther away. She also could see that his earlobe was pierced—but no earring. In spite of his general rep and his grease-stiffened Jiffy Lube jumpsuit, he looked very clean, and she liked that. The longer she stared at him the more he reminded her of Stuart Sutcliffe from the Beatles' Hamburg days: artsy, mysterioso, and handsome—a beatnik greaseball but without all the grease or the beard—and bound, above all, to die young. Same high white cheekbones, same black-on-black plastic shades. (Although Hank didn't wear his in class, he did almost everyplace else.) She had been a big fan of Stu Sutcliffe ever since she'd come across his pictures in Maggie's old fanzines (and then, after that, found her own). There was this one picture in particular, taken just before he died, at twenty-one, of an aneurysm or brain tumor, or something like that, in which he had—

"Yes, Mr. Rendeck?" said Strobe. He seemed slightly less pleased than he usually did to be entertaining the Jiffy Lube Man's impudent but (usually) intelligent questions.

Hank took one final drag from his cigarette, then dropped it in front of him. She could tell he was making Strobe wait. "Yeah, well, this business about God, or whoever this eternal spirit guy turns out to be, about him being a mathematician? . . ."

"Ye-e-es? . . ." said Strobe, oozing mock-patience. He was kidding the length of Hank's question.

She watched Hank grind out the butt of his cigarette with the sole of his paint-spattered shoe. *Would Sir James Jeans's jeans look the same on Stu Sutcliffe,* she wondered, *as they would on the Jiffy Lube Man, or James Dean?*

"Anyway," said Hank, "isn't all Jeans is doing here is getting ready to admit that nature, whatever, *is* quite a *bit* like a musician who's writing a fugue or a poet composing a sonnet? Just like the 'sheer beauty of the physical world' makes guys like Feynman draw pictures, or like Jeans . . . I mean, he says so right—"

"As a matter of fact, Hank," said Strobe, continuing his mock-patient schtick, "he *is* getting ready to say something like that, just as *we* are just about ready to get there ourselves, if you'll be kind enough to wait for the rest of us."

There were whistles, applause, scattered hooting.

"However," said Strobe, apparently changing his mind, "since Hank here insists, why don't we all skip a few pages ahead to . . ."

Hank had already started reading aloud from the article, but Strobe cut him off, speaking to the class as a whole: "Second-to-last paragraph on page eight, three lines down."

Linda located the paragraph, read a few words, looked at Hank. What she wanted to know was—but he suddenly looked right back at her. His eyes were amazingly green. Was he trying to let her know something important? Did he want her to see that—

He turned back toward Strobe.

She could feel herself blushing and hated herself, hated Rendeck, hated the way—

"Have we found it?" said Strobe.

She calmed herself down, found the place.

Strobe was reading: " 'To my mind, the laws which nature obeys are less suggestive of those which a machine obeys in its motion than those which a musician obeys in writing a fugue, or a poet in composing a sonnet. The motions of electrons and atoms do not resemble those of the parts of a locomotive so much as those of the dancers in a cotillion.' " He pushed back his glasses and put up his finger. "Notice here that Sir Jeans is making a *relative* comparison between a poetic or musical picture and a much more mechanistic way of looking at things and finding the former to be *somewhat less inadequate,* but that—skipping ahead to the end of the paragraph—he says '. . . then the universe can be *best* pictured, as,' um, 'as consisting of pure thought, the thought of what, for want of a wider word, we must describe as a mathematical thinker.' " Again Strobe looked up at the class. "In other words, understanding nature as music or poetry, or dancing or painting, may be *somewhat* more adequate than understanding it, as our nineteenth-century forebears did, as some vast machine, and it is *certainly* a clearer picture of things than gods tossing thunderbolts, but that the best of all possible ways, according to James Jeans at least, is to think of reality as pure mathematical thought."

"In the mind of some eternal mathematical spirit," said Hank.

"Exactly," said Strobe.

Five or six hands had gone up, but Strobe stayed focused on Hank, the main reason being that Hank had just taken the chair desk between him and Linda and was rattling it against the tile floor.

"As in, say," he said, once he had finally stopped, "the pure mathematical *thought* of this chair here?" He patted the blond wooden desk part.

"Exactly," said Strobe, who was grinning. Was he pleased, Linda wondered, by Hank's strident counterexample or relieved that he'd ceased and desisted? "As difficult," said Strobe, "or perhaps impossible, as that idea may be to apprehend via one's astonishingly feeble human brainpower."

He was clearly referring to Hank's. There was laughter.

Strobe went on. "Because a hard metal chair and the noise that it makes when it's rattled are merely the thrice or so removed *extensions* of what remains primordially a mathematical idea. . . ."

She briefly considered writing *primordially* down, but did not.

As Strobe went on talking, Hank fished around in his battered old satchel-style briefcase. Suddenly Linda smelled pastry. Galvanized, starved, glancing sideways, she watched as Hank noisily—on purpose—produced from inside a crinkled white bag an orange-glazed half-eaten longjohn. "As in, for example," he asked, "the original, virtual, primordial, and *pure* mathematical idea of this baked good?" He proceeded to take a large bite.

This ploy apparently amused Strobe even more: he was visibly struggling to keep a straight face.

Hank grabbed the desktop again, but this time he chose not to shake it. Instead, still melodramatically chomping the longjohn, he said, "Becaw wha *I* wu li to su'geh—"

Strobe interrupted him, making his own chomping noises while droning out "Ye-e-es? . . ."

Spectacular obnoxia was a respectable way to make points, Linda gathered, so long as it was *really* spectacularly obnoxious.

Hank, having swallowed, continued: "—that it makes as much sense to think of this primordial creator guy as a baker"—he raised what was left of the longjohn—"or a carpenter"—and he rapped on the wood of the desktop—"as to think of him as this prodigiously talented sculptor working in all kinds of forces and waves. . . ."

"In other words," said Strobe, taking a few steps toward Hank, "what God does isn't necessarily mathematical, but rather is something that pretty much fits the description of what Hank Rendeck does."

"Now that you mention it," said Hank. "Yeah, that sounds about right. That's the ticket."

Much groaning. Even Linda was a little dismayed at the extent to which the discussion had (or at least seemed to have) degenerated.

Strobe seemed delighted, however. "Now we are getting somewhere," he said. He was back in the front of the room.

"Because if you've been paying attention these last several classes, you'll have noticed that most if not all of the theories we've looked at so far can be seen, at least to a certain extent, to be little more than egocentric extrapolations by each of the theoreticians. Tribal warriors posit systems in which warrior gods make things happen. Indian gods look like Indians, African gods look like Africans. Along comes Plato, the idealist philosopher, and posits an abstract reality in which the *ideal forms* of all things are really what matter, any disputes about which to be settled by—who else? Idealist philosophers. Then there's Spinoza, then Berkeley, the bishop, who both posit God as the primordial essence of nature. James Jeans and Einstein, the math wizards, posit pure mathematical elegance. Just as Hank here, the sculptor, is positing sculpture as the basis of all our reality. . . . Do you see what I mean?"

Linda did and she didn't. And the rest of the class? From where she was sitting there was no way to tell. They were silent. Even Hank had no comment, though she sensed he was working on one.

"To put it more simply," said Strobe, "things have a way of turning out to be pretty much what we will make of them."

Hmm.

"To which Jeans would say 'bearshit,' " said Hank.

"Not really," said Strobe. "To which Sir Jeans would probably attach the proviso *mutatis mutandis.*"

The proviso mutatis mutandis. She had written it down before Strobe had gone on but did not look it up after class. She was pissed. She had wanted to follow along, but after a while she hadn't been able to keep real close track of who was replying to whom, let alone what the issue still was. The discussion—Hank and Strobe, for the most part—had continued until people from the class after theirs had arrived, which was the way most of these spiels ended anyway.

Anyway. There had not been a chance to say even one word to Hank, or for Hank to say one word to her.

She was pissed.

His fisheater farts every morning. Void where prohibited.

RICHARD WAS standing alongside the door to her stairway, more or less blocking her path. She was on her way out to 2D class and was running a half hour late. She could tell something fishy was up.

"Hello, Linda."

"Hello, Richard."

"How's school been going? All right?"

"Not bad."

"So I hear. Glad to hear it."

Long pause. Where was Maggie, she wondered. And why is he home at 9:30?

He suddenly held up a match. It took her a couple of seconds to recognize it. Then she smiled.

Richard didn't. "What, just exactly, is this?"

Did he want her to take it or hold it himself? Hard to say. It was midway between them, exactly.

She took it.

"This," she said, rolling the burnt sulfur head between her index finger and thumb, "I'd say, is a light. A dead light."

"That's correct. It's a match for the lighting of cigarettes. More specifically, Merits. You know where I found it?"

"No." *I mean No,* she was thinking, *I don't want to know where you found it.* "Where did you find it?"

"I found it—"

"I mean yes," she said. *Words!* "Yes I want to know where you found it. I mean yes I do know where you found it." *I also know what you can do with it.* "You found it in your office. On your carpet, in fact. Your priceless Iranian carpet. By your priceless computer and copier that are *so* supersensitive to cigarette smoke."

They stared at each other. Four seconds. Richard was two inches taller. Eight seconds. Neither looked down or away.

"Two things," Richard said. He dropped his eyes briefly to look at the match, then retook it. "First, if there's—"

"Yes?" Linda said.

Richard glared. They were two feet apart, nose to chin. "If there's something you need in my office, I would very much appreciate your asking me to get it for you myself."

"Fine. Though there's nothing I *needed,* your office or anyplace else."

"There wasn't."

"Ah ah."

"So then why were you in there?"

"So then what was the second thing?"

"What?"

"You said there were two things."

"I said what were you doing in there."

"How do you mean what was I doing?"

"At my desk. In my office. Smoking cigarettes. What were you doing?"

"Let me get this straight," Linda said. "There are certain rooms around here that we need your permission to enter?"

"Permission's got nothing to do with it, Linda. You know goddamn well what I'm talking about."

Linda blinked but kept staring. Then she purposefully batted her lashes. Then she stopped batting them and examined the smudge of gray soot the match head had left on her thumb. Then, looking up, she admitted: "I was admiring the view from your window."

Richard glanced over the railing, down the two flights of stairs, at the oil-stained concrete that had once been the service department. He could feel the blood pulse through his choroidal vessels. A long way to fall and a hard place to land, he concluded. Linda was frightened but tried not to show it. He really did look pretty pissed.

"Listen, you—"

"Listen you what?"

She could tell he was going to hit her. She decided she wouldn't fight back, changed her mind, and got ready.

"Don't misunderstand me," he said.

"Don't worry."

"And don't underestimate me. I understand perfectly well exactly what it is that you're up to."

"You do."

"Yes I do."

A long pause.

"Can I have back my match now?" she said. She could tell it surprised him. A lot. She could tell that he never would hit her and understood why. They both knew that Maggie would freak.

She held up her palm. "I appreciate your concern for my things, for my needs, but I really do need to be going. To class."

"Go then," he said. *Go and get some.* He inhaled and exhaled, controlling his pulse rate, then dropped the match onto her palm. "By all means then please do be going."

"Thank you," said Linda, politely. She tucked the match into the hip pocket of her jeans, stutterstepped past him, and went.

Assholerics are rewarded if and only if they are sufficiently incredible. Necessarily and sufficiently? In Rick Dick Rich Richard's case, most most most certainly.

FOR THE drive out to Fermilab Thursday, she somehow got stuck riding with Strobe in his Volvo, up front, along with a pink infant carseat. There were three other students in back, Gordon and Paul and Suzette, none of whom Linda was friends with or even knew very well. The remaining eleven or twelve of their classmates were following the Volvo in three other cars. They had met in the lobby at ten and waited around almost forty-five minutes for Hank and another guy, Tim, who Strobe then found out had just called in sick. So they left. Hank simply never showed up.

They headed west out of the city on the Eisenhower, through Maywood and Broadview, then picked up the East-West Tollway and headed southwest toward Batavia.

She had set her alarm for 7:15 (about two hours earlier than usual) to give herself plenty of time to tart herself up, deal with the pimple that had inevitably emerged on her forehead, then make it by ten down to school. And she had. What she hadn't had yet, though she'd been up now for almost four hours, was a cigarette (her hard-and-fast rule was never to smoke before noon). And to make matters worse, her period was just coming on. She felt groggy and bloated and ornery. She also was sure there were parties in the three cars behind them, or at least the opportunity to just yawn and stay silent, whereas in Strobe's goddamn car you might just as well have been sitting in class. In addition to his running commentary on the "visual environment" of Chicago's West Side, the point spread in that Sunday's Bear game and ways of "disguising the forty-six blitzes," he was treating his fortunate four student passengers to a bonus introductory lecture on antiproton debunchers, Doug Plank, colliding charmed quarks, and the differences between bevatrons, boosters, and tevatrons.

Christ!

Yet in spite of her mood, in spite of the captive conditions, didn't she have to admit that what Strobe had to say about where they were headed was interesting?

Categorically, unequivocally, absolutely, most definitely *not.*

Ah ah.

No way.
Not a chance.

Strobe stopped the car at a tollbooth and tossed in some coins. They were now out by Oak Brook. Could you hitchhike from here back to school, Linda wondered. Or walk?

The tollgate went up and Strobe shifted gears and accelerated. "Please let me know if I'm getting too technical," he said. He was only half kidding.

"Oh no-oo-ooo," said Gordon, who apparently felt pretty much the same way as Linda. Paul and Suzette, though, were writing things down in their notebooks, merely the idea of which made Linda feel carsick. And as if that weren't bad enough, they were actually asking Strobe "follow-up" questions in order to make him talk *more.*

She sipped her black coffee and wanted real badly to scream. She stared out the window awhile, but the tollway-side scenery could not have been too much more boring: vast shopping plazas surrounded by still vaster parking lots, complexes of très moderne condos, between which lay flat brown dead nothing. She did not feel like chatting, however, even less like attending a lecture on charmed quarks and Bears while seated right next to the lecturer, let alone taking notes or "participating." What she did feel like doing was (literally) puking. Because all of a sudden she had started to feel pretty carsick. She opened her window a little and took some deep breaths. *Very* carsick, in fact. Whatever James Jeans (whose essay she'd finally read Wednesday night) had to do with all of this technical stuff, or the Bears, or Enrico H. Fermi's damn lab, Strobe hadn't gotten to yet. But Linda was sure that he would. Would have bet the whole rest of her life on it.

Would have lost. Because by the time they turned north off the tollway at the Eola Road exit, Strobe had at last lightened up and the air in the car had begun to do Linda some good. She was hungry, in fact. Even the scenery had improved: it wasn't the ocean or mountains, of course, or the Thames, but at least there were trees around here, changing color, and every so often a pond or a barn or a stream.

Ten minutes later they arrived at the Fermilab entrance. Strobe said good morning to one of the guards, was corrected with "good afternoon," and drove through. James Jeans's theories had still not been mentioned. Just as amazing, perhaps, was the fact that the other three cars were still with them.

She was doing her best to get pumped: any place with an official security outpost manned by uniformed (albeit female) armed guards could not be *all* boring, she figured. But the first thing she saw, as they came around a bend in the road, was the last thing she'd ever expected: a medium-sized herd of—what?

Buffaloes?

Yup. (Had she seen one before in real life? Aside from a pair in the Lincoln Park Zoo, she had not. And that had been when she was ten.) There were five or six dozen, it looked like, grazing quite nonchalantly on a green sloping pasture, and in all shapes and sizes to boot. The largest, the bulls, were gigantic, the size of at least two large cows, with magnificent humps on their shoulders and thick chocolate manes surrounding their horned massive heads. They looked like a cross between lions and rhinos and bears, assbackward throwbacks of some sort, but gorgeous: beautiful strange shaggy monsters from another whole epoch. She loved it.

Strobe slowed way down as they drove by the pasture,

though his tour-guide routine was now very much back in fifth gear. He even had taken to waving and shouting to the students who'd pulled up behind them. Linda was content just to look and so managed to phase out his spiel. It was still sinking in that she'd come all this way to watch quarks get collided in tevatrons and but here she was gawking at . . . buffalo.

The Fermilab cafeteria was on the ground floor of an atrium that featured mottled gray staggered-board concrete hung with patches and streamers of ivy. It was enclosed on two sides by glass and on the other two sides by vaulted twin towers rising up over the treetops, then coming together several more stories above them. She had never seen anything like it. The atrium in the State of Illinois Building was larger, she figured, but this place was somehow . . . sublimer.

Gordon was sitting across from her at the end of a long empty table. He had already wolfed down a burger and was talking nonstop about school. Was he flirting with her? Yes he was. He also was managing a better than fair imitation of Strobe's lecture manner: beaming, beneficent, talking five words a second about six things at once—hard not to like but still more than a little ridiculous.

She assumed the effect was intentional, so she shook her head, nodded, and smiled. Gordon looked baffled, then pleased, and she knew right away that meant trouble.

She concentrated on her food. She had ordered the special: potato-tomato-and-green-pepper omelette, onion croissant, and the medium drink of her choice; since Bombay and tonic was not on the menu, she'd settled for Dr. Pepper. After three bites of omelette, however, with Gordon still blabbing and staring, her appetite somehow had vanished.

She lit up a cigarette, her first of the day, and stared through the trees and the plants and out the glass wall at the sky.

"*Cats,*" Gordon said.

Huh? She said nothing.

"You look sorta just like the chick who was playing the lead in the, you know, the white one. Grizabella. In *Cats.* Did you see it?"

She suddenly felt very dizzy. The sky was so blue. And she hadn't.

"Awkward silence," said Gordon.

Though she still felt real dizzy, she took one more drag. She hadn't a clue what to tell him. The sky—

"This is your captain," said Gordon. "Your captain says we are going down. . . ."

Still dazed, she refocused on the concrete, then looked up at the point where the vaults came together. "Do you know what you call that?" she said—God knew why. She thought she was going to vomit or faint.

"Big Science?" said Gordon.

Or vomit *and* faint. Or faint and *then* vomit. Or maybe she'd simply—

"Call what?" Gordon said. "You mean—"

"Nothing," she said. She breathed out and in very slowly, put out her cigarette, swallowed some New Dr. Pepper to put some cool fizz in her stomach.

"Call nothing?" said Gordon. He looked toward the top of the atrium. "You mean what do you—"

"Yeah," she said, wincing. What else could she say? The sugar and ice in the drink were zapping and zinging the cavity in one of her upper left molars. "Where the two concrete vaults come together." Wherever.

"The chancel?" said Gordon. He was clearly intrigued by the question. "No, not the chancel. You mean there, at the top of the atrium?"

"I don't think the chancel," she said. She could not keep her tongue from exploring the hole, from trying to warm it a little. "I can't—"

"So what do you call it?" said Gordon.

"The chancel?" she said. The hole in her molar still throbbed, and *still* the guy wouldn't shut up. So she shrugged. It was lame but the best she could do. "I don't know."

"Not the chancel . . ." said Gordon. She was touched he was trying so hard. "It's . . . *shit.* It was just on the tip of my tongue." And he stuck out his pink tongue to prove it.

More awkward silence.

"I just thought you'd know what you called it," she told him.

Whatever.

The tour Strobe had promised commenced at 1:30 sharp, as he'd promised, in a room with a screen in the front. Linda sat down near the back, by herself. She sipped Dr. Pepper and breathed. The woman conducting the tour welcomed the class to Fermilab and introduced herself as Helga Fife. She was right around Strobe's age, late thirties, still blond, a little more handsome than pretty. But pretty. She was wearing a plaid pleated past-the-knee skirt, a bone-colored turtleneck sweater (cashmere, it looked like, from where Linda was sitting), and a navy blue blazer with a small purple iris stuck through the lapel hole. Somehow she just didn't fit Linda's image of a middle-aged female nuclear particle physicist.

But hey, there you were, Linda thought. Maybe she's really Strobe's lover, his excuse for the trip in the first place.

Helga Fife passed out a stack of white folders with a (competent) line drawing of Enrico Fermi on the cover. Inside each folder were five or six stapled (long) articles, photographs of a pagoda and a geodesic dome, a six-inch-long sample of niobium-titanium alloy.

Oh boy.

Somebody switched off the lights. There was silence for five or six seconds, then whispers. An unfocused slide came up on the screen: an aerial photograph of the Fermilab complex. Helga Fife focused the slide, then started her lecture by asking them to stop her if things got too technical, at which point Gordon yelled, "Stop!" There was laughter. Helga Fife seemed unflustered; she was apparently used to such antics. She began again by stating that the facility was funded by the US Department of Energy, that construction (new slide) had begun in 1973, that the project was completed (new slide) at a cost of some very large number of dollars. If the Superconducting Super-Collider (new slide: a drawing this time, not a photo) were to be built here, the current collider would be used as an injector facility (new slide). It would also give people the option of retrofitting the magnets in order to . . .

In the light from the next several slides, using her black extrafine Pilot pen, Linda gave Fermi more hair, sweeping it back off his forehead and filling the sides in a little. Positive capability, she noted. With a few more deft strokes she added some slant to his eyebrows and took away most of his smile. Then she wrote down the last thing she thought she heard Helga Fife say: *earthen berk.*

The slide show took twenty-five minutes. The next stop on the tour, for which they left Wilson Hall and were herded through a parking lot, was the pre-accelerator area. Strobe and Helga Fife walked ahead, close together, Strobe (as always) talking and gesturing with great animation, Helga Fife nodding her head. As a couple, thought Linda, they didn't look half bad at all.

The inside of the pre-ac, as Helga Fife called it, was the first place that Linda had seen on the field trip that looked like a place where scientific experiments would actually go down. There were hums, a low buzz, in the background, and much shine and dark all around: meters, beepers, gauges, CRT screens, lots of small flashing lights and dim corners, with strange words and figures—the weird hieroglyphics of ultrahigh tech—stenciled in black on smooth metal. One sign said CAUTION: 480 VOLTS. Another said RADIOACTIVE.

"This is your captain," said Gordon. "Your captain says we—"

Somebody shushed him, and Linda thanked God half out loud.

Gordon blushed.

The actual pre-ac itself was housed in a thirty-foot pit lined on its top and four sides with red bricks, with a single glass slit of a window too small for more than two people to look through at once.

"This is our Cockcroft-Walton Pre-Accelerator," Helga Fife told them. "It is capable of producing . . ."

Okay, Linda thought. This was a little more like it. When it was her turn in line, she stood next to Paul and peered in. Ten feet below her, glinting in silence inside a glowing white room, was a huge soft-edged cube, about eight feet by eight feet by eight, very smooth, very shiny, supported by four thin black legs; its five or six arms were protruding in different directions. It was stark, vaguely scary, and massive. Both the legs and the arms were ringed at two-foot intervals with the same gleaming metal the cube was cut from. She didn't know about Paul, who had just turned away and said nothing, but it reminded her of a headless (though still very smart) metal X-Oid in the secret controlsless control room of some alien starship. Or something like that. She had never liked sci-fi stuff much, but she had to admit that the Cockcroft-Walton pre-ac-whatever impressed her.

After the pre-ac came a more spacious, better-lit area manned by technicians and doctors and nurses with acid-green plastic ID cards clipped to their lab coats, together with what were apparently—because of their pale, tufted scalps—cancer patients. Correcto. Because according to Strobe's low-key whisper, they were now in the Neutron Therapy Facility. Once again they had rounded a corner and discovered themselves in another whole world.

Helga Fife was explaining—even tone, normal volume—that the second step of the process, the linear accelerator, spun off some highly charged neutrons as by-products; after being ricocheted off a beryllium target, the neutrons were used to treat hypoxic tumors. The stages of this treatment were illustrated in the gruesomest trio of before, during, and after photographs—all color, all close-ups—that Linda had ever laid eyes on. There were whoas, groans, and gasps from her classmates. Two guys were already sketching the photos, one on the back of his Fermilab folder, and Suzette was unscrewing her lens cap. The first picture showed the lower back portion of what was clearly a woman. Bulging out over one hip was a tumor—"sarcoma," as Helga Fife called it—that looked like a large baked potato, only bluish and veiny and millions of times more grotesque. It stretched the pale skin that contained it to a transparent thinness that gave Linda the willies to look at; she forced herself, though, to keep staring. In the next picture—Seven Weeks Later—the tumor had shrunk to a blue jumbo egg, and the hip had what looked like a sunburn. In the third picture—Fifteen Weeks Later—all that was left where the tumor had been was the sunburn, which Helga Fife assured them had eventually disappeared, too.

Linda swallowed.

They moved on in relative silence. They were shown through the central control room, then two other rooms of computers. After that came the booster accelerator. Gradually things lightened up. Linda, however, could not get the tumor, or whatever it was, off her brain, just as nobody else could, she figured. Goddamn.

The next thing she knew they were outside again in the parking lot with some very bright sun in their eyes, being herded back toward Wilson Hall.

From the east-facing side of the fifteenth-floor observation deck, by looking as far to her left as she could, Linda could see the buffalo pasture. She could even make out, though just barely, some buffalo. She had eaten a chocolate chip cookie while riding up here in the elevator, so she now felt a little less woozy.

When she let her eyes scan the horizon, she could see for what looked like forever, since there were no other tall or even medium-sized buildings for miles. She could even see weather blown in off the plain to the west. It was winter, she realized. Wonderful holiday visits. Dry skin. It also reminded her of looking out over the Loop from the top of Sears Tower: from fifteen stories or ninety, you wanted to focus convexly in order to take it all in, but you couldn't. The other thing was, when she tried to look down she got dizzy.

To the east, closer in, was the four-mile-long oval of grassed-over dirt: Helga Fife's "earthen berm." Eleven feet under this berm were the rings through which protons and antiprotons were zooming along at something like 99.995 percent of the speed of light. Gee. No. Less than *c*.

Helga Fife snapped her fingers. "Fifty thousand times," she said. She made a quick loop with her hand while snapping her fingers again. "Fifty thousand more times," she said. She paused for effect. "Every second."

"Which is three times as fast as anyplace else in the world now," said Strobe.

Helga Fife said, "In effect."

"In effect," said Strobe. "Right. But so inside that ring is the place on this planet where *E* comes the closest to actually equaling *mc* squared."

Some of her classmates were still taking notes. Linda wasn't. Others were staring down out at the berm. She couldn't see doing that either.

"There are two rings, actually," said Helga Fife. "Protons in one going one way, antiprotons going the opposite way in the other."

All of a sudden Linda was hungry again. She felt as if she were going to faint. She knew that she actually wouldn't, but still. She was thirsty, bored silly, and starving.

". . . as a series of superconducting pulsed magnets suck them along through the aperture," she heard Helga saying. "When we decide to collide them together they produce almost two trillion electron volts of energy, which gives us three times the luminosity of the second most violent collisions now being—"

"For what?" Gordon said. "I mean, you know, what for?"

"That's a good question," said Helga.

Gordon glanced over at Linda.

"That's a *very* good question," said Strobe.

"One of the things that we're looking at," said Helga Fife, looking at Gordon, "is what amounts to the angle of ricochet as the hadrons get broken apart into their constituent quarks, from which we are able to draw certain conclusions about what's come to be called the Big Bang. The reactions we see here, in other words, are analogous to those which occurred when the universe was, quote, being born."

"Excuse me," said Strobe. "That's certain quote unquote, correct?"

Helga shocked Linda by simply ignoring Strobe's question. "The scintillation detectors in the spark chamber," she said, "are able to sense when the hadrons have managed to—"

"So then what's a hadron?" said Gordon, inducing fifth-grade-style tittering in the three guys around him.

"*Another* good question," said Strobe, who was grinning, as ever, at Helga.

"A hadron," she said, unperturbed, "is either two or three quarks, quarks being the smallest particles we now are aware of, bonded together by what we now call the strong force."

"Things do be getting more and more interesting," said Gordon.

Linda half-rolled her eyes in disgust. As she did there appeared, just over Helga Fife's shoulder, Hank Rendeck. She could not keep from doing a triple take. Because standing with Hank was a tall crewcut guy with bad acne: Chester Treasure, she knew. And between them, much shorter, was a beautiful Japanese woman.

Oh boy.

"We got a late start," Hank told Strobe.

Chester Treasure said nothing, apparently content to just stand there looking as sullen as humanly possible.

"Sorry," said the Japanese woman. Her voice was like porcelain sculpture: from just the one word, Linda deduced she was smart, self-assured, and terribly terribly sexy. Proceptive. The other thing was, she really did seem to be sorry. Then to top it all off, in response to Strobe's welcome, she smiled, letting her big white teeth glimmer straight into Linda's crazed brain.

Helga Fife had continued her lecture. They had turned one more corner and were examining a scale model of the tevatron system in cross section. Linda had positioned herself so that she could face Helga Fife and pretend to be paying attention, but could also keep one eye on Rendeck and friends (they *were* just three friends, were they not?) and figure out who was with whom.

Hank was now listening to what Helga Fife said with what seemed to be great fascination. He was wearing a wrinkled gray raincoat and blue jeans in place of his Jiffy Lube jumpsuit. Chester Treasure was talking to one of the guys in the class. The Japanese woman was nodding at something that Strobe had just said. She was wearing a scarlet wool blazer to go with her glossy black hair, which she wore in a braided chignon. Her skin was a flawless white gold flushed with pink stretched tautly across what were, from Linda's perspective at least, some truly astonishing cheekbones.

Linda was certain she wasn't from SAIC: if she had gone to school there, or taught there, she'd have noticed her long before now. She also was certain the woman was older than Hank. Her best guess was thirty, though perhaps she was even much older—but so what was she doing with Hank then? Weren't these Japanese women supposed to be—what was the word for it? Chaste? What a laugh. The longer she thought about it, the more the woman reminded her of a sleek stunning version of Yoko.

Helga Fife was describing how liquid helium kept the niobium-titanium magnets cooled down to 3 degrees Kelvin, or 450 degrees below zero, and how the magnets were "trained" by a series of pulsed excitations and quenches.

"Coldest stuff on earth," said Strobe, "surrounding the smallest and fastest and hottest."

"For now," Helga said. "We're waiting to see what works best."

Though she wished she had not as the words were escaping her lips, Linda asked Gordon, "Who's that just showed up with what's-his-name?"

Awkward silence.

"Do you really want to know," Gordon said, "or are you just practicing for one of those performances of yours?"

Fair enough, Linda thought. Then she smiled, exposing, on purpose, her snaggled and off-white bicuspids. She did not even care anymore if her bangs were still hiding the pimple.

The next stop on the tour was an arrowhead collection from what had once been the Indian camps on the site. The stop after that was a mock-up of the scintillation detectors inside the spark chamber. The stop after that was the north view, from which the buffalo pasture could be seen more directly, and at which point Helga Fife asked if anyone in the class wanted to adopt a baby buffalo, since lately the dating service for the Fermilab herd had been getting "a bit *too* successful." A joke.

Linda was no longer paying her *too* much attention. It was almost 3:30. She'd been up for eight hours but still had hardly eaten. She was dizzy, exhausted, and beyond-hungry queasy. She did not even feel like a cigarette. And she still had to face the hour and a half drive back to school in Strobe's car, then walk—or take the el—to Wolf Point. She did not want to think about that. She did not want to think about Hank. She did not want to think anymore.

Home, in bed, after midnight, when she tried to recall what the Japanese woman had looked like, she was unable to get her face to stand still. It would either start shimmering out of focus or flash off and on very quickly. Sometimes it just turned away, frame by frame, in slow motion.

She did not think at all about Strobe, in whose car she had finally puked, or James Jeans. She did not think about antiprotons. The hypoxic sarcoma on the wall of the Neutron Therapy Facility kept flashing back to her. Spooky light blue. Shine and dark. All that cancer.

And Hank. Just what was up with that guy? She was frantic for five or six seconds, then calm. She was wasted and sick, but the room was not spinning. Her eyes were wide open. Her guts felt swelled up. She was thinking.

She got up and went to the bathroom and looked at her face in the mirror. One pimple. Her eyes were all bloodshot and puffy. She was neither real stunning nor grotesquely ugly, she thought. She was bleeding.

And then: she was crazy. She glared at herself till her eyes stung, then blinked. Was she crazy or wasn't she? No, she decided, just ugly. Not stunning, just stupid.

She opened the medicine cabinet and her face disappeared, just like that. She did not have the right kind of pills.

She put a small gun in her mouth. It was loaded. It tasted like oily metal. Its hyacinth cold zapped her teeth.

She leaned on the sink for a second, then held on with all of her might. It was hard.

When she took the gun out of her mouth, she could taste it.

And somehow she knew that her face was still there.
In the water and silver and mucus and blood.
Puffy and shining and dark.
In the mirror.

I privatize
my private eyes
I menstruate
my man's true hate

I cancer us
in Japanese
I'm on my knees
to cancel us

4

THEY CRUISED out the Kennedy, into the sun, cutting through Jefferson Park, toward O'Hare: Richard and Maggie and Linda in the back of a black Fleetwood Brougham. It was Linda's first ride in a limo. She and six other girls had hired one once during their sophomore year at Steinmetz in order to arrive at the Horizon in style for Katrina and the Waves and the Bangles, but at the last minute something came up involving the expiration date of a credit card, and they ended up having to be driven and later picked up by Patsy Fasano's big brother, who then did his best to grope Linda after dropping off everyone else.

The guy driving now was much older and was wearing a jacket and tie and a cap. He had dozens of tiny black freckles on the back of his neck, constellations, along with a trio of boils, and strange shiny mouse-colored hair—a wig, Linda suddenly realized. He did not say a word as he drove.

They passed Narragansett, then Harlem. The old

Northwest Side. Linda could tell Maggie noticed: without even glancing her way, she could feel it. A six-car B train kept up with them for a while between Harlem and Cumberland, then fell back behind when the driver changed lanes and accelerated.

She felt Maggie's hand squeeze her arm. "Isn't this exciting?"

She nodded. It was.

"I mean, did you ever think we'd be flying off to *Paris* like this?" She was more pumped than Linda had seen her in ages.

"Not really."

"Me neither," said Maggie.

Richard laid a hand now on Maggie's right knee. He was reading a page from a printout. Maggie just patted the hand —and then stroked it. When he put down the printout, Linda looked out the window. A sand-colored Quantum blew by.

And then, very briefly, they kissed.

"I worked in a place like this once," Maggie said.

Richard smiled. Linda looked at her watch but did not see the time. They were sitting at a miniature table in a hole in the wall called COCKTAIL LOUNGE in the new international terminal.

Their waitress, a slender young black woman with three different-colored barrettes in her hair, arrived with their drinks: Diet Coke, gin and tonic, a Beck's. Their table was a foot and a half in diameter, less, with room for their drinks and one tiny ashtray, no more. The barrettes were scarlet and yellow and aqua.

Richard gave the waitress a bill, creased in two, and she left. He held up his stein for a toast. "To Paris," he said.

Maggie held up the Diet Coke Linda had ordered, looked over at Linda, and sipped. And vice versa.

"To Paris," said Maggie. "To our wonderful honeymoon trio." And then, as a joke: "To The Honeymooners."

Richard smiled.

Linda took two more big sips—she could barely taste gin—and looked at her watch one more time. It was 6:56. They'd be boarding in thirty-four minutes. If only she could be—

Suddenly Maggie was standing. She'd grabbed her purse and pushed back her chair before Linda had time to react. "Be right with you," she said.

What *is* this, thought Linda. Couldn't we go pee *together?* She glared up at Maggie and said with her eyes: Are you nuts?

Didn't work.

"Make sure you don't take off without me, you guys," Maggie said, then squeezed past their table and headed out into the concourse.

Linda sipped gin and tonic. She very much wanted to kill her. Richard sipped beer. It was awful.

"So," Richard said.

Linda nodded. She ran a hand back through her hair, scraping her scalp with her fingernails. Richard uncrossed his legs, put his hands on his knees, then recrossed his legs. He was blushing.

They sat there.

Dozens of brisk international passengers, plus their colleagues and loved ones and friends, were using the concourse to move through their silvery time zones. Few, Richard figured, were walking with persons they hated. To a woman and man, Linda noted, they had on expensive new clothes.

And they waited.

"I guess we two guys ought to wait," Richard said.

The waitress came back. At last. Just in time.

Linda said, "Maybe I'd better go too," and stood up.

The waitress gave Richard his change on a plate. She was taller than Linda, and in Linda's opinion quite gorgeous. In Richard's opinion as well. Her aqua barrette was unclipped.

"I'll be back," Linda said. Just like Arnold. She took one more sip, then another, before putting her glass on the table.

The three of them looked at each other.

"Are you nuts?" Linda said, in the john. "I mean—"

"What?" Maggie said. The innocent matchmaker washing her hands of it all at the little white porcelain sink. She looked in the mirror at Linda.

Linda was about to point out that Maggie should not have left her sitting with Richard, that she could have and should have invited her along, or at the very least asked if she had to go too, but she realized how dumb this would sound out of context. It would also amount to admitting she gave eight-seventeenths of a fuck about what Rick Dick Rich Richard might think about *anything,* or even about what Maggie might think about whether she cared about what he might think, or . . . Besides: three sinks from where they were standing, some ditz Maggie's age was making no bones at all about listening.

Maggie took out her brush and said, "Pretty darn soon now."

Fine, Linda thought. Keep up the who-moi routine. It just made it all the more obvious that she had, in fact, staged it. No problem. She could play games like this a whole lot better than Maggie could, and it pleased her that both of them knew it.

"Right," she said. "Pretty darn soon."

Maggie leaned forward and brushed back her hair. Linda watched. The blushing young bride bending over in her new white-on-white Fila warmup. Her mother.

Oh God.

Maggie straightened back up and shook out her hair, then looked at her face in the mirror. She looked . . . like she always had wanted to look, Linda realized. Lean, tan, and loaded. And happy.

Ecstatic, in fact.

Linda said, "Meet you back out there, okay?" and went into one of the stalls. It was clean. She slid the lock over and hung up her jacket, then heard Maggie say, "Just don't stay in there all night." As a joke. And then, farther off: "Should I wait?"

Once again, and as always with Maggie these days, there was simply no way to respond.

She peed and perused the graffiti. GOETZ SMART. GET CRACKING. TOM WAITS. XTC. DOES JANE BYRNE? OR DID JOE COCKER? Plus a half-dozen sketches of crotches and a couple of Rock Hudson jokes.

Was Maggie still out there, she hoped.

The jets on her wing whined and revved, pregnantly pausing, then roared and surged forward. Linda stared out the window, pressing her forehead and nose to the plastic, shading the glare from inside by saluting. She was mesmerized, scared, way too sober. Bumps on the runway ticked through her seat, and she felt the huge thrust and compression pulsing along her intestines. She swallowed. Behind her somewhere, back toward the wing, something banged. There was no way this wasn't disastrous, a major and fatal malfunction. The whole airplane rumbled and shook, its parts getting ready to scatter, but it kept moving faster and faster. Were they still on the ground? In a flash of good sense and composure she realized it would not really do her much good to start screaming. Outside the window, small lights and structures flew by as the plane picked up speed; the rumble and roar both got louder. For six or eight seconds she knew she was going to die.

Seatbelted tightly, Maggie leaned past Richard's shoulder and looked out his window. He kissed her left cheekbone, and she kissed the bridge of his nose. Her guts buzzed with tension and pleasure. He had offered to give her the seat by the window for take-off, but she'd wanted to stay between him and where Linda was sitting. As the plane left the ground she turned and looked back—two rows behind them, across the wide aisle—at her daughter. This was exactly the sort of rush that they always had shared with each other. All she could see was the top of Linda's head, facing forward, but she knew what she must have been thinking.

With his thumb, through two-ply velour, Richard buffed and explored his wife's wicked and intricate kneecap.

The Alec Guinness premonition (or early deja vu) that James Dean would total his Porsche the day before it happens good reason for Shane to drink Guinness.

MAGGIE WAS sipping club soda and paging through *Time* while Richard made notes on some printout. She didn't exactly appreciate him and Linda keeping up their Maggie-in-the-middle routine. She had simply asked the flight attendant not to serve Linda more than one drink, and so now she was sulking. What was worse was that Richard had been hypocritical enough to pretend to be on Linda's side—"Aw come on. You've gotta relax on these flights"—but both she and Linda had already seen through that gambit, and it pleased her that Richard now knew it. About time. Plus she hated to have to take sides.

She'd been married for almost three weeks, but sometimes she still felt—what? Single? Still married to some other guy? Not exactly. Not "widowed" either; she'd never felt that to begin with. With Mike it all happened so fast:

getting stoned before math class that day (when they showed them the movie on fractions), the graduation party at Jen's (the first time they actually "went all the way"), his draft notice next to that upside-down *Look* on his mother's mahogany end table. The next thing she knew they were married, Michael had gone off to boot camp, come back with his hair gone, got sent overseas, and she started missing her periods. The next thing she knew he was gone. Ever since the morning the platoon leader's letter arrived she had tried to decide things according to how they affected their daughter. Her daughter.

Their daughter.

She also decided that Richard and Linda's infantile posturing didn't surprise her, but nor would she let it depress her. She fingered the orchid the muscular steward had pinned to her warmup. She was flying on Air France to Paris—"in the sharp end of the pencil," according to Richard. She'd be staying at Hotel de Crillon. There was simply no way she would let either of them ruin it.

Linda was counting her francs, sipping Mumm's. One thousand one hundred in traveler's checks, two hundred forty in notes. The seat next to hers had stayed empty. Thank God. And she liked the idea of fifty-franc notes being actually physically larger than twenties. Not two and a half times as large, but still larger. And each denomination had its own slick design, wash of color, and etching of old famous writer. Plus Mumm's didn't count as a drink.

She winked at the gay flight attendant. He didn't wink back but did smile.

Plus none had been bought with *his* dollars.

The last time Maggie had been on a plane she was helping to chaperone ninety-six eighth-graders on Linda's class trip to Washington—to see, among other things, the new Vietnam Wall. St. Rita's had booked them on some sort of no-frills supersaver group tour apex economy package: there were certainly not any frills. It was also the last time she'd seen Linda cry.

On Air France First Class there was no sitting elbow-to-shoulder with fourteen-year-olds or passing around plastic glasses. The drinks were poured into crystal from full-sized quart bottles. Mumm's, Schweppes, Guinness, Remy Martin, Martell, and anything else you wanted. Plus menus! This evening she could choose between fillet of swordfish stuffed with a pink salmon mousse and whole fresh foie gras—"Only goose livers of the very best quality are used for foie gras. First they are left to steep in port, then a seasoning of salt and pepper is added, and finally they are cooked in a special earthen bowl. Air France chefs advocate this authentic country-style preparation which permits us to serve you a truly top quality delicacy"—and this stuff was only the *appetizer.* The main course selections were Carré d'agneau aux herbes de Provence and Longe de veau au basilic—"Carrie D. Agnew Hawks Herb da Provincial," according to Richard, "or The Long View of Bacillus." For dessert there was tarte au citron et aux kiwis. Not to mention French cheeses, French wines, Caesar salad, a fruit basket, and decaf Colombian coffee.

The one thing that wasn't much different from coach was the bathroom, which was so cramped and eensy she wondered how fat people managed. A vase of cut tulips was screwed to the sinktop, though all this accomplished was reducing what little freshening-up space there was to begin with. But still, a nice touch, she decided.

The seats were like La-Z-Boys, better, with plenty of elbow and leg room and a wide V-shaped aisle between rows. There also were real woolen blankets, not the see-through synthetic babushkas they gave you in coach. Plus slippers, a decent-sized pillow, some warmed-up Grand Cru for a nightcap . . .

They were seats you could actually sleep in.

The sun came back up after midnight. They'd taken off just before eight, around dusk, so it hadn't really set in the first place. Linda's yawn tasted like Mumm's. *Living with Elvis,* she thought. *Her fingers on Elvis's Levi's.* She couldn't remember the last dawn she'd seen, and she wondered if this one should count.

The captain announced on the intercom—first in French, then in English—that they were flying 10,500 meters above the Atlantic. An unbroken blanket of pinkish gray clouds was spread out below them, so she'd have to take his word for it. Ocean. She'd still never seen one, she realized. Plus she certainly hoped he was sober, at this height: she would not like to fall through pink brains. *Plus live shows saved lives, Dave.* She thought she could make out the curve of the earth to the south, then told herself that was impossible. Was it? She decided it probably wasn't.

The movie was *Raising Arizona.* She'd already seen it but decided to watch for a while: the headsets were free and there wasn't much else going on. She pushed down the shade on her window. Okay. The guy's boss's kids were trashing his motor home and nailing his crotch with a squirt gun. She put on her headset, clicked through the stations, checked out the chase scene in French.

Foreign reporters could call into question her sworn affidavits by asking if Elvis wore Levi's or Lee's. Was he still having sex with his ex? She could say she could not understand them.

She could tell that the short hunky steward was keeping his eye on her.

Photographers everywhere.
Watching.

Richard read *Bright Lights, Big City.* He always liked the way the guy would redeem himself in the end, with the mother and girlfriend and all. And the bread for the sunglasses trade! It was the fourth or fifth time he had seen it or read it, but it kept getting better and better.

She couldn't quite place him, but a famous musician was three rows behind her. She hadn't even known he was there till she got up and went to the john. He was black and not young, with half-gray elaborate dreadlocks and symmetrical scars on his forehead. He was strumming an ampless Les Paul, mostly chords; she assumed he was working some song out. The two younger women he seemed to be traveling with had on headsets but were not really watching the movie. They were both wearing third-world-style caftans; their hair was in cornrows and braids. There was also a boy, nine or ten, whose D-shaped head was shaved like a basketball player's. He was wearing Air Jordans and laughing out loud at the movie.

The guitarist looked up, hit a bar chord, and smiled. She smiled back but turned away quickly. Kept going. She knew she'd seen him somewhere—on stage at some concert, on the sleeve of a Byrne-Eno album—but did not want to stare to make sure.

In *Musician?*

She went back to her seat and watched the last scene of the movie. She was tempted to turn around and peek, but resisted. It bothered her not to know who the guy *was*, though. There was something else, too, that was strange, but she couldn't say what. And then it made sense: she was flying first class. If somebody famous was going where she was that night, the odds were not bad they'd be sitting by her on the plane.

They were flying through turbulence now. She put on her seatbelt, took off her headset, and listened.

A monster with black stumps for arms—a man, a young guy—staggered toward her. His sockets were teeming with maggots. She tried to run, couldn't. Her lungs and shins burned with the effort, but her feet wouldn't budge. Could she scream?

A guy with a javelin sticking up through his chest was coughing dark blood from the back of his throat. It was spraying up into her face. His hands clutched the shaft of the javelin, and her hands clutched his. They were screaming.

She watched Linda rubbing the side of a No. 2 pencil against a sheet of green looseleaf. Instead of the opposite happening, shapes of blank space would emerge where the pencil had *been.* She asked Linda how this could happen. Linda explained that the process was called negative chiaroscuro. She apparently knew what she was talking about. She was good at this drawing style, too, and she knew it. So she must have been learning some things at that school after all. Which meant everything she had put up with—those jobs, the tuition, not getting married, the trip to DC—had been worth it.

Linda kept drawing. A vertical diamond appeared on the looseleaf, then fifteen neat letters: Mike's name. But Linda could not get the face. The eyebrows and nostrils were wrong, plus the hair was so long it was *moving.*

The problem, she realized, was that they had shifted locations. The black granite wall that her daughter was drawing against had been moved from DC to Chicago because Maya Ying Lin, its designer, had married the first black male mayor. The good news was that now she'd be able to visit Mike's name on the wall every day. Admission was free, the designer was pregnant but would still be on hand to explain things, the No. 2 bus made a stop only two blocks away.

She set her watch ahead seven hours to Paris time. It was more or less dawn there as well. She wondered what bands would be there.

But she wasn't in Paris yet. Non. She'd be flying through time zones and dawn for another three hours at least.

She wondered what time it was *now.*

A young guy whose arms had been shredded above the elbow by a booby-trapped doll—a St. Joseph statue from a life-sized Nativity scene—staggered toward her. She ran but he caught her. He wrestled her down to the floor of the jungle and forced back her legs. She was too scared to do much and sensed that he knew this, which made her more frightened, determined. She twisted and punched him but couldn't resist his fierce strength. He was biting her lips and her neck as he struggled to enter her. *No!* V-ed back and open, in spectacular pain, she gouged his eyes, scratched him. He laughed and just leaned on her harder. Strips of his charred greasy flesh tore away from his rib cage and skull and attached to her breasts and her face. She was gagging. "Hey Maggie?" He kissed her and bit her, drawing blood from her tongue and her lips, tearing off soft little pieces, then started caressing her shoulders and hair with his stumps—so what that he knew what her name was. She'd swallowed a piece of burnt skin while he kissed her, and now she was puking. It burned up the back of her throat. She could feel a ferocious erection inside her as vomit ran back down her neck. It was him. It was Michael. She could tell from the shape and the aperpendicular ways it was angling into her. Hard. But it worked. She could take it. From their mouths to their thighs they were slick with each other's warm blood. Then another impossible angle and rhythm and *Jeez.* If he didn't let up he'd destroy her. Then harder, too hard, and she clung to him, whispering, kissing him, begging him please not to hurt her, *no please,* as it sank in how much she still missed him. Then faster, so much, he was tearing her, bearing down into her faster and *oh God* and hard and she knew he would soon disappear like he always did, wait, so she ground her hips frantically, *ungh,* so that pulsing and thrashing against him, please wait, he was *no,* she was *ungh,* he was . . . *wait!*

Richard was nudging her. "Honey?"

Hunh?

He massaged her left shoulder and arm.

What?

"Hey babe?" She was moaning and trembling. "Maggie?"

He was kissing her face. She was sweating. Where was he? And panting. Richard kept rubbing her shoulder, then put his cool palm on her forehead. She had slid halfway out of her seat.

It was dark in the cabin. Where was she?

She blinked, shook her head. The gay flight attendant was looming down over her, smiling.

The plane dropped in stages over England, the Channel, then France. Linda's tonsils and ears throbbed, she was dying of thirst, her whole head ached. She'd hardly slept at all. She'd come close a few times, but the clinking of china and glasses, the movement and hum of the recycled air, kept her up. (No matter now large and lumbar-supportive the seats were, or how far fucking back you could tilt them, she just couldn't sleep sitting up.) Her eyes were bone dry, her forehead and nose were sporting an oily film, and a chalkier slimier version had settled in inside her mouth. She was wasted.

Brushing her teeth in the john seemed to require three hands: one to work the brush with, one to constantly press down the cold water tap because otherwise it wouldn't stay on, one to hold open the weird suction drain of the paste-spattered sink when you spit.

At this stage she only had two.

LINDA WAS around the corner in Room No. 5. Just a single, of course, but a great one: two nice big windows, a desk, a small dining nook, and a fireplace. Even Linda seemed almost half satisfied. She had already changed and gone out.

Their suite, No. 9, had four rooms. The antechamber featured bookshelves with actual books, an Old Master print, and a wet bar. Their six matching bags were neatly lined up to the side of it. There was also a basket of fruit with a handwritten card from the manager welcoming them to the Crillon. As soon as he'd read it, Richard had run downstairs "to take care of something." Why not call, Maggie wondered. He also had taken the key. But he wanted to shower, he'd told her, as soon as he came back upstairs. Did that mean alone or a deux? She would see.

The main room was thirty feet long, at least half that wide, with four tall French windows. It was divided into a sitting area (two chairs, divan, marble fireplace), a writing area (large ornate desk with matching leather blotter and wastebasket, small chandelier overhead), and a sleeping and lovemaking area (twin beds pushed together to form one fancy king). The walls were pale gold and ivory, the upholstery canary and eggshell, the carpeting springy and cream-colored. Maggie was tempted to try a few cartwheels but realized that that was the old her; the new her was haughty and dignified. Very. She did a half-decent one anyway, then another, another, for fun.

The dressing room was the size of her bedroom on Eastwood. It had carved walnut cabinets for closets, his and hers suit racks, an exercise bike, and a vanity table equipped with a magnifying mirror that left nothing to chance or your vanity. She took off her warmup and checked herself out—in profile, straight on, then in profile again—in one of the regular mirrors. Her hair hadn't held up too well to the flight, but the rest of her looked pretty decent, considering. Right? She exposed her left armpit and puckered her lips, which gave her the urge to take off the rest of her clothes. So she did.

The floor and walls of the bathroom, plus the sinktop and bathtub and shower, were all cut from pink marble. It was like being inside a refurbished cave. There were two sinks, a toilet and matching bidet, a hair dryer, plenty of towels, a kilogram scale (on which she weighed forty-nine), and a phone. Plus two plush white terrycloth bathrobes with the Crillon's posh logo stitched in blue on the left front breast pocket. The whole wall behind the two sinks was a mirror. Plus controlling all this très swank "atmosphere" was their very own Honeywell thermostat.

This was how rich people traveled, she realized. She exposed her right armpit, tensed her abdominal muscles, inhaled.

This was how rich people *lived.*

Between 1793 and 1795 the heads of 1343 people were severed by guillotine in the square just outside the hotel. It was now called the Place de la Concorde. Linda had read this in Michelin and wanted to go out and look.

It had been raining when they rode in the cab from the airport, but now it was sunny and gorgeous. The Place de la Concorde was as big as Grant Park but was one solid network of little French cars: no checkered taxis with tailfins, just dense—unbelievable—traffic. Was this where they'd gotten the name for the plane? She sure hoped not. To the east was the old Jeu de Paume and the Tuileries, to the south was the Seine, to the west was the Champs Elysées, Arc de Triomphe, Eiffel Tower . . . At least that's what Michelin said. She did not feel like strolling, however.

Right next door, just across the street on the corner of rues Gabriel and Boissy d'Anglais, was the American Embassy. Which meant terrorists and diplomats probably used the Crillon, did it not? Caspar Weinberger stayed there, according to Maggie (according to Richard, Linda figured), and always took Suite No. 9. Like they knew. But some Middle Eastern terrorist *had* been convicted in Paris last week of masterminding a series of bombings that had killed some Americans. The judges had given him life, the maximum sentence allowable, and his comrades had vowed to retaliate by killing a few more Americans. Preferably diplomats, right? Semtex city. Or mow down some wealthy American tourists?

The embassy building was four stories tall, mostly white limestone and glass, Stars and Stripes flapping up top. Large cubes of concrete studded with long iron bars had been placed every ten or twelve feet along Boissy d'Anglais. The point, Linda gathered, was that you could drive past the Embassy but could not park your car bombs beside it. Or else you would have to get—

"Hey!"

She turned and looked up. Maggie was waving from a second-story window. Her torso and hair were swaddled in white Crillon towels. She looked like an ancient Egyptian.

Richard was soaping his armpits. He was jumpy but happy: he was going to show Maggie Paris. He was not fond of glass shower doors, though. He always imagined himself slipping somehow, spastically crashing through soapy and naked, slicing off parts of his body on jagged and tinkling shards, his own bloody kneeprints crisscrossing over the marble as he groped for his severed left testis. He cringed.

The hotel had provided Cerruti shampoo. He knew that shampooing too often made hairlines recede even faster. Three times a week was his rule, and he'd just washed it yesterday morning—was that already yesterday?—so it wouldn't look flat on the plane. For his honeymoon, though, he decided to make an exception. He tore open one of the packets and squeezed out a third of a portion. It was amber and smelled good, but what did that prove? About nothing. (Did Connors have any more hair, for example, just because he endorsed it? Would he have any less if he didn't? Of course not.) Using only the padded tips—not the freshly trimmed nails—of his fingers, he worked it down into his scalp.

A sudden loud squawking surprised him, and his feet almost slipped on the tiles. It took him a second or two to remember the bathroom had come with a telephone. Smart!

The phone squawked again. He hoped it was Davison calling with the afternoon close—Jesus Christ!—as lather ran into his eye. He had plenty of stop orders in, but he wanted to hear final numbers from the mouth of a guy he could trust.

The phone squawked a third time. This time he shouted for Maggie, politely requesting she do him a favor and get it. He put his face under the shower and tried to rinse out the shampoo.

When it squawked for the fourth time he yelled Maggie's name, just her name, and as loud as he possibly could.

He suddenly wasn't so sure you could trust guys like Davison, either.

Amazing. Two out of two of the soldiers standing guard on the corner were handsome: clean-shaven, lean, with great cheekbones. One had black hair with brown eyes, the other one brown with dark blue. Both had machine guns slung across their waists, and both were encased crotch to chin with concave armored vests that reminded her of blue cooling towers. Their pants cuffs were tucked into their boots. They looked tough.

As she passed in front of them she smiled at the closest one to her, the one with brown eyes. He looked for a second but didn't smile back. His index finger was an inch from his black metal trigger. His partner did not even glance.

Ten feet beyond them, at the embassy gate, there were several more soldiers and cops: helmets, walkie-talkies, more guns. Behind them was a twelve-foot wall topped with a wrought-iron fence wrapped loosely with coils of concertina wire. Everyone clearly meant business.

She skirted them slowly, walking west on the rue Gabriel, but did not try to seem nonchalant. There were squirrels and sparrows in the trees just behind the high walls, but it didn't make sense to wear bulletproof vests on the *outside*, she thought. Like Chicago.

A pair of large buses was parked on her side of the street, up ahead about twenty-five yards. She kept walking. She also heard low distant rumbling. She looked at the sky. Except for some high cirrus clouds and some darker stuff way to the south, it was clear.

She kept walking. The buses were painted a beautiful deep Kleinish blue. From the sidewalk beside them, through blue-tinted windows, she could make out a few silhouettes. A cigarette flared. When she squinted and shaded her eyes, she saw that the buses were both filled with soldiers in helmets, sitting in rows two by two.

She moved slowly past them—the buses were longer and wider than CTA buses—thinking about those blue vests, then stopped and looked back. She was spacey from not having slept but could not have been more wide awake. Then it hit her: the rumbling noise she had heard was the motors of both buses *running*.

She turned and kept walking. Traffic heaved not far away on the Champs Elysées. Sparrows cheeped. Paris. She also was hearing, she realized, the kind of percussion—muffled highhat and vibes, snared syncopation—that they put on the soundtrack of predictable thrillers when the heroine starts to get frightened.

Other things started to hit her. Wars had been fought around here. Some wars were still going on. The buzzing of minibikes was, when you listened, quite separate from the dull thrum and drone of small cars.

Plus a half block from where she was staying a couple of busloads of soldiers were ready to go all the time.

sympathy
contempt
sympathy
contempt

THE HOTEL Sale, which was now the Musée Picasso, had been built, Richard noticed, with the same kind of limestone their bathroom was cut from, though somewhat less pink. It was white, as a matter of fact. It was great. In addition to three floors of paintings and sculptures (and all by one guy!) there were notebooks, chronologies, photographs, and explanatory displays to show how Picasso had lived.

One thing he liked was how short he had been: in some of the drawings he barely came up to the young model's elbow. And all of the women he'd had! And he kept getting them younger and better looking. Apparently his baldness hadn't bothered the guy *or* the women. It was just no big deal. Picasso was old, fat, short, bald, and rich: a combo, it seemed, that drove women crazy. Yes sir.

He was also impressed by the fact that his paintings got better—more lively and colorful, larger, more *touching*—the older Picasso had got. And the richer. By the time he was fifty he was practically a one-man cartel: buying whole wardrobes with drawings, or a villa with one decent painting. Even now, several years after he'd purchased the farm (at age 91!), he still had these exquisitely tailored and well-preserved French women marching around giving lectures to small groups of succulent French girls in knee socks and pleated wool skirts about all the wonderful things he had done. Not too shabby.

He also was proud that Picasso had once been a *Cub*ist.

Linda loved Picasso's Braque: *Nature Morte à la bouteille.* She remembered reading how it was Braque, after all, not Picasso, who had introduced letters and musical instruments, even notes, to his canvases. This one was earlier, though; they still were restricting their palettes to umbers and beiges. It was practically monochromatic, with neither collagework nor colorful pointillist patterns. (Just to the left of the bottle, however, she thought she could make out some burnt umber wedges of lime.) The basic brushwork was uniform half-inch-long rectangles. The lines that divided the planes were darker but much more uncertain, breaking up into obscurity the farther he got from the center. By the time he got out to the edges, in fact, he was letting the canvas show through.

She wandered alone through the crowded museum, determined to take enough time, letting the jet lag ooze through her skin. She was happy. She moved for the most part against the grain of the numbers and arrows designed to get people to follow the work chronologically. The effect was like swimming upstream, but at least she could set her own pace. She even doubled back a few times. There were so many wonderful pictures! And, although it could have been just her imagination, she seemed to be feeling less thirsty.

It was great to be seeing the actual paintings. *La Mort de Casagemas* was tiny, a looseleaf-sized sketch. The candle flame's shimmer was rendered, she noticed, in van Gogh impasto, so why not *compare and contrast the two brushworks, tracing the albeit posthumous influence of the "late" work of the former on the "oily" of the latter, paying especial attention to M. van Guhghthphth's buying the farm, checking out, cashing in, hanging up, or what have you, plus its radically touching déjà vu vis-à-vis Señor Pickasshole's self-whacked young friend vis-à-vis what we note* . . . She noticed a dark purple bruise on Casagemas's temple that she couldn't remember from artbooks or slides. It was stunning.

In the 1901 self-portrait, the one with the buttoned-up overcoat, she could make out the part in his long thick black hair; she always had thought it was one solid swath of black paint. It also was strange since she usually thought of Picasso as bald. But at that point he'd only been *her* age. Goddamn. There also were dozens more delicate, fox-colored beard hairs than she'd ever suspected from looking at "great" reproductions. She also could tell that the coat was a deep midnight navy, not black.

Some of the drawings were eensy: crosshatched wedge faces, two or three inches square max, displayed in glass cases alongside the African masks that inspired them. (Some turtlenecked Frog guy was checking her out, but she sensed he'd fuck off if she coolly ignored him a while. And it worked.) There was also the story, in French, of *Demoiselles D'Avignon,* along with the drawings and sketches he'd made to prepare. He'd even done actual paintings.

But there wasn't enough of the matte and drab cubism she'd always liked best. *Buste de Femme* wasn't bad, though. In fact, after nonchalantly looking both ways plus behind her, she reached up and touched it, running the pad of her left index fingertip back and forth, once, on the crack that had formed next to one of the eyes. Eighty-year-old huile sur toile, by Picasso no less, though it sure didn't *feel* like anything terribly epochmaking. Suddenly fiercely strong arms had wrenched hers behind her and wrestled her onto the floor, while a deep-voiced woman radioed in gruff, rapid French for assistance. Like they needed it. One of the security assholes kneeled on her neck while another one viciously tightened a thin plastic handcuff that cut off the circulation in her wrists. Plus it *hurt.* What was worse was that six dozen people were watching. A man then arrived who spoke English. Thank God! She tried to look up, make some eye contact—*please!*—but she couldn't. With her cheek pressed against the cool limestone, she was made to understand very clearly that, because of her background and age, she would be prosecuted not as a minor, and to the fullest extent of French law.

The synthetic collages were larger, more colorful—busier—than the straight analytical ones. The subjects were mostly acoustic guitars, violins, mustaches, pipes. The one she liked best was the small oval job framed with rope: *Nature Morte à la chaise cannée.* The letters JOU warped back and forth between the stem of the pipe, the fake caning paper, and the fading-in fading-out planes. She knew from Art History that in French *jou* was the first three letters of play . . . also cheek, gamble, joy, pleasure, journal, day, daylight, time . . . and hundreds of other French words. Cheek, she deduced, would make sense with the caning, but she guessed that Picasso had loftier meanings in mind. She was tempted to touch the rope frame, or the paint, or the contact paper, but they'd hung it inside a glass case to protect it from people like her. Just as well. She stared for a couple of minutes into the jumbled, kaleiding matte planes, trying to spot a fourth letter, to make any one meaning make any more sense than another.

Besides the one Braque, Picasso had owned a Rousseau, a couple of decent Matisses—were *all* the great artists men? Jesus Christ!—and three just amazing Cézannes, including a frieze of male bathers she could tell had been modeled after a composition by Mo- or Manet. Manet, she decided. She was clear on the difference between their two styles but sometimes still mixed up their names. But then she remembered her way to remember: *a* before *o*, so Manet. Was the one she was thinking of his *Luncheon on the Grass*? She distinctly remembered a green and blue painting with a half-dozen guys exposing themselves around a pond in some forest (so it wasn't the *Blonde with Bare Breasts*). It was one of Manet's later works, around the time of the *Asparagus.* Wasn't it? If she were taking an Art History multiple choice quiz, she knew she'd guess wrong, but here, in Paree, with the pressure off, she was sure it was . . . *after Manet.*

Downstairs again in the bookshop, Richard bought thirty-nine copies—all they had left—of a black-and-white poster of Picasso's left hand. He was going to have them framed in black lacquer (the same stuff his three Tasset cowfur pieces were framed in), then give them to traders as gifts. Stenciled blue letters like you'd see on an overseas crate were laid sideways and vertically against the black background: MUSÉE PICASSO up one side, PARIS up the other. But the hand was what counted, of course. It was raised and extended, fingers together, palm out. It was perfect.

"It's called *Picasso Gets Short,*" he told Maggie.

"I got that," she said.

The stubby hand's lifeline was long and emphatic, she noticed, which seemed to prove *something* since he'd lived to be ninety-one-plus. But the really amazing thing was that this one single hand had done all the work they'd just seen, plus much much much more. Plus the way it was raised in a gesture of greeting, or maybe a brief wave goodbye. Or a pledge. Plus she knew why her husband adored the damn thing. It was really a wonderful poster. It was small, understated, but expressed what Picasso had done, how he'd done it, more succinctly than a huge color poster of any one painting. Besides. There were too many like that already.

"That's how he *got* short," said Richard.

"I gets it."

It secretly pleased her that he liked it so much. Because the more she stared at the sample, the more its sharp contrasts intrigued her. It looked like a great person's hand, but it also reminded her of an aerial reconnaissance photograph of mountainous farmland, with runways and gorges and streambeds and roads that was taken at sunset or dawn.

It was also an omen, she thought, since her daughter was also left-handed.

141

Naming or painting these ghosts sometimes seems a way to stop their nagging.

ON THEIR third day in Paris, while Linda went off to look at more paintings, Richard and Maggie shopped the couture shops around their hotel. You could hardly avoid them in the district the Crillon was in: there were seven or eight every block. Sweatshirts cost nine hundred francs, men's loafers over five thousand. And that was the *cheap* stuff at places like Gucci, Cerruti, la Renta, Paloma Picasso . . .

"No relation, I trust," Richard said as they turned left on rue Saint Honoré. He had just bought his third pair of shoes.

"Actually," said Maggie, "his daughter, I think."

"That so?" Richard said. "By which of his wives?"

Maggie did not really know. She was dazed. She had already bought some Picasso perfume, perfume and a belt from Chanel, two Hermès dresses, a Nam Uong Dong sweatshirt for Linda, a jacket by Lagerfeld, a jacket by Issey Miyake. For a while she had tried to divide things by 5.85, that morning's rate of exchange, and when that got too hard, by just 6. She wanted to be at least slightly cost-conscious, but Richard was forcing the issue, so what could a poor girl do? Whenever she'd protest or hesitate, he'd slap down the platinum trump card.

They bought two tennis sweaters from Fred: green, blue, and white his and hers. They were nice. Then Richard insisted on buying a long paisley scarf as a gift for Fred North, his 345-pound former Abilene Christian offensive tackle acquaintance who now traded soybeans. Because the pattern on the scarf, when you looked at it closely, was a neat grid of paisley-shaped FREDS.

"North'll shit," Richard said.

Maggie considered this gross possibility and concluded it wasn't unlikely. Because according to flatulent Fred, anything chicer than tucked-in blue shirts was "more faigbait," and anything faigs wore or baited was cause for a noisome reaction.

"He'll go absolutely nuts when he sees this," said Richard, excited. "Probably want to nuke all of Paris, drop some big AIDS bomb or something, very least change his first name . . ." He handed the salesgirl the Amex.

"Don't doubt it," said Maggie, more or less to herself. "Haute couture reaches the pits."

Richard wrote out the gift card: *Yo! Fred! This is you all over, we thought. RBaum and Maggie.*

Maggie watched as the salesgirl refolded the scarf and laid it in baby blue tissue. From the way she was smiling at Richard, you could tell that she understood English.

In the *Pieta de Villeneuve-les-Avignon,* the three female saints all had neat white round halos that looked just like notary public seals, while Jesus's halo was long and short spikes of gold light. And it bugged her. She had heard of the old boy art network, but the Louvre was a little ridiculous. She could see things like *Venus de Milo* and Delacroix's bare-breasted *Liberty*, but the Jean-Baptistes Greuze and Carpeaux and Chardin, Hyacinthe Rigaud, Honoré Fragonard —who *cared* about lecherous frogmold like these guys? Then there were *Esther at Her Toilet, Diana,* Ingres's *Turkish Bath,* a long wall of boring Courbet-types . . . French guys, she gathered, to judge by the Louvre and the Métro, were big on bare breasts (and probably bullish as well), especially when sculptors or admen or painters had bared them *artistically,* only one at a time had been bared, or when critics called tit shots *La Nude Bust* (central panel, 1607–11, a detail).

Nor was she in the right mood to pick her way through the dense throng around *Mona Lisa.* She was jetlagged and thirsty, but still: did you come all this way and just skip it? She angled diagonally into the crowd, regretting each half-step she managed. Persons from various continents were crowding each other and sweating, flexing their elbows, having flashless photographs taken of themselves with corners of Mona behind them, or tapping back curryous belches. A few of these persons had not had a shower or bath in some days, so Linda tried not to inhale. Didn't work. The painting was hung in a steel and glass grotto the grunge paying homage made her pray was machine gun- and Krylon- and funk-proof. She angled and shouldered in closer, trying to stay in her own little pocket of air. Didn't work. Seen from the side, between cameras and heads, the painting was drabber than she had expected, and maybe a little bit larger. She could see how it got to be famous. But the closer she got, the more it still looked like the image she'd seen all the hundreds of versions of, except for the way— The back of a hand brushed her hip and lingered an extra three seconds. She turned around quickly, left fist cocked back, nails on her right hand all ready, but the pock-nosed guy standing next to her was holding a camera above him: apparently innocent. They glared at each other a moment. He was all Banlon armpit, nose hair and pores and black eyes, and she couldn't be certain that he was the one who had groped her. Even if she was, what could she do in this crush? Start a brawl? And besides: his b.o. was *worse* than a feel job, much more intrusive and potent, Class X, a first-degree rape of the sinuses. It had even seeped into her lungs. But enough! As politely as possible, she shouldered her way toward the mob's outer fringes, shimmying, wriggling, holding her breath, excusing herself while she waited for fissures to slip through, and, when none opened, just shoving. Whatever you do, she was telling herself, do *not* get all frantic and shrill. DO NOT PANIC. By the time she'd emerged from the crush she was gulping down mouthfuls of half-decent air, thanking Christ there was *any,* and composing herself in order to look, once again, enigmatic. . . .

Without any pattern or plan, she wandered around the first floor, getting spaced out and thirsty and dazed. There were too many fabulous masterpi! The Bosch *Ship of Fools,* Breughel's *Beggars,* plus Goya, Velázquez, Van Eyck, Botticelli, Van Dyck. But why didn't people take baths? Suppose you ran into somebody? Wasn't the Louvre like the best of all possible places? Suppose you picked somebody up, got invited to lunch and then up to their empty apartment . . . *St. Joseph in the Carpenter's Shop:* it was hokey, of course, but what light! There were also some really nice Rembrandts: *Bathsheba,* the *Old Age* self-portrait . . .

Then, out of nowhere, *Pogues II.* It was crowding the wall floor-to-ceiling, one and a half times as wide, as in-your-face massive as anything she'd seen by Manhattan's big Art Stars, and all the more startling compared to the cassette-sized version she had thought was original art. Because live and up close it was *wild.* Crashing green waves, outstretched hands, desperation: a Board of Trade pit, only windier, wetter, and crowded with one less large asshole. Could you make it *more* melodramatic? She hoped not. It was all done in browns, greens, and beiges: a camouflage pattern almost, when you squinted. It also had full frontal nudity, *male,* plus marbly shoulders and back muscles that made you unsquint pretty quick. Boy oh boy. The half-naked bodies no longer had Pogues heads, but she figured she'd have to accept that. She'd also have *both* versions now, as soon as she picked up the postcard. This one was painted in 1819 by some French guy, Théodore Géricault, who called it *The Raft of the Medusa.* What else.

But all things considered, the Louvre surprised her by how much it put her to sleep. She did like the bas-relief work on the walls, like neat concrete ribbons of brain, and the mazes and windows and gargoyles. There were too many funkmonger foreigners, though, and too many miles of old paintings. Plus all you could see half the time was light glaring back off the varnish.

The most interesting part, at least in her hungry opinion, was the outside: a two-pronged Napoleon palace with a huge see-through pyramid set smack in the middle of the courtyard, a courtyard already congested with networks of muddy archeological digs and sullen French hardhats taking their time building new stuff. Talk about states of transition! Newfangled pink-and-black cranes twice as tall as the Louvre's highest towers were wheeling and tilting between the two prongs. It was strange. GAY PRAYING MANTES FROM PLUTO PREY UPON ART IN GAY PARIS. The plywood construction barriers were plastered with posters and smeared with dried mud and cement. The most common graffito was جهاد . The second most common was WOZA.

She stood for a while on the quai, watching barges move

up the gray Seine. She thought she could see the rhinoceros, the one with its foot chained, in front of the Musée d'Orsay, but did not have a very good angle.

The sun disappeared to the south, then popped right back out.

She was starving.

With their hee-haw sirens preceding them, two blue police cars, Peugeots, darted and lurched through the Champs Elysées traffic. The drivers both leaned on their horns. So did others. Sounds like Europe, thought Linda. But louder. It pleased her that all this was happening *live.* The cops in both cars looked incredibly tough, Maggie thought. Needing shaves, wearing leather, not smiling, they leaned out their windows and said things they looked like they meant. They couldn't be *too* much less street, she was thinking, less scary, than the guys they were chasing. Go get 'em, thought Richard.

In the wake of the second police car was a convoy of minibikes, helmeted messengers taking advantage of this authorized part in the traffic. As the convoy went by, one of the messengers turned and very frankly looked over Maggie or Linda, or both; you couldn't see into his black helmet's sheer plastic surface to tell. But probably Linda, thought Richard.

Straight ahead several blocks, decked out with several French flags, was the Arc de Triomphe. To Maggie, compared to what she'd expected, it looked rather grimy and . . . medium-sized. The rest of the Champs was fast food, souvenirs, car dealers, airlines, bleeping arcades next to seven-screen theaters, with packed brasseries on each corner. Heathen Town city, thought Linda. Wide sidewalks perhaps, Maggie thought, world-famous Arc at the top, but still: just like Rush Street.

They strolled. The Iran Air display window featured a fundamentalist realist portrait of Ayatollah Khomeini, though he looked just a smidgen too grouchy, in Richard's opinion, to get you to want to vacation in Qom or Teheran. Perhaps Farsi Island . . .

The Aeroflot office next door featured a mosaic tile portrait of a stern, goateed Lenin, who always made Maggie think of John Lennon, Marx Brothers movies, and her second-best friend in third grade, Suzie Engles. But she *would* like to travel to Russia someday. Her mother's great-uncle was from the Ukraine. Plus for years she had wanted to take Linda to Poland . . .

A five-year-old girl walked by with her father. They looked at the picture of Lenin. Linda hated the little girl instantly, out of habit, then caught herself. No. Not her fault. The girl asked a question and pointed; her father leaned over and answered. They were not speaking English or French. Not her fault.

Richard hunched up his shoulders to make himself look like a female bolshevik weightlifter and said "Aeroflot girl, you're a gray weight to fly" with a marble-mouthed, Volga-boatman inflection.

Not bad, Linda thought. Though I'd start to worry if my impressions of sex-changer bulldykes were quite that convincing.

"Not bad," Maggie said.

Next door to Aeroflot was Pizza Hut, and suddenly Maggie was starving. She turned first to Linda. "You hungry?"

"Jay tray tray fang," Richard said. "Let me tell you."

The air came alive, ripped apart by a brightness that stunned her. Next came the impact, a pair of concussions that punched Linda sideways. In very slow motion, Richard flew upside down past her. What was left of his torso was caved in and twisted. He'd been torn into three by the blast. What had happened?

Linda was bleeding but didn't much care. She knew that the phrase was "in shock." The sidewalk was littered with bodies. She thought she heard sirens. Were they two blocks away or two miles? Getting closer or farther away? Both the girl and her father were dead.

A blond woman tried to get up to her knees. It was Maggie. She was sobbing hysterically because she couldn't stand up; she did not know her husband was dead yet. One cheek, her neck, and the front of her blouse were soaking with blood. Its dense scarlet luster against the pearl-colored silk of the blouse startled Linda. She'd always thought real human blood would look . . . matter.

She could see Maggie's wound wasn't deep, that her forehead had merely been grazed. She knew it was never as bad as the gushes of blood would suggest. She'd recover.

She helped calm her down by wiping the blood from her cheek and her eyes.

And she held her.

They're both just obsessed with their bodies. Like they're not gonna lose it someday. Get old and die. Or die young. It's like they both think they're exempt from all that.

FROM THE top of a neat stack of tabloids at a newsstand on Boulevard Haussmann, the London *Mirror*'s headlines leapt up at Maggie:

MOM SLAIN ON HONEYMOON

DAUGHTER FLEES SCENE IN HER DRESS

There were also two black-and-white photos. One showed a plain English schoolgirl, thirteen or fourteen, smiling in three-quarter profile. The other one, not quite in focus, showed a bride and groom cutting a cake.

Maggie was too loaded down with Printemps bags to be able to point, so she nudged Linda's elbow. "Hah," she said, nodding toward the *Mirror*. "They're onto you finally, it looks like."

"Onto me what?"

"In London at least. Lookee there."

Linda spotted it, got it, and smiled. Couldn't help it. Then, before Maggie saw her, stopped smiling. They'd been shopping for three and a half solid hours without once ever mentioning Richard.

Maggie transferred two bags to Linda and picked up a *Mirror.* Linda protested, but under her breath, regrabbing handles and juggling shoeboxes to get these new items in balance with what she was already carrying, managing—barely—not to drop the whole load. "I would say bloody slaying's too good for them."

Maggie paid for the paper, took back her bags, said "Merci."

"Jesus," said Linda, re-readjusting her load.

"Souvenir," Maggie said.

"For either of them," Linda said.

According to Richard's new guidebook, eight hundred years of French history had been made in the Bourse du Commerce. Louis XII owned it first but lost it in a cribbage game to his chamberlain, who converted it into a convent for repentant sinners. It later became a hotel, a bordello, then a gambling hall, before Louis XVI turned it into a wheat market—not a place to trade futures, of course, just some stalls where you'd go to buy wheat. This was replaced in 1889 by the present rotunda, which was designed for real trading.

The very tall woman at the information desk told him, in very good English, that wheat would be traded on Wednesday. But what was so special about Wednesday French wheat, Richard wondered. The answer was that in Paris, the capital of France, the largest free country in Europe, wheat was traded one day a week. Only on Wednesdays, that is. He found this quite hard to believe.

It was true. The trading floor looked like a genteel and intimate bar. Eighteen or twenty guys were sitting around on tall stools, watching price fixes come up on monitors. The stools were surrounded by couches—*couches!*—and telephone carrels. Some guys were smoking, making blasé conversation. A pinup-girl calendar was hanging from one of the walls.

Seeing such a low-key and amateur-hour operation in a city like Paris made him stupendously proud of Chicago. Even prouder, that is. He wanted to rush in and announce how much volume got generated *each day* on the CBOT, how liquid the whole market was, how much you could make on each tick . . . but he figured they couldn't speak English.

She spread out her loot on the bed. Five books, twelve tapes, wintergreen Lifesavers, *Elle*, *Wet*, the *Tatler*, blood red silk bullfighter tights, four pairs of shoes, two sweat-shirts, some wonderful crow-feather earrings, a Métro-ticket keyring, and a men's large Brando-style motorcycle jacket, lined and with plenty of zippers. A decent day's shopping, all things considered. The thing was that so far she hadn't been able to spend more than seventy francs, on cheap stuff like cigarettes, magazines, tampons. Almost everything on the bed had been charged to Madame M. Baum, who'd *insisted*. So she shouldn't feel like *too* fucking much of a hypocrite, should she. Because all Madame asked in return was to *be sure to say thank you to Richard*.

I'm sure.

She tried on the tights with a pair of black crocodile pumps and the earrings. Yes ma'am. She posed in the wide floor-length mirror, flexing her calf muscles, turning and standing on tiptoe, feeling more and more strange and ass-miserable. Shit. Were you supposed to feel guilty about not feeling guilty about things you could never do otherwise? Huh?

She put on the jacket. She'd had it on twice in the store but forgotten how heavy it was. She tried out each pocket, each zipper, making the sleeves creak, inhaling the dead calfskin richness while she checked out the total ensemble. Not bad. But where (*where*) did she get that blank *(blank)* expression on her face?

She was thirsty and nervous but did not want to drink. A jacket like this would be old hat at school, a cliché, but so what. It looked great. There were plenty of places to wear it besides SAIC. She pouted and posed, mussed her hair up, noting the radical angle of dangle of the glossy black feathers, throwing her shoulders back, hunching them, whanging some bar chords and humming, feeling horny and thirsty and silly and guilty and pissed.

She hitched the silk pants up succinctly, turning and looking behind her to see if a flex showed beneath the black leather.

It did.

"Whoa," Richard said. He was nervous. He pretended as though they were strangers. "I see we've got major league leg talent here."

Maggie slapped him.

"All I wanted—"

She slapped him again, just as hard. "I told you to keep your mouth *shut.*"

Her hair in the light from the candle was yellow and amber and black. (In daylight, he knew, it was wheat-colored, a lion's mane tasseled with silk.) The rise of her femoral muscles shone taut nylon black, unforgiving, then was suddenly lusciously golden. Oh Ceres! The forces that swelled there could easily choke him unconscious. He wouldn't be able to cry out for mercy or help. She could kill him.

She continued to pull up her nylons, hitching and stretching them, making the seam straight in back, snapping them into her garters. She knew that her legs were terrific: long, lean, and shapely, with kneecaps and tendons that made Richard ache. He had told her.

The thing was, she didn't mind rough stuff, by her *or* by him, but she didn't like props. Plus was this what you did on your honeymoon? The Story of R, she was thinking. It really was kind of pathetic. Then she slapped him again, for good measure. Any less and she knew he'd be miffed.

She could force him to masturbate, strangle him, whip him with leftover rope. Put him on the exercise bike, make him pedal . . .

"Kneel down," she said.

Though his arms were bound smartly behind him—the new nylon clothesline wound tight around his biceps, his neck, and his chest, symmetrically pulleyed and knotted, his wrists crossed and wrenched cruelly high—he managed to do as she told him.

Linda had taken three Dalmane, 90 mg altogether, plus cognac, then had gone to bed early. She wanted to wake up on French time.

She was dreaming that Richard was yelling at someone. She couldn't make out what he wanted.

He was hugging a red-headed woman who was trying to pull free and slap him.

Someone said, "Richard, speak up."

He was panting.

LINDA TOOK the Château de Vincennes line from Concorde to Hôtel-de-Ville, then the Mairie des Lilas out toward the Pompidou Center. The Métro was cleaner and quieter than el trains, and cheap. Most of the seats faced each other, like restaurant booths without tables. She'd taken it down to Sèvres Babylone the day they'd arrived, just to see where it went. It was the first thing she'd liked about Paris.

The Louvre stop had statues and paintings and mummies behind glass on the walls of the platform, but the billboards at most of the stations featured half-naked girls, reproductions of cheeseball Impressionists, and Pop exclamation points: WOW! The ads for some florist called Linda's used big yellow dew-covered roses.

A couple of guys gave her looks—petals on a wet, black

bough—but did not make them into productions. Just checking.

She liked that. She also was proud of herself for making poetic connections.

Norb and Shannon Wiener took Richard and Maggie to the roof of the Montparnasse Tower. From here, fifty-nine stories up—fifty-three higher than just about anyplace else—you could see all of Paris: Luxembourg Gardens, Sacré Coeur, Arc de Triomphe, La Défense . . .

"Ninety percent of Parisians," Shannon told them, "simply loathe this here little old building."

"Subverts their architectural integrity," said Norb. Two years before he had traded financials with Richard but now had retired to Paris. It was not a short story. "Rends their precious organic integument."

Maggie nodded and shrugged. She could see how the Tower was different from most of the rest of the city, but the view still just blew her away.

"As you can see," Shannon said.

"Right," Richard said.

Norb said, "It ruins the roofscape, they say."

"They wouldn't say roofscape," said Shannon. "A Parisian would *nhevah* say roofscape."

She had two gin and "Indian" tonics in a bar in the Forum des Halles, which was one massive underground mall. She was shopping for something she couldn't get back in Chicago, but all they had here was the same old Guess? denim and Reeboks.

Across from Les Halles (on rue Berger!) she had a late lunch at McDonalds. Except for the fact that the names of the food were in French and ninety percent of the customers were wearing black clothes, it was like a Chicago McDonalds. A Quarterpounder with cheese and a medium Sprite cost her 22 francs, tax included. The burger was spicier, and much less well done, but ten minutes later, as she rode the glassed-in escalator up the side of the Pompidou Center, the synthy Mac's aftertaste was exactly—*exactly*—the same.

Five or six years ago, when they were both getting started as traders, Norb and Richard had both cleared through Refco. They went to some parties together, put over some trades on each other, conspired to back-door a few people, had fun. Richard met Shannon while bailing her and Norb out of the Lake County jailhouse, after she got arrested for doing 105 on the Tollway, he for "just shoving, not punching" the highway patrolman. During one twenty-seven-month span Norb had made, lost, then made back again five "count 'em" eight-figure fortunes. Shannon had threatened to leave him if he didn't retire from trading. When that didn't work, she persuaded his doctor to threaten him: the stress of the trading would shorten his life, or, even worse, make his "little old" penis not function. When threats didn't work she hired a lawyer and filed for divorce. And that worked. He finally got out at a point about forty-nine million ahead—"about fifty points short where I'd counted on finishing up." They took their two kids and moved to a place in Wisconsin, forty miles northwest of Madison. "Idyllic," said Shannon. Norb said, "My ass." Because within a few months he was trading again on the phone. Even worse, he was *losing.*

"What else do you do up in fucking Wisconsin?" he said. You could tell he was proud of the story.

"Certainly not too much of *that,*" Shannon said.

Too much of *what,* wondered Richard.

Too much of what, Maggie wondered.

"Either lose all your money," said Norb, "or go stalking wild birds through the brambles."

In less than eight months he had lost back three-fourths of their stash, by which point Shannon had—"luckily," according to Shannon, "finally," according to Norb—"figured out a way to empty whatever accounts I'd foolishly set up as joints."

"Which was all except one," Shannon said.

"Took Susan and Lew and just took off for gay fucking Paris."

"As far away as I could get from this boy and stay civilized."

Richard asked Shannon, "Isn't Paris where you guys had gone on your honeymoon?"

"Sure enough was," she said, winking.

Norb said, "Just give 'em that one little taste . . ."

"Three short days later this boy was over here with his little old tail 'tween his legs, lookin' *whupped.*"

Norb shrugged and nodded. "The manipulating bitch."

Shannon winked.

Maggie was listening: the story, she knew, had mostly been told for her benefit. But she'd also discovered that ten francs would get you three minutes of looking through a telescope powerful enough to see the escalators moving up the side of the Pompidou Center, the cross on the Sacré Coeur dome, the Crillon, and the people almost two miles away on the Eiffel Tower who were looking out over Paris through exactly the same kind of telescope.

Norb put his hand over Maggie's and lowered the tip of her scope half an inch. "See that park there, Champ de Mars?" He excused himself, peered through the scope. Once he had aimed it for her, he stepped to the side, let her look. "See the white buildings . . . those white ones?"

She saw them. The base of the tower was directly behind them. She nodded, said yes, and then lost them. The shield had slid down through the finder. Time's up.

"That's our house," said Norb.

A twelve-foot-tall Giacometti, a woman, was standing with her arms at her sides. The black-tinted bronze looked deliciously craggy and fragile, but Linda did not want to touch it.

The smaller galleries had a lot of the early cubism the Musée Picasso was missing. It was just so incredibly subtle. She loved it. It made her want to be back in those days, and be painting. She also liked the way Delaunay's *Eiffel Tower* was rising up out of and tumbling down into the very same chimneys and rooftops she had seen riding up on the escalator. But the earliest Braques and Picassos made most of the other stuff, even their own, seem somehow a bit *imma-chur*, at least in *her* humble opinion.

"But so all we are talking about," Shannon was saying to Maggie, "is applying a Zen-type philosophy, honey, to big-money money and business." She laughed. "Fear and greed?" Shook her head. "That's all business *is* anymore. . . ."

Shannon was somehow from LA *and* Houston. Her son was seven and her daughter was five and a half; they were "sharing" a nanny "from Sussex." (Were Shannon's two children in Sussex? Maggie did not understand. Could she ask?) Her father was a "miserable failure" as a TV producer. Her mother had died of leukemia.

"I'm sorry," said Maggie.

"Because all these boys do," she went on, waving away Maggie's sympathy, "is assume a little fiduciary responsibility, underwriting the risks for the farmers and such, all the little chickenshit sandwich-eaters of this life, if you know what I mean . . ."

Maggie asked how her kids had adjusted to living in Paris, but Shannon would get to that later. "I will, hon. I promise." Right now she was bent on explaining the "too-brilliant stunt" Richard and Norb had once "pulled" before Maggie met Richard. "As basically the securitizer, they took a few indicators, figured out a way to make an effective offering . . ." Pregnant pause, rubbing thumb and index finger together, "and here comes the mucho dinero."

Maggie nodded.

"Way I look at it, it's like being the property guy on a big-budget flick," Shannon said. "Make sure everyone's wine glass is as full as it was when they cut, got the same lipstick smears too, that their cigarettes have burned down the real-time amount. Gotta stay away from mirrors, of course, though the weirdest thing is, it's all *done* with mirrors . . ."

"Always seemed that way to me," Maggie said. She heard herself drawling a little.

"Plus it helps if you're just the weensiest bit sadistic, you know what I mean."

Maggie did.

Shannon winked. "Though the *real* trick, of course, is to get them to quit when you're way way ahead."

Maggie nodded again.

"And I do mean way *way* ahead, daughter."

Maggie yawned, but it wasn't because she was bored. "I agree," she said, yawning again, then apologized. She was tired, that's all.

"Speaking of which," Shannon said, "how *do* your Richie and Linda get on?"

———

After forty-five minutes of staring at oil on canvas, she had to sit down, close her eyes. Her retinas felt semidetached.

No smoking, of course. And no drinking. Just as well, she decided, since she'd started to feel a bit queasy.

Things started spinning when she got up and went to the window. There were fists clenching down in her gut. It did not feel like something her period did to her, either.

She stared out across all the rooftops, with the breast of Montmartre to the north, Sacré Coeur's dome like an off-center nipple . . . Paris was starting to get to her. Each crooked rooftop had four or five little clay pipes sticking out of a lopsided chimney. Except for the Eiffel Tower and some miniature skyscrapers far to the west and the south, the skyline was mostly these rooftops and chimneys, which did have their charm, she supposed. She was trying to picture the towering, geometrical Loopline—with all of its steel, glass, and vertical graphite—superimposed on this low rolling limestone horizon.

She could tell she was getting real sick.

According to Richard, the Marines were *too* in the embassy compound: he had seen them that same afternoon from his window. According to Norb they were off in the Bois de Boulogne poking new buttholes in his and hers KGB whores in exchange for state secrets about how to cook snails and lose wars, all this while not wearing rubbers. It was not clear to Richard exactly who wanted these secrets and who would be giving what up to obtain them, but he felt he should snicker and nod, so he did.

Norb was refilling their wine glasses. "But so current business climate being what it is, I go, Jack, let the *Muscovites* pay the darn rent on your seat!"

"*Oh* yeah," said Richard. He was shaking with genuine

laughter. "So but *I'm* like, why not let some of that shit trickle *sideways* into my *wife's* Bern account!"

Norb exploded.

The windows in her room were closed. It was dark. She hunched and curled up in her bed, fighting off waves of fierce nausea by taking deep breaths through her mouth. She was trying to hold very still. Sometimes she groaned as the next wave came on to help take the edge off. She figured fresh air would help too, but for that she would have to get up and open a window. She knew if she moved she would puke.

The thing was, she knew what was coming. A breaded veal cutlet from the Steinmetz cafeteria had zapped her like this three or four years ago. She remembered the episode vividly. She had popped a small vein in her eye from puking so hard and lost thirteen pounds in two days. Some of the vomit had stained the cloth part of her left jungle boot, which she should not have even been *wearing*. . . .

She wanted to total McDonald's with shoulder-launched ground-to-ground missiles. Whoever was responsible for letting the patties go bad, especially that one in particular—but even the thought of that pattie, or the pickle or cheese or the bun, even the *seeds* on that bun, even *one* . . . just the *idea* of that seed brought the horrible aftertaste rocketing back to her gullet and left her more desperate to retch.

Thin ten-inch-square strips of smoked North Sea salmon, plenty of mineral water, and an avocado salad with white Russian dressing were served by the Philippine maids. Norb did the wine. Next came a perfect Beef Wellington.

Maggie was pretty impressed but also a little embarrassed. She had once had a job with a North Shore caterer serving these same kinds of dishes in Glencoe, Winnetka, and Kenilworth, though the salmon back then was Chinook and the . . . Once! It was already two *decades* ago, before she got married to Michael. The worst thing about it had been the ridiculous uniform the guy, Mr. Howe, made them wear: black spike heels, black nylons, lacy white apron over little black dress—clearly designed to make you look like a saucy French maid. Plus the dresses were hemmed way too short, even for back in the sixties, so you always felt like you were about to get spanked by the guests. . . . But the beef was so tasty. You could cut it with the side of your fork. There also were artichoke hearts.

"This is great," she said, swallowing. She sipped more red wine. "I mean, this is—"

"Really," said Richard.

It had her now coming and going, three ghastly churnings at once. She was trying to hold it all in, hold it back, at both ends, just to deal with the looseness and tightness another five seconds, *oh Christ* . . .

Should she run for the bathroom or puke off the side of the bed? As she tried to decide, up it came, rushing viciously, choking her, burning her, heaving from deep in her bowels, and out.

A little off-key, Richard was belting the national anthem, italicizing *amber waves of grain* for comic, ironic effect. He and Norb had retired to Norb's giant den, which looked up and out at the Tower.

Norb sang along for a couple of bars, then suddenly blurted out, "*What?!* A position like that and you're *here?*"

"It's my honeymoon, fella," said Richard.

"That's my whole point. You just got short, what, four million bushels?"

"Four million two."

Norb exhaled, rolled his eyes, drank some cognac. "Fucking eight hunnert twenty-some contracts, go out and get *married*, Chrissake?" He shook his head, sighed, grabbed his crotch. "Takes big ones."

"*Got* big ones. Also got stop orders up the wazoo."

"*Bet* you do, guy. Bet you do. Even still."

"I can follow it practically tick by tick on the phone," Richard said. "Get the close . . ." He could feel all his sweat glands rev up, especially the ones near the top of his forehead, where they soon, he was sure, would be drowning some more of his overmatched follicles.

Fuck!

She knelt on the floor of the bathroom, heaving up nothing, hugging the vomit-streaked bowl. Her eyeballs bugged out with each heave. She was bleeding.

The last cheese-flecked fragment of ginburger had long since come up. She was working on stomach, intestinal juices, an acidy liquid that burned up the back of her throat.

Between dry heaves and gagging on bile, she was crying. She would never drink gin again—*ever!* Her teeth chattered hard. She was dying.

"Plus you *still* get to smuggle this scrumptious young thing of a daughter along on the *honeymoon?*"

"A man's gotta do what a man's gotta do," Richard said.

Norb was refilling their snifters for the umpteenth last time. "Heard that they look more like sisters than, you know . . ."

" 'Swhat everyone says," Richard said. "Not *quite* how I see it. Just more like a—"

"Just make sure you don't get them mixed up."

"That's the only way *to* get them, Norbie."

"Ouais . . ."

"Girls will be girls, after all."

"Don't tell me," said Norb. "Adjoining suites, right? Or you all bunking down in one bed?"

"Adjoining," said Richard. "That way they both can be—"

Maggie and Shannon came into Norb's den.

Richard and Norb swallowed cognac.

Shannon grinned. "*What's* a man gotta do, Richie honey?"

She was back on the seat, leaning forward, hacking hard clots of puke from the back of her throat and spitting them onto the floor while warm blood and hot diarrhea squirted and leaked out behind her.

The fluorescent bathroom was glistening. Her chattering teeth made the puddles and chunks by her feet glow and vibrate. There were tracers whenever she shivered.

It couldn't get worse, but it did. She held on. Streaks of dark blood were all over her legs and the towels. A reversed monoprint of her foot—the ball and her three largest toes—had been stamped in her own bloody shit on the marble.

She shivered.

165

NOT THAT much light was making its way past the curtains, but Linda could tell it was morning. She must have been able to sleep for a while, though she couldn't be certain: the last several hours had merged in her mind as all horror. It surprised her that she had survived it. Her watch was a few feet away, next to her purse on the table, but she sensed it would be a long time before she'd be able to reach it. She was also ferociously thirsty, for anything wet except gin.

She dreamed she was back in Aesthetics and Physics. Hank looked right at her and told her he thought that he loved her, but since he still had a particle of doubt, they couldn't get married yet—could they?

If you're rich, I'm single, he told her, then laughed. She

didn't know what he was saying. Like the rest of the guys in the class, he was wearing brown-and-red camouflage bikini-style briefs. His stomach was hard and his hipbones stood out. He also had pretty big balls.

The girls were all wearing conventional Y-front white jockeys. Some had on navy blue Zara Baines T-shirts in order to cover their breasts. Sandra was wearing a DAT sweatshirt from Seoul. She didn't know what *she* was wearing.

Her father said, Who's Zara Baines?

Make tapes, not war, was her answer. Then, since Hank hadn't laughed, she said, Get it?

Nope, Hank said coolly. I really don't know what you're saying. Then he called her a poor little rich girl.

She suddenly understood that French guys had started the Vietnam War, then had left. Guys like her father had had to replace them. And now it was up to their daughters to get some revenge for their deaths.

The class was discussing this issue.

Strobe said, Where first there is nothing, suddenly there is everything. Lord, Giacometti, Amen. He was naked.

Or vice versa, said Hank.

Or vice versa, said Strobe.

You mean, Lord, God Almighty, she told them.

The angle of light looked the same, though it seemed as if she'd slept a long time. It was curtains. Her watch, she remembered, was right over there on the table. Her thirst was now coming from every square inch of her body.

Another dream. Nothing much happened. Where was she? She couldn't speak French and was terribly terribly thirsty. English felt strange in her mouth. Even, at times, in her head.

167

She ordered two ginger ales and managed to get out of bed: she would have to be up when they came. She staggered a little at first, then took two normal steps, getting used to how dizzy she was. The bedsheets were mottled with blood.

Even from ten feet away, the fume from the bathroom was scary: blood, vomit, shit, and ammonia. When she stood in the doorway, the mess and its stench almost floored her.

She ran the cold water while she peed and changed tampons, then gargled. The water felt great in her mouth, sluicing around her parched tongue, but her stomach forbade her to swallow.

The ginger ales came before she was ready. She still hadn't taken a shower, gotten dressed, brushed her teeth. She pulled on the white hotel bathrobe and answered the door.

She could see right away it would not be enough: two tiny black Schweppes cans, two glasses, a few tiny ice cubes in each. The guy who had brought them was her age and was wearing a charcoal tuxedo. She thanked him and signed the receipt, then gave him a twenty-franc tip. He thanked her in French, turned to go.

"Pardon, s'il vous plaît." She knew that her breath would be awful, mass murder, so she backed up a couple of steps. "Parlez-vous anglais?"

Yes he did.

"Could you please bring me five more large ginger ales, please?" She held up five fingers. "Five more?"

He nodded and sniffed. Though he'd done it discreetly, she could tell he was smelling the bathroom.

"And also more ice. Much more ice."

He nodded again. "Mademoiselle is okay?"

Thirstily, desperate, she nodded.

Even before she had finished the first glass of ginger ale, she could feel its gold coolth effervescing down into her guts, flushing her acidy stomach, soothing her ravaged intestines, seeping into her bloodstream and organs and tissue. The second glass, sipped slowly at first and then gulped, made her coo and moan gratefully. More!

Ten minutes later the same guy returned with five more. He also brought maids—three little white ones, not young —unless it was just a coincidence. In any event, here they were. She tried to apologize for what they would find in the bathroom, but they didn't know what she was saying.

She sat on the couch with the TV remote while the maids stripped her bed, did the bathroom, and whispered about her in French. It was awful but what could she do? There were game shows, cartoons, and some news. A couple of white "Hill St. Blues" cops were hassling each other in French while Washington gnawed on his toothpick. She sipped two more ginger ales, went through the channels, sucked ice. The commercials were like what you saw on the Métro: saucy and sassy blond gamins artistically stripped to their undies. It made her appreciate American spots, which at least managed to cook up scenarios in which *guys* took key parts of their clothes off.

The news had some footage of an airlift of food into Africa. As the sacks of wheat burst on the ground, people went scrambling frantically after them, scrounging the wheat from the dirt, while soldiers in camouflage shot at them. After that, women's hockey. She could not understand what the reporter was saying, but she got the big picture: bare tits. For the minute the segment was on, they never showed the girls playing hockey: no slap shots or checking, no goals, not even anyone *skating.* What they showed were the giggling girls helping each other into their protective equipment, with plenty of closeups on their white plastic breastplates, concluding—with typical Parisian logic—with full frontal shots of them lathering up in the shower.

After the maids left she finally took her own shower. She'd planned on a lengthy and hot one—sort of a stand-up sauna with soap and shampoo, something to steam out the last of the bad shit and puke—but ended up cutting it short when she just couldn't shake the idea that perverted French soldiers were spying on her with hi-tech, and therefore undetectable, cameras.

Was she hungry? Not really. Plus she still felt too weak to go out. She decided to catch up on her A & P homework. She wouldn't be back for another six days, and had already missed four or five classes, but she wanted to know the material before she got back in case Strobe asked her questions in class, especially now that she sat next to Rendeck. She might even ask Strobe a question.

The biggest assignment was the "Parts of Things" chapter from Strobe's book, four Xeroxed pages from Roland Barthes' *The Fashion System,* and a weird crisscrossed poem by John Cage based on a Jasper Johns statement about how to get things into paintings: read each at least twice, underlining the salient points and examples, then write a hundred-word precis of each, emphasizing common ideas and motifs. Hey, *no problem.*

She tried the Barthes first since it had the most interesting title and by far the least number of pages. Bad choice. The guy didn't know from seams about clothes, she decided, plus the way he wrote what he did know seemed designed not to ever make sense. The stuff was like *we must first determine which are the syntagmatic (or spatial) units of the written garment, and second, which are the systematic (or virtual) oppositions.* Precisely. According to Strobe, the guy had been killed by a laundry truck in front of the place where he'd written this. Good. Or was it a dune buggy? No, that was O'Hara, the artsy American poet (not the old-fashioned one who wrote novels). Who pronounced it O'Hada, of course. In any event, even considering the crazed Paris traffic, letting yourself get run down by a truckload of diapers and bloody hotel sheets made about as much sense as his book did.

As she reread the sentence and gloated, an amazing idea came lightbulbing on in her brain: cash in the first-class return ticket, fly back on coach, pocket the difference in cash. Yes! Voilà! When her menstrual brain started racing this way she knew she could get into trouble, but she had to get out of this city, and quick. Paris bugged her. A lot, as a matter of fact. It was really that simple. She also sensed Rendeck was ready to make his big move.

She called up Air France. Of *course* she'd be able to downgrade her ticket and still fly back early. And be handed the difference in cash when she got to de Gaulle? No, Madame. To O'Hare? Not exactly. The 6617 francs would be credited to her account. Motherfuck. But there *was* one more seat on that afternoon's 3:10 flight if she wouldn't mind sitting in smoking. Were there any more seats in first class? There were not. She would take it.

Okay. It was just after one. She could make it. She'd screwed herself out of the big tilting seat, free champagne, and maybe some fancier food, but so what. She wouldn't be eating much anyway. Plus with all the time she would gain flying west, she'd be back in Chicago by just after five. She *loved* it when things happened fast.

Did she have enough francs left for cabfare? About. Had

she taken her key to the loft? Yes she had. Her story for Maggie would have something to do with her schoolwork. Don't know how I forgot, but I'll see you next week, blah blah blah.

She worked out more details while packing. A follow-up field trip to Fermilab, required for science *and* studio credit, wouldn't be offered again until . . .

She took out a sheet of blue Crillon stationery and started composing the note.

THEY'D BEEN looking for L'Eclipse, a restaurant Shannon Wiener had told them about, for the last thirty minutes, and now it had started to drizzle. They had given themselves a few hours to wander and shop Montparnasse before they had lunch, but now they were hungry and cold.

Richard cursed each time they turned a corner and found that the name of the street on the "rustic" blue plaque wasn't the one they were looking for.

"Please relax," Maggie said.

"I'm plenty relaxed."

"Just relax."

At the corner of rue de Vouille and rue Cronstadt, a tall slender gentleman passed them. He was old and well dressed. Maggie decided to ask.

"Excusez-moi, s'il vous plaît."

The man turned and stopped.

"Parlez-vous anglais, s'il vous plaît?"

He nodded, paused for a second, said "Yes." He had piercing blue eyes behind thick rimless glasses. His close-cropped white hair was brushed back from his forehead; a half-inch-wide streak on the left was still black. He seemed to be in a small hurry.

"We're looking for L'Eclipse?" Maggie said. "It's supposed to be on the rue de l'Abbé Groult?" She showed him the pad on which she had written the restaurant's name and address.

"Seventeen," Richard said.

The old man repeated the name of the restaurant, then nodded his large narrow head. In profile he looked like a calm but still fierce bird of prey.

"Jay tray fang," Richard said, rubbing his stomach. He knew you could tell that he didn't speak French, or even appear all that hungry, but that was the point. A small joke.

"It's around that corner," the old man said, pointing.

Maggie looked where he'd pointed and pointed herself. She thought she was hearing a brogue. "So it's that way?"

"On the right."

Yes she had. Was he Scottish, she wondered. "Merci beaucoup," she said, smiling up into his eyes. His cheekbones were simply incredible.

He began to walk off. "De rien."

Richard considered the possibility that the guy didn't even speak French. "Thanks a lot," he called out.

Maggie could tell that in this old guy's time, in his prime, he had probably been quite a specimen. She watched him turn briefly and wave, then keep walking.

Still was, as a matter of fact, she decided.

as it Were
anotHer world
A whole or
The best one can of it

suddenlY
sOmething
. . .

5

"GONE DEAD Train," Randy Newman, attacked her from six different angles through six Alpine speakers strategically aimed at her head as she lurched east on Wacker in the black Lamborghini, fighting the traffic, unclutching too quickly in second, getting stopped by red lights at Clark, then at State, then at Wabash. The Countach was testy and hard to control, but she loved it. She had not had a drink in six days.

She was glad she was not claustrophobic. Her knees were between the front wheels, where the engine would be but was not, and the tight bucket seat was slung down so low that her butt could feel each little pebble and crack in the asphalt. (Let's see. Could it "read" the design on the manhole cover she was now passing over? . . . Almost.) She also liked the silver steer logo up front, the way it snorted and bucked like the rest of the car. It was *wild.* Of all his possessions, including the Wang and the Porsche, this was the last thing that Richard would want her to fuck with.

That it had a customized Alpine DAT sound system and the key was in the ignition were the other two reasons she took it.

She turned left at Michigan Avenue as "Downtown Train" started. The tires tracked smoothly across the grilled bridgework, Tom Waits started singing, she swallowed. The tape she had brought, *Cruising Licks Volume VI,* was *the* perfect vehicle for the mood and the car she was in, and vice versa.

The Countach was getting her looks now: double-takes, stares, pointed fingers. She put on her best blasé face and tried to pretend to ignore them. The Wrigley Building, on her left, was lit up and looked real well scrubbed, but what did it do for your *teeth?* On her right, Tribune Tower, invisibly gargoyled and turreted, an elongated medieval fortress laid siege to by six or eight pickets . . .

Could she smoke in this car? She fished her cigarettes out of her pocket, shook one up from the half-empty pack, and lit it with one cardboard match while not crashing—a major accomplishment, even if she did say so herself, of digital-Indy dexterity—then located, retracted, and *used* the too cold and square to be vaginal, no longer quite virginal ashtray. She could.

The next song was "Solitude Standing." Even with the volume on four, the pocket of air in her cockpit was swollen and pulsed with the bass. Vega's voice wasn't awesomely strong but still sounded def and intelligent, even more like no-frills Laurie Anderson than it usually did. Floor tomtoms pounded her eardrums, the two sets of chords zinged her scalp. She ached to drive faster, but the buses and lights wouldn't let her. She rolled up her window and boosted the volume to seven.

Between Grand and Ohio she managed to scoot past two buses then made the left turn at Ontario without getting caught by the light. She was starting to get used to the gears and the clutch, not to mention the ferocious acceleration you got from just tapping the gas. She sang along under her breath, ripping chords off the steering wheel, grinding and jacking with the drums and the trans and the bass. It was great.

Heading west past the Hard Rock Cafe, rumbling under the Ravenswood viaduct, past Ditka's, past Rose, she was glad she had come back home early. Maggie had called the next day. She'd been pissed, *very* pissed, but no more than Linda expected. She of course hadn't purchased the field-trips-to-Fermilab story, but once they had talked for a while and Linda apologized—twice—and explained she'd "just *had*" to get back, Maggie'd chilled out a degree. It was always that first one that counted. . . .

Bagpipes droned under the hot mandolins and the pennywhistle, and Ms. Kate O'Riordan was lulting for all she was worth—*another* girl's voice, Linda noted, that was not gonna blow you away, but still *worked*—as she roared down the ramp to the Kennedy.

She was not even feeling that thirsty.

She had cruised these expressways in Maggie's old Nova since she first got her license. She'd done most of her cruising at night, while Maggie was out on her dates. She knew the whole Sheridan-Kennedy-294-Lake Shore Drive corridor like pilots knew stretches of continent. O'Hare, Half Day Road, the Ravines, Bahai Temple, doubling back to check out the crowds around the Pavilion, the Vic, the Horizon—her turf. At least it was much more her turf than Lawrence and Cumberland was. Or Wolf Point.

That the Nova was never a flash cruise machine didn't matter: the skankier, less yuppie-ish, and louder it got, the more she had liked it. She even was fond of the jagged crenelations of rust above the rear wheelwells, especially the flaky and delicate lacework of slow oxidation under Rusty Jones's shit-eating grin. Plus it always had started right up, went where you steered it, stopped when you put on the brakes. Four or five dollars for gas, you were good till you had to be home. Most important of all, it had FM, a cassette deck with auto reverse, and two decent speakers up front: not the highest of fi's, but with tapes and a flask and some cigarettes there was no better way to just cruise to some hard stuff and think.

She would pick up a hitchhiker, maybe, provided he was alone, over twenty, mean and lean chiseled without looking too much like a model, and had something about him that said he had just stepped out of the shower, was on his way someplace intriguing, and that the very last thing on his artistic, intelligent, and heterosexual mind was to cause her the wrong kind of trouble. So far, in over three years, no guy with his thumb up had managed to meet these requirements, but she hadn't stopped keeping an eye out.

As the Edens forked right, she stayed to the left on the Kennedy. She was heading for 294—fewer cops, wider lanes, fewer cars—to see how fast this one would go. Only two lanes were open down here (some pile up? emergency midnight construction?) and she couldn't get out of third gear. She was tempted to drive on the shoulder but did not feel like getting arrested. She'd been pulled over three times in the Nova—once for wrong way on a one-way, two times for speeding—but never had gotten a ticket. She figured tonight might be different.

She also had never been strip-searched.

"Cut Across Shorty" came on, one of her all-time fave raves, but the O'Hare congestion and Rod Stewart's latest assholerics made her FF to "Side One of *Wave.*" (The last time she'd seen them, at Clubland, the Pogues had done "Maggie May" for their encore, with Joe Strummer—who else?—playing rhythm on a miked black acoustic guitar.) And where the heck *was* Patti Smith? Living with her mom in New Jersey like she'd heard down at school? Hanging out in Detroit? What had *happened?*

Another thing bugging her lately was that she couldn't get herself to paint anymore, or even make sketches, whereas the energy she was able to muster for things like making Greatest Hits tapes was almost unlimited. She often spent days on one tape, coming up with slick titles (there was no *Cruising Licks Volume V,* for example), endlessly revising the table of contents, working out intricate segues ("Crosstown Traffic" by Hendrix after "Uptown" by the Crystals after "Downtown Train" by Tom Waits, followed by something by Traffic), or concocting such gin-inspired medleys as Five Celtic Dirty Old Towns, Chicago Garage Bands Spell Gloria, or Songs with Parentheses in Their Titles: "(I Don't Want To Go To) Chelsea," "Eat (Your Heart Out, Stephen King)," "(You Make It So) Hard On Me," "(I Can't Get No) Satisfaction," etc. Deep down she sensed this was all a perverse waste of time, but that only made her more driven. If a song occurred to her that she didn't have in her collection, she was unable to focus on anything else till she'd borrowed or boosted or bought it. Even the boring techno-mechanical business of producing a tape could absorb her for ten or twelve hours: cleaning old vinyl, typing up tables of contents, patching together components and adjusting the frequency levels, designing the cover and doing the miniature artwork, deciding whether to Dolby or not, adding up minutes and seconds of playing time to use each side of tape most efficiently—the more time the process consumed, the more things it *kept* her from doing, the better she liked it. This was the way she went about everything: her guilt about not doing one thing turned her into some frantically anal-compulsive perfectionist while doing some other thing. Sick.

The same thing had happened in high school, she realized, when she'd blown off her classwork to paint. Once she had seen those van Goghs, those Picassos, those Johnses, something kicked in and took over: it was like her whole nervous system had been dowsed with some hyper new enzyme. Even the sledgehammer headaches she got from fifteen-hour sessions breathing in Brera fumes mixed with cigarette smoke hardly fazed her, because nothing else mattered but painting. But once it became what she was *supposed* to be doing, of course, she suddenly had zero enthusiasm. She still was obsessed about painting, about being an artist and all, but she didn't know how to trick herself into feeling that driven to *do it* again. The trick was, it wasn't a trick, and she knew it.

Winged Eel Fingerling and Zoot Horn Rollo's guitars chugged and whistled, a single twelve-stringed locomotive, as Drumbo whapped di-rhythmic tempos behind them and Beefheart gnarled "Click Clack" between them. She jiggled the mirror till headlights appeared in it. There. The wicked superbness of the Magic Band's musicianship made her burn to drive faster, but there was still too much traffic on this part of 294. She was already out past O'Hare, around Touhy, but as soon as she took it past seventy-five she'd be up under somebody's bumper. With the concrete guardrail on one side and the middle-lane cars on the other, there was nothing to do but back off.

She couldn't help wondering what would happen if she simply quit painting and "officially" took up guitar. What a joke. Knowing her, she would probably make all her lessons and practice quite diligently for two or three months, then decide that what she *really* wanted to do after all was make videos, except once she'd enrolled in the video courses she'd tell herself that watching TV and movies should count as "her work" and she'd spend all her time doing that—all this while hatching her *next* big artistic career change.

And but what if she were a real rock star? Wouldn't she soon get fed up—with the traveling, sycophants, teenagers, various rock-star-type assholes? The chaos? Eventually wouldn't she settle for, settle *down* with, something less hectic? Like painting?

Captain Beefheart said "Come back, baby" as she passed a Corvette on the right and then swerved to just miss a Mercedes, barely avoiding the front of the car alongside it. Fuck me. Horns blared to note the near-misses. Them too. She was kidding herself being in art school because what had she ever created? The Mercedes was showing its brights as a protest. She downshifted, gave it some gas, and held on: Janet Ray Guthrie Andretti. The Countach surged gratefully, seemed to stall for a third of a second, then rocketed forward, staging what felt to her eardrums and Fallopian tubes like roadbound but vertical liftoff. Captain Beefheart said "Baby, come back," and Linda thought, Why the heck not? Plus his harp sounded *just* like a train. The brights of the Mercedes faded, went out as she banked to the right and arced along into the darkness, alone, steering between blurred reflectors and thrummed by her own valved adrenaline. *Grr.* What better place, after all, than an art school to learn to be a rock-and-roll star?

"LaGrange," ZZ Top, volume at 8 1/2, causing pain. She was buzzing past cars doing ninety, using the steering wheel to follow the chord changes on. It was great. She knew it was pig-fucker raunch but could not think of anything better to melt down the wax in her ears and burn its way through to her vermis, her pons, to her spine. The speedometer was at 115. The thrill of this volume and headlong velocity had lodged itself high in her chest, then strummed up the back of her throat. It tasted metallic, delicious, like oysters. It also was pleasantly choking her, stopping her jaws with a humbucking out-of-phase density and chilling the throb in her lap and her palms by making her sweat little crystals: 130. She was way up past Willow, the TriState had banked to the left, she wanted some gin very badly—or, even better, some oyster shells filled with champagne. Ooh la la. She was reaching to turn down the treble when something centrifugal happened to how she was steering. Then something else, something else. The Countach leaned slightly, then hard, to the right, then swerved back and started to fishtail. She swung the wheel back to the left and went for the brake, but hit gas. This wasn't her fault, she concluded. She'd been going too fast. She'd been drinking.

The Countach careened on two wheels through the middle and far right lanes before it finally went perpendicular and cartwheeled along the shoulder for eighty-five yards, winged something metal, and ricocheted up in the air, maintaining an imperfect spiral. Linda believed she was screaming. She was. G-forces shoved back her lips, exposing her top teeth and gums, but she still had some powers of reason. Through my fault, through my fault, through my most grievous of faults. She could hear herself think in slow motion.

The tracers and flash of the crash were resolving themselves into pictures that also had words. NO EXPLOSION. The Countach, SPECTACULAR SCULPTURE, buckled and crunched with her in it. You could not tell the back from the front. Her skull, DENTED TRANSLUCENT WHITE CARTON, protruding through windshield. HER EYES.

CUT TO: overhead point of view, a hundred fifty feet up, later on. A slow lane of gawkers urged on by state cops with bullhorns. A tow truck, an ambulance, people. Squad cars are parked every which way. Bright beams of headlights cut through the darkness at melodramatic angles. A news crew arrives with a minicam. The Alpine has auto-reverse, it's as tough as a 747's black box, so the tape keeps on playing: Del Fuegos, *so baby now don't you ru-u-u-n* . . . There are blue and red rotating blips.

She could picture all this. Each image, each detail, entranced her, made her drive with more grim concentration. The staticky crackle of cops' walkie-talkies, the glint of her blood when their flashlights first hit it, the look on the youngest cop's face at the sight of her torn-up complexion. She always had thought it would not be a bad way to go. Princess Grace and Jayne Mansfield had cashed in like this. So had Richard Fariña, George Ormsby, James Dean, and Mary Jo Kopechne. John Bonham? Since she wouldn't be covered by Richard's insurance, he'd be out the whole cost of the Countach. And what about Albert Camus?

It was not hard to die, she concluded. But you had to make sure you didn't wake up in some nursing home seven years later, drooling and relieving yourself on yourself, unable to finish the job off. That would be not very good. You'd have to come up with the right stretch of tollway, generate some serious velocity and have a good time for a while, get yourself in just the right mood, then sort of accidentally-on-purpose turn yourself into a car bomb. The spectacular rush of the Mumm's and the speed and the music was the last thing you'd ever remember. No pain, no more hassles, maybe make the ten o'clock news.

"Brothers in Arms" made her ache to drive faster, but she knew she had to slow down. (In her studio version she got the effect of her old—stolen—National Steel out of her new Paul Reed Smith Custom by gently caressing the sweet switch.) The cars in her way seemed to be backing up toward her *on purpose.* She'd been pulled over twice in the Nova for speeding, but neither cop gave her a ticket. She also had never been strip-searched but figured tonight might be different.

A doctor with a neat red dot in the middle of her forehead pronounces her dead on arrival. Two handsome guys with acetylene torches cut her immaculate body from the splintered black fiberglass, transfixed by the translucent whiteness of her flawless complexion, the deadly calm glint in her eyes. Both guys take days off from work (without pay) to attend her cremation, to something her terrible beauty.

She made a fast loop through O'Hare, paying an extra toll for the chance to check out the Wednesday night traveling public. There was no one around, though, to mistake her for some big celebrity. Even United was more or less dead at this hour. Ho-hum.

Procol Harem's "Memorial Drive" started up as she headed back east toward the city.

She got off at Ogden, doubled back over the Kennedy, cruised into Area 4. No Man's Land. The Shakespeare Police District. Damn. She'd been in here before but not for a couple of years, and never this late or while driving a car that was bound to attract some attention. She turned off the music, drove slowly. She didn't remember the streets. Tool-and-die factories, huge truck docks, warehouses with half their windows stoned out, still waiting for loftrification. Her nose said there also were bakeries. Not many three-flats or houses, however. No mid-rises, either. No people. Disciples and Vice Lords graffiti, Insane Unknowns, Kings . . . How far could she be from the war zone at Sedgwick and Larrabee? Cabrini was five blocks away,

SuHu eleven or twelve. The city was strange, Linda thought. She licked her index finger and used it to moisten her forehead and nose, then rubbed it all dry with her sleeve. A white girl like her could get killed around here, and that might be if she were lucky.

She pulled into a parking lot at the corner of Ogden and Milwaukee. The only other thing in the lot, an old van, looked abandoned, but how could you tell with a van? She drove past it anyway, making sure that at least the front seats were empty, then mussed up her hair in the mirror.

She parked in a space directly across from the warehouse at 756 N. Milwaukee. The building was fifty yards long and three stories high. Rectangular, gray, nondescript. Only the top two floors had windows. There were lights on: two on the second floor, one on the third. None of the windows had shades.

As she turned off the Countach and mussed up her hair a bit more, she understood that this was where she'd been headed since she first turned it on. The cruise and the tunes were all prelude. This was the building Hank lived in.

She sat there and waited and stared. Smoked a cigarette. No one went in or came out. She was thirsty. She had gotten the address just that morning by calling the Registrar's office and saying that she was his sister.

Nothing happened. And she still didn't know what she'd do, what she'd say, if it did.

"If what did?" she said to herself.

A mufflerless Oldsmobile cruised up Milwaukee. Young black guys. House music stuttered and rasped from blown speakers: Denise Motto, or something like that. Xaviera?

The Olds slowed way down as it passed her. One of the guys in back yelled something that Linda could not understand: magic wand? The driver ducked down and looked over. The guy riding shotgun was shaking his hand like he'd burned it.

Linda looked up at the warehouse. There was nobody there, no one in all those windows, but she waved toward it, moving her lips. Then she waved again, nodding, pretending that someone had answered.

The Olds stopped at Ogden. It did not use a signal, but Linda could tell it was waiting to make a right turn. She looked at the warehouse again. On the second floor, far to her left, a guy in a baseball cap was looking out over the street. Was it Hank? No: a guy who was wearing a baseball cap backward stood with his back to the street. Was it him?

The Oldsmobile turned, growling and rumbling, and moved east on Ogden for twenty or twenty-five yards, very slowly. She watched it. She knew what was going to happen, but still, when it happened, it stunned her. The Oldsmobile's headlights bounced up and down twice as it turned right and entered the parking lot.

Why had she turned off the engine? She didn't have time to restart it. Plus she'd have to back up now before she'd be able . . .

The Oldsmobile pulled up behind her and stopped. Its absurdly loud engine kept running. She turned around to look but could not. She looked at the warehouse. Second floor, to the left. Anywhere. The guy in the window was gone.

They turned off the engine. Big silence. She decided to try to be "cool."

Two guys got out but did not close their doors. They came around to her side of the car and stood about six feet away. One had on Adidas hightops, a shiny gray suit, and wraparound black and red shades. The other wore Ray Charles–style shades. He had very light skin and red hair; his beard and the sides of his head had been shaved into blunt geometrical patterns.

"One flash black ride that you got for yourself, little white girl," he told her.

She nodded. She did not tell him *hey, what I say.*

The one in the suit said, "Hey, what's the frequency, brick?" Or that's what she thought he had said.

She said, "Fine."

"Fine?" said the one with red hair. They looked at each other. Then: "What's it, Italian?"

She could tell that the question was addressed to his partner, but she wanted to answer it anyway. If she talked to them, got them to say things to *her* . . .

"Countach," said the one in the suit. Not to her.

Two other guys had emerged from the Olds. Did it matter? All four were older than she had expected. Middle twenties, about. It was always so hard to tell, ha ha ha. The guy with red hair had on a blue leather jacket, black pants, blue socks, and blue hightops. The two latest guys were both giants. They both had on translucent shower caps and black-and-red Adidas warmups.

One of them told her, "Slick ride."

"Lamborghini," she tried to say, swallowing. She only got out about half of it. "I think." She shrugged and tried smiling. "It's my mother's."

"So you think it's your mama's ride, huh?"

She nodded. But why was she saying these things?

The guys in the shower caps both seemed insane and unfriendly. They had started to dance, juke around, mimicking each other's movements. The other two guys were staring at her and the car. They did not seem to have any weapons, but why would they need even one?

"Countach, Jack," one of the shower caps said. "Mo'-fucken Countach, my man. Mo'fucken ride cost like two hundred mo'fucken grand."

"Sheee-it. Costed no mo'fucken two hundred . . ."

"You wan mo'fucken *bet,* Bubba Haid?"

Linda stopped listening. So *this* is how you die, she was thinking.

"How much?"

The one in the suit thrust his hand inside the Countach. Her heart tom-tommed hard, and she couldn't help cringing. The back of his hand was black in this light, and the inside was white. His knuckles were inches away from her chest. About two. Her plan all along was to scream and fight back—to concentrate mostly on yelling as loud as she could—when they grabbed her, but to definitely wait till they'd done it. *Bap bap bap bap* went her heart.

"My name Jamaal."

Bap bap bap.

She suddenly found she had put her right hand into his and was squeezing to keep hers from shaking. Jamaal's hand was huge, warm, and hard. She had almost passed out but was glad she had not. She must have hyperventilated from breathing so hard, from working so frantically to keep herself from breathing too hard. To be cool.

"I'm Linda," she said.

He let go her hand. "My partner name Patrick."

She shook hands with Patrick. The guys in the shower caps also shook hands, with themselves.

"We admire your car very much," Patrick said.

"Thanks," Linda said, when he too had let go her hand. "It's sort of my stepfather's actually."

"It's your stepfather's car?" Patrick said. He seemed deeply disappointed, to the point of real anger. "It isn't your mama's car then, like you said?"

"You steal this ride, girl?" said one of the shower caps. He stared at her, glaring and furious.

"What is the frequency, brick!" said the other.

Bap bap bap bap bap bap bap.

"I didn't!" she said.

"You sure you don't steal it?" said Patrick.

The guys in the shower caps mimicked her, holding

their hands up, protesting "I didn't!" in squeaky white chickenshit voices.

Jamaal said, "You sure now?"

They were toying with her. She understood everything clearly. They were going to mess with her head for a while, then fuck her a few times and kill her. She was glad she was still in the car but realized that this would prevent her from making a run for it—though a lot of good running would do her. She figured they'd probably snatch her right out through the window, stuff her in their trunk, then drive her someplace where they could take their sweet time. She imagined the things they could do to her.

Bop.

"We teasing you, Linda," said Patrick.

The four of them looked at her. Silence.

As firmly as possible, she told them, "I really do have to be going."

"You do," Patrick said.

"Really?" Jamaal said. He looked back at Patrick. A streetlight the size of the head of a pin reflected four times off their lenses. Convex, Linda realized. But how many angels could dance there?

"Really, I do," she said firmly. "My stepfather and I really don't get along very well." In order not to say the wrong thing, she decided to tell them the truth. "I don't get home soon, they find out I'm driving this car . . ."

"What will happen," said Patrick. It wasn't a question.

No squad cars cruised by. No one grabbed her. Nobody came to Hank's windows.

"That's a very good question," she said.

"What's the answer," said Patrick.

"Don't know," she admitted. At least she had not said *Je ne sais pas, Paddy boy.* "But I really don't wanna find out."

The shower caps mimicked her, mumbling some

squeeky *dunnos* toward their chests, then all four got coolly hysterical.

"Don't wanna see her get whupped, do we now."

"Don't wanna see her get *spanked.*"

"No ma'am."

"Not *Linda.*"

"Not white girl."

By now only Patrick was laughing.

"Sure don't wanna see no blond-ass jackaroni get spanked."

"That is about the lastest thing Bubba Haid wanna see."

She turned on the Countach. It started. The engine roared loudly, then idled. She could feel their collective amazement tingle the side of her face, like cool wind on sunburn. She swallowed and looked at Jamaal; he was the one she had gauged was the friendliest. She suddenly realized that she hadn't asked *him* any questions, shown any interest in *his* life. Could he possibly understand that she'd just been too scared, or how badly she wanted a drink? She reached her hand toward him.

Patrick took it. He held it. Didn't shake it or squeeze it. Just held it—hard, tight—inside his. The shower caps also shook hands.

"Nice to have, you know, to have met you," she said. *Bop bop bop.* Then, to Jamaal, "And you too." Patrick still held her small hand. "Really. Like all of you guys."

"Nice to meet *you,*" Patrick said. "*And* your car."

Jamaal said, "*Wherever* you got it."

"Right. Well . . ." Patrick was shaking her hand. He was not gonna rape her *or* kill her.

"As a matter of fact, we must be off now ourselves," said Jamaal. "Pressing appointments, you know. No offense."

Patrick let go of her hand. "We've received our instructions," he said.

"No offense," Linda said. She tried to shift into reverse,

but her hand was too shaky and damp. Her whole arm was numb. Plus *their* car would have to be started and moved before she could leave. She tried not to think about that.

"Get home now before you get hurt," Patrick told her.

She shook her head, nodded.

Jamaal moved behind her, *hopefully* back toward the Olds. The guys in the shower caps yawned. Were they nervous? She heard metal scraping on metal. Patrick was looking right at her, but she couldn't make eye contact because of the shades. He did not look at all like Ray Charles.

The Olds started tapping and rumbling. Her heart *bapped* and raced along with it.

It backfired twice but kept running.

Patrick was shaking his head. Not like Ray Charles *or* Stevie Wonder. More like a boxer did after the bell. Like someone who didn't fight girls.

She shifted into reverse, but left in the clutch. *Bap bap bap.*

"Well then," said Patrick.

Those four homeboys killed me. And so where was Hank Rendeck, that shit, to defend me?

FRIDAY AT 12:43. Linda was in the school library to do an assignment for her A & P class: analyze the colors of one of your paintings (or other works) in terms of their dominant wavelengths. It was due in—what? Seventeen minutes. She'd still been in Paris the day Strobe had talked about dominant wavelengths. The books he had put on reserve weren't there. She did not have the relevant handout.

She went and asked Rollie Tennaqua, one of the library's student workers, for help.

"Dominant wavelength?" he whispered. "Thing for Strobe's physics class, right?"

Right.

"Check Chicago to Death, under Color."

She must have looked puzzled.

He pointed to low shelves behind her. "Volume sixteen of *Britannica.*"

"For the thing about dominant wavelength?"

He nodded. "Page six sixty-one. Better hurry."

She thanked him and turned to the shelf.

"That's Colour with a *u,* don't forget."

The pages of the encyclopedia were almost as thin as a phone book's but larger and crammed much more densely with print. A continuous two-column footnote, it looked like. She groaned.

She turned to page 661: Dominant wavelength, reflectance, and purity. She skimmed it. Basic color specification, it said, was provided by three tristimulus values. Made sense. It was necessary, when analyzing color, to specify the quality of the reflected light as well as the quantity. Quality was specified by occupying a comparison field with a mixture of white and homogeneous light. Colors were quantitively analyzed by adding an appropriate amount of white light to an appropriate amount of homogeneous light of the proper wavelength. One possible use for such analyses, the article noted, was that the colors of the pigments used by the old masters might have been preserved forever in terms of their dominant wavelengths, and would thereby . . .

She didn't have time for the benefits. She also kept losing her place in the dense blocks of type. She looked at the clock: nine to one. She was more or less thoroughly baffled but decided to make some notes anyway: she had to have *something* on paper. She wrote down *wavelength of light = dominant wavelength of sample.* There was actually a mathematical formula, but to use it you had to be able to . . .

Wait! Up in the corner, at the top of the next block of type, was a table. She scanned what it charted, reread its headings, then kissed it, smacking her lips on the paper. All you had to do was look up your colors then read off the numbers beside them. Emerald green, for example, had a dominant wavelength of 511.9 millimicrons, a reflectance of 39.1 percent, and a purity of 22.8 percent. Ivory black had a dominant wavelength of 494.5 millimicrons, a 2.2 percent reflectance, and a 1.7 percent purity. Okay. The other two colors of her camouflage painting, tan and brown, weren't listed, so she changed them to colors that were. Zinc yellow's numbers, for instance, were 575.8, 32.6, and 79.7. Burnt umber's numbers were 589.5, 5.1, and 34.2. Autumn camouflage.

She took out a blank sheet of looseleaf and copied the names of the colors in order of dominant wavelength, making her own little chart, putting the highest (most dominant) first. She figured that such an arrangement of colors and numbers would have to amount to *some* sort of "color analysis."

Her homework completed with almost three minutes to spare, she flipped through the rest of the volume. Columbus, Combinatorics, Confucius ("Filial piety begins as the natural and early exercise of the *jen* sentiment, leading to an attitude of respectful affection toward one's parents"), Constitution and Constitutional Government, Constitutional Law, Copernicus, Crime and Punishment ("In England, for example, two-thirds of female victims of violent crime were attacked by relatives. . . . Homosexuals and other sexual deviants appear to be especially prone to violent attacks"), Cromwell, Crusaders, Crustaceans, Cryptology ("concerning the methods and devices employed to camouflage communications"), Cyprus, Czechoslovakia, Damascus, Dance, Dante, and Darwin.

And Death. Which, according to the article at least, wasn't simply not life. What it was was a number of things. A transition from one phase of life to another. When a mass of cytoplasm containing a membrane-bound mucus stopped replacing itself, Linda learned, it was curtains. If a land mine blew up underneath you, you died. It was also the case that a widow often died soon after the death of her spouse—but not always. It was also the case that, in a person near death, the Purkinje cells of the cerebellum swelled initially when deprived of oxygen but underwent irreversible shrinkage degeneration if hypoxia was prolonged, whereas the cells of the medulla or spinal cord would show little or . . .

She turned back to the front of the book, to Chicago, and skimmed. The typical American city, it said. (Hadn't Paschke said something like that?) Catastrophic fire in the Iroquois Theater. Al Capone, John Dillinger, the St. Valentine's Day Massacre—at the Biograph Theater, she knew. The Mercantile Exchange and the Chicago Board of Trade —the latter harbored bald clueless sphincters. "Here," Carl Sandburg had written, "is a tall bold slugger set vivid against the little soft cities." *Okay* . . . A stroller through present-day Chicago would find a complex city, a kaleidoscope of neighborhoods mirroring the ethnic and racial diversity of American life. The Windy City was an accurate nickname, meteorologically speaking. The city proper occupied 228.1 square miles (590.8 square kilometers). The three branches of the Chicago River originally flowed into Lake Michigan, but when the Sanitary and Ship Canal was dug in 1900—exactly?—it began to flow backward. Which made it a true, perhaps *the,* twentieth-century river. There was also a map of the city which explicitly named, among other significant places, the spot where the mighty Chicago's trio of backward-flowing branches came together: Wolf Point.

She was late.

tougher to look
than to leap

THE LIMOUSINE got them home from O'Hare by eight Friday night. Their bodies were still back on Paris time, so it felt more like three in the morning. Maggie wanted to go up and see Linda, then take a hot bath before going to bed. Richard carried most of their bags to the bedroom, then went down the hall to his office.

It was good to get back to his Wang. He realized how much he had missed it: it was *not* like he'd never been gone. While he and his bride had been kicking up their heels in Paris, here it had been—quietly, solidly—waiting to get back to work. The market would open again Monday morning, and he realized how much he'd missed *that.*

There'd been three stacks of mail in his box, gathered neatly together in rubber bands by Renny, his trusty Barbadian carrier. (He made a note on his December 18 calendar page to tip Renny $50.) He did not want to deal with the mail now, however—till he spotted the light purple corner of a very small envelope near the top of one stack. No return address, general 606 postmark, his name and address written out in neat rounded penmanship. Jacqueline's.

She had been Refco's best-looking runner the summer before Maggie had come on the scene, and they'd had some wild times. (She was prone to strange spasms and cramps in her thighs and the small of her back if she twisted or bent the wrong way, which had forced them to improvise several new uses for stairs.) But what was she sending him *now?*

The answer: an Andre Dawson Sportsflics baseball card from the days when he'd still been an Expo. No letter, no note, just the card. But he got it. Their four or five dates had revolved around the fact that they were Cub fans.

The card looked brand new, and he wondered where Jackie had got it. When he moved it around in the light it showed three different stages of Andre's fierce swing: bat cocked and ready, striding forward while snapping his wrists, knees bent and following through. Richard loved it. He flicked it back and forth between the last two positions, interpolating Andre's shoulders and hips turning hard into the pitch, the buggywhip wrist snap, the crack of the ball off the bat. He pictured the barechested mob in the left-field bleachers standing and screaming with their fists in the air as the ball carried out onto Waveland. He even could picture Andre's no-nonsense home-run trot. He could hear Harry Caray: "Cubs win!"

The longer he played with the card, the more Richard hoped Dawson's knees would hold up. If they did and he had a good year, he would make another couple three million (including endorsements), maybe six hundred thou if they didn't. These were not far from the numbers he himself had been bouncing between for a while, although none of *his* bucks were deferred. He always had thought he and Andre were pretty much on the same wavelength: same Porsche, same loafers, same city, big Cub fans, wives with sharp clothes and great legs. . . . According to the back of the card, Andre was seven years older than he was. In two or three years they would both be retired, which was doubly strange when you thought—

The floor creaked behind him, and he thought he heard breathing. He felt it, in fact, on his neck. The last time Maggie snuck up on him like this, playing guess-who, he'd reacted with so little amusement (he had actually gone into a rage) he was sure she had gotten the message. Didn't she realize she could startle him into a heart attack when he was at his desk trying to strategize? Could she not understand how exhausted he was from the flight, how *not* in the mood for these games? (Shouldn't *she* be as tired as he was?) There also was the open purple envelope sitting right out on his desk to consider: what fellow male Cub fan would use such a candy-ass color, or dot all their *i*'s with small circles?

She tapped his right shoulder.

"Have you seen these new kinds of cards yet?" he said. Trying to hide it would only make Maggie suspicious.

When she didn't respond right away, he turned to his left and looked up. No one there . . .

For a moment or two, he was nervous.

"*Gotcha!*" she said, and he jumped: *Jesus Christ!* Having anticipated his contrarian guesswork, she was standing behind his right shoulder. "And, no I haven't."

Her hair was still wet. She was barefoot. The white Crillon bathrobe was open enough to reveal beads of water or sweat on the flushed middle part of her chest.

"Let's see," Maggie said.

And he showed her.

Linda heard footsteps. Not Maggie's. They had just gotten back a few hours ago. She and Maggie had sipped some hot chocolate together, Maggie gave her a watch and a sweatshirt (with no further hassle about her coming back early), then they both went to bed. Plus it had to be three in the morning by now. Had the jetlag just woken her up? But she'd known Maggie's footsteps since before she was born. All it took now was a couple for her to be sure it was her. And it wasn't.

The footsteps were not Richard's either. Richard's heels clicked slightly irregularly, and he always wore loafers or tennis shoes. These footsteps sounded like heavy men's boots on the bare concrete floor, getting closer, echoing up the steel staircase, then down her long hallway. Plus Richard would never come up to her room by himself. Not at night.

The footsteps got closer and louder, then stopped. For a minute or two (maybe it was eight or ten seconds) she heard nothing. She listened as hard as she could as her pulse pounded back through her veins. What a cliché, she was telling herself. What a chicken.

She peered from her mattress through the leaden light outside her door and fought the temptation to cover her head with the blanket. But she saw and heard nothing.

Then: "Easy now. Easy."

She jumped. Her father had moved through the doorway and was standing right next to her mattress. His voice sounded friendly but scared. "It's just me," he was saying.

His forehead was bandaged and filthy. Though he seemed to be shivering, and his teeth to be chattering, his chest and face glistened with sweat. There was also a stench in the room—a fierce combination of shit, gasoline, burning hair—like nothing she ever had smelled. Plus some of his features were missing.

"You're Linda, right?"

"Yes."

"I'm your father."

He didn't have arms, though. One of his charred, bloody stumps swung toward the other as he tried to point out where his wounds were. "Forgive my condition," he said.

There was gunfire, chattering voices, a thumping explosion close by. Then another. Her father was jerked back and forth like a puppet. His neck seemed to snap. He was writhing face down on the floor. "Forgive me," he groaned. "Please forgive me."

She shuddered. Her scalp felt electric. She always had hated her father for leaving, for dying before she was born. She did understand that it wasn't his fault, but she still—she didn't know *what* she still wanted.

It was quiet again, and the stench had let up, but her father was still on the floor. He was trying to turn himself over. She watched him there, helplessly writhing. She had lost some control of her bladder. She knew what had happened. He really was there. She could see him.

A stun of pain seemed to go through him, and he raised his head toward her. "Please," he said, gasping. Pink-flecked white drool foamed from the side of his mouth. "Linda, I beg you!"

She tried to reach toward him, to let him know how much she loved him. More than anything else she ever had wanted, she wanted her father to hold her, just once, to be hugging her terribly hard, absorbing her sobs with his arms and his hands, with his body, to make all those wanting things better. But her sobbing was tearing her throat up. She couldn't.

"Please . . ." He was wheezing and panting. "Oh Linda, oh *please* . . ."

She couldn't. She loved him so much. She wanted to, wanted him, *Daddy*, for him to have always, forever, to *know* that . . .

Roaring, not knowing, ferocious, he trembled like heat waves and faded.

6

IN THE last nineteen months, Richard had purchased six paintings from the Zara Baines Gallery: an Ashleigh, a Jackson, a David Sedaris, three Kripkes. His invitation to that evening's opening for Togrul Farmanovich Narimanbekov, an Azerbaijani painter, had arrived in a hand-addressed envelope that included, in addition to the usual four-color postcard and biographical material on the artist, a personal letter from Zara that saluted him as Richard, chatted him up for five sentences about his aesthetic and professional acumen vis-à-vis Sovart and Azerbaijani agriculture, then offered a preferred-buyer's discount of twenty percent as well as an invitation to meet Mr. Narimanbekov's personal representative from Sovart at a private post-opening gathering at Zara's Bucktown triplex. Since the envelope had been addressed to Richard Baum, Esquire, he inferred Zara still didn't know he was married.

He blowdried his hair (he reserved this destructive procedure for when he was on his way out someplace artsy), then undid the third and fourth buttons of his blue Oxford shirt. Forget that. Showing chest hair, he thought, made him look too provincial. He put on a pea green silk tie, neither narrow nor wide, this to go with his gray herringbone Donegal tweed jacket and the jeans Maggie had bought him in Paris. The bottoms of these jeans were narrower than he was used to, but he decided he liked them that way: they looked très New Wave, and they didn't cover the buckles on his new suede Cerrutis.

Maggie came into the bathroom. She was wearing yellow Lycra gloves, a chrome yellow WilliWear micro stretch dress zipped to the top of her throat, blue Lycra tights, and her cobalt blue suede Gucci thighclimbers. She did not look provincial, to Richard.

"You look terrific."

"You too."

What Maggie was wondering was whether, at thirty-six years and nine months, she could still get away with this look. She couldn't ask Richard, of course. She wouldn't ask Linda. She knew there were people she *could* ask, but right now she couldn't think who. She would find out tonight, she supposed.

"We ready?"

"One second."

Four big TV screens overlooked Cadillac Cucina's mobbed bar. The first and third screens had the Bulls-Cavaliers game, the second and fourth screens the chefs hard at work in the kitchen, an *abab* action quatrain. Linda watched, turned around, lit a cigarette; she pretended she was waiting for someone. She knew that she might not get served—she'd never been in here before—so she wasn't in too big a hurry to get a bartender's attention. She could feel men's siberian eyes on her body as she looked back out into the street.

Orleans and Huron, just after six Friday evening. Pink and gray sky, jerky traffic, yellow and red neon tracers. It was warm for November, but crisp. Within two or three blocks of this corner, she knew, twelve million people were doing the same SuHu Crawl through Phil Collins Michelob Country. Tonight. Six or eight gallery openings per block, jammed wall to wall, overflowing onto the sidewalks. Limousines, miniskirts, Cherokees, briefcases, Saabs . . . Heathen Town. A CTA bus braked and farted. It had barely missed hitting a woman who had just gotten out of a cab. Another was just getting in. Huron ran westbound, one way, but cabbies had sly ways around this. Ho-hum.

She ordered a Bombay martini. The bartender—mustache, a Mediterranean—wanted to see her ID. She winced and half smiled, acting surprised but amused, asking him if he was kidding. He apologized, smiling, for having to ask, but insisted.

"I'm flattered," she said.

A guy two stools over said *he'd* like a Bombay martini. He had reddish blond hair, and had on a red tie and tortoiseshell glasses. He seemed to be sitting with two other guys; all three had turned and were facing her. Lawyers. The guy who had ordered the martini was about Richard's age. All three had mugs of dark beer.

The bartender looked at the guy. He seemed to be neither amused nor dismayed. He was about to say something, but waited. On the screen above Linda, Scottie Pippen stood at the free-throw line, sweating. He looked like a young Masai chieftain. The referee bounced him the ball.

"Mushroom?" the guy said. He glanced up at Pippen, then back down at Linda. "A twist?"

Pippen's first free throw rimmed in, back around, and spun out. People cursed. Linda smoothed salt from an oyster cracker, brushed off her fingers.

"Or how about one of those little white oniony guys?" Pippen's next free throw went swish.

Richard and Maggie excused their way into the Baines. Personal invitations from Zara did not count at this stage *at all.* A banner and posters outside had announced that

SOVART
ZARA BAINES GALLERY
DEUTSCH BANK
IBM

were presenting Togrul Farmanovich Narimanbekov. The *Sun-Times* and *Tribune* both had reported the opening, and so had the 4:30 news. It was packed.

Maggie picked up right away on the two separate camps in the gallery. The gay young things and the art-student types, Camp One, favored gray, olive drab, basic black: black denim, black leather, black cotton, black wool—or a combo of loud clashing plaids. They had vertical hair and pale skin, and wore work boots, sawed-off black dress boots, or sneakers, and nondescript pants with tight ankles. The ankles of the pants of the men from Camp Two, the buyers, were wider and more sharply creased. The women wore dresses or skirts: mostly designer stuff, pricey, but in color and cut much more frumpy than what *she* now had on. Tut tut tut. Camp Two liked the art, Maggie gathered, Camp One did not, but there also was some intermingling.

It took Richard almost ten minutes to bring her a mineral water. In the meantime she stood there and looked at one painting—a wheat field with birds, clouds, and sky—getting furtive (from Camp Two) and frank (from Camp One) second looks.

She wasn't sure whether she liked it.

Linda looked at the paintings. They were not very large, so you didn't have to stand too far back, though you wouldn't have been able to anyway. They all had that pulsing, irregular glow that reminded her she was sober.

The one in the least crowded corner was a landscape that featured a woman and a horselike creature alongside a tractor. The figures were facing away from each other, and everything seemed to be floating.

Another one featured gold haystacks. The paint was globbed on rather thickly, but the brushwork was not all that wonderful. Ugh. Horses or satyrs or unicorns tended to make an appearance. As the paper had noted, they looked like Chagalls. Only hokier, she thought. More provincial. She realized she couldn't do better, but still. These were nothing.

Where was Zara, he wondered. She was rawboned and tall, he remembered, with thick wavy reddish brown hair and a face like a pony's. She wore things like polka dot skirts.

"Look at this one," said Maggie.

"You like it?"

She started to nod, and then stopped. It looked so old-fashioned, and the paint was so messy and thick, but she knew that this might be the point. (But wasn't the "expressive hand of the artist" no longer allowed to show through?) Richard's friend Ivan Kral had paintings of faces that looked just like photographs but were fifteen feet high. Some works of art were nothing but words spelled out in six-foot-high letters, or phrases that ran across message boards. Richard had one in his office that was really just neatly framed cow fur.

"Shall we take one?" he said.

"You mean buy one, you mean?"

Richard looked out the window. "Yeah, buy one." A

gleaming white van was double-parked outside the gallery. He also could see his reflection.

"Hmm," Maggie said. Was he kidding? He'd sounded a little sarcastic. Plus she didn't like standing this close to plate glass in spaces this crowded. She did not like these thin plastic cups. "I'm thinking," she said.

"They aren't half bad," Richard said.

Which one was Zara, she wondered.

A voice she recognized instantly said to her, "Linda." Her fornix and nodes trembled faintly. 'Twas Rendeck. He was wearing his Jiffy Lube jumpsuit and standing so close she could smell him. There were three smells, in fact: a wood-limey combo of men's shaving cream and deodorant, a vague petrochemical fume she figured must be from the jumpsuit, and cognac. She had turned and looked up at his face while her nose sorted through them, but she didn't know how to address them. Him, that is. *Him!* There was also a fourth smell she couldn't make out yet. And where was the Japanese woman?

"Hank," she said finally. "Right?"

From across the main room of the gallery, past two dozen heads, Maggie spotted her friendless and renegade daughter. She was talking to a Camp One–type rake with a box-office caliber profile.

"Lookee who's here," she told Richard.

Linda was nodding, *agreeing* (it only seemed fair to assume) with something the young man had said. It was also the first time this decade she'd seen her poor daughter look *shy*.

"Who?" Richard said.

Linda was saying, "What are you doing here?" Her emphasis fell more on the *you* than the *here* than she'd wanted. She shook her head no. "I mean—"

"Just doing the SuHu Crawl solo, I guess."

She nodded. "Me too."

"What else does one do of a Friday?"

"Nothing, I guess. I don't know."

"*No* one knows."

"What?"

"No one *knows.* And speaking of which, did you know I've been looking for you?"

She wanted to look at him now, at his eyes, his green eyes, but she couldn't.

He looked at his watch. "Had my eyes peeled 'bout a week or two now," he said. "On the, you know, the lookout for you."

She attempted to process this strange information. She couldn't. She could, but she couldn't. She couldn't.

He pulled a small platinum flask from one of his Jiffy Lube pockets. "You're a gin man, correct?"

She nodded. But how could he possibly know that? She shrugged. Should she say that they had the same flask?

"Nice flask," she said.

"Duty-free VSOP. Have a taste."

Her thumb brushed two of his fingers as he passed her the flask. It was heavy, she thought. He'd been *looking for her?* Then she thought: No, it was light. She unscrewed the cap and inhaled some. The aroma was lovely enough to provide her its own little buzz. Then she sipped it.

The cognac was cool on her tongue for a moment, then icy, then soaked in as fiery smoothness. The sequence repeated itself as it moved to the back of her throat. From the back of her throat it passed straight through the top of her spine, her medulla—bypassing somehow her stomach, intestines, and bloodstream—and vibrated into her brain.

"That tasty or what?" Rendeck said.

She sipped it again, and it vibrated half a step sharper.

"Should be warmer, of course," Rendeck said. He looked back again toward the door, so she knew he was waiting for someone.

"Quite tasty," she said. She didn't know what she expected.

Their hands didn't touch when she handed the flask back. She did know she wanted to kiss him.

"So," he said, suddenly businesslike, slipping the flask into his pocket. "What do we think of these pictures?"

She looked at the painting before them. Colorful minarets, spiraling gyres: the Kremlin? A tall woman's shoulder was blocking two-thirds of her view. And she wanted to kiss him so badly.

"Socialist Chagall's what it looks like," said Rendeck. "The humble but mystical farmer." He took on a thick Russian accent: "The humble but mythical farmer by the mystical Mr. Farmanovich."

Hank Rendeck acting this hokey? She loved it.

"Pre- or Post-Chernobyl, you think?"

She earnestly nodded, said "Nyet." Can I have three more sips of that cognac, you think?

"Nyet that it matters, of course," Rendeck said.

"Of course nyet." How could it?

"Sorry," he said. "I only talk this way when I'm nervous."

She watched him look back toward the door. "What have you got to be nervous about?" There. She had said it. They now were on more equal terms. "Not that it matters, of course." That was perfect.

"Good point," he said. Looked at his watch. "Not to change the subject or anything, but would you like to see something real interesting happen?"

She knew he was going to kiss her. "Like what?" She hoped she had half-decent breath.

He put his large hands on her shoulders. She stood there and looked at him, blushing. He held her. She could feel what he wanted now coming right out through his hands. He was trying to turn her around.

Sudden and stunningly loud, a quick burst of staticky gunfire exploded into the gallery, echoing off the eight walls. Then there were two longer bursts, even louder. You couldn't tell where it was coming from. Most people got to the floor: some dropped, some squatted, some dove. Men tackled women and covered them. Others edged back around corners.

Linda was down on one knee. She could feel Rendeck crouching behind her. He was still holding onto her shoulders.

"Watch this," he told her.

She watched and heard shouting, hysterical screaming, followed by two more quick bursts. The floor was now covered with bodies. There were two men in camouflage outfits and ski masks; a third man was wearing a green army jumpsuit. All three brandished high-tech machine guns: stubby black barrels, long squared-off handles, not shiny. Sort of like old-fashioned bicycle pumps, Linda thought, without hoses. Like tubular, lopsided T's.

The three men were expertly covering people with precise, rhythmic movements, shouting phrases that weren't in English. She could feel Rendeck's breath in her hair; she could feel his strong hands on her biceps. She watched.

The guy in the jumpsuit selected a man from the floor and pulled him up onto his knees. He whimpered and gasped, "Christ no no *please!*" He was wearing a gray pinstriped suit and had stringy gray hair; his glasses had half fallen off. "Please, oh I beg you, my heart!" One of the camouflaged guys took hold of his collar and yanked him up onto his feet. His face got all red and his eyes bulged. The other inserted the end of a gun in his mouth.

They began to move backward, dragging their hostage and shouting something like *Free Dr. Afghan Abdallah Farah!* The one in the jumpsuit ran forward and opened the door. The man with gray hair gagged and whimpered; you could hear his teeth click on the muzzle. His glasses were all the way off.

They shoved him and dragged him outside, and were gone.

Richard tried to get the license plate number as the van pulled away, but his angle was blocked by the hood of a Jeep parked on Huron. People were still on the floor, but most were now up on their knees. Maggie was shaky—she still couldn't talk—but okay. Neither of them had been hit.

He had lain there on Maggie (on top of the mother of one of the people he assumed were responsible) for what seemed like two hours, till he'd sensed it was safe to get up. Now, with fresh hindsight, he realized they probably had been cowering against the parquet for no more than forty-five seconds.

The police arrived one minute later: black guys and micks in black leather, young crewcut studs in blue SWAT suits, then pocky and cool-eyed detectives. Most of the cops had their guns out, which pissed Richard off. They were clearly too late to do shit.

Ambulances pulled up in front. Then minicams, lights, and reporters. Despite all the gunfire, the huge plate glass windows were both still intact. He couldn't spot one hole or crack.

Maggie was suddenly desperate to know *where was Linda?*

So what else was new, Richard wondered.

7

THEY KISSED in Hank's room, standing up. The door was closed and the lamp was turned off, but his two windows facing the Kennedy didn't have curtains or shades. There was light. His room was way back in one corner of a cavernous warehouse or factory. She guessed that, like hers, it had once been the manager's office, although hers wasn't quite half as large. He had put on a Bach cello suite, No. 1, and was kissing her much much less hard than she'd thought he would be, but she liked it. She loved it. She wanted to look at his body and face, but mostly she kept her eyes shut.

They were still standing up. He was holding her chin in his palm, caressing her throat with his thumb while he kissed her. His other thumb kneaded the small of her back. She could tell he was terribly strong. She opened her eyes for a second and noticed that his were not closed. She put her hands onto his shoulders, looked him right back in the eye, and hung on.

He pushed back her hair, kissed her temple, her eyebrow, her chin. They weren't real kisses exactly: he was touching the skin on her face with his lips, very lightly, all over. First slowly, then quickly, then slowly again. And then quickly. And then he was kissing her eyes, and she closed them. Through the stiff cotton jumpsuit she moved her hands over his biceps. His shoulders. His chest. His neck and his face and his sternum. His shoulders again. He was hard.

Was it actually finally happening? Yes! He was kissing the back of her neck, nipping her shoulder, coaxing her head to the side. She felt a sharp stab in the back of her mouth; she winced but ignored the brief pain. It stabbed her again; she ignored it. She opened her eyes and looked out the window. She also could see their reflection. Hank was now standing behind her. White lights moved toward them and through them while smaller, red lights moved away, through the rain, on the Kennedy.

When his right hand moved under her sweatshirt she reached back and grabbed his thick hair. Grabbed his ears, grabbed his neck . . . Then both hands were under her sweatshirt, fingertips seizing one nipple, other hand tracing the contour and cut of her stomach. She twisted and moaned, couldn't help it, exhaling hard through her mouth.

She had these irrational thoughts. The Japanese woman walks in with her hands on her hips. Hank wants to get to know Richard; he's using the gullible slut of a stepdaughter to learn how to get rich trading futures. The people Hank lives with are watching through peepholes. They're making a Japanese film. Or her father . . .

She disengaged herself, gently but firmly, and turned round to face him. "Listen," she said.

"Okay." He smoothed down her sweatshirt and listened.

There must have been two thousand books in shelves on the wall by his bed. It was too dark to read any titles. On the windowsills: two empty vases, a baseball glove, books. There were books on the floor by their feet. "I ain't never done this before," she admitted.

"I'm happy," he said.

She looked in his eyes, taking a black-and-white picture. Her arms had dropped down by her sides. "And I want to, believe me, with *you.*"

His fingertips combed through the hair on the back of her head, massaging the sides of her neck as he whispered, "But what?"

She decided he didn't have AIDS. Either type. Contraception? She decided that virgins got one dispensation.

His thumbs brushed her earlobes.

She hoped.

One minute later she witnessed her first live erection. It was lit by a streetlight and, indirectly, by the northbound cars on the Kennedy. She touched it. Stretches of it were so cool, talcum smooth. Other parts weren't. It was twitchy and thrumming and lovely.

She was drier now than she had been, and it hurt going in. A lot, as a matter of fact. Both of them had all their clothes off. Hank held her right leg way back, and she hooked her left calf round his neck. Once it was all the way in, it hurt less.

Somewhat less.

They adjusted.

"Okay?"

Oh yeah. She nodded. Oh *yeah.* She shifted the tilt of her pelvis as more and more pain got converted somehow into something she didn't have words, even thoughts, for. When he started to pull it back out she went No please no, *stay,* then realized that this was all part of the plan: he'd already bumped it in deeper. Oh God. She found herself panting again, and letting these whimpering noises escape. Couldn't stop. Hank's fist held her biceps against the wool blanket; his shoulders were pressing her thighs back. She shivered.

The pain in her mouth had got worse, but she understood now where it came from: her moaning and panting had vacuumed the hole in her upper left molar. Goddamn. CAVITY COMPROMISES LUSTFEST WITH RENDECK. She tried breathing more through her nose. Didn't work. Because of the things Hank was doing, and the way he looked while he did them, she couldn't help breathing like this. Couldn't move.

The music slowed down, Hank did not. Forces encouraged her sliding away, but he always found others that held her in place, rocking her more or less steady.

She shuddered and clutched him however she could as they moved on against one another.

Oh boy.

He accompanied her to the bathroom. They held hands, kissed twice, didn't talk. He'd told her to put on her shoes and some clothes, and now she saw why. It was not a short trip. They walked past dark corridors, forklifts, long rows of empty steel shelves while sharing a Marlboro Light. A battalion of tailor's dummies were lined up ten deep along one of the windowless walls. It was cold. Punch machines were bolted to the bare concrete floor, wooden skids stacked toward the forty-foot ceiling. With any more light she was sure that her breath would be visible. It was like taking a stroll through a cold metal forest—flying monkey wrenches, wicked gook witches, lost dollies, Dorothy Gale without Toto—though she *was* holding hands with the Wizard.

They went through two doors, round a corner, then up a short flight of steel steps. Suddenly Hank reached around her and switched on the fluorescent lights in what turned out to be an enormous industrial men's room: eight stalls, three showers, eight urinals, a long row of gleaming white sinks.

Her sense, heading back, was that they were more or less retracing their steps—till a day-glo stalactite loomed up, made her duck. What it was was the front of a CTA car in the fiery light of a blowtorch.

Hank said, "Yo, Teddy *Boy.*"

The guy who was wielding the blowtorch was down on his knees on the floor. He was wearing a black welder's mask and a Sox cap, on backward. His gruff voice was muffled: "Yo, Hanky."

"Got someone I want you to meet."

The blowtorch went off with a pop. The only light left was from a trouble light hung from a hook on the el car. The guy pushed the mask from his face and stood up. He was short but astoundingly muscular.

"Linda, this is Teddy Boy. Teddy Boy, Linda."

"Linda Krajacik?"

Hank nodded. "I already told him about you," he told her.

She shook hands with Teddy. "What did he tell you about me?"

Teddy Boy shrugged. He was wearing a white sleeveless undershirt, filthy and soaked through with sweat. He was almost real handsome. His shoulders were hunched and his neck was tucked in—like he was standing outside in the rain, Linda thought.

"We're thinking of flooding this over this winter for hockey," said Hank, gesturing out toward the darkness. "Isn't that right, Teddy Boy?"

"He told me you were the most interesting girl at that school he goes to. That he thought he was falling in love."

"*You* know," said Hank, "paint some blue lines and face-off circles, then open some windows and turn on a couple of faucets."

Teddy Boy yawned. "We won't even have to *open* the windows, the heat we don't get in this joint."

They took sips of cognac while watching the traffic go by on the Kennedy.

They tasted its fire on each other's tongues when they kissed.

They thirstily fucked with each other, licking and teasing, trying new tacks, making love.

They smoked and played back their strange rendezvous at the Baines, the look on the face of the man taken hostage, the first time they'd ever made love.

"You weren't exactly clawing the sheets," Rendeck said.

"I was scared."

She told him about Picasso's Braque, the Picassos, *The Raft of the Medusa,* the big Giacomettis, the Pompidou Center, the Braques.

They did imitations of Jonathan Strobe as dawn came up over the city.

Made love.

Became hungry.

Smoked and sipped cognac and water.

Dozed off.

One more time, slowly, with Linda completely in charge, they made love.

Ooh.
Ah.
Ooh.
Ah.

SEVEN OF Hank's umpteen roommates were up having brunch in the kitchen. It was late afternoon. Was it *Sunday?* The fat Sunday *Tribune* was sitting right there on the table.

The kitchen and dining (and bike parking) area took up most of one wall at the opposite end of the warehouse, one floor upstairs from Hank's room. She'd been up here with Hank in the dark, but this was the first time she'd seen it in daylight. There were three sinks, two refrigerators, several industrial sewing machines, a hot plate, a coffeemaker, a breadbox, a radio with WSAI on, a color TV with the sound off. Stacked on steel shelves were neat rows of soup cans, boxes of cereal, packages of hot dog buns, pots and pans, glasses and dishes, and hundreds and hundreds of books. The two picnic tables around which his roommates were sitting were covered with red and white checkerboard oilcloth. Clean, Linda noticed. And homey. A fire was going in a big iron drum by the window. "No gas," Hank explained. Hot dogs were roasting on long three-pronged skewers while industrial fans overhead efficiently sucked out the smoke.

Hank made polite introductions. Teddy she'd already met. Emily and Muster Mark were a couple, it seemed: they were wearing identical (scarlet plaid) bathrobes, and both had wet hair. Willa was Irish (from Belfast) and looked like Mick Jagger with short hair and regular lips. Visa was Norwegian, which explained at least part of her stark, preternatural blondness; she was also a graduate student at Circle in the History of Art and Architecture. Eusebio Vargas Jimenez Pedroza played bass, or at least kept a white Fender P in his lap while he ate, plucking some notes between bites. Bruce, who was doing the cooking, was an ophthalmologist "taking a little sabbatical," according to Hank, and a sculptor. Bruce was also the oldest—by twelve, fifteen years, Linda guessed. Everyone else looked to be more or less Hank's age.

Bruce handed Linda a mug of black coffee.

She thanked him, then asked, "You're an eye surgeon?"

"Yup," he said, turning a skewer, "but we only have nondairy creamer."

"Black's fine." She sipped some. The idea of working on eyes with eensy sharp instruments gave her the wriggling willies. She hid them. "Do any, I mean, other folks live here, besides—"

"Besides us?" said Bruce. "Yes. An uncertain number."

"Too many," said Willa. She dabbed at her normal-sized lips with a napkin, stood up. She was short and was wearing a gray pinstriped suit.

Hank said, "Officially, five."

"Depends on which bill has arrived in the mail," Teddy said.

"Or which Bill," Willa said. "Or which male. We're obviously not all that choosy."

"Or whose rich uncle Gary just died," said Eusebio. He made a fast sign of the cross.

The silence that followed was broken by Teddy: "Each person has 34,600 cubic feet of space and pays two hundred and seventeen dollars for rent, about twenty-eight more for utilities."

"And what could be fairer than that?" Visa said.

And who could be fairer than you, Linda thought.

"More or less," Muster Mark said. "No-neck Ted, for example, gets more, owing to the nature of his project and the fact that he's burliest."

When no one disputed this claim, Linda shrugged. Would they change the subject or was she—

"I'm off," Willa said, excusing herself and skirting the smoldering drum. "Very nice, Linda, to meet you."

"To see the wizard?" said Visa.

"The wonderful Wizard of Oz," sang Eusebio while playing his own bass accompaniment.

"You too," Linda said.

"Actually," said Willa, "today it's the wonderful wizard of Standard Oil of Indiana." With that she hoisted an aluminum briefcase from the floor and marched from the kitchen.

Linda asked Hank, "She works Sundays?" She knew that people like waitresses did, but not usually people in suits.

Hank explained that Willa was from Belfast; that she painted, wrote plays, and repaired ceramic microcircuitry for macro, quadruple-time fees. "Which is why Willa only works Sundays."

"A bleeding computer surgeon from bleeding Belfast," said Eusebio, with an awful Cubanian brogue. There were groans. It did not sound like Willa's at all.

"So what's on the menu this morning?" said Hank.

Louder groans.

"What?" said Hank. "What?"

"In addition to pure beef Vienna-style hot dogs," said Bruce, "we have coffee, a variety of homemade-style soups, one Dunkin' Donut, one Sprite, some more of Renée's Remy Martin Grand Cru, plenty of Budweiser Light, plus Cheerios, Grape Nuts, and Wheaties."

"What!" Muster Mark said. "No just-caught raw yellowtail?"

"And Wheaties with who on the *cover?*" said Hank.

"Just rubber buns and liquor," said Emily.

Bruce turned the box and showed Hank. "Uncle Walter."

Visa squinched over to make room for Linda beside her. Whispering loudly, she told her they usually ate out. Even her breath smelled light blond.

"No milk, though," said Bruce. "Unless Muster Mark jumps up, digs in his one shallow pocket, and runs out and buys some—as it *is* now his turn to."

Muster Mark jumped up, ran out.

Could I live here too, Linda wondered.

She launched into "Will the Wolf Survive?" without introducing it. The Pavilion went nuts. On her friend Keith's advice, she had left the E string off her Gibson GS and was using an open-G tuning: G, D, G, B, D. She could now hang her drone notes right through the chord changes and still keep the other notes ringing. (The thing about this kind of tuning was that all you needed to play it, according to Keith, was five strings, three notes, two fingers, and one asshole. But that was just Keith's sense of humor.) She was wearing a little black slip and red patent take-me high heels to go with her battered red Gibson. She had opened the show in an Issey Miyake crepe-and-cane "satellite" suit, but now that she was down to the shoes and the slip, she didn't hear any complaints. She was letting Hank Rendeck, her studly new bass player, sing the first stanza; she would join him for the second, then take over the singing completely. The girls in the first fifteen rows were jealously checking Hank out, waving bras and torn nylons, but they all understood he was taken.

The song was admittedly hokey, but the crowd always loved it: it filled the arenas and helped sell her album, which allowed her to do her more serious stuff and play a few intimate venues. (Los Lobos had naturally covered it, and had done a good job, but the most acclaimed version was still her own studio track—either that or the live bootleg take from her Montreal concert last spring, when she'd sung the duet with Nile Mansions.) She had just broken her own Pavilion record by selling out all four shows on this "homestand" in something like thirty-five minutes. The album had thirteen new songs and featured a grainy high-contrast Skrebneski photograph of her back on the front and her "jungle" self-portrait on the back; it had already gone double platinum. The local rock stations had been hyping the concert all week—or, rather, hyping *themselves* by playing cuts off the album and giving away pairs of tickets that could be easily scalped for a grand. Minicam crews had set up on stage or stationed themselves in the crowd; all five TV stations would be cutting here live near the end of the ten o'clock news.

Even Maggie had come. She often called Linda for passes when the band played Chicago, but this was the first time she'd dared to show up with her husband. But there they both were, right up front, mesmerized by the lights and the music. She ignored them. She waited until the minicams' red lights went on and the various stations were beaming her image all over the Greater Chicagoland Area. Then, simply by nodding her head to signal a time change, she showed Richard who was in charge—of the band, of the show, of the whole fucking city, in fact.

"That reminds me," said Visa. "How did that thing at the Baines go?"

"Flawless," said Hank. "Ne plus ultra."

"Yeah, we heard it was pretty intense," said Eusebio.

Linda nodded. "It was."

"This was a couple of days ago, right. Friday night?"

"What's this?" said Mark. He was still in his bathrobe but was lugging two gallons of milk. "You guys were *there?*"

"Hank and Linda," said Teddy.

"I already told you this, Muster," said Emily.

"I had a hot tip from DeSanto," said Hank. "Very last minute, of course. Apparently they're this hardcore performance group out of Randolph Street, probably funded by Guggenheim, Ford, NEA . . . I also knew Linda'd be there."

"Yeah, right," said Linda. But had he?

"But so how did they pull off the guns part?" said Bruce. "The news said had actual guns."

"Sure *looked* real," said Hank. "Even when you were looking for them to, you know, look fake. What I heard was, they sampled automatic weapons fire off some soundtrack, amplified the shit out of it, then ran it through speakers they had strapped to their chests."

"It was pretty convincing," said Linda.

"And loud. People hit the deck *hard,* right away."

"Papers say accurate replicas," said Mark. "They didn't say where all the noise had come from. By this time they pretty much knew it was a stunt. Fake guns, hostage they took was a confederate . . ."

"A *performance*, you don't mind," said Emily. "Stunts are what jerks pull. Like whatshername pulled on the news."

"Okay, a performance," said Mark. "A staged perturbation for the *aes*-thetic edification . . ."

"Of performance art people," said Bruce.

"Not this one," said Hank. "These four guys pulled something *off*."

"All terror is is catastrophe practice," said Mark.

Emily put a microphone fist by his mouth. "Tell us, Muster Mark, about terror."

Bruce said, "They've already caught them though, right?"

"Yep," Teddy said. "About a half hour later, trying to switch vans up in Uptown. Still makes no difference. They nailed it."

"So who's pressing charges?" said Bruce. "Zara Baines?"

"The Baines doesn't have to," said Visa. "Anyone *there* could press charges."

"But so what did the people there think," Mark said to Linda and Hank, "when they didn't get shot by the guns?"

"I guess they were too busy shitting their drawers and thanking their lucky stars they hadn't *got* shot," Hank told him.

"The best part was recruiting the old guy," said Emily.

"He was good," Linda said.

"I heard rumor has it," said Mark, "that the hostage was Zara Baines's father-in-law, that Zara herself had been in on it."

"No fucking way," said Eusebio. "Are you shitting me, man?"

"That's what Peter Taub told me last night."

"Plus Zara Baines ain't even married."

"Right. She's a lesbian."

"Wrong."

"Hey. What's this 'wrong'?"

"What it means is, you're wrong. Angel *worked* there, remember? Zara Baines is *notoriously* heterosexual. She also has never been married, which means she doesn't *have* any father-in-law."

"Which makes it even stranger if her father-in-law *had* played the hostage," said Visa.

"This is true," Hank admitted.

"Even old Ludwig and Burt would have to agree about that one," said Teddy.

"The following statement is true," said Hank. "The preceding statement is false. We agree."

"Even still," said Eusebio. "Zara's had some pretty wild folks doing performances there."

"Like who? Jimmy Grigsby?"

"Hey man, I'm talking people like Ellen Fisher, Renzo Ricardo . . ."

"Yeah," said Emily, "didn't Fisher do her Pussy Dance number one night?"

"It's not the same difference," said Bruce. "People's lives were at stake at this thing. I say it's going too far. *Way* too far."

"No people's lives were at stake," Hank insisted. "That they *thought* their life was at stake was the *point.*"

"What about heart attacks? Some old fart keels over and dies?"

"Who, like you?"

"What they had for dessert could've made them do that," Hank told Bruce.

Everyone thought about that. Linda sighed. She knew it was time to call home.

"So what did the po-lice have to say for themselves?" Teddy said.

"Like I said," Hank said. "We didn't stick around to find out."

Linda remembered their exit: racks of canvases in the

storeroom, getting yanked by Hank's fist, somebody's Church's fried chicken dinner spread out on top of a carton (with red-and-white checkerboard napkins just like this tablecloth here), then suddenly out in the alley and into Hank's truck. Romance action!

"We just made real sure we were standing real close to that door when the fun started up."

"I still say the thing was immoral," said Bruce. "To put a person's life in danger, however provisionally, for whatever purpose, is asshole, outrageous behavior. Not art."

"Oh, and Sovart and Deutsch Bank's isn't?" said Mark.

Isn't what, Linda wondered. Not art?

"Your point could be hardly less relevant," said Bruce.

Emily said, "The quote in the *Times* said the artistic integrity of what they—"

"What?" said Bruce. "That it had all the artistic integrity of, say, Elvis Presley? Or perhaps of a Vincent van Patten?"

"You know, since this is turning out to be such a scandal," said Teddy, "maybe we should call in . . . *Pam Zekman!*"

Everyone except Bruce and Linda recoiled in horror, yelling in unison: "NOOOOO!"

"Linda," said Bruce, "you were there. What did you think?"

Visa was still shrieking "NOOOOOOO!"

"I don't know," Linda said. "I mean, at the *time* . . . The thing was that Hank tipped me off, just before. He's like, Watch this. So that made it different for me."

Eusebio, Teddy, Visa, and Mark were still screaming.

"I don't know," Linda said. She liked Bruce a lot, and she wanted to answer him seriously, but she couldn't think quite what to say. "Is there a phone around here, by the way?"

"Not that!" yelled Mark. "Is she bringing in Liver Spots *too?!*"

"Oh no, not *that!*" yelled Eusebio. "Not *MIKE WALLACE!*"

"Not *Liver Spots!*"

"*NOOOOOOOOOOOOOOOOOOOO!*"

Things have a way of turning out to be pretty much what we will make of them.

THEY PLAYED back their messages. Most were for Richard, but none had to do with the incident at the Baines Friday night. The Loeber Mercedes service department called to announce that the magneto was in. Sissy Blackley called Maggie to confirm tennis times. Lynch called three times and left different numbers; he sounded concerned about something. Finally Linda came on: "It's me. So look, I'm staying with friends, so don't, with a friend for a couple of days." Her mouth moved away from the phone: "Where are we?" They heard a voice, male, say, "Milwaukee," then Linda said, "Listen, okay Ma? I'll talk to you." *Beep.*

Richard said, "Typical."

Maggie replayed the message. They listened.

"Doesn't sound like a terrorist who's gone underground to me," Maggie said. "Sounds more like—"

"What do terrorists who've gone underground tend to sound like?"

"Listen," said Maggie. "We've been through this already ten times."

"Yes we have," Richard said.

"I mean, *I* was there, wasn't I? Would she want to subject her own mother—plus she didn't even know we would *be* there."

"Are you serious? You know sometimes you're really naïve. 'A coincidence.' She *clearly* knew that we'd be there."

"How."

"How? A dozen ways. 'How.' She could've gone through my mail, seen the invitation. . . . She goes through my mail all the time."

"How do you know that?"

"Let's just say that I know."

"That's not a good answer," said Maggie.

"She practically fucking admitted it, for Christ's sake. And I caught her once too."

"You caught her."

"I caught her."

"Doing what?"

"In my office. She practically admitted to me she was snooping. She also was smoking a cigarette."

"Smoking a cigarette. Gosh. Call up Pam Zekman why don't you."

"Listen, I've already explained to both of you about the gizmos that read the diskettes, how they—"

"Anyway," said Maggie. "Okay. Yes you did. When was this?"

"When was what?"

"That you caught her."

"Three or four weeks ago maybe."

"Why didn't you say something *then?*"

"I did say something."

"To me?"

"No, to her."

"Why not to me?"

"I said plenty, believe me. It was the first time I really let her know what I thought."

"But why not to me? I thought we agreed that, things like this happen, you come to me first."

"This was different. Purely spur of the moment. She was flaunting it right in my face."

"Flaunting it right—flaunting what?"

"She also was driving the Countach before we got back. I checked my odometer log, and it—"

"What do you mean 'flaunting it,' Richard," said Maggie.

They stared at each other.

"And how was it 'different,' " she said.

Teddy Boy's hand left her shoulder, though she still felt its heated impression. She was upstairs to see his big project. "Stand here," he told her. His footsteps receded. It was cool and pitch black with her eyes closed. She heard him hit switches, then call out "Okay." When she opened her eyes, dozens of overhead lights had come on, and she found herself standing on—what? An el platform? Yes!

"Are you kidding me?"

Teddy was throwing more switches. She heard an el train roar through a tunnel, its metal brakes screech against metal. She looked back and saw the front end of a green and white CTA car emerge from a curved, green-lit tunnel. She looked at the tracks in amazement: there were three iron rails, oil-stained ties, and authentic CTA gravel—grease-blackened pebbles strewn with thousands of cigarette filters. Four feet above this, the platform she stood on was mottled with coins of black gum. It was *strange.* A similar platform, trompe l'oeil, was expertly depicted on the wall she was facing, then merged, up the track, with the tunnel.

"What you think?" Teddy said.

She turned around, taking it in. Next to a one-way turnstile cage was a faretaker's booth with dollar bills, transfers, tokens, and change on the counter. The trashcans and benches all seemed to be standard issue. *Defender* and *Sun-Times* vending machines both featured that morning's paper in their display windows; it would cost her a quarter to find out what day's were inside. Even the signs looked official. NO MAN'S LAND 1550 N 1200 W. Black and yellow caution lines, blue metal CTA maps. The PLEASE DON'T RUN sign had WALK Kryloned over the PLEASE.

"Are you serious!"

There were posters, graffiti, long billboards. One had an ad for *The Texas Chainsaw Massacre, Part II,* showing a chainsaw zigzagging jaggedly through plywood. THE BUZZ IS BACK, it proclaimed. Another one, next to it, said RE-ELECT GEORGE W. DUNNE PRESIDENT COOK COUNTY BOARD. The picture of Dunne showed him sitting at a desk holding bifocals, the American flag draped behind him. He looked ancient and beefy and Irish. The thought bubble over his head said

THAT PUERTO RICAN DICK
I SUCK LAST NIGHT WOW
IT WAS TASTY AND BIG
MMM MMM GOOD

in devil-tailed gangbanger script. The two-foot erection protruding up into Dunne's mouth had been drawn with the same magic marker. It was roughly the same size and shape, Linda noticed, and protruded at much the same angle, as the chainsaw that ripped through the plywood.

"It still needs a lot of distressing," said Teddy, then switched on the overhead heater.

Richard called Lynch from the Porsche but got Lynch's answering machine. He slammed the phone down on the console.

They were cruising northwest on Milwaukee, eyes peeled for Linda, still fighting. They passed Como Inn, crossed the Kennedy. Nothing. There were stores and activity, people, around Halsted and Grand, but much north of that things got bleak. There were certainly not many blond girls about on these streets.

"But it's *gotta* be avenue, honey," said Maggie. "She's not gonna know if she's up in Milwaukee?"

Richard drove silently, shifting the Porsche unsmoothly. Still pissed.

"The city of. You know, *Milwaukee.*"

"We'll see," Richard said.

A sweet warm aroma filtered in through all the vents. She inhaled. "Smell that bread?"

Richard sniffed. "Smells like chocolate," he mumbled.

The streets were getting more and more industrial. They appeared to Maggie to be more or less uninhabited, but since this trip had been her idea, she wasn't about to give up. There also was this to consider: Michael's uncles were both from Milwaukee. His Uncle Jerome still lived in the same little two-flat on Twelfth Street, with the three plaster ducks on the lawn, a block and a half from the tollway. She and Linda drove up every other Thanksgiving or so—although not since the move and the wedding, of course. She hadn't told Richard about it because she *knew* Linda hadn't gone up there. And not in the mood he was in.

"Plus, if she *was* 'in hiding,' " she said, "then why would she say where she was on the phone?"

"She didn't," he said. He'd turned and was looking right at her. "Now did she?"

The Lincoln in front of them suddenly stopped at a light. She pointed and gasped, went for the brake. Richard cursed, hit the brake, cursed again, then shifted to neutral and sat there, unclenching and clenching his fist.

"You seen her yet, Maggie?" He violently shifted as soon as the light turned green.

"No. But so that doesn't prove—"

When he let out the clutch the Porsche lurched forward, snapping her head back. He shifted to second. "Then just keep fucking looking!" he shouted.

"Listen, you asshole, you can let me out right—"

He slammed on the brake. "Or *don't* keep on looking. The fuck should I *care,* fucking worthless two bitches the both of you!"

fear and greed
greed and fear
fear and greed

"WHO WAS that Japanese woman you were with out at Fermilab?"

It was midnight. The rain was beating on the windows. Hank's neck was propped on a doubled-up pillow. He was smoking. Linda was lying on top of him. She was wearing the Jiffy Lube jumpsuit.

"Without what Japanese woman?"

She kneed him.

"Ain't you heard the old proverb? Wise man no go without Japanese woman. That is haiku, I believe. And now, awful tanka."

"What's tanka?" said Linda.

"Sort of longish haiku."

She heard a crash cymbal get whapped.

He took a short drag. "Another example of awful haiku would be, um, who was that Japanese woman you were with out at Fermilab. Kind of an interrogatory, though still very awful, haiku."

"Listen, I'm serious." Her right ear was pressed to his sternum. "I'm jealous." She did not lift her head because she wanted to hear his heart beating. "Who was she?"

"Renée wouldn't be all that pleased to be called Japanese, by the way. Let me tell you."

"She wouldn't."

"No siree, Bob. Nor would the people she works for. Though apparently it happens quite often."

"Who is she."

He took a long drag. "Who's Renée?"

She wanted to tell him how happy she was being with him, that she couldn't *help* asking these questions. "If that's what her name is," she said.

"That's what her name is."

"Who is she."

He exhaled. "Renée is a Singapore girl."

She had no idea at all what that meant, and she knew; her crazed brain was revving, spinning its wheels, going nowhere. He would have to have practiced on quite a few girls to have gotten as good as he was, would he not? Not that *she* would be much of a judge . . . Plus that theory—what was it?—something she'd read in *Ms.* or *Bazaar*, which said that a macho supremo performance in bed wasn't always a positive sign; that it often could indicate an egocentric desire to display a mere technical skill, or worse, a cold heart. If this theory were valid, she thought, they could use Rendeck's ventricles to chill out those Fermilab magnets. Did it also imply that if his *or* your teeth started chattering, it was time to get dressed and go home? If so, in whose clothes? And to whose?

"As in, you know," he said, "a great way to fly?"

"Yes, I know."

"She drops in whenever she gets laid over in Chicago. She's American, though. So she claims—insists, I believe, is the word. God knows why. One-half Japanese-American, one-quarter Vietnamese, one-quarter French."

Since there was nothing she could think of to say for the moment, Linda began to turn over. God knows why *what*, she was thinking. Hank groaned and cursed as she shifted her weight on her elbows, accidentally grinding them into his unpadded ribs. When she was through turning over they were both looking up at the ceiling.

"Drops in on who?" she said finally. Hank brought the cigarette up to her lips, and she smoked it. "Or should I say, drops in on whom?"

Taking his time, with the hand that was holding the cigarette, he unzipped the front of the jumpsuit a foot and a half. "Drops in on whom, I believe."

"Well?" The air on her chest gave her goosebumps. "So then whom?"

Hank blew a smoke ring. Then she did. She watched them both rise toward the ceiling, getting warped by invisible currents, as Hank tugged the zipper down farther. His had been larger, more perfectly circular, but her ring had stayed intact longer.

"It's interesting," he said, half out loud, to himself. He slid a hand into the jumpsuit and surveyed her lowermost rib. "Renée is a stewardess—sorry, a 'flight attendant'—who wants to be an artist, whereas Chet is an art student—sorry, an 'artist'—who wants to be a flight attendant. So maybe they *should* get together."

"Maybe they should." Who was Chet? Chester Treasure? "How old's this Renée, by the way?"

"Actually—Renée's thirty-seven, I think—Chet would probably rather be a stewardess."

"Let me get this straight," Linda said. "You only talk this way when you're nervous, correct?"

He put out his cigarette in the Cliffdweller's ashtray and slid that hand inside the jumpsuit. She felt more cool air on her torso, one more warm wrist—that made two, did it not? and two hands?—his pinkie exploring the rise and divide of her hipbone.

"You say so."

A werewolf was stalking her in the Eastwood apartment. The werewolf was actually Hank. He hadn't metamorphosed completely yet—only one hand was a paw—but as soon as he caught her he'd change all the way. She couldn't decide whether she wanted him to catch her or not. He was going to tickle her hard when he caught her no matter how much he had changed.

When she edged past the dining room corner, he grabbed her. She screamed. He threw her onto the floor and viciously went for her throat. He had changed all the way. It was Richard.

While Hank was asleep, Visa showed her his in-progress sculpture. It was upstairs behind Teddy's welding equipment, surrounded by power tools, glass shards and solder and corkscrews of metal, bootprints of paint, spattered canvas. She was startled by how different it was from his work that she'd already seen, though she realized she hadn't seen much. This piece was iron, rectangular, hollow, a yard long and twelve inches square, with transparent Plexiglas panels on the top and both sides. A long narrow box with four legs. It came about up to her hip. Everything but the Plexiglas was painted a flat graphite black, including the four iron legs, which were screwed to the floor through the canvas. Inside the box, at one end, was a pile of glass shards; an inch-thick cast iron bolt—it looked like a weightlifter's bar—protruded in from the other. The bolt ran back out, perpendicular to the side of the box, through a spring and three chains, then extended another ten inches outside. That end was fitted with a black plastic bicycle grip.

"No red-white-and-blue plastic streamers?" said Linda.

"He calls it *Black Box,*" Visa said. "He tells me he'll probably call the canvas underneath the same thing—with, I presume to assume, some impossibly witty parenthetical title appended."

"Looks vicious," said Linda.

"It is," Visa said. She reached behind Linda, plunged her hand into a crateful of powder blue Styrofoam chips, and pulled out a long-stemmed champagne glass. She breathed on it, polished it up on her shirt, flicked off a fragment of chip. "First one's free," she said, handing it over. "Forty-four percent leaded crystal."

"Merci, I think," Linda said, plinking the glass with her nail. Its note came off ringing and sharp.

"You are, therefore, welcome," said Visa.

Yeah yeah, Linda thought. Ain't you smart. Ain't you blond. Ain't you cute. She plinked the glass harder, letting it oscillate next to her ear. Plus he'd told her his plans for the *dropcloth?*

Visa had opened the door at the end of the box where most of the crystal was piled. Several shards spilled to the floor. Linda winced, then relaxed when the smash was absorbed by the wrinkled and paint-spattered canvas. Hung on a stretcher, she thought, or unstretched from hooks through brass rings like a Golub, it wouldn't look unlike a Schnabel, but why hadn't Rendeck told *her?* She found herself wincing again as she watched Visa squat on her heels, slide her unchainmailed hand in the box, then gingerly pick away three of the shards, revealing a circular pedestal centered a foot from the bolt. She'd clearly known right where it was. She stood up, stepped back, moved aside. "Putting it in's half the fun."

"You say so," said Linda. She squatted, looked in. The bolt was a foreshortened slug suspended above a jagged 3D crystal network; leaden light prismed in bright new directions as her focus receded, got fisheyed. She set the glass onto the pedestal—it barely fit inside the box—then closed and rebolted the door. She wondered if Visa agreed with the magazine's theory, if Hank—

"And to think it's our very best Waterford glassware," said Visa.

Yeah yeah. Linda moved to the opposite end, took hold of the bicycle grip. Eased it back. J-eee-ee-e-z. She could feel the dense mass of the bolt, the torque the big spring was expending. She pulled on it harder, retracting it five or six inches. The spring pulled it back five or four.

"Just like a pinball shooter," said Visa. "Though he seems to have boosted the megatons."

Linda ground a splinter of crystal into the canvas they stood on, her own little wittily titular, impossibly parenthetical (small) contribution to Hank's work-in-progress. And secret. "Nothing like overkill, right?"

"One of *thee* basic laws of the universe, hon."

Hon? "I guess so."

They looked at each other. Linda saw that Visa was blonder by a couple of orders of magnitude. She probably also was smarter. Linda understood that they both wanted Hank, and vice versa.

"Do it to it," said Visa.

Linda leaned on the box with her right hand, bracing herself, then yanked back the grip, retracting it almost a foot. Three-fourths of the bolt was now outside the box; its middle was smeared with beige grease. The spring's tension throbbed up her arm as she looked at the champagne glass, at the point where the cup and the stem came together. (Strobe called these things singularities, right? Yes he did.) She felt Visa watching her. Good. Though the bolt couldn't really be aimed, she was aiming. The spring had retaken an inch of it. She retook that inch, took another two-thirds for good measure, let go.

The explosion was over before it surprised her. The bolt's whang and shudder still rang up her arm. Had she screamed? Crystal plinked faintly, settling into the glistening pile, as the grip kicked back hard in her palm. Visa winced.

"Again," Linda said.

In eighty odd hours, she'd found out a number of things.

Who Renée was, for one thing, although not where things stood now between them.

That he'd clearly had dozens of lovers, in any event.

That Visa was probably one of them.

That for five or six weeks, when he first moved out to Chicago, he'd been a real Jiffy Lube Man. His main job had been lubricating chassis and checking differential, transmission, and brake fluids. He also had had to do vacuuming.

He was born in Sag Harbor. He'd been a big gearhead in high school, then played some guitar in some bands in New York. He got his B.A. in Philosophy from CUNY. The last place he'd lived was Tribeca. And he was, as she'd guessed, twenty-six.

He liked Yo-Yo Ma, *Live at Leeds,* Dick Holiday, Nile Mansions, Glenn Gould, Miles Davis, Ronald Shannon Jackson, Tom-Tom Tully, Tom Waits, Thomas Pynchon, Tom Lux. He hated but loved Stanley Kubrick. He didn't like opera but "wouldn't mind sharing a shamrock shake with" Kathleen Battle. He and Ronnie Spector had (twice) eaten dinner together. He also knew Marianne Faithfull.

The artists he respected the most were Beckett, Kiefer, Duchamp, Ozzie Smith, Picasso before he turned thirty, Isiah Thomas, Jasper Johns, Martin Scorsese before he turned forty, and the African National Congress.

She'd also discovered that if you went in one day, overnight, from no sex to *this*, you could really get tenderized good.

The three male terrorists were stripped to their waists. Their chests were like twinned pairs of flagstones; their pants were now pink-and-blue camouflage. They had decapitated their hostage and were making her look at the head. If she kept on refusing to look, they would shoot her in places that wouldn't quite kill her but would still be excruciating and would probably soon get infected. Plus she didn't want unsightly blemishes or exit-wound scars because Bruce would be taking off her clothes to examine her body for eyesores.

She looked. The top of the hostage's head wasn't bald but looked strange. It had neat little tufts of brown filament, like the hair on a rubber doll's head, planted in rows in the form of a regular hairline.

Since she guessed that by showing her this the terrorists wanted to scare her, she screamed.

"I do swear," Hank said.

"What?" Linda said.

"Nothing."

"Tell me."

"Nothing."

"Just tell me."

"Just tell you what?"

"Just tell me what you do swear."

"That them are about the most scrumpdiddleyumptiousest pair of wheels I have ever laid eyes on. That's all."

"Say that again," Linda said.

"Or you'll what? Or, *and* you'll what?"

"I mean about 'them are about the most . . .' "

"Oh." And he said it.

"One more time." She was posing.

He said it.

When he told her her pussy was scrumptious, she couldn't respond. She was trying to catch her breath. For a minute or so her teeth had been actually chattering.

Later on she was mad that the noise coming out of her mouth sounded so much like whining.

He told her her pussy was lovely.

They did not go to classes or do their assignments. They lost track of time. They did not call the school with excuses.

They went around the corner, just once, to La Primadora, for grapefruit juice, condoms, pizza fajitas, and cigarettes. Linda bought a toothbrush, a sweatshirt, a three-pack of men's Y-front briefs. Willa and Teddy Boy brought them food too. Mark did a load of their laundry.

They took awkward showers together. Rendeck made up awful quatrains about how luscious and plush her skin felt. When the hot water suddenly stopped, Linda screamed.

She liked all the power she had, the control, when her teeth and her lips were slippering over his cock. She also liked tracing the pulsing green veins underneath with the side of her tongue, putting his balls in her mouth, massaging his cock with her nipples while licking his bulletproof stomach.

She liked how his chest heaved, how his spine disappeared in the muscular small of his back, how he writhed on the mattress or floor when she nibbled and tongued him that way.

She liked to stop suddenly, wait, make him ache, make him want, make him ask her to do it some more, and she liked to pretend she might not.

She liked having Hank at her mercy.

Her nickname by Wednesday was Mimi. As in The Screaming Mimis.

"Take it easy, why don't you, you guys," Willa said. "We all thought that you'd been *attacked.*"

Basically Linda apologized, making jokes about nightmares and wolves and cold water, while Hank grinned and bore it.

"I'm ready to run down to see if the person's okay," Bruce was saying, "but you're always afraid to intrude on such ecstasy, in case of, if you know, it wasn't."

"Ouais," said Eusebio. "My thoughts exactly."

"Ecstasy my butt," Muster Mark said. "It sounded like Mimi was getting her fornix ripped out."

"No really," said Bruce, and Linda could tell he was serious. "I couldn't tell which kind it was."

"Oh blown youth!" cried Willa, hand on her heart. "Blasted with ambiguous ecstasy!"

Is Chicago the Warsaw of America, or the Dublin, the Seoul, the Berlin, or the Prague? R. has inquiring mind, and he wants to know.

THE OUTSIDE of SAIC convinced Richard that what went on inside might be worth all the pricey tuition, if not all the trouble. So this was the School of the 'Tute. Long low clean lines, mirrored glass, lots of granite, a moat with a sleek marble fountain reflected back into the building. And right on the lakefront to boot. He assessed its cash value offhand at well into middle eight figures.

Inside, different story. It reminded him more of a fifties-style high school: hallways lined with graffiti-ized lockers and crawling with hairdos, fruitcups of some new fifth gender, and stridently casual attitudes. No wonder the worthless cunt loved it.

The number of people his age or older surprised him. But who were the students and who were the teachers, he wondered. And all this extravagant pussy . . . Excuse me!

The slender young thing he'd bumped into had turned and was glaring at him. She had high Nordic cheekbones and was toting a crocodile briefcase; all her hair but $\sqrt{-i}$ had been shaved from the side of her scalp. When he tried to glare back she just winked, turned around, and was gone.

On the wall near the end of a hallway were two big hexagonal sculptures. The one on the right was spray-painted two shades of black in a slick isometrical pattern to make it appear three-dimensional; below it were four black Helvetica letters, also 3D, spelling GOLD. After ten or twelve seconds, he got it: an ingot, South Africa, blacks. The hexagon on the left was two shades of white and modeled to look like a television. Recessed into the screen part were three (also white, also Helvetica) letters: YEN. The pieces were not uningenious, he thought. They reminded him of the WNE corporate logo. They also convinced him to rethink the nothing design for RBaum.

Somebody tapped his left shoulder. Was it one of the school's strango beauties? He turned to his right. It was Maggie.

"Pretty sharp," Maggie said.

"What, these?"

"You," she said, patting his shoulder.

They kissed.

"Still mad?" he said, suddenly worried again.

She shook her head no and looked brave. "I just want to find out, you know . . ."

Richard nodded.

It was 2:47. Their appointment with Felice Dublon, the Director of Student Affairs, was for 2:45. They sat in a tiny reception area crowded mostly with young Asians who did not, Richard thought, look like students. They did not even look like the type who engaged in affairs.

At 2:49 a green-eyed brunette in a blue business suit appeared out of nowhere, introduced herself as Felice, and ushered them into her office. The director had legs and was younger than Maggie? Hello. And the cut of her suitcoat accented her sleek waist and ass in a way that—forget it. Her office door featured a sox sticker and a drawing of a turkey with a red cancel slash running through it. And those flashy green eyes . . . Was the bottom line good sign or bad sign, he wondered.

Maggie began by explaining (a bad sign) that while she, Maggie Baum, was Linda's Krajacik's "real" mother and sole legal guardian, Richard, her husband, was also—

"I merely pay the tuition."

"Happens all the time," Felice said to Maggie. "Would you folks like coffee or something?"

Nope. No? No thank you. Okay. Down to business. Since she and Maggie had already talked twice on the phone, Dublon was aware of the incident at the Baines and the fact that Linda had not been home since. "She also has not been to class in, let's see . . ." She referred to some sheets on her desk.

"Plus you knew about the week she took off to come with us to Paris?" said Maggie.

"We do and we did," said Dublon. "But I also have talked to all four of her teachers. One of the problems seems to be that she hasn't been to *any* of her classes, even since you got back from Paris."

Typical. "We're especially concerned about the turn of events since, and including, last Friday's opening," Richard said. "What we'd sort of like to know is where your school stands on all this."

He could tell that Dublon had expected this question, so he wasn't surprised when her response seemed rehearsed. The incident had happened off-campus. What was done at the Zara Baines Gallery had not been assigned by a member of the SAIC faculty. The School, therefore, couldn't fairly be expected to assume responsibility—

"Even though one of the admitted participants was one of your graduate students?"

"The gentleman I assume you're referring to," said Dublon, "hasn't been enrolled here for almost two years, though of course we're concerned—"

"Of course," Richard said. "Can you possibly tell us how we might get in touch with him?"

"That we can't do," said Dublon. "Our Registrar's Office is expressly prohibited—"

"What about your Office of Student Affairs? As that seems the most apropos."

"We think the young man she was with went to school here," said Maggie. "Though we don't think she was involved."

"Of course not," Dublon said.

Of course not.

"Could you possibly tell us who *he* is?" said Maggie.

"Who who is?"

"The guy she was with at the Baines," Richard said. "And with or without whom she hasn't been seen ever since."

"You have reason to think he was one of our students?"

"We do," Richard said.

"Mrs. Baum?"

"I don't know," Maggie said. "He certainly looked like he might have—we never got to meet him that night. Plus she doesn't have that many friends. I don't know."

"Do we have to assume that he wasn't?"

"Not necessarily," said Dublon, addressing her answer to Maggie. "Although it might be more productive if we concentrated more on your daughter, since we're certain where *she* was that night, and she is now a student at SAIC—"

"But where she hasn't been once in, how long did you say? Three, four weeks?"

Dublon looked at Maggie, ignored him. "We do, after all, have *some* means for getting in touch with her."

"How?" Maggie said.

Fuck you too, Richard thought. Fuck you two.

"What we usually do in these situations is put up a notice on the doors of her classrooms, requesting that she call your home number." She handed Maggie a small yellow form. "If you'd just fill this out . . ."

Maggie glanced at the form and said, "Sure."

"If we get no response by, say, Monday—"

"I suppose," Richard said, "you'll be needing all this in sextuplicate."

Dublon smiled benignly. "We'll only be needing the one, Mr. Baum." Though please do feel free to fill out as many as makes you feel comfortable.

That does it, you dyke, he decided.

A 2/4 time reggae-calypso heavy on cowbells and rimshots pulsed through the Fenders above Eusebio's bounce-and-slide bass. The chords, played by Hank, were composed of buzzes and screeches sampled on el trains, keyed through a Synclavier 2. Bang and grind, buzz, clack clack clack. Bang, grind and pop, bap bap bap. So on. Teddy played regular chords on a Gibson. Bruce's drum fills were mostly floor toms and high hat. Visa played cowbell and sticks. Sounding like a cross between Van the Man and Mama's Boy Otis, Muster Mark did the singing:

she be Maggie in the middle, yeah she do
play the Maggie in the middle, vap'rize you

do a Maggie in the middle, com tal le vous
ah ah, no way, yeah she do

way she scream like she walk
walk and scream like a left-handed wo-man
ah ah ah ah [girlish screams] no no no
but she walk like, whoa yeah
Lefty jack, Lefty tilt
don't she walk, but she do
yeah she talk like a left-handed girl

she say Lefty don't know from
(she do, yeah she do)
don't know from nobody name Maggie
(hairdo don't matter, no no)
say she don't know nobody like you

want to bite the big hand
(doncha, no no, no no doncha)
hand that feed her
(no no, no no, no no no)
bite that hand
bite that hand jive so badly
bite that hand
bite it hard
yeah she do

she want to be Mag [woman screams] in the middle
she want to be left-handed girl
want to make you wish you never seen her
make you want
make you wish
yeah she do

Linda and three fat black grandmas from the Robert Taylor Homes sang the chorus and screamed. Linda was playing a Gretsch mandolin through a Fuzz Face. The four of them sounded real good.

The crowd in front of the Petrillo Music Shell was spread out for hundreds of yards—all the way back to Lake Shore Drive and Monroe—but was packed in more densely the closer you got to the stage. Chuck Nash and Baxter were there. So was Strobe. They were waiting for Linda to strap on her upside-down Stratocaster and do "Thumbelina," but she wasn't quite in the right mood.

What to do.

Sissy Blackley's first serve sliced in hard toward Richard's backhand, and Richard began to change grips. The ball hit the line, skidded a little, stayed even lower than usual. Bill Blackley moved at the net, pretending—or starting—to poach. Richard stuck out his racquet to block the ball into the alley and burn Blackley good, but the spin on the serve and his lateness made it carom off his brand-new gut stringjob, banana obliquely to his left, and land ten feet out. He cursed himself under his breath.

"Little deuce," Sissy said.

The Blackleys had won the first set 7–5 and were up 4–3 in the second. It was the third round of the West Bank Club's "C" Mixed Doubles Championship. Richard still thought they could win.

"Tough serve," Richard said. "In my next life I'm being born lefty."

Sissy Blackley was better than her husband. Not relatively better for a woman, just better. And Bill wasn't that bad himself. Her serve had more slice, her volleys more accuracy, her groundstrokes more depth and consistency. She was also left-handed. She also looked fifteen years younger. But she still let Bill play the ad court and serve first. Foolishly, Richard concluded. It was why he and Maggie might win.

Her first serve to Maggie was long. Maggie stepped inside the baseline and moved several feet to her left, hoping to get a forehand. She did. She moved her weight into the ball, whipped her wrist over it, driving it crosscourt with topspin. Sissy half-volleyed it back down the middle, but high: a real floater. Was it his or his wife's ball to rip? His forehand, her backhand, though it seemed to be angled toward her. He lunged, then pulled back, still uncertain, while Maggie stepped forward and volleyed. She slashed down and under the ball, aiming for Bill Blackley's toes, but mishit it. The ball warped acutely off the side of her frame, heading out—then nicked the tape, paused, and fell over, landing right next to the line. It was in, Richard thought, but the match was too close for Blackley to give them the call. He could also tell Sissy was pissed.

Bill Blackley stared at the spot. "In by a fuzz," he said finally.

"We'll take it," said Richard.

"Sorry, you guys," Maggie said. "Rather be lucky than good."

"That ceramic's expensive," said Blackley. He winked right at Maggie. "May as well use it, I guess."

"Add out," Sissy said. She was pissed.

Once again her first serve was hard and deep to Richard's backhand, but this time he was better prepared to produce one. Knees bent, shoulders parallel to where he was aiming, he leaned in and drove the ball crosscourt: try volleying *this,* Sissy Suckley! But something went wrong and it plopped halfway up on the net.

"Excuse me while I change my pantyhose," he said, swallowing trios of not-quite-acceptable curses.

"You're excused," Blackley said, winking again right at Maggie.

"Deuce," Sissy said.

VAN GOGH'S LIKE

exaggerate
the essential

leaving (on
purpose) the

obvious vague
plus let yourself

go without thinking

BUT THAT Linda was party to a terrorist act was for Richard the last fucking straw. He'd decided this once and for all on the floor of the Baines, but now was the time for real action. He'd put up with her flagrant attempts to head off his marriage, then taken her along on his honeymoon. He'd honored her mother's request to give her more time to get over the trauma of seeing her father "replaced." He'd paid all the bills and then eaten raw seven-course meals of her shit. Now she had shown him her gratitude by running off with some artfaggot terrorist and further subverting his marriage. It was clear that he had no real leverage, that he'd never have legal authority, and that the schitzed-out frazzle her mother was in had made her incapable of rational action. Neither the cops nor the school were going to do anything either.

Even so, he did not like the looks of James Jackson when they met at Monadknocker Tavern. Jackson's gray shirt was two shades darker than his gray flannel suit; he had big ears, bad teeth, and had not bothered wearing a tie. He was also too young: twenty-three, twenty-four at the oldest. He needed a shave and his hair was too short; he did not have a card or an office. He looked more like one of the artfaggots Linda hung out with than a guy you would hire to find her.

Richard ordered a St. Pauli Girl and asked Jackson "Two?" because he wanted to see him get carded.

Jackson said "One," ordered club soda.

The problem was Jackson came well recommended. According to Lynch, Mel McGuigan, and the two other traders who'd admit they had hired detectives, Jackson was the best guy in town. All four had stories to prove it. The most interesting one involved the thirteen-year-old son of the head guy at Beatrice Foods. The son has been missing for almost eight months. No ransom note, trail of blood, nothing. The cops and the Feds come up empty, as do three or four in-house detectives. The Beatrice guy hires Jackson, he gets back his son in three days. (In one version he rescues him from a porn-film syndicate in San Francisco; in another the kid has been Harold Washington's concubine; in another, Ed Koch's.) The point was that Jackson worked fast and effectively. It sure had sold Richard.

Jackson had told him to bring three recent photos of Linda, a detailed outline of her weekly routine and school schedule, and a tape of her message to Maggie. He also told Richard his fee: thirty-five hundred a week, no expenses.

"You get a half-decent recording, that message?" said Jackson.

Richard handed him an unsealed manila envelope containing the things he had asked for and a cashier's check for thirty-five hundred dollars.

Their drinks came. Jackson looked over the photos. Richard felt very uneasy. It was not what he—

"Hasn't been going to classes since, what?" Jackson said. "This last Friday?"

Richard nodded. He was tempted to say *maybe longer* but did not want to complicate matters.

"Since the thing at the Baines."

"That's correct."

While Jackson made notes on the schedule, Richard told him about the note to call home that Dublon said she'd tape to the doors of the classrooms.

Jackson half-smiled. He looked like Cap Boso, thought Richard.

"That's why I called you," he said.

"You realize what happened that night was a stunt."

"Do now," Richard said. "At that point, we didn't."

Jackson nodded, looked back at the schedule. "No job?"

"Not for two or three months," Richard said. He was guessing.

"No boyfriend."

"None that we know of. Or knew of."

"Only this guy your wife saw her with at the Baines."

"Right."

"Her mother."

"Correct."

"And your wife's not . . ." He waved his veined hand back and forth. "About me."

"That's correct," Richard said. He passed him a card with Lynch's office phone and address. "This is where I'd like you to get in touch with me when you locate her."

"Then what?" said Jackson.

"I'm still working on that," Richard said.

the richard
the hardon
the dick

8

HE'D BEEN up crunching numbers since four, getting nowhere. Trying to stare down his phone hadn't helped too much either. The subsidized EEC wheat was twenty-nine dollars a ton under his, yet Tradex had not made an offer. The exchanges in London and Brussels would close before the opening bell in Chicago. He yawned now, but only because he was dying: he sure wasn't tired or bored. Kerenyev had promised to call him by eight o'clock yesterday morning. None of these prescheduled calls had ever been late by more than an hour or so, and most had come early. He gnawed on his fist and yawned harder.

The Wang churned and ticked, and both printers clattered on softly. Subsidies, strike prices, the triple witching hour spooking the spiraling Dow, Bardeen getting whipsawed in options. So what. He tore off the USU support-and-resistance report. Intermediate high, previous day's high, previous day's close, minor high trend line, inter high trend line, three-day moving averages switch—his eyes glassed over. Without some fresh dirt from Kerenyev, it was all so much calcified dogshit: iridescent purples and yellows, downtown frown brown, tutti-frutti.

He sipped some warm tea and stared out the window. The phone did not ring. Except for the Wang, and his low-pressure system of breath in the mug, it was silent. Wolf Point was glazed with a platinum frost; the river was still mostly black. A two-car Ravenswood train moved south past the Merchandise Mart. It would not be a bad day to walk.

He slid the charts into the shredder. Besides. By this time next year he'd be locked in a Joliet cell with a Rukn or two for a roommate, with plenty of time between gang-bangs to read all the charts ever printed.

Maggie moaned softly and winced. She was dreaming again about snakes, and her closed eyes were remming like mothers. There wasn't much story this time, just a montage of creepy snake weirdness. Right now a series of lateral swiggles, disconnected like sine curves on a CRT screen, were strumming across a tan dune that she realized was really her stomach: the swiggles were sidewinder tracks headed straight for her untan vagina. Then a python had swallowed a live baby boy. The bulge near its tail was stretched thin as a white surgeon's glove, so all the boy's features were clearly revealed. She could tell that he wasn't a girl, for example. That in six or eight years he'd need braces. And by watching his lips and his tongue she could almost tell what he was saying. Then a cobra's head rose up before her, bristling with whiskers and eyebrows and peacock green fur. Its long red forked tongue flicked out between fake werewolf fangs dripping with also-fake venom and blood and saliva. The thing was, the cobra could only attack her in very slow motion; she was hypnotized, though, so she wouldn't be able to dodge even slow-motion strikes to her face—but, since the venom was fake and a cobra could never grow peacock green fur, she was safe.

The dream made more sense when she shifted her head on the pillow. She was shopping with Linda at Field's. The stores along Michigan Avenue were decked out with Santas and baubles and life-sized Nativity scenes, so they must have been shopping for Christmas. Linda had just charged (to Richard) three tickets to a play about struggling Vietnamese wheat farmers, the same gala family extravaganza that the Goodman Theater put on every year at this time; it was such a hot ticket, in fact, that she assumed Linda must have pulled something untoward in order to get hold of three. She also assumed that the third ticket was for Michael, since Linda still always insisted that her father be included in their holiday plans.

This made her sad, and she told Linda so.

"Get a clue," Linda said. "It's for Richard."

"Of course," she said, smiling, doing her best to conceal her surprise and relief.

"Now the three of us can go as one rich happy family of Baums," Linda said. "And besides, we both gotta be there to check out the look on his face when he sees this one scene."

"Which scene is that?"

Linda said coyly, "You'll see."

Then both of them said "I'm afraid" at exactly the same time, so they hooked their left pinkies together.

"Make a wish," Linda said.

"Crack a dish."

"Kill a fish," Linda said.

Then one of the Santas asked Linda to sit on his lap.

Linda blushed hotly. "You, wish!" she said, slapping the Santa's fat face, twice, first—*You*—with the back of her hand, then—*wish!*—with the front, very hard.

"Then how about your friend?" said the Santa. His cheeks were bright rose from the slaps. "She been naughty or nice, would you say, this past fiscal year?"

"Mostly naughty," said Linda. "But she isn't my friend, Saint. Piss off." She cocked her left hand as if she were going to slap him again. When he cringed and shrank back, she patted the side of her hair. "Ho ho ho ho, if you know what I mean."

The Santa did not. "Your sister?" he wondered.

"Nooo-oo-o . . ."

"You're sure?"

"Guess again," Linda urged.

"Her mother, I'm afraid," she admitted.

The Santa refused to believe this. She repeated that it was the case. He protested that surely she fibbed. A crowd of young men had gathered, shouting BULL! and I'LL BET! and NO WAY! They could not be convinced that a woman who still looked like *her* had a nineteen-year-old daughter. She showed them her driver's license, but they claimed it was fake, that she carried it just to buy gin. She told them exactly where she had been (in seventh grade, twelve, in her sixth-period sex education class at St. Rita's) when Kennedy was assassinated, but they introduced notarized documents and sworn affidavits from nuns establishing that St. Rita's didn't *offer* sex ed in those days. "And besides," one guy said, "we all know it could've been Bobby." In the end she was forced to disrobe, bring out her caliper, and extrapolate her percentage of body fat by gauging the flab near the tops of her thighs, on the lower part of her abdomen, and in other embarrassing places.

"And look at these crow's feet," she said, wiping off her foundation with Kleenex.

"BUT LOOK AT THOSE CHEEKBONES!" they shouted.

"Or what gravity's done to my bosom!"

"Even so," said the best-dressed and handsomest shopper. He winked. "If you curtsied on *my* face, I promise I wouldn't say boo."

"ME EITHER!"

"ME NEITHER!"

"ME TOO!"

"You wouldn't say boo?" Linda said. Her left fist was cocked.

"To Santa, I mean," said the guy, backing off.

The Santa said, "That mean the answer is yes?"

"Oh," Linda said, to the guy. "That makes it okay then, I guess."

The guy and the Santa winked at each other. Then the guy winked at Linda, and Linda winked back at the guy. Then the guy winked at *her* . . .

Where was Richard, to save her, she wondered, or Michael, now that she needed him, either of them, more than ever.

Linda leaned back in her chair. Her heels were propped on her dresser and her weight was exactly in balance. If she leaned back another degree, she'd tip over. She knew that her father was standing behind her, but she'd made up her mind not to notice.

She was conjuring up her reflection in a new plastic folder the color of Tanqueray bottles; it was also about as translucent. She'd bought it to cover the autobiographical essay which was due in three hours, at nine, but which wasn't quite done yet. It worked like a green funhouse mirror, only softer and smaller, more private. It frustrated her, but she liked all the ways she controlled it. She'd been at it for forty-five minutes.

She was back at Wolf Point only to pick up some clothes and her schoolbooks; she would move out the other stuff later. She was saying goodbye to her short happy life as a rich girl, toasting Paris, fast cars, and tuition with tap water and wintergreen Certs. Richard was up but had not gone to work yet. She would not talk to Maggie until she could get her alone. If he didn't leave soon, she might have to come back tomorrow.

When she made the green plastic concave her face would appear right side up, upside down when she made it convex. What she wanted to do was get it faced both ways at once (it would make such a great album cover!) by controlling the curve of the plastic. She figured the trick was to catch it somehow in between merging curves. She'd come close a few times, but apparently some big law of physics declared that it couldn't face both ways at once. The best she had managed so far was diagonal pairs of her faces that warped back and forth between quadrants: upper right/face upside down, lower left/face right side up, then vice versa, vice versa, vice versa.

As he strolled down LaSalle Street in milky dawn light, Richard was buttonholed dead in his tracks by an ornery, phlegm-laden drawl.

"Hey, *buttwop!*"

He'd turned and acknowledged the drawler—he *still* always fell for this gambit—before he could stop himself. Shit!

"That's right, Señor Charmin. Must be real clear who we're talkin' to."

Richard found himself surrounded by two dozen farmers: all denim and camouflage, feedcaps and sideburns. The guy who'd been doing the talking hawked and spat.

"My name, case you're wonderin', is Wayne Moreland of Puxico, Missoura." His tobacco-stained, snot-studded hawker was clinging to the tip of the carefully polished left tassel of Richard's right oxblood loafer. "And we certainly all know who *you* are."

"I'm—"

"And we know what your question is, too. Your question is, 'Hey, what's your problem?' "

"But—"

"Well I'm here to say what's our problem. *You* are our problem, my friend. You are our *whole* dadburn problem."

"Yeah," sneered another huge farmer. "What's the frequency *now,* Kenneth Baum?"

"Richard," he said.

"Yeah, whatever."

Wayne said, "You hear me?"

He did.

"Because, *bwah,* we are talkin' to you."

His bladder ached badly, but he managed to say, "I believe you exaggerate, Wayne."

"That so? How is that?"

"Um, when, you know, you say I'm your problem."

"You call me a *lahr,* Dick Baum!?"

"Not really. It's just that it's not all that—"

The farmers moved closer, hawking and drawling and clenching large placards and fists, contracting the circle around him. He could smell the manure on their boots; he could taste their tobacco-stained breath. They had not laid a hand on him yet, but he knew they could tell he was scared. Just like dogs, he reflected.

A snarling white wolfhound appeared at the end of a chain. Richard blinked. Couldn't help it. He couldn't back up, so he'd blinked. But blinking in these situations was never a good thing to do, and he knew he'd regret it real soon.

Moreland meantime had unfolded a printout and was reading a list of complaints to which Richard supposed he should listen. Richard's kind, Richard's ilk, buttwipes and sphincters and dickless-whore arbitrageurs like RBaum were selling contracts for wheat that they never had owned to begin with, *that did not even fucking exist yet.* This was, at least should be, impossible. This was immoral. This sucked. This was artificially depressing the prices the farmers could get for their crops. The farmers could not pay their debts. The banks were foreclosing on loans they had made to the farmers. The farmers were losing their land. They couldn't be farmers no more.

"That's tellin' him, Whine!" drawled a juicy young blonde. She had bangs in her lashes and extra long wheels slanting down from the hem of a half-zippered white denim micro into black-pink-and-blue cowgirl booties; the black parts, he knew, were Ugandan crocodile, the pink parts were patent, and the blue parts were finest Corinthian minotaur. Whoa, mama! he thought. Could feedcaps like these guys have wives looked like *that?* Must be one of those "farmer's daughters," he told himself, smirking. She curtsied on *my* face I sure as heck wouldn't tell papa. But then, when she'd moved a step closer, he could tell it was actually Linda. What was *she* doing up at this hour, he wondered. And where had she *been?* And then he concluded it figured.

"Tell him some more, Mr. Moreland!" she cheered.

Moreland told him. "You," meaning Richard, he said, "on the other hand, really don't produce much of anything, do you?"

He shook his head, nodded, then shrugged. "Depends how you look at it, Wayne."

Moreland showed him his cabbage-sized fist, then extended his thick index finger. Even from two feet away, you could make out every last hitch, swirl, and loop of its print, it was so damned enormous and grimy. "You don't produce shit!" Moreland boomed.

"Actually, that's about *all* he produces," said Linda. "And can that asshole stink up a bathroom!"

She winced, held her nose, and the farmers all hooted.

"That about figures," said Moreland.

"Ick-hay ubique," said one of the farmers. He was wearing a camouflaged World War II helmet and had blood running out both his ears, but his pig-Latin rhyme scheme was flawless.

Moreland ignored him. "And so what we are going to do," he told Richard, "is shut down your slick operation."

This got the farmers excited again, as did stepdaughter's strenuous cheerleading. She executed three expert back flips while waving two pom-poms, then cartwheeled right into hard splits. Richard got jostled but didn't fight back; he just watched her, entranced. The farmers were crowding him harder, applauding for Linda, shaking their fists in his face. Some of them squatted like catchers. Others were standing on tiptoe with their palms in the air. A third group was crouched halfway over. Then all of a sudden it hit him: they were psyching themselves to attack him by making a wave that was "split."

"And we're going to do it *right now!*" Moreland shouted.

"YOU BET!" they responded.

"BID TWENTY!"

This threat heartened Richard immensely. He'd been scared about shitless a minute ago, but it had finally dawned on him that Moreland was bluffing. He also had realized he *liked* being crowded. There also was simply no way, after all, that this deluded little crew of dungareed dungkickers, these *farmers,* could close down such a bastion of American capitalism as the Chicago Board of Trade. If push came to shove, the Chicago police would serve and protect their best interests; in the unlikely event that they couldn't, you called out the National Guard. A mismatch of major proportions was what we were talking here, right? So the fact that the farmers had threatened to do such a thing made them seem just a little pathetic.

"We know not seems!" Linda cheered, vaulting sideways this time into splits. There were groans and grabbed crotches when she bounced up and down on her vulva, but she grinned and kept cheering. It *seemed* like it hurt, but it didn't.

"WE KNOW NOT SEEMS!" came the cheers.

"Bwah, I'm still talking to you!" Moreland said. "Pay attention!"

Richard smiled. The poor dude had written a check with his mouth that his raw farmer's ass couldn't cash. It was all so incredibly typical.

"What you girls fail to understand," he said boldly, "is that commodities exchanges don't *set* prices—they merely *reflect* them. Any attempt to close down the CBOT would jeopardize the only real markets you farmers still *have* for your crops."

"What about farmer's markets!" shrieked Linda. She was clearly hysterical. "This is just typically cryptic Richard Baum bearshit. Don't listen!"

The only way of dealing with Linda, he knew, was to ignore her. He did so. "In fact," he said, raising his (clean, well-trimmed, civilized) finger at Moreland, "if you girls would take the opportunity to educate yourselves as to how these commodities instruments operate—learn things like hedging, the difference between implied and historical volatility, how to read your Fibonacci numbers, decipher the ratios between your three- and ten-day moving averages—you just might find them a useful tool for averting the very price volatility you came here to bitch about."

"But, but," said Moreland, harumphing.

"But *no-oo-ooo,*" Richard said. "Instead what you do is you plant wall-to-wall, borrow yourself into a hole to buy up more land than you can possibly hope to afford, let alone efficiently manage, then hide behind Chapter 12 or come crying to us when—"

"Would you listen to this guy?!" Linda said. "He's in cahoots with the Russians, the Soviet Union, the same Evil Empire that subsidized the slaughter of my father and fifty-five thousand-odd other American soldiers in South Vietnam nineteen years ago!"

"Am not," Richard countered.

"ARE TOO!" cheered the farmers in unison.

"Even before I was *born,* " Linda sobbed.

"Shit, change the subject why don't you," he said. Had she sussed out his deal with Kerenyev? "Although while we are on it, would she have us believe that without Russian aid to the North Vietnamese, our invincible young GIs would have 'nailed the coonskin to the wall'?" He snorted. "Is *that* what she'd have us believe?"

"Exactly what sort of *coon*skin you talkin' about, Mr. Baum?" Moreland said.

"LBJ's coonskin."

"Words, words, words," Linda sighed.

"Oh, speak!" interjected the farmer with the World War II helmet, to Richard. "If thou art privy to thy country's fate, which happily foreknowing may avoid . . ."

Richard ignored him. "Mac Bundy's in Saigon same time's Kosygin's up there in Hanoi, both of them trying to get Ho Ho Ho Chi Minh to agree to some sort of reasonable trade-off."

"Exactly what sort of *trade*-off you talkin' about, Mr. Baum?"

"Well, for one thing, our surplus wheat in exchange for their leverage on Ho and Hanoi, to make them back down a small bit in Geneva. Most folks agree that something like this might've worked."

"Yeah, like who?"

"Well, as Kissinger pointed out later—Henry Kissinger? I assume that you've heard of him—as Kissinger said after Nixon took over, American wheat was *far* more important national-securitywise to the Rooskies than a bunch of zip gooks ever were. Eventually Brezhnev understood this—all too well, one might add—and it is upon this very understanding that our current complex but essentially viable international relationship is founded."

"Yeah, right," Moreland said. "We're supposed to ship Brezhnev *our* wheat, let him feed his cowed masses, then trust him to persuade Ho Chi Minh to do something the man has been fighting for thirty-five years to prove he is *not* gonna do? Who's being naïve, Mr. Baum?"

Hmm, Richard thought. And how come he's losing his drawl?

"There isn't that much wheat in the *world,* Mr. Baum."

"At least we could've got Brezhnev to stop supplying them with SAM missiles and radar."

"What's radar got to do with it?"

"What's radar got to do with it?! Don't you farmers ever watch the MacNeil-Lehrer News Hour!?"

"Just answer the question, McButtwipe," said Linda.

"That's right, McFarland," said Moreland.

"Fine, fine," he said. "Radar's the radio waves the NVA gunners beamed up to bounce off our bombers during Operation Niagara, or something like that. Or the Phantom runs over Khesanh. Their very own gook SDI."

The farmers convinced by this answer seemed to outnumber the farmers who weren't.

"But don't, please, be calling me gook," said a short, bony, slanty-eyed farmer, politely.

"I'm sorry," said Richard. "No, really. Forgive me. I am. So but the point is that Gorbachev always had plenty of—"

"Who?" Moreland said. "You mean Brezhnev?"

"Who'd I just say?"

"Garbachev."

"Sorry. Forgive me," said Richard. "Meant Brezhnev. The point is that Brezh—"

"Hold it," said Moreland. "Ain't Garbachev the fella with the map a Vietnam tattooed right up there on his forehead?"

"That's *Gor*bachev."

" 'Swhat I *said,*" Moreland said. "Mean, Jesus, 'sgotta prove *somethin'* you got the map a the country they're supplyin' the radar an' stuff to plastered right there on their general fuckin' secretary's *head.*"

"Good point," Richard said, somewhat baffled. "He used to be a wheat farmer himself, by the way: forty-six through fifty, I believe. Just before—"

"I thought it was a map of Northwest Afghanistan," said Linda, "and that Stingers were now the big issue."

"I'll make a big stinger the issue," said Richard.

"Buzz, buzz," she said, flipping him off.

"Wouldn't you love to," he said. "I mean, am I having a premonition or a déjà vu here or what?"

She smiled. "I'd exhaust you, you grotty old wankoff."

"Like Edge?" he retorted. "Besides. It would cost me my wife's love. So fuck off."

"Al*leged,*" she said. "Mark it. Al*leged* love."

"You say so," he said. "But mark this: you begrudge me my rake-off, I notice, yet would Amex your sprees, plus tuition and fees, without groaning."

"Please, spare me!" she cried. "Having made your big killings on AIDS stocks . . ."

"I was bullish on latex because of your ilk, not mine own. Them thar boots you wear cost me a hedging. To buy back my shorts now would—"

"Piss off, spineless sludge, or these boots'll do more than just nudge your weak spine, if you've got one!"

"Tell him, Nancy!" yelled one of the farmers.

Richard (aside): "The bitch wants chap'roning, but piss off my Maggie I'll nary. Detective? She never would budge on that issue."

"But now just hold your water a second," said Moreland. "Just realized: this Garbachev fella weren't even their president then."

The farmers all nodded and spat. They agreed.

"And weren't the fella 'fore him named, like, Masturbov?"

The farmers all nodded and shrugged. They forgot.

"Anyway anyway anyway," said Richard. "As I was saying, Brezhnev had plenty of leverage, if only he'd wanted to use it. He'd just *proved* it, in fact, by wiping out Dubcek's supporters in Prague that same spring."

"But ain't the bottom line here the young biological fathers we sent off to die in the jungle when perhaps there were other ways of pacifyin' them slopes and *still* keepin' our markets in Russia?"

"Good question," said Richard. "Because while personally I regret the loss of human life as much as the next man, the fact is we *had* to spend a few grunts in the jungle in order to waste a few slopes, this in order to win the hearts and minds of the indigenous Vietnamese peoples, or, failing that, to search and destroy those we couldn't wherever we happened to find them: in their huts, tunnels, paddies, wherever. The problem was that, as the siege of Khesanh got more and more hairy, General Moreland was preparing to actually use—"

"*West*moreland, I believe, was his name," Moreland said.

"Right, right," said Richard. "Whoever. The point's that West*more*land was itching to use tactical nukes on those four, five divisions of zips who'd surrounded Khesanh."

"I didn't know that," said Linda.

"I'm stunned," Richard said. "Because the parallels with Dienbienphu had Westmoreland just freaked out completely. When LBJ vetoed the nukes, his only alternative was Operation Niagara, using mucho conventional ordnance and spending some grunts mopping up. Unpleasant but necessary, unless you'd've preferred him to—"

"Nuclear weapons are *never* the way, Mr. Baum, but—"

"I agree."

"But," Moreland said, pointing his finger again. "And it's a very big but, I'm afraid."

"Lay it on me then, Pee Wee," said Richard.

"This here girl's father was one of those grunts, as you call them, whose lives were laid down to uphold the principles you so smugly and comfortably count on in order to sell off *our* wheat."

Linda sighed. "What can I tell you?" she said. "It's the new Age of Avarice. And this mother's All Fucking World."

"What can I say?" Richard said. "I mean of course I feel awful about—"

"Yeah, I'm sure we're all very impressed by—"

"Furthermore, by using *our* wheat as a bargaining chip, the administration raised farmers' hopes about gaining new markets, so *naturally* we all bought more land, new equipment, and planted a few extra acres."

"A few, Mr. Moreland?"

"Well . . ."

"And besides: in seventy-two you ended up selling them seventeen million tons of your wheat, more than anyone realized till *after* the deal had gone down."

"That was *you* guys that let us get robbed!" Moreland whined.

"Which is ironically why I continue to maintain the importance of working hand-in-glove with the Exportkhleb buyers in London, in Brussels, as well as right here in Beirut on the Lake."

A cold-eyed young man in a cheap navy suit cleared his

throat. "I would remind you, Mr. Baum, that using insider information, most especially if it has been obtained from KGB field agents posing as Exportkhleb buyers, in order to encourage and subsequently profit from shifts in the price structure of certain foodstuffs, would not be looked upon very favorably by the Department of Justice."

"Or the SEC, I might add," said a second cheap-blue-suited man.

"Or the FSLIC," said a third.

"Or the KGB, I might add. Or the National Security Council. Or the CB of T."

"Or the IR of S, of the IA of C, or the S of the AI of C . . ."

"Or the FB of I, I might add."

"Or a ghost with a fucking agenda," said Linda. "For 'tis sport to have the enginer hoist with his own petard, Mr. *Baum.*"

"Actually," said Moreland, not drawling at all, "the possible prosecutorial permutations are slightly unlimited." He giggled.

"Call Pam Zekman why don't you!" yelled someone sarcastically.

"Yeah!"

"Plus the weirdest thing is, this asshole actually believes he's pretending, I think," Linda said.

"Wha?"

"Huh?"

"Duh?"

"What!"

The man from the Justice Department said nothing. He was too busy glaring at Richard. One of his assistants was recording what Richard was saying. The other was taking his picture.

"What's this got to do with the price of our hard red spring wheat in the USSR?" someone asked.

"Yeah. Or some grunt getting greased in Khesanh."

"Or the price of wild rice in some paddy."

"Or the plight of some small family farmers."

The blue-suited men didn't answer. They had what they'd come for. They split.

When he was sure they were gone, *very* sure, Richard said, "Shit, change the subject why don't you. Because the fact is, sirrah, that the Wayne Morelands of this world have never seriously even *considered* the possibility that, churning and burning aside, there is ample opportunity for one and all in the pits to achieve what one wants to achieve, i.e., financial security for oneself and one's stepfamily."

"But what small family farmers believe," Moreland said, "is that this country will *be* in the pits, will be the pits *period,* if this sort of ubiquitous commodification isn't curbed quickly."

"That's just not the case," Richard said. "Go ask the families at Cargill or General Mills."

"Hey, ick-hay ubique, okay?" Linda said.

"Well *I* say ogwash-hay," said Maggie, who was suddenly standing by Richard. She was wearing her scarlet Ellesse triple-ply terrycloth running shorts, her white Fila brushed-cotton tanktop, and her navy ROOS sweatband. She must have been out for a jog, Richard figured, secretly lagging behind him in order to surprise him with a last-minute kiss for good luck before he arrived at the Board. In any event, she sure was a sight for sore eyes. Chest still heaving from running, hands on her full but trim hips, she demanded to know, "What's the aggro, you berks? What it is?"

The farmers all gaped at her Teflon-smooth femoral acreage, her Ellesse's succinct scarlet plushness, then upraised their covetous eyes to the synclinal oval of sweat on her tanktop—to the saucy yet thimbular nubbins protruding tangential through loose moist white single-ply weave to that still-heaving, sweet-smelling ring. One farmer whistled respectfully. The rest were dead silent. They were all set to hear this girl *out.*

Richard introduced her as "Th' imperial jointress to this warlike state, whom, as 'twere with a defeated joy, with an auspicious *and* a dropping eye, with mirth in funer-al and with dirge in marri-age, His Highness hath taken to wife."

"Yeah, tell us about it, *M. Baum,*" Linda said.

"With pleasure," said Maggie. She established firm eye contact with Moreland, and then, as she spoke, with each of the farmers in turn. "Because what *real* men like Richard here do is provide us a viable marketplace for buyers and sellers of foodstuffs, creating some much-needed pricing stability. Think of the American housewife why don't you for once in your life! Think of the US of A for a change! The Chicago Board of Trade is not a casino. I repeat: it is *not* a casino. It simply provides an arena for buyers and sellers to gather and trade your commodities; all they are doing is providing a little liquidity, *whatever* Paul Volcker might say. Can't you manure artists dig that? Because if the FTC, the ERA, the IRS, the EEC, the SEC, the SSC, the EROS, the CBOT, the SAIC, the CFTC, or the Fed were to accede to even a single one of your silly demands, it would nefariously jeopardize the delicate infrastructure of the entire agricultural economy, not to mention your hard-won world markets, as well as an untold number of ancillary sectors of the West's cherished free-market system. Or look at it this way: you seen any mangy Shiite camel-jockeying *mullahs* trading commodities lately? *Huh?* Didn't think so. And remember how long half you chumps waited in line for a gallon of gas for your tractors back in the seventies. Just think how long you would wait for some *food.* There'd be riots, acts of out-and-out terrorism, and possibly much much much worse. Why, without men like Richard . . ."

There were cheers from the traders who'd arrived and surrounded the farmers. Most were long wheat, and they'd all had the foresight to put on identical sheepskin-lined trenchcoats so Richard could spot them as targets. They also were wearing the trenchcoats because it had started to drizzle while Maggie was making her pitch, and now it was coming down hard. A crack team of Rangers in camouflage wetsuits arrived and arrested the farmers; the sentences they would receive were not gonna be any picnic. Then the sun came back out. LaSalle Street was now back to normal.

Except for one thing. Linda was whaling on Maggie with her fists and her fingernails, and Maggie was forced to fight back. Richard grabbed Linda's shoulder. All he was doing was trying to pull them apart, but what happened was that four-fifths of Linda's bulky wool cheerleader's sweater unraveled somehow in his hand, leaving her torso clothed only by the turtleneck collar, the elasticized waistband, and tattered ribbed cuffs on her wrists. Thus unencumbered, she pressed her advantage on Maggie, viciously ripping her terrycloth outfit to shreds. Both were now more or less naked. But instead of covering themselves up or conceding, as he'd hoped and expected, they flew at each other with retrebled fury, using wristlocks and thumbholds and whatnot, dumping and flipping each other, executing Huey-propeller-style bodyslams and half-gainer kneedrops onto each other's temples and tracheae.

Round one was wild but dead even. Both had weighed in at 112, with 63-inch reaches. The prebout caliper skinfold had shown Linda's percentage of body fat to be 5.67 percent less than Maggie's, but in structure and texture and amplitude their buttocks and breasts were identical. And both were still blond, undefeated.

As round two began there were whoops, hoots, and whistles from the men in the trenches, nine-tenths of whom were bidding big dollars (on margin) against the possibility that Maggie would come out on top. They also made clear their allegiance by chanting the baritone chorus from Jan and Dean's cover of "Linda." As the match referee, Richard was prohibited by SEC statute from suspending the trading or breaking the fight up. There was also no way he could keep all these dickfors from gawking. Besides: whatever he did would be seen as an effort to either grope his "poor" stepdaughter or keep his new bride's spread position from losing more leverage. Because as round two wore on, Maggie had managed to get herself tangled in the ring's too-loose ropes. Bent over just about double, with an arm wrenched behind her back one way and her hair being yanked in the other, she was helpless and cruelly exposed.

As he pondered his options, Richard was clipped from behind by a trader who'd gone long on Linda, then checked through the ropes to the sidewalk. The stampede was on. He drew himself up in the fetal position, but this didn't keep them from viciously kicking his spine. Such kicks, he knew, if delivered at just the wrong angle, could cripple or kill him, even if the person who was doing the kicking had on loose-fitting loafers with tassels, but he made up his mind not to give them the satisfaction of hearing him holler or whimper. For a while it surprised him how little it hurt to be kicked in the spine, but then something told him the reason he felt so courageous was that he hadn't felt anything period, or been able to move, since the reinforced toe of a certain black-pink-and-blue cowgirl bootie had been planted with murderous leverage in his second coccygeal vertebra.

And still the longs wouldn't let up. If anything, their kicks now came faster and harder. He'd be dead in a matter of seconds, he realized, and this sent a strange sense of peace coursing through him. He knew things these longs simply couldn't, and that was enough. The market would still move against them that day, whether RBaum was dead or still kicking.

He staggered into the bathroom and switched on the light. He was still half asleep, the last tattered frames of his dream blasted white by fluorescent exposure. That he hadn't been paralyzed was, he supposed, a relief, but he still had to piss rather fiercely. He yanked down his jockeys and lifted the seat up, then stood there for several long seconds, wincing and aching and waiting. His dick was absurdly erect, its green and blue veins pulsing up through its right-tilted, purple-tipped arc. And it *hurt.* The problem was that he couldn't piss through it until it subsided a little, but it wouldn't subside till he pissed.

He contorted himself over the bowl, hunkering sideways and squinting, coaxing his bladder, aiming himself in the general direction of down. Didn't work. There were three dusty floaters—no, four—in his vitreous humor; he blinked them away and kept straining. He tried to relax for a while, tried forcing the issue again, then thought about waking up Maggie—about making the best of this painful and strange vascularity. Hmm. He barely remembered a tenth of the dream anymore, but enough of this tenth to deduce where the hardon had come from. Or was it vice versa, he wondered.

Back in the bedroom, as his rods realigned in the darkness, he could gradually make out the sine curve of Maggie's swell torso in warped planes of eiderdown quilt. He stood there, still hard, marveling over how well she'd defended his honor, watching the quilt fall and rise as she breathed. The side of her face shone in moonlight.

A man's head appeared next to hers. It had long straight blond hair and a mustache. With its wide mouth and eyes it was laughing at Richard's erection. Richard hung tough for exactly one second, letting everything register—*gaa!*—

believing his eyes absolutely but determined to face down his fear, then screamed without making a sound.

The man had sat up in the bed—no, he was hovering, legless, above Maggie's head. He was handsome, with well-defined pecs and abdominals, square bulging shoulders and biceps. And worse: his enormous erection dwarfed Richard's with laughable ease; its uncontained throbbing looked forged out of live ammunition. He was roaring and choking and sobbing with desperate and echoing laughter.

Richard's mouth made a whimpering sound; as scared as he was, it still shamed him, and he knew he could not take it back. He heard Maggie murmur his name, saw her reach back to find him. He gulped. Alternating current buzzed up his shins, then blazed through his rib cage, dropping him down to one knee. His left arm felt hot. He was having a stroke and was going to die. He was freezing.

"Richard?"

He huddled and clutched himself, panting, then staggered back upright. His scrotum and penis had shrunk to the size of three chestnuts. He was trying to calm himself down, to respond to his wife, but he couldn't.

"Look at this guy," Maggie said. She had turned and was up on one elbow, awake and a little amused. "Are you nuts?"

Her face was in shadow, his own, but Richard could tell from the sound of her voice she was laughing. He knew who the blond guy was too. He was—

"Honey?"

He shivered.

Angel will watch over us.
Angel?
I can see the space
to live with you.
Why not staff the past
above, the future
below, the present
plunging through us.
No answers prepared!

9

STROBE HAD made five decent drawings in powder blue chalk on the board: a strip of film, an open book, a painting, a CDT screen, a guitar. "*Nothing* could be further from the truth," he was saying as Linda sat down near the back. She was barely five minutes late, but he was already up to full speed. "Pun intended. It's like what gets lost when we translate a spoken, let alone a sung, double negative. 'I can't get no satisfaction,' " he sang. "Logically, the two minus signs will cancel each other—" he held up his index fingers, crooked but parallel, then crossed them— "forming the logical positive, 'I can get satisfaction,' but of course that is not what's implied. 'You get what you need' might be closer."

She took out her notebook. It was the last day of class before the final exam. She doubted she'd ever catch up, but she still—

"Another example," said Strobe. "The case of the double

affirmative, 'Yeah yeah,' which means something along the lines of 'I *don't* think so' or 'I *don't* want to hear about it.' "

A chorus of yeah-yeahs rose up.

"That's more than two," Strobe responded. "Too confusing. And now that you've gotten them 'out' of your system, I infer that I'd better continue. We've got too much to cover for this—"

"Okay," said Paul. "We don't think so."

Ha ha.

Where was Hank? They had met at Lake Street and taken the el down together this morning. He had something to do at the foundry while she checked the Student Employment Office about a job at the State of Illinois Gallery that a friend of a friend of one of his friends had just quit; she had gotten the number and made an appointment for Wednesday. Their plan for today was to meet in Strobe's classroom at one. So where was he?

"But let's not forget the main point," said Strobe, getting serious, "which is that in Einstein's world everything that happens has a reason, even if you don't know what it is."

"Do you," sang Gordon basso-nasally, "Mr. Jones," an awful, obnoxious Bob Dylan.

Strobe just ignored him. "This is where it starts to get spooky," he said. "Because the term Einstein coined for the forces he hypothesized would eventually explain all these gaps is Gespensterfeld—ja?—or Gespensterwellen. Both words are found in the letters he wrote to Niels Bohr." He turned and wrote *Bohr* on the board, eliciting take-offs on real and feigned boredom. "In English, then, ghost waves," he said, printing the term in block letters. "Even better, the French call it *densité de presence.*" He wrote the French phrase, kept on talking. "Mathematically they are represented by"

$$\Psi^2 = \text{amplitude}^{\,2} = \text{probability}$$
$$\text{probability} = \text{possibility}^{\,2}$$
$$\Psi > c$$

"their most extravagant attribute being—and please get this down—that they are *superluminal,* i.e., they move faster than 671 million miles an hour per hour." He circled the lowermost symbols. "At velocities greater than *c.* And which, if my gradebook is any indication, is a few mph. quicker than some folks in *this* class are moving."

Hands went up. Groans. He acknowledged both sorts of response with eye contact, nods, but wasn't quite ready to call on them yet—a sign, Linda guessed, that what he was saying would probably be on the final.

"What does this mean? If ghost waves exist it would mean that, just as a film or a piece of music can be played backward, or a painting be seen in a mirror, subatomic particles could send messages to one another *backward through time.* They could respond to each other nonlocally, to use the pro physicists' term."

Most people wrote this down furiously, but Linda just listened.

"It happens, it *doesn't* happen, depends on, if Einstein's correct, a kind of vague, veiled, or virtual reality. On ghost waves." He circled the Ψ on the board. "Or, continuing our earlier notion of Keatsian negative capability, they define what does happen in new, much more radical ways."

"What about the other way around?" Wanda said.

"Good question," said Strobe. "In other words, you're saying, can past things occur in the present."

"Or *re*cur," said Wanda.

"And if so," said Strobe, "how's it different."

"Good question," said Wanda.

"The present, of course, being the now, the here, through which future things plunge to the past."

"Riiight," Wanda said.

"Though is 'plunge' the best word for what happens?" Strobe sounded suddenly dazed, off someplace else by himself. "Is *that* what we're doing here? Plunging?" Good question. "Because elsewhere he has Stephen say—this is Joyce again, right—that it might be the other way around: that Life, that Reality, just may be the Afterlife of the soul. Granted that Stephen is saying this in order to rationalize not paying back the pound he has mooched . . . Nonetheless, as we weave and unweave our bodies, their molecules shuttled to and fro, so does the artist weave and unweave his own image. As a mole on my breast is still where it was when I was born, though my entire body has been three times rewoven, he says, so through the unquiet ghosts of our parents do we now see the world, i.e., do we now see the world *as an artist.*"

Without being called on, someone up front asked, "So what's all this got to do with that trip out to Fermilab?"

Dead silence. Strobe closed his eyes, shook his head.

"A bad way to answer such questions," he said, "would be to point out that beams of antimatter produced at our sister facility are central to the feasibility, for example, of the SDI program. That an antimatter bomb containing a single pellet of antihydrogen weighing a millionth of a gram could vaporize the Loop in a tenth of a second. No, faster. That it would be, in the typically redundant words of Cap Weinberger, 'a highly lethal kill mechanism.'"

Okay . . .

"Another way to answer would be to suggest that what particle physicists and artists both do is track the transformations between physical reality and our inner experiences. Okay? That neither are in the business of giving out too many answers these days. They describe things in ways that make us all more aware of more possibilities—of more, and more interesting, questions."

"So—" But the person who'd said it was shushed by the class. Strobe merely shrugged. He seemed to be out of his trance. Had he plunged, Linda wondered. Was he plunging?

"So there very well might be a parallel between the ways the subatomic physical world and the human imagination both work. Does that sentence parse?"

"Not really," said Hank. He'd slipped in and taken the seat behind Linda.

"Didn't think so," said Strobe.

"That one parses," said Hank. "Implied subject. I."

"Danke," said Strobe.

Hank squeezed her shoulder. People had turned and were staring. She blushed but did not touch his hand. He let go.

Strobe was writing:

what do you see?
what does that make you see?
what does *that* make you see?
dot dot dot

"The anomalon particle," he was saying, plunging back into his trance, "the zeta particle, the aesthetics of assimilation, the voodoo priestess's iridescent rainbowlike python with its tail in its mouth standing for the great big wide world . . ." He tapped what he'd written with chalk: tap tap tap. "Dot dot dot. The longer this list gets—and perhaps we could change *see* to *get*—the more potent the object has turned out to be, the more pregnant the mind of its audience."

"And vice versa," said Hank.

"And vice versa," said Strobe. "Any questions?"

People were too busy writing. How pregnant were they, she wondered. Or was she.

"Okay then," said Strobe, in a hurry. "One more quotation before we review for the final. From Barthes."

She put up her hand. She wanted to know if the quote would be taken from one of the handouts she'd missed. If so—

Strobe ignored her. "Fashion, read physics, resolves the passage from the abstract body to the real body of its reader in three ways." He held up one finger, read slowly. "The first solution consists of proposing an ideal incarnate body, i.e., that of the model, the cover girl." He paused and looked up—right at Linda, it seemed, making a point of her absences, of ignoring her hand, of knowing all about her and Hank. He went on: "Structurally, the cover girl represents a rare paradox: on the one hand, her body has the value of an abstract institution, and on the other hand, this body is individual, and between these two conditions, which correspond exactly to the opposition of Language and Song, there is tension, anxiety, and sometimes a supercharged violence. More and more often, the event of this no longer virginal cover girl rock and art star alcoholic threatens the structure of everyday life, so that we no longer know whether the structure is inspired by or determines what is real. . . ."

She lowered her hand and just listened.

What is a ghost? I said with tingling energy. One who has not faded away through a chord change, bad manners, or death.

HEADACHY, NERVOUS, Linda stood still and alone in the main exhibition room of the State of Illinois Gallery. Dozens of glass gallon jugs filled with water were arranged on the floor in a grid, squares within squares within squares, intersected by fragments of plumbing. A maze, then. Light from the ceiling and windows opped through the jugs every which way: off metal pipes, through water and glass, around corners, then back through reflections and shadows. When you walked alongside it, or shifted positions, the entire maze shimmered arhythmically.

Which was why she was trying to stand very still. She'd had to go back to Wolf Point to change clothes, which had made her a half hour late for her interview. She also was getting her period. The angelic young black male receptionist had invited her to "check out the show" while she waited to see the associate director, but this maze only made her more nervous.

Other full jugs, up on shelves, were refracting small objects the artist had centered behind them: a convex half-inch section of bright yellow felt was becoming a tennis ball, a red cancel slash the infinity sign, the beam from a nightlight a penis . . .

When Linda thought no one was looking, she popped one last peppermint Cert.

Roger Winfrey, the associate director of the gallery, was gay. So what else was new, Linda thought. He had longish gray hair and a small turned-up nose. He was also humungously fat. In his brown V-neck sweater and turtleneck he looked like a slow-motion mudslide. He apologized for keeping her waiting and offered her coffee. She accepted.

Winfrey got up with great effort—an effort, however, that he seemed more than happy to make—poured coffee, made small talk about SAIC, SuHu, the weather. He looked at her funny and glanced down through bifocals at her work-study voucher and hurriedly typed application. And talked. He was low-key and friendly but smart, Linda gathered. He would not be a bad guy to work for, she thought, though she knew she would not get the job. The view from the window behind him was onto the Clark and Lake el station. The people who waited for trains were not bundled up but were breathing out plumes of gray breath.

"Have you spent any time," Winfrey said. "I mean, we hate to ask personal questions." He paused. "Do you know how to use a word processor?"

"Not really," she said. She thought about Richard's computer and wondered how much she should lie. "But I think I could learn. But not really."

"Because all we end up with is processed words anyway, right?"

She shrugged, smiled, and nodded, cursing herself for not having planned better answers. She wanted a cigarette desperately but decided it would not be a real good idea. There wasn't an ashtray in sight.

"We can type, though, of course . . ."

She nodded and shrugged. What's all this *we* stuff? "Okay, I guess. Decent."

He wrote something down on a pad. She tried to decide what to say when he asked her how fast. Was twelve words a minute too slow?

"Charlie can teach you the Apex in no time," he said.

What? Sipped her coffee. He can?

Winfrey went on to explain that her duties would mostly involve answering the telephone, keeping the mailing list up to date, looking terribly smashing at openings, unpacking the occasional carton . . .

"You mean, are you saying, I got it?"

"You got it," he said. He smiled and then wrote something down.

"Jeez, Mr. Winfrey, I'm happy," she said. Don't gush, she thought. "Thanks a lot."

"We're happy to have you," he said. They shook hands across his neat desk. "There still are a couple of things—"

"I just didn't think—"

"And please call me Roger," he said.

In the drugstore upstairs from the gallery she bought cigarettes, deodorant, Tampax, razors, Certs, and shampoo, plus *Artnews* and *-forum* to study and *Spin* and *Musician* to celebrate. She was almost unbearably happy. She had a job at a high-profile gallery in a world-famous building working twenty-one hours a week with a schedule that wouldn't conflict with her classes. (She had gotten the job in the first place, she knew, because SAIC's work-study program paid sixty percent of her wages. They also made sure that the job would fit into her schedule.) It was perfect. Nonasshole boss, decent pay, nobody grabbing her body. She would not have to wait on dinky tables. She would not have to live at Wolf Point.

She was meeting Hank in the mezzanine by the top of the escalators in eleven more minutes, at three. It was going to be their first date since . . . their first real date ever, she realized. She was going to ask him—

A guy in a navy blue suit was following her. She'd first sensed it, vaguely, about forty-five minutes ago, when she'd noticed him outside the gallery. He had taken her elevator, gotten off at her floor. She was sure of it now. Which meant he had waited for her during the interview. He was now standing ten or twelve feet to her left, paging through *Newsweek.* He'd positioned himself so that she couldn't get out of the store without walking past him.

He was young and not bad—not bad at all, as a matter of fact—but there was something about him that made her feel queasy. He was not like a regular guy, someone whose eye she had caught and who wanted to grab a few glances. This guy was much too unshy in the way he watched her: he *would* turn away when she caught him, but he made no attempt to pretend that he hadn't been looking. Like a cop or a killer or something.

She collected her change and walked out. Turning left, the wrong way, on purpose, she started to merge with the crowd on the concourse, then suddenly veered to the right, walking as fast as she could without running. She was desperate to know if the guy was still following her but did not turn around to find out. If he was—and he was, she was certain—she figured she'd be much better off if he didn't suspect that she knew.

She stopped at the first bank of elevators. A half-dozen people were waiting. A door opened and the car emptied out. She got on it. So did a black woman carrying a baby, a middle-aged man with a briefcase, two other people as well. Not the guy. The car started upward. Okay.

The car only stopped at floors ten through sixteen. The highest three buttons already had been pushed. She suddenly sensed that the guy had been someone she knew. From the School? She ran through the guys in her classes. Was it possible she'd seen him with Hank?

The car stopped at 10. The man with the briefcase got off; two others, just like him, got on. Up they went. She would ride to the top, then go down.

Two-thirds of her headache had moved to her stomach. It had gone into remission while she was with Winfrey, but now it was back with a vengeance. To keep from looking down and making herself even sicker, she studied the building's cylindrical skylight. It was surely a huge cubist breast, she decided, although more Stellaesque in its palette and shape than Picasso- or Braque-like. But cubist. (Either that or a Helmut Jahn hardon, a take she found much much less pleasing.) The geodesic lacework of rose salmon girders was slashed every which way with sunlight. Some breast! She was jumpy and frightened and happy. There were hundreds of thousands of surfaces caroming light in her face: marble and glass, painted girders, three shades of tacky blue plastic, plus the slightly smudged Plexiglas wall of the car she was riding in, all lit by fluorescent tubing, everything else, and the sun. She wanted some gin and a cigarette badly, and Hank. She could smell the black woman's perfume as she looked back down into the building, the place that she now had a job in.

Mistake. Drunk on the Orbit Room dance floor—literally, that is, *on the floor,* as the mob strobed and spun far above her—was the feeling she had in her guts and her legs and her brain. She was 'dozed.

Three floors below her, in one of the other glass cars, she spotted the guy from the store. Navy blue. He was looking right at her and smiling.

The building was spiraling madly as her own car rose through it, transparent as all get out too.

Rose white and four shades of blue.

Bap bap bap.

She got off at sixteen, the last stop. Her temples were pounding in time with her vibrating tubes. Could she walk? The flesh on the back of her neck and inside her forehead was crawling. With what? She figured it must have been fear. Because no gin could tempt her, no cognac, champagne. The straighter she was now the better, she realized; she had to be able to think straight.

She could, and did, walk. She had to find Hank. She edged herself up to the navel-high parapet, swallowed, peeked over. Seventeen stories below, through the rotating swirl of the atrium, was a brown-and-gray marble rosette. A dilated iris, she realized, looking back at her, not blinking. The floor. She felt herself falling, a low-voltage thrill through her shins and the soles of her feet. She could picture herself hitting the marble dead center: her spatter, the crunch of her skull, the hideous posture of all that was left of her body. For Hank.

She even could see where he'd told her to meet him—and now it was one after three! Someone was standing there too, looking up. A guy who was not wearing navy. She squinted but still couldn't tell: tall or short, brown or black hair, Hank or not.

And the building was moving again. She knew she was going to puke, almost smiled when she thought *all that way!*

She backed up and leaned on the wall and just breathed. Closed her eyes: *but please do not please go away!* So but why would some guy want to *follow* her?

To get a more level perspective, she looked at the bank of elevators she'd just ridden. All cables and pulleys and girders. Three cars. One car, empty except for one man, arrived, going up, at fifteen. He was wearing a navy blue suit.

Hugging the walls and clutching the bannister, she raced down the stairs to fourteen. Since the building was mostly a circle, she realized, it didn't provide her with too many places to hide. Exposed stairways or transparent elevators were the only two options it gave her for moving around, up or down. If he maintained the right points of view, the guy would be able to follow her while blending right into the background.

She ran down another half flight, looking behind and above her, trying to pick out the navy blue shape in the hundreds of thousands of others. She still felt quite dizzy, but a wave of adrenaline had wiped out her headache completely. Okay. She was trying to catch her breath, but she couldn't.

Let's see.

She peed long and hard in the john on thirteen. It was just what she'd needed, she realized. She sat in the stall for a while, totting the pluses and minuses of sitting and waiting much longer. She was hidden here, sort of, but she also felt cornered and vulnerable. She needed to ditch her pursuer but did not know how long Hank would wait. And if someone walked in now, she didn't know *what* she would do.

The walls of her sanctuary had been spackled by the manufacturer with whipmarks of paint to make them graffiti-resistant. All you needed, however, was a wide-tipped felt pen or a knife. Some lines had been rubbed off with bleach or steel wool, but she still could read what they'd once said. One had said JEREMY IRONS. A fresher one said YO GOTTA NICE CHI CHI. Below this, still fresher: WHO GIVES.

She really had to laugh at herself. Here she was shaking in her black leather booties and Stewart plaid skirt and no nylons, holed up in some stall reading wisecracks and come-ons from strangers *because some guy had looked at her strange?* Maybe he'd followed her a while, or looked up her skirt as they rode past each other in new-wavo transparent lifts, *but so what.* Plus, knowing her, she had probably only imagined that he'd been outside the gallery to begin with, that he'd ever been actually "following" her, that he'd meant any harm if he had been. It was all just a bit too *I Spy,* although now that she thought of it she hoped it would not become *Witness.* And but when did she start running *from* guys like that? She opened the new box of Tampax. The answer, of course, was *since Hank.* So she had to get out of here, quick. Plus she couldn't help thinking it had something to do with the richard.

She peeked out the door of the john, looked both ways, then walked toward the elevator. Deodorized, Tampaxed, nose and forehead degreased, Visined and Certed and lipsticked. She was moist in the right places, dry in the others. All set.

She rode the next elevator down to the concourse. No problem. It was *good* to be late for first dates, though she sure hoped that Hank hadn't left. It was already 3:21. The more she thought about how he'd been treating her, though, the surer she was that he'd wait.

A hand clapped her mouth. Its sinewy fingers locked on her jaw as its thumbnail dug into her cheekbone. A hard wool-clad arm raised her chin, locking her throat in its crook. Her head was wrenched sideways and back.

"Do not scream."

Her right arm was pinioned in back of her head. She had to get up on her toes and rotate her neck just to breathe. Her left arm was more or less free. Should she scream? Could she? It wasn't a voice that she recognized.

"I am not gonna hurt you."

She struggled. She sensed that she probably shouldn't but still couldn't help it. His grips on her throat and right arm were absolute, painful, but she could move the rest of her body. She twisted round thirty degrees, tried to kick back with her heels, yanked on the ironhard arm. Didn't work. With a spasm of violence and power he wrenched her neck sideways, collapsing her windpipe and raising her heels off the ground. She couldn't get purchase to kick anymore. Couldn't breathe.

"Okay?" He shoved her and dragged her along a blue wall—part of one word stenciled on it was STAR—around a corner, down a short darkened hallway. "If you scream I will kill you."

She nodded, or tried to, relaxing what muscles she could, trying to show him she wouldn't.

"I am not gonna hurt you," he said.

Where the fuck *was* everybody! She suddenly felt very drunk.

"I just want to ask you—"

She cocked her left elbow and plunged it back down as viciously hard as she could, then recocked and nailed him again. He roared and let go of her face. And again. She had gauged where his crotch would be, roughly, and seemed to have scored one close hit. (The way he'd held her originally had hoisted her elbow too high. When she'd relaxed and stopped struggling, though, her entire left side had been able to slide a bit lower. He also had loosened his grip.) But she wasn't quite free of him yet. He was still holding onto her neck and right arm, though less firmly. As she elbowed and kicked him, he suddenly let go and ran; and she chased him. He tripped, almost fell, but kept running. Her fist hit the back of his head as she lunged. Then she fell down too, started screaming.

He was gone when she looked around the corner, but a pair of policemen ran up. Had they seen him?

"A man, has been following, me," she gasped, catching her breath. "Attacked me, just now, over there." She pointed toward the dark corridor.

"Just now?" one cop said. The other one said, "What'd he look like?"

"Navy blue suit," she said. She held her hand up to his height.

"And this man attacked you just now?" The other talked into his radio.

"Yes," she said. "Yes!"

They seemed to be taking her seriously.

"Choking me, practically breaking my arm. I think—he was trying to rape me."

She saw him. He was walking across the rosette, trying to look nonchalant. "There he is!"

They said, "Where?"

He had shoved someone over and was taking the stairs of the escalator two at a time. "That's him!" she said, pointing.

The policemen looked at each other, then one sprinted after the guy. People in the concourse backed off and watched him.

The other cop's radio crackled with static, but Linda could make out some words: ". . . seven, that's go, *go* . . . come *on!*"

He started to run through the crowd. "Wait here!" he yelled back. "Just wait there!"

She ran toward the bottom of the escalator and watched the cop race up the stairs. He was fast. People leaned back to get out of his way. He was already close to the top.

She got on the least crowded escalator. Two little girls with balloons—identical twins, Linda realized, though the outfits they wore didn't match—were riding in back of their mother; their silver balloons were bobbing in front of her head. Linda remembered the tiny balloon man outside; he had winked at her on her way in, and she had winked back. He was well over sixty and harmless. If she hadn't been late for the interview, she thought, she just might have bought a balloon, then realized she wouldn't have even if she had been early.

She thought she heard gunshots as she got to the top of the escalator. She watched as the second policeman burst through the mezzanine door. Where was his partner, she wondered. And what if—

He pulled out his gun as he ran past the Dubuffet sculpture.

"Okay," Maggie said. She had called Richard at his office. "I'll admit that, right now, she might be a little bit nuts."

"At least that's a start," Richard said. There were runners and staffers around, so he whispered. "She needs both our help."

"I agree, which is why—"

"All along she's been poisoning our, like right now, at every and each opportunity. The girl never misses a trick."

"But so now that we know where she's been—"

"So but, you *ask*, that's why I *hired* the guy. In order to find out exactly—"

"Richard, *okay*. That was then." She found herself whispering too. "I admit it made sense at the time."

"But you *still* don't know where, what she's up to, or where she's run off to *this time.*"

"She hasn't 'run off' anywhere—"

"Then what do you call moving in with the same sons of bitches who pulled—"

"She's moved in with two other students."

"Two guys, though, honey. Two guys."

"It's supposed to be a very big place. There's six or eight—"

"But she doesn't say where? She doesn't provide us with names, the address . . ."

"Well didn't this guy of yours find out who, you know, where it was?"

"He hasn't been in touch with me yet."

A pause.

"What do you mean?" Maggie said, speaking up.

"That he hasn't been in touch with me yet."

"Then how were you going to tell him she's back?"

"As soon as I talk to him. It's just that—"

"When will that be?"

"Soon. It's just that—"

"When, Richard? When."

"You're right, Mag. I'll call him right now."

"Because if you don't I'll, I'll have to—"

"You're right. As soon as we hang up I'll call him."

She finally found him, with Teddy, in the restaurant part of the concourse. They were sitting at one of the Slice of Life tables. Hank nodded, saluted. She waved.

Teddy got out of his chair and gestured that she should sit down. She'd forgotten how large, wide, he was.

"The Great White Girl has . . . a-rrived," he announced.

Hank said, "Great skirt."

"Thanks," she said. Should she wait to be kissed, kiss him, or what? If so, where, for how long, and how wetly? "Sorry I'm late."

Shake his hand?

"That's okay." He sounded and looked like he meant it. No kiss, though.

Teddy had grabbed a third chair. He swung it around and sat with his arms on its back. "You okay?"

"Me?" she said, sitting between them.

"You. You look like you've just seen, ooo *wheeeeeee* ooo-oo-o, or like you've just had An Interview For A Job As A Gall'ry Slave."

"Well I have."

"Get the job?"

"Yes I did, as a matter of fact."

Hank said, "That's good."

"Way to go," Teddy said. "Want some coffee?" They were both drinking coffee, she saw. And Teddy was offering to go get her some: to leave them in private a moment.

"I wouldn't say no, I suppose."

"You got it," said Teddy. He left.

Hank put his hand over hers. She did not want to tell him about the guy in the navy blue suit. She didn't know why, but she didn't. She wanted him to think of her as a serious person. She did not want to come off hysterical.

He played with her knuckles a moment, then took back his hand. "Somebody's looking for you."

Before she could think what the best thing to say was, she blurted out, "Tell me about it!"

Hank looked surprised. "So you already knew?"

"Knew what?" Way to go. "I mean, no."

He gave her a look, and she blinked. "Somebody told you already?"

"About what?"

He gave her a slip of pink paper. It was folded in three, with a smudged strip of tape at the top. *Linda Krajacik,* it said. *Call Maggie at 763-2273.* "It was taped to the door of your English class. Treasure's friend Cynthia spotted it."

She nodded, reread it.

"Maggie's your mother, right?"

"Right."

He gave her another pink slip. It said the same thing.

"The door of your Life Drawing class."

"No date?" she said.

"Date?"

"What no date?" Teddy said. "This *certainly* counts as a date." He had coffee and six giant slices of pizza. He passed her the coffee, two napkins, two slices. "Two for you, three for me . . ."

"Merci beaucoup." She was hungry.

"De rien," Teddy said. "Maggie's your mother, right?"

"Right."

She and Hank looked at each other. She winked, but he didn't wink back.

"The plot thickens," said Teddy. "Ooooo *wheeeeee* ooo-oo-o."

Hank said, "There's also this guy who's been asking around about you."

"Was he wearing a navy blue suit?" Linda said.

Hank and Teddy looked at each other, melodramatically raising their eyebrows.

"Ooooooooo WHEEEEEEEEEE oooo-ooo-oo-o . . ."

Linda looked up at the skylight. The building seemed much more benign from this angle. The rosette looked much less like an eye. She blew on her coffee. She wasn't quite ready to ask either of them if she could *briefly* move into their warehouse, so she looked at Hank's pizza, said: "What do you—yeah yeah, I know—so but what do you think of this place?"

Teddy Boy stage-looked at Hank. Was she *always* this strange, he was asking.

There was silence. No one was touching their pizza. She wanted to say—

"Be nice if it worked," Hank said finally. His eyes were cool green, almost gray. "What do *you* think."

"I like it," she said, right away. "The inside much more than the outside. And I like it a *whole* lot better from the bottom up than I do—"

"Who doesn't," said Teddy. He took a big bite of his pizza.

"But how do you mean, if it worked?" she asked Hank.

"If the guy who designed it remembered heat rises, for starters."

Where was the bag with the things she had bought in the drugstore? And where was her purse! She had lost them.

"Insufficient AC," Teddy said, between chews.

"Oh."

"In the summer."

She nodded. She could feel Hank's cool gaze on her earlobe.

"Though it *does* have its pan-moderne charm," Teddy said. He was using the inside-joke tone of the loft. "Or, as DB would put it, 'evincing Jahn's Edifice Complex.' "

Hank peered around at the concourse, then up through the building, shading his eyes with his hand. "Yon Edifice Complex? But where?"

"I mean, after all," Teddy said, part Oxford professor, part Cockney. "There *is* a certain 'rad' corporate 'bang' to it, what?"

"Bang?" Linda said.

Hank made a gun with his index finger and thumb and pointed it at her. Bang, he said silently. A hammer clicked inside her brain.

"Bang," Teddy said.

"Or, how shall we say," Hank was saying, "sort of a gauche, perhaps goyisher, Guggenheim?"

Bang.

The three of them gazed, sipping coffee, through the crosshatched, cylindrical skylight.

Am I wanted
or wanton
or wonton
I wonder.

HE HAD his good feeling this morning, Christ knew why. In spite of the bullshit at home and his dreams, it wouldn't surprise him if the market opened up limit down and stayed put. He was pumped.

He got out of the elevator and walked toward the floor. The only real problem was that he'd just reached his limit position at yesterday's close. Maggie's account was maxed too. The backup accounts he had opened with Refco and Hagerty against this very contingency were already close to their limits. In order to get any shorter, he would need to open at least one more account by tomorrow. Perhaps it was time to get even.

Carl Gottlieb jogged by and punched Richard's shoulder. Gottlieb was also short wheat. Richard knew this, and he knew Gottlieb knew that he knew it. That's what the punch had been for.

"Do it to it," said Gottlieb, waving behind him. He disappeared onto the floor.

"You got it," called Richard.

Adrian Dennis was walking ahead of him, talking with two other bond guys. The word on the floor was that A.D. was snakebit of late, but he wasn't a guy Richard spent time feeling sorry for. During the late seventies he'd been part of a six-member team of British and American investment bankers who managed the personal portfolio of King Faud of Saudi Arabia. His wife, Diane Dennis, was one of the stunningest women that Richard had ever laid eyes on. When the family moved back from Riyadh to Winnetka, she had gotten a job as one of the weekend anchors on the Channel 5 News. They were one of those couples. Their oldest child, Marcy, had worked as a runner last summer. She was well groomed and beautiful and had excellent manners. Apparently she was also intelligent, since he'd heard she had just gotten early admission to Michigan, Stanford, and Radcliffe. He also assumed she was *theirs.*

She hated to have to write papers. She had things to say, but she didn't like to have to put them into well-organized paragraphs that had things like transition and structure and closure.

For her English final, she had to write an autobiographical essay, six–eight pages, on some aspect, event, or trauma that had affected her life and or her ideas about art. It was supposed to be concrete, specific, and honest. You were not supposed to leave out the dirt. It was due half an hour ago.

She read through her measly false starts:

My mother's new husband trades futures. She wants to get pregnant again so she hopes they have upward motility. I myself was a semi-immaculate conception, or so I've been told. The one time my parents made love they had me.

The ghost of my father has appeared to me three or four times. He died nineteen years ago, a few weeks before I was born. He was in Vietnam to fight "Charles" and was killed by a mine near Khesanh. He probably never knew what hit him. He did know my mother was pregnant, but he didn't die fighting for her.

My mother didn't want to be a war widow. She and my father were hippies. They got married when he came home on leave before he got sent overseas so she could get his insurance in case he got killed and I'd be legitimate in case she got pregnant. That's what she tells me at least.

She didn't get married again all these years because of the money the VA, ADC, and Social Security were giving her to support me. The fact that she was a hippie and a feminist also had something to do with it. She wanted to be independent. Plus because, she claims the right guy

When I was twelve or thirteen I started to read Vietnam novels. I wanted to find out what it was like to be over there. To die over there. My father had died over there a few months before I was born. He never knew I had been born (leaves me where?)

I read them compulsively for two or three years. There were as many sex scenes as battle scenes. (This was how, more or less, I learned about the birds and the bees.) The impression you got from reading these novels was that American soldiers screwed water buffaloes, whores, Vietcong POWs, each other. Vietcong women would put razor blades in their vaginas. There was one in which the hero went on R & R to Tokyo and had an affair with a Japanese prostitute. They got along so well together it turned out that he probably wouldn't have to pay her anyway. She gave him three baths and scrubbed him until he was raw before she would let him make love to her. The point was that even though he didn't treat her like a prostitute, he still had to pay her.

It has caused me to wonder if my father made love with any women, prostitutes included, after he made my mother pregnant with me. The more of these novels I read, the more I believe that he did. I wonder if the women became pregnant (leaving me?)

American soldiers often took Vietnamese wives and had children with them. Sometimes they came back to their American girlfriends or wives as though nothing had happened.

His camouflage uniform has given me ideas for drawings and paintings.

The amazing brutality. Bamboo splints under fingernails. American soldiers stuck flares up their prisoners' assholes, or chopped their arms and legs off, then dangled what was left out of helicopters. The Vietcong did hideous things to their own prisoners. Made them play Russian roulette (from a movie).

I am thankful he hadn't been captured.

The year I was born, 1968, was a strange one. It was also the year my father got killed. Vietnam. Woodstock. The Beatles began to break up. In April Martin Luther King was assassinated. Lyndon Johnson was president. Two months later Robert Kennedy was assassinated while running for president. His brother John F. had been assassinated five years before while he had been president. This was just before Johnson, in Dallas. Johnson was Kennedy's vice-president. Johnson wouldn't run because of his Vietnam policy. Then, in Chicago, in August, Hubert Humphrey, who was Johnson's vice-president, was nominated to run for president, but the hippies and yippies went nuts, staged these big riots, and Mayor Daley gave the "shoot to kill order," which was one of the reasons that in November, ten days before I was born, Spiro Agnew and Richard Nixon were elected vice-president and president respectively (neither are no longer president). Also Morrison died around then, Brian Jones, Hendrix. Altamont too. Janis Joplin.

She had one decent title, "Art in Heaven," but could only come up with six words to go with it: *Our father who art in heaven.*

She also had pages of sketches and doodles and scribbles, but these wouldn't do much good either.

Dec wheat was at 2.20A—limit down. The pit was inert but still seething. It wasn't quite ten yet, and some guys had already left. Richard felt jumpy but tried not to show it. He figured he now needed 4.16 million bushels to buy back his shorts. It was time. The trick was not to spook the suckers too soon. Forty-five minutes ago he had casually found out from the wire-house fillers how big the pool was—how many many sell orders there were to be had at this price. No big deal. Nah. No pen or pad out, kept both his hands in his pockets. Who moi? He was just being idly curious. He could tell guys were scouting him, though, eyes peeled for chances to tear a short piece of his spine out.

The facts he had gathered were roughly as follows. The Smith Barney order-filler had eighty-five contracts to sell: 425,000 bushels. The guys from the other wire houses didn't have much—maybe two hundred thou at the most. Forget them. The interesting news was that Danny Boy Zervos from Bunge was sitting on a one million eight lot, and Dreyfus's guy, Shawn Tellier, needed to get short two million.

So. Okey dokey. All righty. Four hundred thousand from Smith Barney's chump, plus the whole schmeer from Tellier and Zervos, would do it—though not in exactly that order. He kept both his hands in his pockets. No need to start the stampede before he'd got even himself; after that they could do what they wanted. That honchos like Gottlieb also were short was both bad and good. Even mooches like Elliott Saunders—who'd wet-dreamed himself into being short wheat simply by trading in front of RBaum for a week and didn't know from short or Shinola—were starting to look a byte twitchy.

So it had to be an all-at-once hit: surgical, swift, and real final. He was confident that none of the worthless-pud locals would try to pick up the pool ahead of him. They knew his position would waste them. They'd stand on their heels, as per usual, let good old RBaum start the bidding, generate all the momentum, then pussyfoot after like women.

He knew this territory like pilots knew stretches of continent, but he had to admit he was nervous. Was the RBaum stealth system infallible? The fundamentals were still pretty bearish, and the Wang had advised not to buy yet; its advice was, in fact, to get *shorter.* The Soviet wheat harvest had been running 34 percent ahead of even the most optimistic estimates. The new British polyploid strain was giving them almost twice the yield per hectare in Azerbaijan alone. Not only that: the rest of the EEC wimps were going to help the Evil Empire cut their own throats by providing *more* subsidies. It was more than a little bit strange. But fuck it, he thought. Sell the rumor, buy the fact, discount the old fundamentals. Discount the new ones as well. And while you were at it, may as well discount the fractals. Where's your testicular fortitude? Fuck the Wang, fuck the facts, fuck the charts, fuck the fracts. What the heck. Everything in moderation, including moderation. Every thing *I* know is wrong, so fuck *them.* Get even, get up, and get out.

He stepped up in front of Tellier—and at least he could say it had sounded like a good idea at the *time*—positioning himself so that Saunders and Gottlieb et al. wouldn't see what went down right away. They'd know soon enough what was up.

Tellier gave him a how-'bout-them-Bears look.

"You need to get rid of two million?" said Richard. On a move this substantial he *had* to confirm his reconnaisance.

Tellier was surprised but all business. "Two oh seven."

"Buy 'em," said Richard, that quick, then wheeled to engage Daniel Zervos.

Zervos had already caught on. "One million seven at twenty," he said, perfunctorily holding one palm up.

"Buy 'em!" yelled Richard. The pussy was out of the panty, he realized, *so just don't go limp on me now!* He turned to the Smith Barney guy: "Twenty bid on how many!" But Saunders was desperately trying to horn his way in: "Can I have fifteen?" he was whining. Only seven or eight seconds had passed, but it was already all but all over—all but the shouting, of course. Richard got right into Saunders's pink face and roared "Pay up first, mooch!" loud enough to melt down the wax in his ears, then turned back again to Smith Barney: "Buy four hundred thousand at twenty!"

Smith Barney actually hesitated. Looked at Saunders, at Gottlieb, at Richard. Tick tick. Richard was stunned for a moment. Everyone here knew the rules: by moving the market off A, he had purchased the option to buy all the bushels he wanted. Everyone, of course, except Saunders and *this* teething ditz. Tick tick tick. Richard gave Smith Barney one final look: it would cost you some grain trades to piss off RBaum, and that, my good friend, was for *openers.* Smith Barney blushed, blinked back at Richard, croaked "Sold."

It was done. He looked at poor Saunders and grinned; he no longer wanted to plunge out his cum-clotted thorax. At Gottlieb, he winked. But Saunders and Gottlieb and just about everyone else were too busy unloading their shorts to much notice. It was already $2.27 and counting. Tut-tut.

He could not trust Honora to card these three trades, so he wrote up the orders himself. The din in the pit was electric, but he phased it all out with ceramic din bafflers and switched on his digital abacus. Let's see now. He'd sold the Dec wheat at an average of $3.10 a bushel and had just bought it back for $2.20. Eight hundred and thirty-two contracts, 4.16 million bushels, minus twenty long contracts already plus seven cents meant he'd just taken . . . hmm . . . $3,741,982 from the market. Minus his round-trip cost of $832 and expenses of oh let's say $8,320 (including EEC research in Paris) times 72% IRSless came to approximately . . . ahh . . . $2,687,637.60.

Time for lunch.

Skank.
Grotty.
Skanky.

Sixty-eight.
Paint it black.
Crunchy.

AROUND 11:15 Friday night, as Linda was hunting and pecking on Willa's electronic typewriter page one of her seven-page, five-days-late autobiographical essay (while Hank worked on *Black Box* upstairs), Renée, *the* Renée, arrived in a cab with a friend, a cold, four open magnums of Mumm's and one of Perrier-Jouet, two leather suitcases, an aluminum purse, and much circumstance. Had she called, Linda wondered. Her shiny black hair shone with rain; her gold cheeks were pink from the air. So who cared. Her friend, named Daphne, was also an SAL flight attendant and had one canvas YSL suitcase. Teddy Boy carried all three up the stairs, in one trip. Within forty-five seconds the place was abuzz with arrival. Renée was still wearing her blue-and-white uniform, but Daphne had changed into a peacock blue silk peplum jacket and a short flirty black-and-white skirt. Daphne, of course, was quite gorgeous, but was not in Renée's league for class, even when Renée had the sniffles; she also was fifteen years younger.

"Gianni Versace," she said, turning around in her heels, skirt, and jacket. "You like?"

Teddy Boy groaned. So did Bruce. Linda forced a big smile. Visa and Muster Mark whistled. Willa and Hank started clapping.

"Looks like she's been on her Bobby Sands diet again," Visa said. "Think I'll try it."

"You mean her boat people diet," said Mark.

Daphne giggled, kissed Bruce. Did she get it? "You artist," she said, meaning *them.* "You too goddamn easy to please."

Linda found out by talking to Teddy and Willa that Renée and Daphne (and sometimes another one too, Gabriella) usually ("Usually?" said Linda. "Almost always, I guess," Teddy said) stayed at the warehouse when they were furloughed into O'Hare, which happened about twice a month. Most furloughs lasted a day and a half. Some lasted almost a month.

She did not ask how long this particular layover, furlough, whatever, would last. She did not ask whose girlfriends they were. She did not find out (yet) who they slept with. She noticed, however, that Daphne and Bruce seemed completely shook by the prospect of breathing in each other's germs. As were, she could tell, Hank and "Reb."

She did not ask how long *she* could stay.

While buzzed on champagne, she complained that she hadn't been able to sleep. It pleased her, albeit briefly, to realize that she already felt comfortable enough with these people not to think long and hard before she opened her mouth (it usually took her a couple three years), though she did understand that what she'd just said could be taken two ways. She also understood that she might not be around here much longer.

"Can't sleep take Xanax," said Daphne, who'd taken it the way she'd meant it. She proffered a small square white bottle.

Linda examined the label. Xanax R Tablets, it said. Complimentary package. Alprazolam, 0.25 mg, 30 tablets.

"Just say no to drugs, dearie," said Mark, expertly imitating a prissy old woman.

"That's telling her, Nance!" said Eusebio.

Bruce shook his head at such naughtiness. Renée sneezed, blew her nose. When Hank said "Tut-tut," it sounded like he was insane.

Linda took two, knocking them back with more Mumm's, then handed the bottle to Daphne, toasting her —thanks—with a nod and her crystal champagne glass.

Emily, Mark, and Eusebio whistled and clapped their approval.

"Never lick a gift horse with your mouth," she managed to enunciate properly.

They laughed. Even Hank. She was happy. Although

not-drinking drinking, she thought, was not easy. And what did that fucking R stand for?

"That's what *I* always say," said Renée.

Oh *do* you? She smiled without parting her lips.

"I was just reading 'Pet Milk' last *night*, " Visa said. Some writer named Dybek was on David Letterman. "The guy *looks* like the Polacks he writes all the stories about."

"Hey, I heard that," said Emily "Watch it."

"Yeah," Linda said. The guy on TV sounded just like her Uncle Jerome.

"I am I am," Willa said. "And I like it."

"Sucker can *write,* " Visa said. "Ever read 'Sauerkraut Soup'?"

No one had.

"Looks like he works *out* with Polacks," said Willa. "Yum-yum."

Linda watched, sipped champagne. This Dybek guy sure seemed familiar. He was telling a joke about flies and karate —exactly the same kind of joke that her lunatic uncle would tell! Maybe she *had* read a story of his, seen his picture on the back of a book . . .

"Yorba Linda!" cried Muster Mark suddenly. "Xanax y Mumm's!? Vutt a mensch!"

She scowled, flexed her bicep. She'd forgotten she'd taken the Xanax.

"But so *now* what's the frequency, Kenneth?" said Teddy, to her and or Hank, and everyone yukked except them.

What did that mean, Linda wondered, as Letterman started to snicker. Would Hank now be able to take sexual advantage of her? Of Renée? No Xanax needed for *that.* Who was Kenneth? Would *he* if Hank wouldn't? Would Teddy? Would Dybek? Would David?

"Who's Yorba Linda?" she said, and all the guys knowingly snickered.

Renée went to bed before one, by herself, with her cold, as the party began to wind down. She had said she was tired and looked it. Exhausted, in fact, Linda noticed.

Renée, it turned out, had a room of her own in the warehouse; it was back by the second-floor john. So did Daphne, it seemed. Daphne, however, would be spending the night with Der Bruzer.

"Getting her fovea czeched by Der Bruzer," said Mark, continuing one running joke about Bruce's Slavo-Jewish heritage, another about his ophthalmological practices, a third about how he played tennis, and a fourth about Daphne's frank cuddling—all this as soon as Bruce and Daphne had turned, holding hands, past the skids. Linda got them.

"Having her young ciliary body examined," said Willa. She stood up and made herself cross-eyed.

Hank yawned.

"What about her posterior chamber?" said Visa.

"Why, you sexist mothers!" huffed Mark. "You two *bitches.* For your penances I want you to say five Our Fathers, five Hail Marys, and cause ten ejaculations."

"In a row, Father Mark?" Willa said.

"You say so," said Visa, then yawned.

Emily poured three droplets of Mumm's into hers and Mark's glass as Mark put his hand on her waist. "Plus he mustn't neglect Daphne's limpid yet aqueous humor," she said. She knocked back the droplets, licked her top lip, then looked down at Mark for her penance. "Plus he mustn't neglect—"

"Hey, I *heard* that," Linda could hear Bruce as saying, having snuck back to listen and spy.

"Me too, and I'm *hurt,*" Daphne goes, hotly blushing. Yeah, right.

It turns out Renée's with them too, cold and all, and will be through dawn and beyond.

And she yawned.

She made love with Hank. There was that. The Xanax made things more emphatic, but she tried not to come off too wanton. It worked.

Afterward, smoking, he asked her a question about the Musée Picasso, implying that maybe they'd go there together some day. But Paris now seemed so provincial. She pretended she'd fallen asleep so as not to embarrass herself by wanting to do what he wanted.

And what would've happened if *she* hadn't gone to bed early?

315

Woe is me.

MAGGIE WAS thirteen days late. She felt bloated with thick backed-up blood, plus her skin didn't look all that hot. Was she sick? She'd been nauseous a couple of times, and jumpy from not being able to sleep. She'd attributed this (mostly) to nerves about Linda, though she guessed PMS would better explain how she felt. Which was also, she knew, about how it felt to be pregnant. Oh boy. As she counted again on the calendar, she couldn't decide *how* she felt.

Having sex on a regular basis again had, among other good things, made her menstrual cycle like Swatch pulsar clockwork. Which was why she thought counting might not be totally pointless. For the last several months she'd had neat five-day periods once every twenty-nine days. They had also become much more bearable. Ninety percent of the bleeding got done in the first eighteen hours or so, so the other four days were a picnic. Whereas during the times between men, especially that year and a half between Janos and Kenny, she'd never known *when* they would come. Some months she'd even get extras, then go ten or twelve weeks and have none. Then—surprise!—she'd have soaked through her double-stitched denim. She also remembered the two-year-long stretch during which she and Linda would get them within one or two days of each other, sometimes the same afternoon. It was like it was somehow contagious.

If she was, in fact, pregnant, she figured it must have transpired their last night in Paris. Richard had not worn a rubber, and when she'd tried to *insérer* that French foam it just hadn't seemed to go in right. Richard, for his part, she knew, would chalk it up to something along the lines of "the RBaum sperm's patented upward motility," its "hardiness running the spermicidal gauntlet," as proof of his "consummate semenship."

He would also be very excited.

Linda caught Maggie undressing. It was strangely embarrassing too, for them both. She was trying on outfits in the downstairs bedroom with the door two-thirds open. Japanese Christmas shoppers were being unwittily interviewed on the 4:30 news by Bob Wallace. All of a sudden there was Maggie's white bottom confronting her sans pantyhose or underwear. Charming. No top on, no bra, boobs jutting out every which way. Sorry, excuse me, closed door. The afterimage Linda was left with disgusted, unnerved her. She could also tell Maggie was ticked. Six months before they'd have whistled, ignored it, or traded some Northwest Side jive: Posing for holy pictures? or, Gross me out *more,* Ma, why don't you. Not these days, however. No way.

Maggie came up to her room. She was pinkeyed from swimming in West Bank Club chlorine, it looked like.

"I just came to pick up more clothes," Linda told her.

"We don't say hello anymore?"

She was stuffing her black leather jacket into a bag with some sweatshirts. "Hello." She had *Marilyn* on, but not loud.

"So," Maggie said. "Where've you been? *How've* you been?"

"I told you. I've been staying with friends from the School."

"Decent place?"

Linda nodded. "I just got a job."

"Great," Maggie said. "That's good, is it not?"

"Yes that's good."

"So, at a—where?"

"No, not at a restaurant, Ma."

"Okay . . ."

"At the State of Illinois Building. The Gallery."

"Whoa. That is great. At the art gallery?"

Linda nodded, kept packing.

"Plus so close."

Linda nodded.

"What about school, though?" said Maggie.

What Linda now wanted to ask her about was the first time she'd made love with Michael, to ask if it *was* the first time. "What about it," she said.

What Maggie could not keep from asking was, "Didn't you get all of those messages?"

"You've got a very fertile imagination," said Maggie. She was happy that Linda at least didn't seem to be drinking, but still. "Do you know that?"

Linda was stuffing her heaviest clothes into black plastic bags. She'd filled two already, plus two smaller brown ones. She smoked. "Oh No Ophelia" was playing. It was Maggie's favorite song on the tape. Linda's too.

"You know that?" said Maggie.

No answer.

"Because the only reason *you* never had them was, yes, because *I* just could never afford them. Whereas *now* . . ."

"Yeah," Linda said. "And so look where your braces and all your jazzercise classes have got you."

"You tell me. I mean, what's *that* supposed to mean? Where did they get me? You mean why did I marry him, right? Why not just come out and say it?"

"Because that, as you'd say, is your *business,*" said Linda. "Don't think I don't know it. Plus also because that's your *problem.*"

"Ah ah. That's *your* problem, kid. *All* your problem."

"Dalmane" was playing, but Maggie was no longer listening. "Plus also because," she was saying, "quite frankly, there really was no one that tempting till he came along."

"Tempting? You gotta be kidding."

"In the first place, that's what you've said about all my men friends."

"That's not true."

"Afraid it is, kid. You couldn't stand Kenny because of your problem with—"

"What about Janos?" said Linda. "I never had nothing but good things to say about Janos. I always thought Janos was great."

"Yeah, so did Janos. And he felt the same way about you was the problem."

"So? So did you, I might add. At least it sure seemed—"

" 'So'? You were thirteen years *old,* 'so.' My God . . ."
"What's your point?"

"Look, and I've said this before, but this here is Life Part II for me, kid. For us both."

"Not for me," Linda said. She had turned off the tape deck. She shook her head no. "Not with him."

"And you want to know why?"

"Don't believe it," said Linda.

Michael appeared next to Maggie. Heat shimmered off him. She could see through him too. He was wearing a gleaming white shirt.

"Believe what?" Maggie said.

She just stared.

"But I'm asking, you want to know why?"

"Because it seemed like a good idea at the time?" Michael said. Fresh blood from wounds underneath had soaked through one side of the shirt. He was pale.

She waited for Maggie to answer him. When she saw that she wouldn't, or couldn't, she asked, "Because what did?"

Maggie glanced toward the spot at which Linda was staring transfixed, then looked back at Linda. Michael put one trembling hand onto Maggie's left shoulder. His other was stroking her hair. Linda moved toward him, but he stepped behind Maggie and held her. He was trying to turn her around.

"Because what?" Maggie said. "Believe what did?"

"He loves you!" said Linda. She pointed. "*Still* loves you, goddamn it! His blood's dripping onto the *floor!*" And it was. Six drops had already splashed next to Maggie's right foot. The pattern they'd formed, Linda noticed, was very much like the Big Dipper.

Maggie looked where she'd pointed. She figured it might be the aftereffects of the gin, but she wanted to leave that alone since they seemed to be getting somewhere.

"Honey, look. It's okay. It's okay."

"It's his *blood!*" Linda screamed.

She looked. There was nothing. But the look on Linda's face, in her eyes, made her shiver.

"You see! He's been bleeding there, right through his shirt!"

"Honey, just tell me." She was forcing herself to speak calmly. "Whose blood?"

"You can't see him!?"

More quietly. "Who?"

"Ma, Jesus Christ!"

As she stepped toward her daughter, her foot smeared the small oval puddle. She did not seem to notice, however, which made Linda's heart very sick. Then Michael did too, as he followed. He was wearing his green and black boots.

"Linda, now this isn't funny. See who?"

"My *father,* you fucking, you ignorant—" Lunging, she punched her, kept punching her, wildly and roundhouse and harder. Michael threw both his arms around Maggie, hugging her, trying to kiss her, protect her from Linda's attack. "Linda!" he cried as he held her. His voice echoed: Linda!

She was looking right into his eyes as they struggled, wondering what to do next. Maggie refused to fight back. They were screaming and whispering things to each other, but she couldn't tell what. He was stronger than she had expected. His hands were all over her—hungrily, bloodily, terribly. With his mouth and his body, he touched her. Through her hair, up her legs, on her face. She was trying to ward off the punches and scratches. He held her. They were smeared with each other's warm blood.

"Linda! Please talk to me! *Listen!*"

10

SHE REVIEWED her six pages of notes from the last half of Strobe's final class, translating word parts and scribbles as well as she could into points. All or nothing. Film is the artform with highest percentage of juvenile second-rate minds flourishing as its practitioners. The novel is probably second. Mine eyes have seen the gory of the coming of the word. God or whomever is not a performance artist. Lowest is sculpture or physics. My eyes and my mind come together. Nothing is unstable. Give it enough time, nothing will collapse into something. In the beginning the cosmos was symmetrical with respect to matter and antimatter. Big Bang made cosmos collapse into former. It could just as easily have gone the other way. I'm so sure. Therefore I am. What. So sure. But how sure. So so sure. Which could mean I'm only so-so. If ghost waves exist, things could move backward in time, and vice versa. If things could move faster than light. Three kinds of symmetry are degree-rotational (W), left-right (in mirrors), and glide (across pages or planes). Six quark flavors are up, down, charm, strange, top, and bottom. Top is the heaviest flavor. Each flavor has its own spin and color, its own mass and charge. Each has its very own antiquark. Nothing or all. Seated Nude, 1910. Girl with Electric Guitar. Yeah yeah yeah. Chromodynamic analysis. Yeah. Private eyes. But. Nothing is unstable. Given enough time, it will always collapse into something. We're here, after all. Where is that. Kaluza-Klein 11-D universe: three that we already get, seven compressed into tiny invisible hyperspheres, time. Tick tick tick. Quanta the dreams stuff is made of. Suzie has no guts. She's a dreamer. A kind of confusion of realms. Very spectral. The universe may be this huge mindless mother field that generates patterns and laws and whose language is silence. That's why we need mindful artists. Rock is the artform with highest percentage of infantile seventh-grade minds flushing down half its parishioners. The Bible is probably second. That's why we need artful minds. Was Jesus a cubist PR guy? Who gives. My own eyes plus light are required to make bottle green Tanqueray bottles come off that green. My quantum mechanical eyes.

Maggie zipped up the back of her navy blue Vicki Tiel sheath, turned around. The song on TV was "The Take Off" by a girl called E.K. With her shoulders thrown forward, then back, she looked at her side in the mirror. Was it possible Linda saw Michael? With her hands on her hips, she looked at her shoulders and back. It was not. She stood up on tiptoe. She hoped so.

Richard strolled north on LaSalle Street. It was cold when the sun wasn't on him, not bad when it was. Lynch had come up just this morning with three courtside seats for the Bulls and the Celtics that evening, and his wife had surprised him by saying she wanted to go. He decided that things could be worse.

the detective

THE BANGS in her lashes. It was what Hank had told her he liked most about her that night. That and the way her lower lip looked when she blew them up out of her eyes. So she now had a subject to paint for her goddamn 2D final project.

She traced the pattern on her camouflage jacket then carboned the green, tan, and brown parts onto a regessoed tray (she forgot what had been underneath). In place of the black parts she drew the words BANGS IN MY LASHES in roughly the shape of a halo, using a tilted and jangly cursive to make them look part of the pattern. The tail of the *y* looked like Italy, and the top looked like Ψ; both the *n*'s and the *m* looked like π. She liked how the shapes all disrupted each other, how you couldn't tell which were in front, which behind. A few of the shapes looked like pieces of puzzles or countries on maps, others like profiles or numbers. Strobe called this sort of stuff Slash Art, as in verbal slash visual. Yeah. If it was good enough for Braque, Jenny Holzer, Jap Johns, and soldiers, she figured, it would sure do for someone like her.

She set up her mirror, combed out her bangs, made some sketches. All worthless. Her usual method was to build up her face by accretion, trial and error, erasing mistakes, going slowly, keeping the marks that made sense. But she hadn't really painted or sketched for so long that her rhythms were off. She had made herself look like a squaw. She needed to get this done quickly, *right now,* plus her face had to be just as slickly exact as the camouflage.

She stuck her head under the cover of Richard's big IBM copier. Damn. She thought for a second about what she was doing. (His office was eerily quiet. Weren't the printers turned on? Where was Maggie?) If she was, in fact, pregnant, it wouldn't be up in her *head.* And besides, she was not. She was not.

With her forehead and nose pressed against the cool glass, she felt with her hand for the start button. Found it. She remembered what Hank said and pursed out her lip. Then she closed her eyes hard. This was nuts, but she needed to do it. She pressed it.

Gizmos below her made plastic, mechanical noises. Small motors whirred. An aura of cranapple backlit with neony cyans and yellows flashed through her eyelids, sliding across left to right: 4D Paschke. She was sure to get brain cancer now, and the skin on her face felt like magma. Then the light disappeared and the glass became cool. She had done it.

The image was grainy but sharp, and her cheekbones looked pretty dramatic. It looked like a black-and-white photograph but without all the fisheye distortion of SLR closeups. What also was nice was its being *exactly* 1:1 with her face. Every last freckle and hair left a line. Where her bangs reached down into her eyebrows and lashes, it distinguished between the three gauges.

Using this copy instead of her head, she made several more, working with No. 2 pencil and gray liquid paper to introduce changes in each. By blackening some areas and highlighting others, graying out lines and redrawing them, she gradually divided her features into four distinct shades: white, light gray, dark gray, and black. It was something like making a squashed contour map of her face. Mount St. Linda's. She could darken the overall image by adding more toner, or enlarge it by twenty percent; she also could tone it back down, add some contrast, reshrink it. Where the changes in shade were most subtle she just split the difference, drawing the line down the middle.

She danced back upstairs to her room, put on *Trust.* She was pumped. She cut out her silhouette, trimmed it, then traced its perimeter a couple of inches inside the four-word-long halo. After erasing the pattern inside this new line, she traced on her camouflaged features. Okay. There she was. She felt like she had a slight sunburn.

She mixed her four colors in yogurt cups: black, muddy brown, olive drab, marsh grass tan. She matched up the tones and gray values as close as she could to her jacket. The dark gray would have to be brown, she decided, the lighter gray areas olive.

She drew more black areas freehand to balance the halo of letters. She was working at high fever pitch, chain-smoking, headachey, happy. Forget drawing, she thought. IBM!

She sat there and stared at the camouflage sections and letters, deciding what else she could add. Vietnam? Ireland? An upside-down Strat? Nicaragua?

She shuffled *Tattoos,* reread some and winced, cut them up into confetti.

Okay. She was ready to paint.

She was ready.

ON HER first day of work at the gallery, she reported a half hour early. A show was going up. Painters were rolling two walls, carpenters hanging a huge 3D word on another. The letters so far were GE. Maybe, just maybe, she thought, she could get some of *her* slash art hung here, or at least into local group shows. At least *some* day she could. She understood that it was possible. In the meantime her life would be different. She resolved to arrive at least ten minutes early each day she worked here, and get to know artists and dealers. She would go home and paint every night. Plus, next semester, she would not fall behind with her schoolwork. There was going to be a new Linda.

Roger Winfrey rushed up and put his soft hand on her shoulder. He looked glad to see her—so glad, in fact, that the poor guy was practically wheezing. She knew she looked good in short skirts, but wasn't all this a bit much?

"Hi," she said.

"Hi."

Was it *too* short, she wondered. No way. It was tweed, for God's sake, hazel gray, and barely came up past her knees. Her green V-neck sweater could not have been much more demure. Roger, for his part, was wearing an XXXL scarlet blazer, this to go with his black patent leather bow tie and white shirt. It was great. He looked at her funny, then smiled. Was it possible that he was straight?

"I tried to call you," he told her. There was mint on his breath. What *was* this already? A *pass?* "I mean, I've been trying to call you all over the place."

They looked at each other. It was suddenly clear he was going to give her bad news, but she still had to ask. "There a problem?" The new Linda understood things like this. All too well. Her attire, she knew, was appropriate.

Roger winced. Then he nodded. He ran a hand back through his hair. "Oh Jesus, I *hate* things like this!"

"I'm fired, right?"

With his teeth biting into his thin lower lip, he closed his eyes, nodded. "I was hoping she'd already told you."

"The financial aid lady?"

He nodded.

"She hasn't," said Linda.

"Your financial aid package? That form? Apparently this past semester your status just . . . changed."

So. That was it. She was now under Maggie's new "income." She was too rich for work-study money. The catch was there wasn't a catch. She was out.

"Meaning I don't get the work-study now." Her eyes stung. She knew. But she wanted to hear all the words.

"Apparently your eligibility . . ."

Yes. Right. Apparently.

Winfrey turned up his palms, shook his head.

"Meaning I don't get the job," Linda said. She knew that she didn't, but still. She was hoping that somehow he'd . . . something.

She heard him say relevant phrases. Two-for-one matching grant funds. Other students. The people in Springfield and Washington. "Though it all must be *sort* of good news, I mean, since your status improved so dramatically . . ."

She shook her head. Nodded. She knew she was going to cry. "I don't suppose . . ." No. Though perhaps she had merely imagined . . . She pushed her bangs sideways. She hadn't.

Winfrey was listening hard, waiting to answer her questions, completely—absurdly—concerned. On her side. She was trying to calm herself down, but her breaths were too frequent, too large, for her lungs. So they fluttered. When he put his hand onto her shoulder again, she knew that he wanted to hug her. She wanted to slug him or run.

"I wish there were something . . ."

She smiled but could feel herself losing it. Don't! Just do not. There was nothing. She couldn't. He wasn't—

"Linda, I really am sorry."

She understood—*no!*—that he was.

She was way out of breath when she got to the top of the steps at the Clark and Lake CTA station. She pushed a dollar bill under the slot, saw the PAID light go on, then figured she might need a transfer: she didn't know where she was going, but it seemed like you always could use one. Still puffing and trembly, she took out a quarter and bought one.

Both of the platforms were crowded with (mostly) black people waiting for various trains: Ravenswood all-stops, A and B Lake Street-Dan Ryans, Evanston Express trains making the loop headed north. Mostly women. A few seemed pissed off about something. Others were bouncing and cheerful. Two blocks west of the platform and half a block north was the back of Nuveen's glassy lime wedge. Below, down on Lake, through the tracks, she could see the sun flashing off windshields.

She crossed the bridge over the tracks. No trains were coming from either direction. She waited. Should she throw herself under the wheels? Make a splash? The billboard beside her depicted a talking end table. IT WOULD SAVE YOU A WAXING TO DUST ME WITH PLEDGE, it advised. The overhead heaters were on, but she chose not to stand underneath them.

There were dozens of places to waitress within walks of Wolf Point or the School. Up by Rendeck's, as far as she knew, there was only Nepenthe and General Foods, and neither place seemed like they catered to spenders or tippers. A woman brushed past her and said something under her breath. She was cool. Plus she'd sworn up and down all those times she would never wait tables again.

If she got on a southbound Dan Ryan, the A or the B, she could ride back to school, maybe try to explain things to the Financial Aid people in charge of . . . Yeah sure. Were there dorm rooms available at Hefner or Crown next semester? She could also check out Roommates Wanted.

The Ravenswood train would get her within seven (long) blocks of the warehouse. The Evanston train, on the opposite platform, would express her right out of the city. Downstairs, underground, was a train that went up to O'Hare, where airplanes were parked, the owners of which might take credit if she mentioned a certain account . . .

In the last seven weeks, she was startled to realize, she had lived in the Eastwood apartment, Wolf Point, the Crillon, and with Rendeck and friends on Milwaukee. Some of her stuff was up there, a few things were down in her locker, but most was still back at Wolf Point. If she had to say where she lived now? Clark and Lake el stop, platform right under her feet, Chicago Sic Transit Authority.

She looked at her transfer. The woman had punched the hour outside the blue circle and exactly between three and four. Plus the hour it legally gave her . . .

The other thing was, it would not be a bad day to walk.

A Dan Ryan A train lurched toward the station, sparking and clacking against the steel rails. She realized it looked just like Teddy's. It stopped. Passengers quickly got out. Its solid steel wheels looked like car brakes.

From a couple of stations away, down by Wabash, a Ravenswood rounded the bend. Should she hang out at school for a while, maybe work on her camouflage painting, or see what was up at the warehouse? It would not be a bad idea, either, to go get some more winter clothes from Wolf Point. She looked at her watch and then back at the transfer. She couldn't decide what to do.

A tiny old black man settled down, facing backward, in a seat on the Dan Ryan train. With all of his wrinkles and shaking, he looked at least eighty or ninety. He peeked inside his green and red Field's bag, stuck in both hands and rummaged around for a moment, then took off his watch cap and nodded. He had steel-colored hair on the sides of his head and white woolly sideburns; his bald scalp was dark brown and shiny.

He spotted her smiling and winked as the Ryan pulled out of the station.

He watched a door open in front of her. The platform got crowded again as people poured out of the Ravenswood. He watched her step back. He could tell she'd get on from the way she had moved toward the door as the train had pulled into the station.

He had her—which meant, in his mind, among other good things, that she didn't *know* that he had her. He got on the car behind hers as the door swiveled closed. Its rubber edge nudged his bad shoulder.

He moved down the aisle, peering ahead through the car, making sure he could see into hers. And he could. Two guys in bubble-head caps paused in front of him, laughing and cursing and jiving. Tinny, staccato percussion leaked from their phones as he passed. But he had her.

The train started forward, lurched back six inches, stopped dead. Thrown sideways and forward, he tried to grab onto the overhead bar. The guys in the caps had to catch him.

A warning buzzed twice as both doors swung open again. Five seconds later they closed. The voice on the intercom that he hoped would explain this had turned into ear-piercing feedback. The doors swung back open. He peered up ahead into her car, trying to spot where she'd sat.

The absurdly loud buzzer went off three more times. Nothing happened. He glanced out the window. A woman, a girl, pretty juicy, was standing there holding a transfer.

The way she was framed by the window, he saw only torso and hip. There was something about her, however. Unzipped black jacket, wool skirt . . .

He ducked and looked out. It was her. The thick lower lip, the bangs in the lashes, the works. He rushed back to try to get off, but too late: the doors had already swung shut. He knew where she lived, though, and where he could find her again, if he had to.

The train moved ahead several feet, slowed down, lurched forward, then stopped. He stayed by the door, just in case. She was standing right there now, just outside the narrow vertical window. He quickly looked down, turned away.

With the car swaying sideways, seemingly poised to move forward, a buzz interrupted the voice feeding back through the intercom. He stopped up his ears with his pinkies, winced as the feedback got louder, more fierce, then reached up and pulled the emergency knob. Didn't work.

He glanced out the window. Still there. She looked like a Slavic Madonna, he realized. A virgin, built solid, but spooky, less sure of herself. A little bit less . . . beatific. Her left hand was up by the side of her face. Had she made him? The train started forward again. She was looking right at him, straight through him, fixing her hairdo and waving goodbye in the glass.